P9-CDY-305

"I ADORE YOU, VINCENT NAVARRO . . ."

He led her through the low hanging branches of the willow oaks. Suddenly, Karita beheld a sight of splendor. Towering above them was a waterfall; its waters flowed over the boulders into a deep green creek below. Wild ferns and verbena and other wildflowers grew profusely.

Karita was speechless.

Vincent sank down on the blanket and placed a blossom behind her ear. "Lie still while I tell you something about this place of magic. This is where my grandmother and grandfather stood when they were first in love. When they noticed how the silver moonlight shone down on the waterfall, they decided to name their ranch Silvercreek."

The touch of his fingers on her cheek made her tingle with excitement.

He whispered in her ear. "I brought you here . . . because this is where I wanted to make love to you the first time." He bent his head to capture her honeyed lips in a rapturous kiss. His hands moved to caress the soft curves of her young body and she felt herself swaying closer to him as she called out his name softly and lovingly. "Oh, Vincent!" she cried. "I want you so! I love you, Vincent Navarro. I have always loved you!"

Once again, this magical spot had cast its spell . . .

THE BEST IN HISTORICAL ROMANCES

TIME-KEPT PROMISES (2422, $3.95)
by Constance O'Day Flannery

Sean O'Mara froze when he saw his wife Christina standing before him. She had vanished and the news had been written about in all of the papers—he had even been charged with her murder! But now he had living proof of his innocence, and Sean was not about to let her get away. No matter that the woman was claiming to be someone named Kristine; she still caused his blood to boil.

PASSION'S PRISONER (2573, $3.95)
by Casey Stewart

When Cassandra Lansing put on men's clothing and entered the Rawlings saloon she didn't expect to lose anything—in fact she was sure that she would win back her prized horse Rapscallion that her grandfather lost in a card game. She almost got a smug satisfaction at the thought of fooling the gamblers into believing that she was a man. But once she caught a glimpse of the virile Josh Rawlings, Cassandra wanted to be the woman in his embrace!

ANGEL HEART (2426, $3.95)
by Victoria Thompson

Ever since Angelica's father died, Harlan Snyder had been angling to get his hands on her ranch, the Diamond R. And now, just when she had an important government contract to fulfill, she couldn't find a single cowhand to hire—all because of Snyder's threats. It was only a matter of time before the legendary gunfighter Kid Collins turned up on her doorstep, badly wounded. Angelica assessed his firmly muscled physique and stared into his startling blue eyes. Beneath all that blood and dirt he was the handsomest man she had ever seen, and the one person who could help beat Snyder at his own game.

Available wherever paperbacks are sold, or order direct from the Publisher. Send cover price plus 50¢ per copy for mailing and handling to Zebra Books, Dept. 3312, 475 Park Avenue South, New York, N.Y. 10016. Residents of New York, New Jersey and Pennsylvania must include sales tax. DO NOT SEND CASH.

WANDA OWEN

Tempting Texas Treasure

ZEBRA BOOKS
KENSINGTON PUBLISHING CORP.

This book is dedicated to a very special lady and a very rare breed of doctor whom I admire very much. This is my simple way to tell you how much I appreciate you and how glad I've been that you were there when I needed you, Dr. Barbara Hastings!

ZEBRA BOOKS

are published by

Kensington Publishing Corp.
475 Park Avenue South
New York, NY 10016

First printing: February, 1991

Printed in the United States of America

Part One

Chapter 1

There could be no sky as bright and blue as the one above the Pedernales River nor could there be any more beautiful, colorful wildflowers than those growing around the banks of the river. At least, this was what Karita Montera thought as she sat there this warm summer day and daydreamed, as she often did.

There was a young man she always daydreamed about, even though she knew it was an impossible dream, and one that would never come true for her. Yet, she dreamed as she had since she was sixteen. The handsome Vincent Navarro, son of the esteemed Navarro family, would never come to court her. His father was a senator in Washington, but the family spent much of their time here, at Silvercreek Ranch—the grandest ranch in the region. Karita had heard her own parents talk about the parents of Vincent all her life. Her father had been Senator Danton Navarro's houseboy when he was a young lad and her lovely Mexican mother, Yolanda, had served as a maid to Vincent's mother, Kristina Whelan, before she married

Danton Navarro.

Eighteen year old Karita was the middle daughter of Abeja and Yolanda. She wished that she had been named Kristina instead of her older sister, because each time the Navarro family came back to the region, and Karita caught a glance of the magnificent lady with flaming auburn hair and sparkling green eyes, she was convinced that Kristina Whelan Navarro was the most beautiful woman in the world.

Karita knew that the two sons of Danton and Kristina were twins, though they bore little resemblance to each other. Vincent had his mother's green eyes while Victor's eyes were as black as his father's. Both had jet black hair.

Somehow it had always been Vincent she'd envisioned as the handsome caballero who'd come to woo and win her heart. She had no wish to be courted by the young men on the neighboring ranches near Whispering Willows, nor did she wish to marry any of them, as her sister had done last year.

Cara, her younger sister, seemed content to follow in Kristina's footsteps and marry one of the local young men. Constantly she taunted Karita about thinking herself too good to keep company with the Gomez and Lorenzo boys who were always coming over to the ranch.

Of all her daughters, Yolanda had always considered Karita the most beautiful. Her features were softer and more delicate than the other two, and her skin was smooth and fair. But she also worried about her more than the others, for she knew that with great beauty came great expectations, and she feared life was going to disappoint her.

Yolanda never had the high expectations that her middle daughter did. All her life, until her marriage to Abeja, she had been a servant to the wealthy. She worked in their large and elegant homes, first in the kitchens, and later as a chambermaid, surrounded by finery which would never belong to her. She knew her place in life, and was content. She worked hard and was delighted in all her duties, and was rewarded by becoming lady's maid to Kristina Whelan. She counted this as the most fortunate event of her youth, for the beautiful lady was always generous and kind to her. Despite the differences in their lives, they became devoted to one another. She met her dear Abeja when Kristina Whelan married Danton Navarro, and they had been young brides, and then new mothers, together. Danton Navarro had given them this ranch as a wedding gift, and she and Abeja would love Danton and Kristina Navarro forever.

But despite the affection between them, she was wise enough to know that no son of theirs would marry one of her daughters. It would be some lovely young lady from a wealthy family of their status; but she could not hurt Karita by telling her that. Let her have her dreams while she is still young, Yolanda thought. Life will steal them away soon enough.

A few weeks ago, Yolanda had received a long, newsy letter from Kristina Navarro telling her that Danton was giving up his seat in the Senate and they would soon be returning to Silvercreek Ranch. She was elated about it.

Yolanda knew Señora Lucia Navarro would be happy to have her spacious ranch house filled with her family again after they'd been away all these many years. Once again there would be many gala fiestas drawing beautiful women and dashing young men from all over the region. The twin sons, Victor and Vincent, would soon be taking brides, Yolanda thought. Getting Señora Kristina's letter had put her in a reflective mood and she thought of her younger days, and how she and Abeja, with their humble background, had been bound to the grand Navarro family.

She strolled to her kitchen and glanced out the window to see beautiful Karita with a yellow flower tucked to the side of her black hair, and knew she'd been down by the river. She watched her walk toward the house and observed the blossoming curves of her figure. Her full gathered skirt swayed to and fro as she walked, and her thick black hair fell around her shoulders.

Karita had been only sixteen when the Navarro family came back for a visit at Silvercreek Ranch, but Yolanda recalled how Karita's black eyes sparkled when she saw handsome young Vincent Navarro. Yolanda prayed that their return to the region would bring no problems to the two families, but she could see how it might happen—and how easily a young romantic girl like Karita can get her heart broken!

Abeja was also feeling a mixture of emotion about the return of the Navarro family to Texas. To Abeja, Danton Navarro had never been Senator Navarro—he was Señor Navarro, and there was no man on earth that Abeja admired more than the señor. But Abeja had only to remember the time their families had last been together to share a picnic lunch down by the river bank. He'd noticed one of his daughters looking at one of the Navarro twins, and Karita had seemed mesmerized by Vincent Navarro.

He could certainly understand why his sixteen year old daughter would be so entranced by the handsome young man. He was much more handsome than his twin, Victor. No eyes were any greener than Vincent's. It made for an interesting image with his light olive complexion and jet black hair. There was a devil-may-care air about Vincent that his more serious brother, Victor, did not share.

But what troubled Abeja were the same things that troubled Yolanda, for he knew that his daughter was dwelling in a land of fantasy to think that young Vincent would come to Whispering Willows to court her. That just wasn't the way life was.

He also knew that of all his daughters, Karita was the one who did not allow herself to be ruled by the conventional ways of life. She never had!

Being a doting father, Abeja did not want his pretty eighteen year old daughter to feel the pain of heartbreak. But how would he save her, he pondered?

Danton Navarro had watched his wife eagerly supervising the packing of their belongings for their preparation to leave Washington and return to Texas. Her enthusiasm and the happy look on her face were enough to satisfy him that he'd made the right decision not to run for another term as senator. He was ready to go home to Texas and enjoy a leisurely life at Silvercreek Ranch. Obviously, she was too!

Their sons were now grown and he would like to think that they would take an interest in the vast ranch, but he had doubts about that. Vincent would most likely become a lawyer and wish to live in Austin when he returned from the tour of Europe he was taking right now. As for Victor, Danton wasn't at all sure what he would want to do.

His and Kristina's sons might be twins, but they were as different as day is from night. But it had been the same with him and his own twin brother, Damien.

All Danton hoped was that neither of his sons had inherited the evil traits of Damien with his sinister, devious nature. Rarely did he allow himself to think about his twin for the memories were too unpleasant. He could not forget the way Damien's jealousy and determination to possess Kristina had almost destroyed the Navarro family.

But his love for Kristina and her love for him overcame all Damien's wicked plots and trickery. In the end, Damien was the one punished, and took his own life.

Danton's sorrow had been not for Damien but for his dear mother, Lucia. But the Navarro family had been strong and they put those years behind them. His marriage to the beautiful auburn-haired Kristina Whelan had been a most happy one.

He was sure that his mother was just as excited as his wife about them returning to Silvercreek. Señora Lucia had always adored Kristina.

Danton found himself weary just watching Kristina fluttering back and forth through the rooms of the townhouse. When she fell exhaustedly into the chair across from him, she moaned softly, "Oh, Danton—it is going to be so grand, getting back home with spring approaching. I can just see all those meadows and pastureland bursting forth with all the wildflowers!

It—it will be so nice and mild there, with none of this chilling cold weather we have here."

He laughed, "Vida mia—I should have taken you back home a long time ago, I think. I'm glad you are so happy. Your happiness is all I want—all I ever wanted."

"I know, Danton and I am happy. I can't deny it. Why, I feel younger than springtime this miserable March day," she laughed.

"And you look it, too," he declared. It didn't seem possible that she was forty years old. The years had not changed her as far as his eyes could see. When her two sons towered over her, he found it amazing that she was old enough to be their mother. She was far more alluring and attractive than any of the ladies he'd seen his sons escort to the elegant galas here in the capital.

"I'm anxious also for our sons to return, Danton," Kristina confessed as she relaxed by the cozy fire.

Danton gave her a slow, easy grin as he remarked, "I'm truly surprised that the two of them have lasted all these weeks together on the tour. Can we dare hope that they will learn to get along?"

"I doubt that, Danton. I would venture to guess that Vincent has gone his way and Victor has gone in a different direction."

Danton would not disagree. They talked a while longer before Danton suggested that they enjoy a quiet dinner and retire early, for he knew that Kristina must be exhausted after the last few days she'd put in.

Danton found his beloved wife in a reflective mood during dinner as she spoke of the people dear to her back in Texas.

"It won't seem right not seeing old Santiago there

11

at Silvercreek, Danton," she sighed sadly. Danton agreed. For as long as he could remember old Santiago had been there.

"But he lived a long time, querida. He was eighty. I'd like to think I'll be around as long as he was. I don't want some other man marrying my beautiful wife after I'm gone. I'm still the selfish man I was when we first met, Kristina."

She smiled as she gazed at him. The only thing that had changed about Danton was the silver in his jet black hair. His face was still as devilishly handsome as it had been when she first saw him, when she was in her teens.

His fiery black eyes could still have an instant effect on her when they pierced her. Her son, Vincent, reminded her of Danton in so many ways that Victor didn't.

Victor was the quiet one of her twins. Vincent had always been the little hellion, so alive and spirited. Those sparkling bright green eyes of his had only to look at her and her heart melted before she could punish him.

"It will be wonderful to see Abeja and Yolanda again, won't it Danton? Can you imagine that their oldest daughter is married now? Why, they could be grandparents by the time we get back to Texas!"

"So that leaves two at home now," Danton commented.

"Yes, Karita and Cara. Karita reminds me very much of her mother when she was young. She is the loveliest of their daughters."

"I think our two sons noticed that the last time we visited with Abeja and Yolanda. I saw both of them staring at the pretty Karita."

Kristina had to admit to her husband that she had not been aware of that. A crazy thought rushed through her mind that she would not have dared voice to Danton. It was something she would not be able to dismiss lightly. She'd known the reckless passion of a man or a woman when they were attracted to one another. What if both of her sons were attracted to Karita?

Danton noticed that his wife had become very quiet and thoughtful but he had no inkling of the thoughts going through her mind.

Many miles separated Yolanda Montera and Kristina Navarro this night, but both were thinking about things of the past and the apprehensions of what the future might hold for their two families.

She might be middle-aged now, but Kristina Navarro knew she would always be a sentimental optimist so she tried to quiet any worries she was having by telling herself that the things that worried her would probably not happen.

The bond of friendship she shared with Yolanda Montera went back twenty years and she cherished it dearly.

Chapter 2

Karita Montera had no idea that she'd been observed as she sat at her favorite spot by the river this afternoon. The same black eyes had also watched her walk away through the pasture. Only then did Ricardo Valdez start walking back to where he'd tied his horse and head for home. The Valdez ranch bordered Whispering Willows on the south.

For more than a year, Ricardo had often stood back in a grove of trees just to watch Karita on the grassy bank. He wondered what she thought about as she stared out over the rippling stream. She was so very beautiful with her thick black hair falling around her shoulders. Sometimes she stretched out on the ground, and the sight of this was enough to enflame desire within Ricardo. The lovely curves of her young body were so sensuously displayed!

He wanted to rush to the spot and sink down on the ground beside her, taking her into his arms. He could imagine how thrilling it would be to kiss her lips and feel her soft, small body pressed against him as he made passionate love to her.

But he did not dare to do this. Karita had never invited his attention when he'd been around her. In fact, she seemed a bit of a snob when their families attended the same fiestas.

Ricardo could not understand her rejection of him. He knew he was considered a rather handsome hombre by all the other señoritas. But the snobbish Señorita Karita had never fluttered her long eyelashes excitedly when he was around her as the others had.

Perhaps this was why she had aroused his interests more than the others had. Although he was pleasuring himself with feisty little Carmella Sanchez, it was Karita Montera he intended to possess someday and he didn't care how long it took.

Karita's younger sister, Cara, had certainly given him some inviting smiles at the Sanchez's fiesta about a month ago, but then the sixteen year old Cara was a terrible little flirt. Señor Montera was going to have to hold a tight rein on her.

When Karita entered her mother's kitchen, Yolanda had moved away from the window where she'd been standing to watch her daughter stroll up the path.

"Well, dear—you have surely been down by your river bank again. That old Pedernales seems to hold a certain magic for you—si?"

"Yes, mama, I guess it must. I love it down there by that little grove of trees. It is so wonderfully peaceful."

"I know about such places, Karita. I have my special little spot—my haven of serenity. It is out on the little patio your father built for me where I can sit and think

16

as I rock in my old wooden rocker. I'm surrounded by all my lovely flowers and I watch the colorful butterflies coming to take their nectar. Oh, yes—I find a peace out there."

Karita smiled at her mother, knowing that she understood how she felt. Since Cara was not in the kitchen helping her mother prepare dinner, she asked if there was something she might do to help before her father came in from the field.

"No, dear. We're having a simple meal tonight. It is all cooking in that one big pot," Yolanda told her. So Karita left the kitchen to go to the room she shared with her sister, Cara. There she found her lazy sister taking a long siesta.

Cara's clutter lay everywhere around the room and Karita knew she should just leave it until her sister finally picked it up and put it where it belonged. But she couldn't stand the disarray of the room, so she picked it up and flung it on the foot of Cara's bed, not caring if she woke Cara up. Before she sat down on the stool at the dressing table, she placed her wide-brimmed straw hat on the peg on the wall.

Her sleepy-eyed sister sat up in bed to greet her. "Well, Karita! I've news for you that should thrill you—knowing how smitten you are by Vincent Navarro. They're going to be back here sometime next week. Mama had a letter today from Señora Navarro. Did she tell you?"

"Next week?" Karita stopped brushing her hair, but she dared not let her devious little sister see how excited she was by the news. Cara could be a little devil when she wanted to be.

In the kitchen of their cozy stone cottage, Abeja had

17

come in from the fields, greeted his wife, and washed his face. Dipping the dipper into the pail to fill the basin, he told her about meeting Ramon Valdez in the pasture that afternoon.

"His Ricardo is taken with our Karita. Ramon says he is always talking about how beautiful she is," Abeja laughed.

"She *is* beautiful! And young Ricardo is a very handsome man. I hear that all the young girls find him so, but our Karita has not been impressed, Abeja. There is another who occupies Karita's thoughts and I don't think I have to tell you who that is."

"I know, querida. I know that it is Vincent our daughter has her heart set on. But that will never be, and we both know that."

"But how do we tell her that, Abeja?"

"Madre de Dios, I don't know!" her husband confessed.

"That is the only thing that takes the joy out of their homecoming for me, Abeja," Yolanda declared as she lifted the lid of the huge cast iron pot to stir the simmering beans and peppers. A delightful aroma drifted up to her nose as she smelled the peppers and onions mingled with the beans.

Abeja too smelled the wonderful aroma. "Yolanda, there is no better cook in the world than you, and to think I've had you all these years still amazes me!"

Her doe-like eyes glanced his way and she smiled. "Abeja, I think you must have learned many things when you were in the service of Señor Danton. Señora Kristina always talked about his silken, silvery tongue," she laughed.

"Oh, I'd dare not lie to you, querida. I always

admired Señor Danton. It will be good to see him again."

She gave him a nod of her head as she turned from the stove to summon her daughters to dinner.

For days, Señora Lucia Navarro had kept the house-servants busy cleaning and polishing all the rooms of the spacious two story house at Silvercreek Ranch. The grounds and gardens had been attended and mani-cured to perfection in anticipation of Danton's arrival.

The despair that her son Damien had caused her had been more than made up with the pride she felt for Danton when he went to Washington to represent the state of Texas. She swelled with pride about her wonderful family. Her daughter Delores and her doctor husband had given her four delightful grand-children and their marriage was a very happy one. For over twenty years Danton and his lovely Kristina had been married and their twin sons, Vincent and Victor, were very special to Señora Lucia. They were her first grandsons.

She was already planning a grand fiesta for their homecoming. Her guest list would be a huge one and she'd written to Kristina's mother to come to Silver-creek from her home in El Paso. Her visit would be a pleasure for Lucia, for she and Florine had been friends long before their son and daughter met and married. She wished she didn't live so far away so they might see one another more often.

Now that Kristina would be living here at Silver-creek, perhaps Florine might be persuaded to move to this part of Texas, especially now that she was a widow.

19

Kristina had been Florine Whelan's only child and she was a doting mother.

Everywhere Lucia walked in the house there was an aroma of beeswax and polish. Everything gleamed from the extensive cleaning Miranda had been doing this last week. She already had two of the other Mexican servant girls baking, for those two robust grandsons were hearty eaters.

A few miles away at Whispering Willows, there was the same aroma of beeswax as Karita and Cara polished the furnishings of their parlor. Cara had grumbled and complained ever since her mother had left the room to go outside to tend her garden.

"Will you just stop that, Cara, and get busy polishing that table. I'll swear you are the laziest human being I know," Karita snapped, realizing that she was going to be the one doing most of the work. Each stroke Cara made was so slow in motion that Karita had already finished two wooden tables and dusted the two lamps sitting on them before Cara had polished a single shelf.

"Oh, you are just like mama where the Navarros are concerned. You act like they're gods or something. I know why you're so excited," Cara said.

Karita gathered up her cloths and jars to leave the room but she couldn't resist taking one of the cloths and giving it a sharp snap against Cara's behind.

As she listened to her sister shriek, she hurried on out of the room. "You rat! I'll get you for that, Karita, and you better plan on that!" Cara screamed loudly. She was glad that her older sister was leaving the room so she'd quit nagging her.

When she finished the table, Cara sank down in one

of the chairs and made no effort to follow her sister into the dining room. Let her do that room herself, Cara mused. She stretched out full length on the settee and propped her head against the arm of it. A devious smile broke on her face. She'd show Karita just how smart she was!

She relaxed there in the pleasant quiet for several moments. A lazy languor came over her.

Yolanda finished weeding her garden and as she strolled back toward the house she saw buds bursting forth everywhere on her flowering shrubs. Sprouts were coming up from the earth, springing with life. Soon the grounds around the stone cottage would be covered with a magnificent array of red, yellow and purple. It was the perfect time for Danton and Kristina to be coming back home, she thought as she untied her straw hat and wiped her brow.

She knew that this region was the most fertile blackland of Texas. The land Abeja tilled always yielded a bountiful harvest of grain for their livestock and cattle. The pasturelands always had sweet grasses to provide grazing for their cattle. Yolanda had enough poultry to feed her family as well as to provide money from the weekly sale of fryers and eggs to local merchants.

She and Abeja lived very well, she considered. A far better life than she'd be having back in El Paso if she'd never met Abeja and Kristina Whelan.

Now that she had the chores of her garden behind her and her two daughters were doing the household tasks, she could spend the afternoon sewing, for she was going to make herself and her daughters pretty new frocks and a shirt for Abeja.

The moment she stepped inside the house she smelled the fragrance of the polishes and she went to survey her parlor and dining room.

She came in from the back of the house and glanced into the dining room first to see Karita still working away. She turned to go to her parlor.

She saw Cara on her settee. "Well, niña—are you tired after the polishing of only one room?" she addressed her youngest daughter. She feared Cara was spoiled, and Yolanda could not tolerate a lazy person.

Cara jerked up, startled by the sharp tone of her mother's voice. She had only to look at her face and those angry black eyes to know that she was in trouble.

Yolanda did not have to be told what had been going on. It was Karita who'd done most of the work.

"Well, since you have obviously had a rest while your sister has continued to work, she can rest this afternoon while you start working upstairs in the bedrooms." Yolanda turned to go to her kitchen.

There was a disgruntled look on Cara's face as she watched her mother leave. It was Karita who'd always been her mother's pet. Karita was always so perfect as far as her mother was concerned, Cara thought as she got up off the settee.

All her life she'd resented Karita because she was so beautiful and her figure was so graceful and slim. She'd never gone through those awkward, gawky stages that she and Kristina had gone through. She and her older sister both had a tendency to be chubby, but not Karita!

Cara knew one thing, though: Karita was not going to have her heart's desire. Vincent Navarro would never be her suitor! That pleased Cara. She was going to laugh her head off when the arrogant Vincent Navarro completely ignored Karita. Maybe then Karita would not be so uppity and stuck-up.

Maybe then she would be happy for the attentions of Ricardo Valdez or Tomas Gomez, Cara thought to herself.

Chapter 3

No one had to tell Senator Navarro that his pretty auburn-haired wife was in a querulous mood that evening. But he applauded her restraint in not showing this mood to their son, Victor, when he'd arrived late in the afternoon from Europe. It had been a wonderful reunion for them and Kristina had been as lighthearted and gay as she could be as the three of them had dined.

In fact, when Victor had explained to them that Vincent had decided to linger a little longer in France, his mother had not even blinked an eyelash. But she seethed within. Danton knew it, for he knew his wife well. He saw the fire in those green eyes. He didn't envy Vincent when he next encountered his spitfire mother.

As far as Victor was concerned, it was a delightful evening and he enjoyed being back with his parents. He was eager to travel with them to Silvercreek Ranch.

It was not until Kristina was in the privacy of her boudoir with Danton that she unleashed her fury. "How *dare* he do this when he knew our plans, Danton! Oh, I could wring his neck!"

"I rather suspected that you felt this way, mi vida." In a deep, calm voice, he told her that they would not change their plans. "He will have to find his way to Texas, and I've no doubt that he will—when it suits him."

By now Kristina was taking all the pins from her hair to let it flow loosely over her shoulders. "Oh, he is so obstinate and headstrong!"

Danton gave a chuckle. "Can't imagine where he got that!"

Her head turned so that her green eyes were piercing him but a slow smile came to her face. "Am I to assume that you mean he takes after me, Danton Navarro?"

"I never met a more headstrong woman in my whole life than you, my beautiful Kristina, but maybe that was why I fell in love with you." He ambled slowly over to where she sat at her dressing table to plant a kiss on her cheek. "And I still find myself just as hopelessly in love with you, querida."

Twenty odd years had never dampened the ardor between these two and even now Kristina soon forgot her fury at Vincent.

Tomorrow, they were heading for home and the thought of that engulfed her with joy and happiness. She forgot about Vincent and thought about the life she and Danton were going to enjoy at Silvercreek Ranch.

Danton and Kristina traveled toward the Blacklands of Texas, as they called the land that lay west of the Piney Woods on the way to Silvercreek with its fertile,

26

rich valleys. Many streams ran through the region, as did the Trinity, Brazos and Colorado Rivers.

Kristina did not know which countryside was more beautiful. She remembered the beauty of Whispering Willows on the banks of the Pedernales River. She remembered when Danton had bought the smaller ranch and later deeded it over to Abeja as a wedding gift to him and Yolanda. She knew that there was no comparing the Silvercreek Ranch with its vast acres and thousands of cattle but, she knew the happy life Yolanda had shared with Abeja there, and she was glad.

When her eyes first caught sight of the rambling two story house with its red-tiled roof, time stood still for a brief moment for Señora Kristina Navarro. Yesteryears were recalled for a few golden moments, and there was a bittersweet taste to the memory.

It was a glorious homecoming when their entourage dismounted from the carriage and their two aging mothers were there at the door to greet Kristina and Danton. Laughter and tears mingled as they all embraced.

Back in the shadows of the tiled hallway, Señora Kristina saw a figure she loved dearly from her childhood back in El Paso. It thrilled her that her mother, Florine had brought her along for this reunion.

When her mother finally released her, Kristina rushed back in the hallway to embrace the magnificent quadroon who'd helped raised her. On her head she still wore her kerchief but her face was ageless and still as exquisitely beautiful as she'd always been.

"Oh, Solitaire! Solitaire! It is perfect having you here!" Señora Kristina told her as she and the tall woman embraced affectionately.

"And you, mam'selle, are just as beautiful as you always were."

Señora Kristina clasped her hand tightly in hers. "Please—come. I want you to meet my son Victor."

"I find it hard to believe that you have a son this old, mam'selle," Solitaire said as she followed her into the parlor.

Kristina could feel the feebleness in her beloved Solitaire as she led her over to introduce her to her son. She suddenly realized how old she was. More than ever she was glad that she and Danton had come home. They'd been away from their families too much and for too long.

Victor was impressed by everything about the ranch at Silvercreek. Maybe it was because he was older now than he had been on their previous visits. Now that he knew that this was to be his parents' home he looked at everything in a different way.

Silvercreek Ranch was a small empire, he realized as he rode over the vast acres of the valleys and observed the cattle grazing there. Since most of his life had been spent in the east he'd not realized the little dynasty the Navarro family had here in the Blacklands of Texas.

After a week at Silvercreek, Victor decided he should think seriously about staying around for a while. Here, there could come a day that he could be a king of these vast lands, and he had only to think about the power such wealth could give to him to make his decision easy.

He hoped Vincent would linger in France for many weeks, beacause he planned to take this time to ingratiate himself with the formidable Señora Lucia. His grandmother was a most imposing lady. Elderly she might be, but she was as sharp as any lady he'd ever met. So the first few days at Silvercreek, he tried to woo and win her favor. He took her for daily buggy rides over the countryside and they talked constantly as they traveled over the vast ranch. She told him of his proud heritage and asked him his plans.

"Well, I like it here very much. I find it quite wonderful after all the years in a busy, bustling city."

This naturally pleased Señora Lucia. She told him of the grand fiesta she was planning for next week. "I wanted you and your parents to have a little rest first, so I delayed the celebration of your homecoming a week. I have to admit that I was planning to introduce both of my twin grandsons. I'm very disappointed that Vincent didn't return with the rest of his family."

Victor understandingly agreed with her, "He should have joined us, but Vincent became very intrigued with France, shall we say."

Lucia Navarro was an elderly woman, but she was still young at heart. Giving a chuckle, she told her grandson, "Oh, I know about the young reckless heart, Victor. I was rather willful myself when I was your age. I did not exactly live the traditional way—as I'm sure you've been told."

Victor gave a hearty laugh as he looked at this aristocratic lady with her classic features and her snow white hair which used to be as black as coal. He still found it hard to believe that she was once the famous Lolita, a lady gambler who worked the tables at the Palace in San Antonio.

He also knew the story about his other grandmother, Florine Whelan, the flame-haired gambling queen and owner of the Crystal Castle in El Paso. It had almost seemed like a fairytale to Victor that his mother was raised in the upstairs of a gambling hall. It seemed unlikely that his parents should have met at all, but they had.

It was no wonder that his twin brother Vincent loved to gamble so much. He was lucky at the tables, so he'd possibly inherited the skills of his Grandmother Florine's and Grandmother Lucia's expertise.

The silver moonlight gleamed over the courtyard gardens of the Navarro ranch house. It was an ideal night to take a stroll in the gardens, which was what Señor Danton Navarro and his wife were doing.

"Victor is certainly charming your mother, Danton. For this I am happy, but I only pray that Vincent arrives in time for the fiesta. She is going to be so disappointed if he doesn't."

Danton patted her shoulder. "Don't rule it out, Kristina. He may show up in time."

"Oh, I hope so!" She cast her eyes up at the night sky above them. "Am I just being silly, Danton, or is that silvery moonlight more beautiful back here in Texas?"

"Oh, chiquita—you are surely right. It is far more beautiful here. Remember that little waterfall that flows into the creek? It was the place where I first made love to you."

Kristina giggled. "How could I ever forget that day or that place, Danton?"

"Think we're too old to go there once again?"

She saw the gleam in his black eyes and without any hesitation she taunted him. "I told you I felt younger than springtime, Danton—remember? Why don't we go for a ride tomorrow and see that little spot of paradise once again?"

He wholeheartedly agreed with her as they turned to go back up the garden pathway.

Vincent Navarro had only intended to linger in France five more days after his brother Victor had boarded the ship to sail for home. But he'd found the south of France to be a most profitable place to apply his skills as a gambler. Lady Luck was riding on his shoulder and he knew it, so he wanted to remain for a few more days. When his instinct told him to quit the tables, he did just that.

He spent one more day in Paris to visit some of the most exclusive shops to purchase gifts for his mother, grandmother, father and brother. He bought his grandmother an exquisite lace shawl, and for his mother he found a magnificent emerald ring to match her lovely eyes. For his father, he purchased a fine cognac. Because Victor was very fastidious about his clothes, Vincent bought him a pearl gray brocade waistcoat.

The next day he sailed from the coast of France on a trim schooner that plowed far more swiftly through the ocean than the ship Victor had booked passage on, and the schooner was going directly to the Texas coast. By the time he arrived in Austin, he was only six days behind his families' arrival at Silvercreek Ranch. But he planned to give himself a gift before he rode on to Silvercreek.

His idea was to go to the Kennison Ranch and purchase the finest young palomino Jake Kennison had on his ranch. He'd wanted to own one since he was seventeen and his father had taken him to the Kennison Ranch during one of their visits back to Texas. Now he had enough money of his own to buy one of those fine horses, and he intended to have one.

Two days later when he traveled toward Silvercreek Ranch, he was astride a magnificent palomino. He named the horse Dorado, for his deep golden coat was a striking contrast to the pale gold of his silken tail and mane. His arrogant, self-assured air matched Vincent perfectly; they made a fine pair. Vincent was swelling with pride as he galloped out of the Kennison Ranch astride Dorado.

Never had he owned anything he prized so much as this splendid palomino. As far as Vincent was concerned, Dorado was worth the extra five days in France. But he knew he was going to greet an irate mother when he arrived at Silvercreek. This didn't worry him for he knew that he could sooth her ruffled feathers once they were together.

The trail he took followed the Pedernales River close to the Whispering Willows Ranch. His fiery young stallion had galloped at a fast pace and Vincent had allowed him to have his way until they came to the banks of the river. Vincent thought it was a good place to stop to allow the high spirited horse to have a drink from the river.

He leaped down from the palomino and led him to the shallow edge of the stream. As Dorado enjoyed the cool waters of the river, Vincent chanced to glance down river some two hundred feet to see a most beautiful girl sitting there, gazing out over the river. She was so engrossed in her thoughts that she had not heard him approach.

As Vincent held the reins to Dorado he gazed at the sultry loveliness of the girl sitting there with her jet black hair flowing around her shoulders. Her delicate features and tawny complexion were breathtaking, and her curvy young body was enough to stir a fever in Vincent Navarro. His eyes savored the sight of her jutting breasts pressing against her sheer tunic and his eyes trailed down to her tiny waist. She excited him more than any young woman had in a long, long time, and Vincent knew he must meet her. He pulled on the reins to urge Dorado to follow him down the riverbank toward this lovely nymph.

Karita was suddenly aware of the handsome young man and the palomino walking in her direction. Long before Vincent Navarro was to recognize her, she knew that it was he leading the prancing golden horse. What a handsome pair they made! Vincent wore fawn colored pants that seemed to be molded to his body and a white shirt that was unbuttoned, displaying his broad chest. His black hair fell carelessly over his forehead, making him look all the more attractive to the romantic Karita.

As he approached her, he thought he had never gazed into a more beautiful pair of black eyes as they locked with his and a slow smile crossed her face. "Good day to you, señorita."

"Good day to you, Vincent," she smiled and gave a soft little laugh.

Suddenly, Vincent realized that he had been admiring the little daughter of Abeja and Yolanda Montera. But there had been drastic changes since he'd last seen her. "You're little Rita—si? Karita, is that right?"

"Si, Vincent—I—am Karita." She knew her voice was probably trembling. The mere sight of him took her breath away.

"Madre de Dios, I apologize for not recognizing you! But you've become so very beautiful, little Rita, since I last saw you two years ago."

She smiled. "Your apology is accepted. I heard that you and your family had returned."

"I've not returned to Silvercreek yet. That is where I'm heading now."

"You did not come with the rest of your family?"

"No, Karita," he replied. He sank down to the ground beside her. The nearness of him made her very nervous and Vincent sensed this but figured that she was just a shy one, for this lovely girl was the image of sweet innocence. Vincent had had his fair share of experience with some pretty sophisticated young women back east and in Europe.

So he played the gallant and gave her a tender kiss on the cheek as he told her that he must be on his way to Silvercreek. "But I shall be seeing you again very soon. Give your parents my best regards, Karita." He rose up from the ground and moved to fetch Dorado.

"Oh, I will, Vincent," she told him as she watched him mount up on the palomino. A tender kiss it might have been but a part of her daydream had come true. She had been kissed by Vincent Navarro.

Who was to say that the rest of her daydream would not come true? Karita was foolish enough to think that they would.

She went back to her home in the highest spirits believing just this. Vincent Navarro would become her suitor and her lover!

Chapter 4

Excitedly, Karita announced the news about her encounter with Vincent Navarro down at the river. She darted a smug glance in Cara's direction which gave her a great deal of satisfaction. Maybe now her sister would stop taunting her about being lovesick over Vincent!

"Yes, we sat there talking for awhile before he left to ride on to Silvercreek. He told me to give you and papa his best regards."

Yolanda saw how excited her daughter was; her dark eyes flashed and her long black eyelashes fluttered as she talked.

"And mama—what a magnificent horse he was riding! It was a palomino, so beautiful and golden! Oh, to own such a horse as that would be wonderful," she sighed.

Yolanda teased her, "Don't let poor Bonita hear you talk like that or her feelings will be hurt."

Karita loved the little roan mare she rode around the countryside, so she knew that her mother was only jesting. Nothing would make her part with Bonita.

She took over the setting of the table as she continued to chatter away, ignoring Cara sitting in the corner of the room in a quiet, sullen mood. The long afternon she'd spent cleaning the furniture upstairs had exhausted her. She did not care to talk to anyone this evening. Sleep was what she was going to do as soon as the evening meal was over.

She welcomed the announcement that dinner was ready and she immediately took her seat and began to eat while her parents and Karita talked about the Navarros during the entire meal.

Karita noticed how weary Cara looked. "I'll help mama with the dishes tonight, Cara. You look tired."

Yolanda realized that her youngest was tired, for she'd worked longer hours than usual. But it was a just punishment for her lazy daughter, Yolanda considered.

Later she told her husband about Cara and what had happened today. "No wonder she was so quiet tonight," Abeja grinned. "I had wondered if she was coming down with something. Cara's never that quiet."

"Well, being the baby she was petted too much by Kristina and Karita, along with me, I guess. But all that changed as of today."

Before they dimmed their lamp to retire, Abeja commented about what a happy evening it must have been at Silvercreek, with Vincent arriving.

"Señora Lucia couldn't possibly be happier right now," Yolanda said as she crawled in on her side of the bed. "I'll wager that Señora Florine is arriving any time now if she's not already there."

But she got no response from Abeja and she smiled;

38

as soon as his head touched the pillow he drifted off to sleep.

It was a very festive evening for everyone gathered around the long mahogany table draped with a linen tablecloth of snowy white. Matching silver candelabra sat at either end of the long table giving off a twinkling glow of candlelight.

Silver urns on the sideboard held colorful flowers. But just as colorful were the elegantly gowned ladies at the table. Señora Lucia wore a black gown trimmed with white lace cuffs and collar. Dangling from her ears were diamond and pearl teardrop earrings. The huge mother-of-pearl comb was tucked above the large coil she wore at the back of her head.

Señora Florine was a more flamboyant lady, and she wore a brilliant emerald green gown. Her lovely auburn hair, now streaked with gray, was piled high atop her head.

Of course all the gentlemen had to confess that the most beautiful of all was Señora Kristina Navarro. Her gown was a rich purple, and the lovely color was repeated in an amethyst necklace and earrings.

They enjoyed a grand feast, and some of the finest wines were brought up from the cellar for this special occasion. Now that Vincent had arrived, Señora Lucia was completely happy. In fact, she was impatient to have the fiesta.

At the end of the meal, Vincent rose to propose a toast. His green eyes sparkled brightly as he glanced around the table at his mother and grandmothers. "To the three most beautiful ladies in all the world."

"I'll drink to that." His father smiled.

The three ladies were naturally charmed by the handsome young man, and proud that he was a part of them.

Victor had only to observe Señora Lucia to know that any misgivings she might have been having about Vincent had vanished once he arrived. The same was true for his mother; she had mellowed. But this was always the way it was where Vincent was concerned.

Vincent would make a magnificent lawyer, Victor thought, watching how his brother could win people over so effortlessly.

When they had all lifted their glasses to join Vincent in his toast to the ladies, the still shapely Señora Florine stood up and raised her glass. "Now . . . I've a toast to make. To three of the most handsome hombres I've known—well, maybe one or two more were just as handsome," she jested.

Everyone exploded with laughter knowing she'd proposed many a toast as the owner and gambling queen of the Crystal Castle back in El Paso. Vincent could see why she had been considered quite a beauty in her younger days.

Vincent gazed from one of them to the other. Each of them had been unusual, never ruled by the conventional ways of life. This was what had made them exciting ladies. This was the kind of woman he must have when he fell in love. As yet, he'd not found such a woman. Until he did, he planned to remain the happy-go-lucky bachelor he was now.

Since he had arrived late in the afternoon and wished to take a bath after the ride on the trail from Austin, he'd not had time to present his gifts. Once he'd arrived and found his grandmother from El Paso here at Silvercreek, he realized that he'd failed to buy her a present, so he'd have to give his gifts privately.

Victor was the first to receive his present. His twin was surprised when Vincent came to his room after they'd all retired. He opened the box and saw the pearl gray waistcoat Vincent had bought for him in Paris.

"It's a fine looking garment, Vincent! I'm—I'm quite impressed!" Victor declared as he held it up to survey the work on it. He liked fine-tailored clothes and Vincent had obviously remembered this. "I thank you, Vincent."

"You're most welcome, Vic. But I must tell you those extra five days were worth it. Got myself that handsome palomino out there in the stable, and a few little gifts for everyone."

Victor laughed as he looked at his twin. "Vincent, I think I've never known anyone as lucky as you always are. I wish I'd inherited a little of it."

"You inherited all the brains, Vic. Don't you know that?" Vincent told him.

"Oh, I wouldn't say that at all. I know no one who has a shrewder or more clever mind than yours, Vincent. You were always outsmarting me when we were kids."

Vincent knew that this was true so he made no reply and just gave a husky laugh and asked Victor how he was going to like living at Silvercreek.

"I haven't been here long enough to say just yet, I guess. How about you? Will you stay?" Victor asked his twin.

"Rather doubt that, Vic. I don't think it would appeal to me year around. As I recall, our father didn't live here when he was our age. He owned his own place in Austin and practiced law there and only came back here to the ranch for a few days' visit every so often."

Victor nodded his head in agreement. "That's right. I remember him telling us about that and how Abeja was his manservant."

"Speaking of Abeja, I saw one of his daughters when I was riding in from Austin this afternoon. Little Karita has turned into a real beauty. She's a very shapely little señorita. Sure doesn't take after old Abeja."

Victor laughed. "Should have known that you would have spotted a beautiful girl as soon as you arrived. I figured that it was that pretty little French girl you met who urged you to linger in France."

"Not at all. It was the rich gaming tables that persuaded me to stay and I'm certainly glad I did. Look at the fancy waistcoat it got you," Vincent playfully teased his twin. He turned to leave the room to retire. He had put in a long day traveling from Austin to the ranch. The hour was late now, and he was ready for the comfort of his bed.

Long after Vincent had left the room, Victor lay in bed thinking. It was impossible to find fault with Vincent, even when he wanted to at times. There was nothing selfish about his generous brother who was always ready to share his bounty—whatever it might be. He'd bought a handsome wasitcoat to give to him. He was sure Vincent had purchased gifts for all the family that were just as nice as his.

He found himself curious about Abeja's pretty daughter. For Vincent to speak about her in such a way told Victor that she must surely be a beauty, for they'd both squired some of the capital's most beautiful ladies over the last few years.

Perhaps he might take a ride over in the direction of Whispering Willows tomorrow. With that in mind, he closed his eyes and went to sleep.

The next morning, Victor made straight for the stables to get a horse saddled up.

Servants were already busy working in the courtyard gardens hanging lanterns on the branches of the trees for the fiesta. Señora Lucia's hired hands were also preparing the platform where the guests would dance on the night of the fiesta. It was a very busy time around the sprawling ranch house, and it probably would be for the next few days, Victor realized.

He could not get too excited about it all, for he would not know any of the people coming to his grandmother's fiesta. It was different for his parents, for they would know all the guests, but these people meant nothing to Victor.

Victor rode along, thinking to himself that maybe little Karita Montera might make the fiesta a more exciting occasion for him, if she was as beautiful as Vincent had said she was. He knew about the Montera family and how they'd received Whispering Willows through his father's generosity as a gift to Abeja. Perhaps, Victor suddenly realized, Vincent had inherited the generous heart of their father. But he was not like the two of them. Victor had accepted something about himself a long time ago and admitted to himself that he was a little greedy. He found no reason to feel guilty about it, and he never had!

He spotted the Pedernales River right ahead of him and he knew that he was already riding over the land of Whispering Willows. Willow trees lined the riverbank,

43

their long draping branches reaching down to touch the ground.

He could believe that this part of Texas, called the Blacklands, was the most fertile land in the entire state, for everything seemed to flourish and grow so green.

He had no desire to go to the little cottage where the Montera family lived. All he hoped for was the sight of the beautiful Karita!

He could already see the little stone house in the distance. Over in the pastureland, the Montera cattle were grazing on the lush green grass. But he saw no lovely señorita sitting along the riverbank. Somewhat disappointed, he figured that he might as well give his horse a rest before he started back to Silvercreek. He halted his horse when he came to a pleasant spot where he could look out at the rippling waters of the river and leaped down to tie the reins to the trunk of a tree. He sat down on the ground and lit one of the cigarillos he enjoyed smoking.

Quiet surrounded him. The only sound he heard was the gentle breeze blowing through the willows, and it was almost like a woman softly whispering.

Leaning back against the trunk of a tree and puffing on his cigarillo, he enjoyed the serenity. He didn't know how long he'd been sitting there before a soft voice interrupted that silence. "Vincent? Is that you?"

Karita had spied his black head and relaxed, muscled body stretched out there on the ground. Her heart had begun to pound erratically to think that he'd ridden back this way again to see her!

But as she rushed to the tree and the man sitting there turned to face her, she saw that it was not Vincent. Victor saw that Vincent had certainly not exaggerated about the lovely Karita. He had no doubt that this was she!

He gave her a warm, friendly smile as he informed her, "I'm sorry, but I'm not Vincent. I am Victor Navarro. And you must be Karita—si?"

"Si—I am Karita." Her black eyes looked down at him and he could see that she was embarrassed.

"You remember me, Karita? We met two years ago but I must say that you have certainly grown up." Victor's dark eyes surveyed her beauty from the top of her head down to her dainty ankles and her feet shod in sandals.

"I remember you, Victor," she shyly replied. He was a very handsome young man too, she thought to herself as she stood gazing down at him. His black eyes seemed to pierce her with their intensity.

When he invited her to join him sitting on the ground, she felt that she could hardly refuse, but she felt very ill at ease. Something about him was so different, and she didn't know exactly what it was.

She tried to be friendly to him because he was Señor Danton's son, but her conversation was strained and she found herself anxious to leave. Finally, she rose to excuse herself. "I must be getting back to help Mama, Victor. It . . . it was nice to see you again."

"I shall look forward to seeing you at grandmother's fiesta, Karita, and I'm asking for the first dance with you here and now," Victor remarked as he also got up from the ground.

"I—I will look forward to the fiesta too, Victor. Goodbye!" She suddenly dashed away. She made an enchanting sight and Victor's black eyes savored it for a moment before he mounted his horse. It was only as he was riding away that he realized she had not promised him the first dance.

Karita had had no intention of promising him the first dance, for she wanted the first dance to be with Vincent Navarro. She had to believe that it would be that way.

Chapter 5

Señora Lucia was delighted; the weather was going to be absolutely perfect for her fiesta. It was a beautiful day without a cloud in the bright blue sky and tonight there was going to be a bright full moon to shine down on her courtyard garden.

Everything was ready for the gay affair. The platform was ready for the dancers to enjoy after they'd dined on the mountains of food that would be served. Strolling musicians had been hired to entertain her guests.

Three of her servants were busy in the kitchen preparing the last of the foods to be served. Long tables had been arranged in the courtyard and during the evening huge platters of food for her guests to enjoy would be placed on them.

For Señora Lucia, this was special for it brought back fond memories of years when she and her beloved husband had their annual fiestas for all their friends and neighbors. She was enjoying every minute of the planning and preparations, and now that Vincent had arrived and her dear friend Florine was here, she was completely happy.

Across the miles at Whispering Willows, Abeja and his family were boarding the buggy to travel to Silvercreek as the sun was beginning to sink in the western sky. He considered that he had three of the prettiest ladies that would be attending the fiesta right there in his buggy. His youngest daughter was all dressed up in a pale pink dress with a pink satin bow in her hair.

He looked at Karita in her lovely yellow frock and was reminded of the buttercups that bloomed in his pasture. She had picked some fresh flowers from her mother's garden and pinned them to the side of her hair, and she was breathtakingly beautiful.

Of course the lovely lady sitting beside him in the buggy was the most special of all. The first time he saw her he thought she was the most beautiful girl in the world, and he still felt the same way.

Three daughters had done nothing to destroy her lovely figure and her face had not aged as far as Abeja could see. He'd always thought she looked beautiful in the shade of lavender she wore today. It reminded him of wild violets. He only wished that he had the wealth to buy her a magnificent gem of this shade to express the depth of his love for her.

Traveling from Whispering Willows to Silvercreek Ranch took almost two hours, and all the ladies were pleased that it was a calm late afternoon so that their hair was not going to be blown when they arrived at the fiesta.

Back at the Silvercreek Ranch happy excitement was building in Señora Kristina as she was being assisted into her brilliant emerald green gown. Her auburn hair was fashioned in an upswept coiffure and she looked very regal. Emerald teardrop earrings hung gracefully from her ears.

"Ah, señora—you look so beautiful," the young servant girl sighed as she fastened the back of the gown.

"Why, aren't you nice, Catalina! I think I must tell Señora Lucia that I wish you to attend me now that we will be living here. Would you like that, Catalina?"

The young Mexican girl's eyes sparkled with delight as she exclaimed, "Oh, señora! I would be honored to serve you! I—I would try very hard to please you."

"You already have, Catalina, so it is settled as far as I am concerned. I shall tell Señora Lucia of my decision." Kristina was reminded of the young Yolanda, years ago, so eager to please her. This young girl was about the same age and just as sincere.

"Oh, muchas gracias, señora. You won't be sorry!"

"I know I won't, Catalina," Kristina smiled as she prepared to leave the room.

Catalina stood there for a minute in a state of sheer ecstasy. She would be serving this magnificent lady! She'd always heard that ladies like Señora Kristina were overbearing and hateful but such was not the case with this lovely lady.

Kristina joined her husband and his mother in the parlor to receive the praises of both of them as she entered. Trailing behind her was Florine, escorted by her two handsome grandsons. She was feeling very much like Señora Lucia as she surveyed her very handsome family. There was a feeling of overwhelming pride that a love such as hers and Danton's had produced such fine sons.

This was truly one's immortality—that their sons would carry on their ideals and ways long after they were gone. She knew that Señora Lucia felt the same way about Danton.

They enjoyed a toast to their family before the first guests began to arrive and the six of them stood there to greet the arrivals. Señora Lucia was the first in line, followed by her son Danton and his wife. Victor and Vincent stood by their mother and Señora Florine stood beside Vincent.

As each party arrived and was greeted, Kristina anxiously awaited the sight of Yolanda and Abeja.

When they finally entered, she was so delighted to see them that she knew it was going to be a glorious night. A cordial handshake was not enough for Abeja and Yolanda. Kristina shared a warm, loving embrace with Yolanda and Danton gave a hug to Abeja. But after the embrace of her dear Yolanda, Señora Kristina's eyes were immediately drawn to the beautiful young girl dressed in yellow. She had to be Karita. She greeted the young girl and watched her as she moved down the line to greet her mother and her sons.

Kristina could not resist whispering in Yolanda's ear how the years had blessed them both with such beautiful families. "Aren't we lucky, Yolanda?"

Yolanda nodded her head in absolute agreement for

there were certainly no handsomer young men than Kristina's sons, Victor and Vincent. But then how could good looking Danton Navarro and beautiful Kristina not have had handsome sons?

Arriving shortly after Abeja and Yolanda were the Gomez and the Valdez families. Soon there was a flood of guests coming through the courtyard and another hour went by before Kristina had a private moment with her dear friend Yolanda. By then the courtyard echoed with gay laughter and music from the strumming guitars played by strolling musicians. Twilight was now falling over the courtyard, and the lanterns had been lit, reflecting a glowing splendor over the area. It was a most festive gathering.

Yolanda saw Kristina coming down the path toward the bench where she was sitting, enjoying a glass of wine while Abeja was engrossed in conversation with Señor Valdez. Long ago she'd lost sight of Karita and Cara for they had disappeared into the crowd.

As she watched Kristina moving down the flagstone walk with her lovely emerald green gown swishing back and forth, Yolanda thought that she was even more beautiful than she was when she was young.

"Ah, I was hoping that I would find you, Yolanda. I had no idea that Señora Lucia had invited so many people to the fiesta. But it seems our two children have found one another amid all this gathering," she softly laughed.

"Oh, which ones?" Yolanda asked, feeling that she already knew who they were.

"Vincent and Karita are very occupied with one another, it would seem. They have themselves a private

51

corner on the other side of the courtyard but as I was coming this way I noticed Victor going over to join them," she smiled.

"Well, I had no idea where she and Cara went as soon as we came into the courtyard. But you know that they never seem to linger for long around their mama or papa," Yolanda laughed.

"We have no babies anymore, do we?"

"No, we don't. I will probably be a grandmother very soon now."

"I was going to ask you about my namesake. How are Kristina and José doing?" Señora Navarro asked.

"She is very happy and getting plumper every day, and José is delighted that he is to become a father. I do not worry about Kristina or my youngest, Cara. It is Karita who concerns me."

"How so, Yolanda?" Kristina asked her.

"She dreams of things far beyond her reach, I fear. I think she is bound to face many disappointments in life."

"Perhaps she won't, Yolanda. We all had our dreams when we were younger, and nothing is impossible if you want something bad enough. Don't worry so much about Karita. It is good that she dreams. Let her," she urged her dear friend.

Reluctantly, she left Yolanda to chat with some of the other guests before they started moving down the long tables that would soon be covered with platters of delicious food.

Guests at Silvercreek Ranch were always impressed by the graciousness of Señora Lucia Navarro, but no one was more spellbound by her presence than Karita, who observed her from the far corner of the courtyard. She yearned to be such an elegant lady someday. So now she had another dream.

She was feeling very smug as she walked down the long banquet table to fill her plate. Vincent Navarro walked behind her and had asked her if he might share her company as they dined. Without hesitation, she had told him yes. She felt confident that when the music started to play he would ask her for the first dance.

She knew that some of the other young girls attending the fiesta were staring at her and Vincent with envy. This pleased Karita.

This was a night that would give her wonderful memories for a long, long time, she knew. She would always remember how Vincent had so warmly called her "little Rita" and the warm glint in his green eyes as he'd looked at her.

She had also found it exciting when both of the Navarro twins sat with her in the courtyard gardens. She knew that she was the object of many curious eyes. Such wonderful things had not happened often in Karita's life, and she planned to enjoy tonight to the fullest.

She was glad that Cara seemed to be keeping Ricardo Valdez occupied over in another corner of the courtyard. She certainly did not want to be pestered by him tonight. She'd realized that he was attracted to her for a long time, but Ricardo did not interest her.

When Vincent asked her to dance the first dance with him, she took his hand so he could lead her onto the platform. Another of her fantasies had come true, for she was suddenly in Vincent Navarro's strong arms, and they began to sway together across the floor.

Señora Florine and Señora Lucia chanced to see the young couple dancing together, and Florine turned to Lucia to comment, "That is a most ravishing young lady our Vincent is dancing with. She is a beauty, Lucia."

"Si, and I think Vincent must be thinking the same thing right now. Look at his eyes gazing down at her. Madre de Dios, she is a tiny little thing," Lucia responded to her friend. These two former gamblers were thoroughly enjoying themselves.

"Tiny she might be, Lucia, but look at the loveliness of that small figure," Florine said.

"I'm sure Vincent has also noticed that," Lucia said and patted Florine's hand. As gracious and dignified as Lucia Navarro was, she was also earthy and certainly not prudish. Being the famous Lolita at the Palace Gambling Hall in San Antonio had made her worldly-wise and daring. But she'd found it no problem to change from the famous lady gambler to the wife of one of the wealthiest ranchers in the state of Texas. Her husband, Victor Navarro, was so devoted to her and so in love with her that their life had been a very happy one. It had pleased her that Danton and Kristina had named one of their twin sons Victor. How proud her husband would have been!

Danton and Kristina had followed their son to the platform to dance.

Other guests joined the two couples on the platform to enjoy the lively music and dance.

As the dance finished, Vincent was fired with a fever

as he held Karita's soft, petite body close to him. He wanted to see more of this beautiful young lady.

"Let's go on a picnic tomorrow, Karita. I know a most beautiful spot here on the ranch and mother told me that you and your parents were staying overnight before you go back home tomorrow afternoon," he told her.

"That sounds wonderful to me, Vincent. Will our parents object to that—I mean if we go on a picnic?"

"I don't think so. Do we *have* to ask them?" he grinned with a look of mischief in his eyes.

"You might not, but I have to have my parents' permission."

Vincent admitted, "I'm sure they will allow it. You see, little Rita—I forget that I've reached an age where I don't ask approval for what I wish to do."

"That is because you are a man, Vincent." Her smile melted his heart and flamed the desire to kiss her tempting lips. She was a vision of loveliness in pale yellow that reminded him of the springtime jonquils which were always the first to bloom in his grandmother's vast gardens.

Karita was nothing like the young ladies he'd squired back in the capital. This was what made her so beguiling! He knew her gown was simple and handmade—possibly by her mother. There was no fashionable hairstyle but there was a beauty about her that money could not possibly buy.

Never had he seen such thick long eyelashes, such black eyes! Her complexion was such a tawny golden color—satiny and smooth. Karita needed no frills and fluffs to be lovely.

Karita did not mind that Vincent remained at her side all this time. She caught a fleeting glance of Cara dancing now with some young man she did not recognize and it was even more surprising to see her parents dancing to the lively music. Rarely had she seen them dance at any of the fiestas they'd attended, but she knew what a grand occasion this was for both of them. It was nice to see them so gay.

For the first time since she'd arrived at Silvercreek she found herself alone while Vincent went to get some more fruit punch.

Victor wasted no time taking advantage of the opportunity. He came to the bench where she was sitting, and asked her to dance. "Vincent can't have all your dances tonight," he laughed. "That wouldn't be fair. Besides I asked for this dance a few days ago down by the river—remember?"

"I remember, Victor." She smiled as she took his hand and rose from the bench, but she could not help wondering how Vincent would react when he came back to find her gone. But she could hardly refuse Victor a dance.

Victor's arms went around her and his deep voice declared, as they began to whirl around the platform, "You know that you are the most beautiful girl here tonight, don't you, Karita? In case you don't, I'm telling you that you are."

She had to look up at him for he was as tall as Vincent. His black eyes were devouring her as they looked down on her. Karita could not help being affected by his nearness and the way he was looking at her. "Oh, I've seen many lovely young ladies strolling through the gardens, Victor," she responded to his admiring praise.

"But they don't hold a candle to you," he declared as he gave her a quick whirl around the floor. He was a magnificent dancer and Karita found herself having no trouble in following him. The truth was he was a better dancer than Vincent, she had to admit. She sensed that he realized it and rather enjoyed the admiration from the guests who were looking at them.

Back in the shadows of the garden, Vincent had returned with their glasses of punch to find Karita gone and he immediately suspected what had happened in his absence. He had only to look across the way to see that it was Victor who'd claimed her for a dance. They were the center of attraction out there, Vincent noticed. He stood watching Victor whirl her around on the platform.

Putting down the glasses of punch, he went over to claim his grandmother, Señora Lucia, for the rest of the dance, and when he took her back to her table, he asked his Grandmother Florine for the next dance.

"You're pretty good, grandmother," he told her.

Florine threw her head back and laughed," I should be after all the time I've spent on a dance floor, my darling grandson."

Victor laughed," I still find it hard to believe that you were a gambler, grandmother."

"Well, believe it, honey, and I might add I was a hell of a good one."

When he took her back to the table, he bid his two grandmothers goodbye to go seek out his mother. He had to have one dance with her this evening, and he had no doubt that Victor was keeping Karita occupied.

When he was dancing with his mother, she remarked to him that he and little Karita had made a handsome couple when they were dancing the first dance of the evening.

"Well, I can't compete with Victor on that. He was always the better dancer but I thank you anyway, mother." He smiled down at her for she was as small and petite as Karita.

"She is a very beautiful young lady," she remarked.

"So beautiful that I've invited her to go on a picnic with me before they leave for Whispering Willows," he replied.

"Oh, you have?" A slow, knowing grin came to Kristina's face. "I wonder if Yolanda and Abeja will give her permission to go with you unescorted?"

"I'll find out in the morning. I hope they will for I know the most perfect spot here on Silvercreek for a picnic." Her son told her of the spot he was talking about with the small little waterfall that cascaded down into a creek below. Huge boulders, covered with green moss, jutted out from the water and the wild ferns grew profusely there in the shaded woods.

Kristina knew the spot well, for it was the place where Danton Navarro had made love to her for the first time over twenty years ago. She recalled the day as though it were yesterday, for it was an idyllic setting for young lovers.

A generation earlier it was this same place where Señora Lucia and Señor Victor Navarro had stood one moonlit night when they were first married. They had decided to name their ranch Silvercreek when they watched the silvery moonbeams reflected on the rippling waters of the waterfall and creek.

Kristina knew the intoxicating magic this spot could weave on a young romantic girl, and now her son was telling her that he was taking Karita there tomorrow.

Would Karita surrender to Vincent when he made love to her, as he surely would? She had, when Danton held her in his arms and kissed her, Kristina remembered.

Vincent had no inkling of the thoughts and memories weaving through the mind of his beautiful mother when he left her to seek out Karita Montera.

Chapter 6

Everyone was having such a wonderful time that all were reluctant to see the evening end. Some of the guests began boarding their buggies to travel homeward. Others were to stay overnight. When the midnight hour came, Vincent had finally found Karita once again and told her before they parted for the night that he would eagerly await her answer about the picnic.

"Drussie will fix us a delicious picnic basket if I request it. I'll wait for you out on the east veranda at ten in the morning."

"I'll be there, Vincent. I'll speak to my parents tonight," she promised as she turned to go into the house to the guest room she would be sharing with Cara.

"I'll will be waiting for you, Karita," he repeated as he watched her dart through the double doors of the veranda that led out to the courtyards. By now the crowd had disappeared and quiet was descending over the grounds. The lanterns were still burning brightly as the servant girls were busily dismantling the tables and removing the numerous chairs that had been set up for the guests.

Vincent lit up one of his cigarillos, took a deep puff, and began to stroll the grounds. Walking in the dark gardens, he saw across the way a flickering light that looked like a firefly coming closer and closer to him. Suddenly, Vincent realized that it was his father approaching him. In the same instance, Danton recognized Vincent as he moved out of the dark shadows.

"Well, son—it would seem that we both had the same idea, to have ourselves a smoke and walk before retiring. It was a grand night, wasn't it?"

"Yes sir—it certainly was, and no one enjoyed themselves more than my two grandmothers," Vincent laughed.

"Yes, I noticed it too and I only hope the two of them don't pay for it tomorrow. Neither of them is as young as she used to be."

"Oh, but they're young at heart. I doubt that they'll have any ill effects from their celebrating," Vincent assured him.

"Well, your mother tells me that you are planning on taking Abeja's daughter on a picnic tomorrow," Danton said, trying to sound more casual than he was feeling. His wife's news had not exactly pleased him. She'd told him a short time ago, and it was one of the reasons he'd left the house to take a walk and think. He knew his handsome son was quite the ladies' man and he did not wish him to misuse Abeja's pretty young daughter whom he was sure was a sweet, innocent girl. He was well aware that Karita Montera could be overwhelmed by Vincent's charms and silvery tongue. Far more sophisticated young ladies back in the capital had been.

"I will, if her parents allow her to go with me," Vincent said.

"Abeja and Yolanda are very strict parents, I must warn you, Vincent. The answer may be no."

"But it could be yes, and I've never been shy about asking even if there is that possibility of the answer being no, Father."

"No, Vincent—I certainly realize that, but you must be aware that Karita is not like the young ladies you knew back in the east."

"Well, that I noticed immediately, sir. Being around Karita has been a refreshing change."

Somehow, Danton never found a way to give his son the gentle warning he wanted to give him about Abeja's daughter. Danton knew that there was little he could do to stop what could happen between two young people like Vincent and Karita.

It never dawned on the self-assured Vincent that he might be denied taking Karita on the picnic. As soon as he dressed, he made directly for the kitchen to ask Drussie to prepare a picnic basket for him—some of the chicken and some of her fresh baked bread. He quickly added that a few of those juicy little fruit tarts would be nice too.

His next stop was out to the stables to see that a buggy would be ready for him to take in an hour or so. When he had attended to that little chore he went back to the house to have some of Drussie's black, strong coffee.

She teased him as she did not feel free to do with Señor Victor, with his more serious manner. "Well, you are taking some little señorita on a picnic—si?"

"Si, Drussie the most beautiful girl here at the fiesta last night."

Drussie chuckled as she ambled over to fill up his coffee cup, "You sound very excited about this lady, Señor Vincent."

There was a boyish glint in his green eyes as they darted up to meet hers. "You're too smart, Drussie. Did you know that?" They both laughed as Vincent drank the second cup of coffee. Drussie asked if he was sure he didn't want something to eat.

"Some are already gathering in the dining room for breakfast now," she told him.

"You aren't the only one running the kitchen this morning, are you?" Vincent asked her.

"Madre de Dios, no! I have three girls in there now attending to your grandmother's guests."

"Well, I'm glad you told me that. Think I'll just leave by the backstairs. Good coffee, Drussie!"

Back in his room he ran the brush through his thick black hair, hoping to make an unruly lock stay off his forehead.

He looked very dashing when he left his room to meet Karita at the appointed hour. His fawn colored pants looked as if they were molded on his firm, muscled body. Over his white linen shirt which was opened at the neck he wore a brown leather vest that he'd purchased when he was touring Europe.

He was waiting for Karita when she came in sight, and he knew from the pleased smile on her face that she

64

was going to be allowed to go on the picnic with him. Her full-gathered brown challis skirt was splashed with brilliant colored flowers, and swished to and fro as she walked toward him. Her dainty feet were shod in brown leather sandals.

But it was the pink batiste tunic clinging to her firm rounded breasts that ignited a flaming fever in Vincent. His eyes savored the soft flesh displayed by the scooped neckline of the drawstring ribbons closing the bodice of the tunic.

"I can go, Vincent," she excitedly exclaimed to him. "I must be back by four though."

He took her arm to leave the gardens and go toward the stable. "We'll be back by four, chiquita!"

Drussie chanced to be glancing out the kitchen window to see the two young people going toward the stables and she could see Señor Vincent had such a twinkle in his green eyes. Muy bonita, she was!

Vincent lifted her up into the buggy and then leaped up to sit beside her. He gave a slap of the reins to urge the little black mare into action.

"The food in the basket smells wonderful," Karita smiled at him. She still felt rather in a daze that she was actually going on a picnic with Vincent Navarro.

"That's Drussie's special chicken with all those different herbs she seasons it with and her baked bread. Knowing her, she put in some extras I didn't even ask for," he grinned.

It did not seem that they'd traveled very long before they were turning off the main dirt road to enter the wooded area. Willow oaks growing there blocked out the rays of the bright sunshine that had been beaming down on them as they'd ridden along. There was a pleasant coolness in the woods. Everywhere Karita looked, she saw wild verbenas and ferns.

Vincent had picked a beautiful spot for their picnic. There was an air of enchantment in this verdant green forest.

"You like it here, chiquita?" Vincent asked her, for they were nearing the spot where he intended to spread the blanket for their picnic.

"Oh, it is wonderful—absolutely wonderful!"

He pulled up on the reins to stop the buggy.

It was when the buggy had come to a halt and Vincent's hands were lifting her down from the buggy that she heard the bubbling, rippling sound. He watched her lovely face, with that curious look in her black eyes, as she detected the sounds coming from the stream.

"Are we near a river, Vincent?" She turned to him to ask. "I hear the sound of water nearby."

"You will see in just a minute, Karita." He led her through the low hanging branches of the willow oaks. Suddenly she beheld such a sight of splendor she gasped, "Oh, it—it is beautiful, Vincent!"

Towering above them was a small waterfall, its waters flowing over boulders covered in deep green moss. On the incline of earth, the wild ferns and verbenas and other wild flowers grew profusely.

The water flowed into a creak below. It was so clear that Karita could see minnows swimming on the base of the river rock there.

She was speechless as she turned to look up at Vincent's smiling face. He told her, "I know, Karita—I felt the same way when I first came here. This is why I wanted to bring you here today."

"I'm glad you did for I'll never forget the sight of this place as long as I live!"

In the next hour, Karita was to experience the most delightful time she'd ever known in all her life. The two of them sat on the blanket and listened to the sound of the water splashing down into the creek as they ate the delicious food Drussie had put in the basket. Both seem to have a hearty appetite for there was little left in the basket when Vincent carried it back to the buggy. On his way back to the spot where Karita sat on the blanket, he bent down to pluck a cluster of white blossoms.

As he sank down to the blanket, he placed a blossom behind her ear. The touch of his fingers on her cheek made her tingle with excitement. But what she could not know was the mere touch of her had fired Vincent with an overwhelming desire to kiss her sweet rosy lips. They tempted him so much that it was torment to deny himself. It mattered not at this moment what his father had said to him in the garden last night. He was a hot-blooded man who desired a beautiful young girl in this place of paradise.

His head bent to capture her honeyed lips in that kiss he so yearned to take. Karita knew he was going to kiss her for she could see the heat of passion in his eyes as he gazed at her.

The sensations his lips stirred within her Karita had never known before, and she allowed him to continue to kiss her as long as he wished. When he did finally release her, she was breathless and gasping.

"Oh, little Rita—I knew it would be like that when we kissed!" he huskily declared. He did not need to be told that she had never been kissed like that before.

She felt so wonderfully warm as her small body lay against him, his arms enclosing her tightly. His hands moved to caress the soft curves of her young body and he felt the instant response as she undulated and swayed closer to him, calling out his name softly and lovingly.

"Shall I stop, chiquita? You must tell me now, or I won't be able to stop loving you until I have my fill of you," he murmured softly in her ear.

Her half-parted lips started to reply but there was the touch of his heated hands covering her pulsing breast, so all she could manage was a soft moan of pleasure. This was all Vincent needed to hear.

He raised her pink tunic and took the tip of her breast in his lips sending a searing flame of passion through Karita's entire body. She did not care that he was undressing her and that his hands were exploring her. All she was feeling was a wild, wonderful ecstasy.

"Tell me that you want me to make love to you, Karita! Tell me, chiquita!" he gasped eagerly.

"Oh, si, Vincent. I want—want you to make love to me very much!"

Hastily, he rid himself of his clothing and rushed back to meet her warm silken flesh. He thought for a fleeting moment to warn her of that instant of pain he would cause, knowing that she was a virgin, but he knew that he could make that pain fade quickly so he said nothing as he sank down between the velvet softness of her thighs. Unhurriedly, he sought to tease and arouse her until he sensed that she was as eager and anxious as he was.

Without hesitation, he buried himself within her as his sensuous lips captured hers once again. Her fired body stiffened for only a second before he felt the eager swaying of her hips match the tempo of his own body.

He felt the tightness of her hands holding his shoulders as their passion mounted and heightened to that peak of rapture that was coming far sooner than Vincent would have liked.

It was only after they were both lying there breathlessly enclosed in each others' arms that Vincent was plagued with guilt. He had deflowered this beautiful young girl. So he lay there, anxiously awaiting her reaction when she came back to the world of reality from this paradise they'd dwelled in as lovers.

Would she despise him and break into a panic of tears? He could well imagine how it would be if he took her back to the ranch in tears and she told her parents what had happened. He could also imagine what his own parents' reaction would be if they found out what he'd done. He didn't even want to think about that!

She lay in his arms so quietly that he was driven to know how she was feeling. "Querida, are you all right? I pray so. I only wanted to love you."

Slowly, she moved in his arms. "I am fine, Vincent. I'm just pleasantly exhausted!" This eased his concerns, and he relaxed.

"Then lie still while I tell you something about this place of magic where I wanted to make love to you our first time. Legend has it that it was here that my grandmother and grandfather stood when they were first married. When they noticed how the silver moonlight shone down on the waterfall they decided to name their ranch Silvercreek."

"That is a beautiful story, Vincent and I am happy

that this is where we first made love," she softly murmured.

"So am I, Karita," he said as he gently kissed the side of her cheek. "Before we leave to return to the ranch I must tell you that I did not take what we did lightly. Please believe me. I know I was the first and I feel very proud that I was." His eyes devoured her and beseeched her to believe him.

Suddenly, an overwhelmed wave of shyness swept over her and she felt shocked that she'd been so bold with Vincent Navarro. But it was a little late now for any regret; the act had been done.

Now she had to believe that Vincent did mean what he said and that he truly cared for her.

Her sudden quiet mood bothered Vincent. It was time for them to leave so he might have her back before four. "You—you are not now feeling sorry about anything, are you chiquita?" he insisted on knowing.

She turned to give him a warm smile as she rose from the blanket for she too knew that they must be getting back to Silvercreek. "No, I am not sorry, but I guess I am a little dazzled."

He took her in his arms. "I'm older than you and I'll confess to being far more experienced, but I'll confess I'm a little dazzled too, little Rita. You are a woman of much passion."

He could have said more but he didn't. Instead, he suggested that they get in the buggy and start back to Silvercreek.

Once again this secluded little spot had cast its magic on a pair of young lovers.

Chapter 7

Yolanda was pleased that Vincent had brought Karita back to the ranch earlier than the hour of four. Karita was glowing and radiant so her mother did not have to be told that she'd had a marvelous time. Yolanda was certain that her daughter would throughout the entire summer sit many an afternoon on the banks of the Pedernales and daydream about last night and today.

The farewells were all said and Kristina promised Yolanda that they would come to Whispering Willows before too long. The Monteras boarded their buggy to depart from Silvercreek.

Everyone was in the highest of spirits as the buggy began to roll away from Silvercreek. Cara had found herself a beau at the fiesta and he'd promised that he would come to see her in a few days. It was funny that she'd never realized how handsome Alfredo Gomez was until they'd danced last night. Alfredo's father owned the ranch bordering Whispering Willows, so Cara was thrilled and excited about the prospects of having him as her suitor.

She was so engrossed in her own romantic thoughts that she did not tease her older sister about Vincent Navarro as she normally would have done. Abeja and Yolanda were so busy chatting about the wonderful fiesta and recalling the marvelous evening they'd spent at Silvercreek they took no notice of the quiet in the back seat of the buggy.

As they rolled down the river road, approaching their little stone cottage, twilight was descending. The Monteras knew that a number of chores would be awaiting them. They were coming home to their usual routine of hard work, but they'd had a wonderful two day holiday which they'd not had in a long time.

Yolanda and Abeja were so accustomed to being home all the time that the sight of their little house was a joy. They were glad to be back.

"Pretty sight, isn't it, Yolanda?" Abeja grinned at her and she smiled, nodding her head to agree with him.

When the Montera family got out of the buggy to go into their house, Yolanda was thinking that it had seemed like she had been away much longer than just two days. Her neat, clean little house might not be as grand as the spacious home they'd just come from but she loved every inch of it. So much of her had been put into making it the pleasant, cozy haven she always found within its walls. She went to the bedroom to change out of her fancy gown and get into one of her simple muslin frocks so she might get to her kitchen to start preparing their evening meal. Abeja attended to the chores out at the barn.

She gave orders to both the girls as they were going

into their bedroom. "You go help your father with the watering and feed, Cara. Karita, if you'll throw some feed to my chickens and gather up the eggs I'll attend to our supper."

Karita took no time to change her clothes as Cara was preparing to do. Long before Cara had managed to change, Karita had already gathered up the eggs and brought them in from the nests. Without lingering in the kitchen, she went back out the door to get the chickens fed. Yolanda was busily moving around her kitchen and she smiled, thinking how different her two girls were. Karita was feisty and fast-paced about anything she did, but her little Cara was so slow. Yolanda knew not who she took after, but it certainly wasn't Abeja.

Cara finally came out of her bedroom to go to the barnyard to help her father with the chores, but he probably had most ot them done by now.

By the time Yolanda had a pan of cornbread placed in the oven of her cookstove and a pot of water boiling on the stove to cook the ears of corn, Karita was back in the kitchen offering to set the table. "Your hens did well while we were gone, mama. I gathered twenty two eggs."

Yolanda smiled, "That is fine!" She turned back to slicing the cured ham she was going to fry in the cast iron skillet for their supper. She told her daughter to go to the pantry and get a jar of the green tomato relish she'd canned last summer.

By the time Abeja and Cara came into the kitchen there was a platter of ham, steamed ears of corn, green tomato relish and a pan of golden brown cornbread waiting for them. Of course, she knew that Abeja was going to indulge himself with two or three helpings of the cornbread before he even took a slice of the ham or corn. He loved her cornbread!

The Montera family gathered around their table and ate Yolanda's delicious meal. Abeja rose from the table and told his daughters that they could now put the kitchen in order and do the dishes, for their mother was tired.

He took her hand to lead her into the parlor so she might sit down to rest. She gave him a grateful smile. She was tired now since she had been busy in her kitchen for the last two hours. Her devoted Abeja had always been so considerate of her, this was one reason she loved him so deeply.

He could not give her riches and gems like Señor Danton gave to his wife, but he gave his complete love to her thoughout all the years they'd been married, and that had been enough for Yolanda. She was rich in having Abeja's devoted love!

The last of the overnight guests left Silvercreek Ranch by five. Two hours later, the Navarro family gathered at the long dining table for their evening meal. It was a quiet, subdued gathering, for all of them were a little weary of talking. The lights dimmed early in the parlor that evening as everyone sought the solace of their private bedrooms to relax and rest.

Of all those gathered around the elegant dining table, Vincent seemed the most alive and talkative. Kristina thought to herself that he must have had a splendid afternoon in the company of beautiful Karita to be in such a gay mood tonight. In contrast, she also noticed that Victor was very quiet and almost sullen.

It didn't surprise her that all the excitement of last night and today's activities had taken its toll on the elderly Señora Lucia Florine. Both ladies looked weary.

Later, when she and Danton were alone in their bedroom, she remarked to him about Vincent's happy state. "I would say that his afternoon must have gone to his liking. Little Karita must have put him in a very happy mood, would you not say, Danton?"

"I would say so," he said as his eyes turned in her direction. "I well remember how you had the same effect on me, querida. I was the happiest man in the whole world. I'd made love to the beautiful Kristina Whelan with her flaming auburn hair, and I considered myself the luckiest man alive. Ah, Kristina—it was the most exciting time of my life!"

"Need I tell you that it was for me too, Danton? I shall never forget that day. I am only curious now about what might have happened today when Vincent and Karita went to that magical spot. It does have a special effect on young people attracted to one another, as we well know, Danton."

"Ah, querida—but we could have done nothing to stop what fate has deemed will happen in their lives. Vincent seemed indeed like a very happy young man during dinner," he smiled.

"There was no doubt about that," his wife readily agreed.

After they discussed their son for awhile longer, Danton told his wife about his brief discussion with his mother this afternoon. "She is ready to let you take charge of the house, Kristina. The fiesta was her last act as the mistress here, and I think she is really anxious for you to take over."

"Then I shall, tomorrow. I saw the fatigue in her face as well as my mother's face tonight. I also plan to insist that mother and Solitaire come here to Silvercreek to live. El Paso is too far away now that she is growing old and my stepfather is dead."

Danton nodded his approval of her idea. "If anyone can persuade her, you are the one, querida."

As Kristina sat at the dressing table to brush her hair she told Danton of her plans to make the empty bedrooms on the east wing of the second floor into comfortable living quarters for her mother and Solitaire—if she did come to Silvercreek.

"Those bedrooms lead out to a balcony which mother would enjoy so much. Your mother enjoys sitting out on the one off her bedroom to sun herself during the day or in the evening."

"Sounds like that pretty head has been whirling with a lot of ideas in the short time since you've gotten back to Silvercreek," Danton remarked.

"Oh, I have, because Señora Lucia informed me the first day we arrived back that she was weary of running this big house and that she had reached a point where she wanted to be very lazy." Kristina laughed as she rose up from the stool to take off her sheer wrapper and lay it at the foot of the bed. She crawled in beside Danton.

He leaned over to dim the lamp on the nightstand. "I will not go into my plans tonight, but tomorrow I will start a new life here at Silvercreek. It has been something I've given much thought to when we were back east. Silvercreek had been run quite successfully by mother's good foreman and hands, so I have no intentions of changing a thing about that."

"Now you have me curious, Danton—darn you! You know what a terrible curiosity I have. I insist on knowing what you're talking about."

"Sorry, querida—it is too late and I'm tired, so we'll talk tomorrow," he told her. Although the room was dark, he had an amused grin on his face as he lay there for he could imagine the disgruntled look on his wife's pretty face. What she'd said was true for he'd never known a more curious lady than Kristina, unless it was his own mother.

"Goodnight, Danton," she muttered as she turned over on her side.

"Goodnight, Kristina."

Señora Florine and Solitaire had been settled in adjoining bedrooms in the west wing of the spacious house. Tonight, Solitaire was concerned about her mam'selle, as she called her.

"I think we should linger here a few days for you to rest up before starting back to El Paso, mam'selle."

"Oh, we will, Solitaire. I promise!" Florine assured her.

Solitaire was happy to hear this as she helped Florine undress. This lady meant much to her for the two of them had been together for so long. Florine Whelan had given her shelter when she was a young girl not much older than Florine. The only difference was Florine was white and Solitaire was a quadroon from New Orleans. She became her maid when Florine was running the Crystal Castle and before she became the

77

owner of the establishment.

She'd been at Florine's side when her baby, Kristina, was born, and she'd helped take care of the youngster. Solitaire deeply loved both of them. They were her family. It had been an adventure to share life with Florine Whelan. Her entire life had revolved around Florine and her daughter, Kristina. She'd known no other life, but both of them had always been so kind and generous to her that she had no regrets. While she'd never married, she'd had a few men during the years. As pale as her skin was Solitaire knew that in El Paso she could have passed herself off as a white woman but she'd never wished to do it.

It had always been exciting being at Florine's side. She had never wished it to be any other way.

When she had her mam'selle comfortable in her bed and she went to her own bed, Solitaire lay there reflecting on the past as well as the future. She'd enjoyed seeing Kristina grow up and marry a fine man like Danton Navarro. Now their sons were the same age their father had been when he first appeared at the Crystal Castle in El Paso and was smitten by the beautiful young Kristina.

The aging woman wondered what she was yet to witness and experience with these two sons of Danton's and Kristina's. She had observed both of them very carefully the last few days and already a very definite opinion was in her mind about these two. She saw thrilling, exciting times ahead, but a primitive instinct was also telling her that there was going to be trouble between the hot-blooded twins in the days to come.

Those all-knowing eyes of Solitaire saw that these two were completely different and she had already decided which of the two she liked more. Rarely did her opinion change about people.

One of the Navarro twins was going to cause the family some heartaches, she felt. Solitaire always had forebodings, and there had been many times that she'd forewarned Florine in the past. Lying there in her bed tonight, she felt that she knew which twin would do this, and as she had in the past, she would do everything she could to protect her mam'selle from harm.

Chapter 8

Silvercreek Ranch soon felt the impact of the return of Señor Danton and Señora Kristina. After the first week, they began to take charge and the aging Señora Lucia turned over the helm to her son.

Kristina had already managed to ingratiate herself with all the house servants, and they eagerly did her bidding as she told them each morning what she wished them to do. Drussie found her as gracious as the elderly señora. There was an air of new life around the house that Drussie found wonderful—having the younger couple dining there each night and the long table seating five family members now instead of the señora alone.

Drussie enjoyed cooking for a gathering like this instead of just one. Cooking for only Señora Lucia provided many leftovers to pass on to the women who helped her in the kitchen, and the señora did not object to that, for she had a most generous heart.

A week after the fiesta had been held there was no doubt as to who the new patrona was at the house.

Danton Navarro was the new patron.

At the end of the week Señora Florine and Solitaire left to return to El Paso accompanied by Victor. Kristina had convinced her that she should come to Silvercreek to spend the rest of her life so they could enjoy time together. Florine had agreed and this had made Solitaire very happy, because she felt these last golden years should be shared with the daughter Florine loved so dearly.

There was nothing to hold Señora Florine to El Paso now. Her husband was dead and the Crystal Castle had been swept into the past long ago. There was only the ranch that her husband had owned when he'd married Florine. Victor had offered his services to see about disposing of that and Florine had eagerly accepted his offer.

Soon there was no longer any mystery as to what Danton had been thinking about when he was back east. The irony was that their son had got himself a most magnificent palomino. Danton had become very interested and curious about the breed. He found them a most beautiful animal, and it was a little startling when Vincent had come riding onto the ranch astride the finest palomino he'd ever seen. Then he remembered the time he'd taken Vincent to the best breeder in the state of Texas who ran a ranch outside Austin. Perhaps that was the day that he became intrigued with the beautiful golden stallions prancing in the corral. He'd watched their cream-colored tails swishing to and fro as they arrogantly paced and the thick silken manes were so beautiful. Never had he seen more magnificent animals. It pleased Danton very much to find out that his son was also intrigued with the palomino.

Breeding this animal was the inspiration that had occupied his thoughts when he'd returned back east. There was plenty of land at Silvercreek to do this. Cattle and horses could share pastureland as vast as at Silvercreek.

Danton had never said a word to Kristina about this secret interest of his, and rarely had he kept any secret thoughts from her. This was an exception. He felt that he would have plenty of time to tell her once they got settled. Now that they had been back for several days and the fiesta was over, he told her about his plans and she was very excited about his idea.

She was already having the quarters changed to accommodate her mother and Solitaire when they returned from El Paso. Florine had insisted that her own furnishings be brought for her bedroom and sitting room, so Kristina had all the furniture moved out and stored. The adjoining bedroom, where Solitaire would stay, had been left as it was for it had pleased her very much with its soft shades of lavender and white. Everything was ready at Silvercreek for their return.

She had no idea how long it would take them in El Paso to finish preparations for her mother's move to Silvercreek. Florine had no intention of selling her ranch, so that was left in the care of her very dependable foreman and his two grown sons.

"Oh, they are a wonderful breed. Vincent's Dorado is absolutely beautiful." With a sly grin she teased Danton, "You wouldn't be thinking that this might tempt your son to stay here at Silvercreek, now would you, darling?"

Danton shook his head and assured her that Vincent or Victor had played no part in this decision. "I love the palomino myself, Kristina. I have since father took me to the Kennison Ranch as a youth, just as I took Vincent with me a few years ago."

"I thought I knew you so well, but I never suspected that you were as fond of horses as you obviously are."

"Just goes to show you that you've still got alot of things to learn about me yet." He gave her a wink as he started to walk out of the room, leaving her to finish the work she'd been doing at her desk.

Becoming mistress at Silvercreek had not been any more tedious than the demanding routine she'd had to observe as a senator's wife for many, many years. The truth was she had far more leisure time now, and she was enjoying it.

It was gratifying to her to see Señora Lucia enjoying herself without any responsibility on her shoulders. She could putter and stroll in her gardens or sleep as late as she wished in the morning.

It amazed her to think that it had only been a week ago that the fiesta had taken place. Like Danton, she felt settled in. Silvercreek was now their home.

Over at Whispering Willows, it had been an endless week for Karita. The days seemed never to end and the nights were long and lonely. She realized that she'd been foolish to think she would see Vincent riding up to the cottage to see her—as Cara's young man had been doing almost nightly—to sit with her on their front porch.

She listened to their lighthearted laughter and felt more depressed for she wished that she was the one sitting in the oak swing with Vincent.

With long hours to think about that one night and day of enchantment she'd enjoyed at Silvercreek Ranch, she had to admit to herself that Vincent Navarro had made no promise to her. She had allowed her foolish young heart to hope that it would be the way she wanted it to be.

She chided herself severely. "You silly girl, Karita! You always dream such grand dreams, dreams that can never come true, don't you know that?"

But her restless heart found that hard to accept. She did not want to settle for anything less than the heart's desire.

However, when the good-looking Ricardo Valdez came riding up to the cottage a week after the fiesta, she tried to be nice to him. As they sat on the porch talking, the night of the fiesta came up in their conversation.

"I did not get one dance with you, Karita. The two Navarro twins kept you to themselves all night," he lamented.

"Well, now Ricardo—you were pretty busy dancing most of the time. I saw you and Cara dancing many times," she replied.

"Well, I never could get close enough to you to ask you. So I asked Cara. I sure wanted no part of those ugly Ramos girls. They've got to be the two ugliest girls I've ever seen!"

Karita threw her head back and laughed. "You're terrible, Ricardo. Maria and Theresa Ramos are very nice."

"Who cares how nice they are if you have to look at those faces!"

She smiled, for what he said was true. Ricardo had a right to be a bit conceited, for he did have a handsome face and a magnificent physique. She knew he'd been spoiled by the attentions of the ranchers' young daughters since he was fifteen or sixteen.

His black eyes danced over her face as he told her, "Now you, Karita, have the most beautiful face my eyes have ever seen. I could look at your face all night long."

"Oh, Ricardo," she sighed.

"I speak the truth and you know it! We're alike, Karita—do you know that? I want more than my family expects me to want and you do too. I don't want to settle into a ranch life and see nothing of the world. I've sensed this in you too."

"You . . . you aren't just satisfied with living day after day on your father's ranch?" she stammered.

"No! Madre de Dios, no! I want to see more of the country—country outside the state of Texas. It's a big world out there. You can imagine how this riles my father and my mother. But I don't care." The intensity in his voice showed Karita a side of Ricardo that she'd never noticed before. Perhaps she'd never taken the time to notice him in the past.

He did seem very nice this afternoon, and she had to confess that she was enjoying herself for the first time since the fiesta. It was a good feeling not to be so lonely.

Before Ricardo finally departed, he asked Karita to go for a ride with him the next day. He laughed, "And I promise that we will stop down by your river for a while where I know you always go to in the afternoon. But I'd like to take you over to my folks' ranch to see the little colt that was born a couple of days ago. Cutest darn thing you've ever seen. Think you could, Karita?"

"I . . . I guess I could, Ricardo," Karita told him in a hesitant tone.

Ricardo was elated that she was finally accepting an invitation from him, for he'd wanted this for a long, long time. Karita had always been so untouchable and aloof. He knew not how he'd been so lucky today and he didn't care. All he knew was that she'd accepted his invitation, and that was a beginning. There was no girl in the whole of Blanco county prettier than Karita Montera. He rode back to his father's ranch in the highest of spirits.

After he left, Karita was feeling a little more lighthearted and happy. Yolanda noticed her change of mood as she helped in the kitchen that evening. If Ricardo's visit had caused that, then she was happy. It was nice to see a smile on her pretty daughter's face again!

When Abeja came in, Yolanda told him the news that Karita had accepted an invitation to go for a ride with Ricardo Valdez. This pleased Abeja because Jose Valdez was his best friend. A young man like Ricardo was the sort that Karita should consider for a husband instead of Vincent Navarro. Abeja knew that this could never be. He could never have married the beautiful Kristina Whelan nor could his beloved Yolanda ever have married Danton Navarro. This was the way it was and nothing could possibly change it.

Karita would have to learn this truth about life. If she didn't Abeja feared that she would be an unhappy person, and he did not wish this for his pretty daughter.

Besides, if she should be courted by Ricardo and they should get married, it would be nice to have her living over on the next ranch. His oldest daughter lived so far away!

So it did please him that Ricardo Valdez was going to come to call on Karita.

Chapter 9

When Ricardo left Whispering Willows he didn't go directly home. He made a stop along the way to boast to his friend Julio about finally getting the pretty little Karita to go for a ride with him. When he arrived at Julio's family ranch he found Julio and his other friend, Orlando, in the barn nipping at a jug of whiskey.

So he sat up in the hayloft with the two of them and took his turn with the jug, as his two friends had been doing for the last hour.

"How did you manage it finally? You've wanted to get next to that little señorita for the last two years. Luck must have been with you today, amigo," Julio giggled, for he was truly feeling the effect of all the liquor he'd consumed. Orlando was somewhat more sober. The three of them had known each other all their lives, and Ricardo had always been the handsome one that had all the little senoritas eager for his attentions. It had certainly irked him when the Montera girl proved to be the exception, Orlando knew.

With a wicked glint in his eyes, Orlando taunted his friend Ricardo, "Better be careful, Ricardo, for I hear that old Abeja can be a bastardo where his daughters are concerned. He's supposed to be a hell of an hombre with that rifle of his."

"I'm not too bad a marksman myself if you'll recall, amigo. Old Abeja don't scare me," Ricardo cockily declared.

"Old Ricardo here could take care of Montera any day, Orlando. That old man wouldn't stop him from having his way with little Karita. Never stopped you with any of the other neighbors' daughters, has it Ricardo?" Julio asked as he handed the jug to Ricardo.

"Never will, either," Ricardo boasted, and took a generous gulp of the liquor.

None of then were aware that the sun was sinking in the western sky and that Julio's father had come into the barn to start the evening chores. He was in a foul mood because Julio's chores had not been taken care of.

Then he heard laughter coming from the loft and he knew why they'd not been done. His son and that no-good Orlando were up in the loft drinking again. He had a voice that could roar like a lion when he was as angry as he was right now. Pedro Sanchez was a burly, husky Mexican with a fierce look about him. He had the strength and stamina to have taken any or all of the three younger men up there in his loft and beat them soundly.

"Julio, you asno! Get yourself down here and do the work you should have done hours ago, and Orlando, you get your butt home to help that poor widow mother of yours. Madre de Dios, she deserves better than the likes of you."

Julio and Orlando began to move over the hay toward the ladder for the tone of Sanchez's voice was enough to sober them up. Ricardo sat where he was, for old Pedro didn't know that he too was up there in the loft.

There he remained as he listened to the harsh cussing Julio was getting and he could see Orlando scurrying out of the barn door. Ricardo stayed in the loft and enjoyed another sip from the jug as he waited for Pedro Sanchez to leave the barn a half hour later.

As he was climbing down the ladder to make his exit out the back door of the barn, he was glad he had tethered his horse behind the barn so that Sanchez had not spotted his horse.

Darkness was beginning to gather around the countryside by the time Ricardo rode into the corrals of the Valdez Ranch.

José Valdez was prepared to give his son a tongue lashing when he arrived back at the ranch until Ricardo told him that he'd been over at Whispering Willows calling on Karita Montera. Nothing could have pleased José more that this bit of news. Not only was she the most beautiful girl in Blanco County, she was also the daughter of his good friend, Abeja Montera and his sweet wife, Yolanda. If his Ricardo and Abeja's Karita would marry, he would be a very happy man.

Ricardo had been their one and only son and José was the first to admit that he and his dear wife, Antonia, had pampered their only son all his life.

"And you shall bring Karita here tomorrow to see our new colt? Your mama will be very happy to hear this, Ricardo. She will be busy tonight baking something special to serve tomorrow afternoon when you and your guest come back here. I shall tell her when I go to the house."

He turned back to his chores, anxious now to be through here in the barn so he could get back to the house and tell Antonia that they would be having Karita Montera in their home tomorrow.

Ricardo knew his father was excited about the news he'd told him, and he smiled as he watched his father leave the barn.

The minute José Valdez rushed into the kitchen, he called out to his wife, "Antonia—Antonia, I've something to tell you."

Antonia came rushing out of her pantry, wiping her hands on her apron. "Yes, José—what is it?"

"We're going to have a visitor tomorrow. Ricardo just told me. He is bringing Karita Montera over here from Whispering Willows to see our new colt. Is that not good news? Our Ricardo has an eye for Abeja's daughter and maybe finally she is getting interested in him too."

She gave him a slow, easy smile. "Well, it would be nice and you know that would delight me. Yolanda and I have always been such good friends."

"She is certainly the prettiest of all their daughters."

"Karita is the prettiest girl around these parts, José. But then I remember Yolanda when they first came to Whispering Willows. I thought she was so very beautiful. I was expecting Ricardo and she was pregnant with her oldest daughter."

"I remember, Antonia. That seems like a long time ago now." José turned to the basin on a small wood stove to pour some water from the pail so he could

92

wash his face and hands.

Soon Ricardo came in and took his turn at the basin to wash his face and hands before he sat down to enjoy the evening meal.

The Valdez family were all in a cheerful mood tonight and Ricardo knew why, although his parents were probably not as elated as he was tonight. Long after he lay down in his bed and dimmed the lamp, he thought about the beautiful Karita with her haunting black eyes and, sensuous, curvy body. She made all the other girls around Blanco County seem dull and boring as far as he was concerned.

But tomorrow he would have the time alone with her that he'd always wanted and could never seem to arrange until today. Tomorrow was going to change everything around for him, Ricardo believed. He knew he could charm beautiful young ladies, for he had time and time again over the last five or six years. Karita Montera could surely not be all that different. All he needed was the right place and enough time alone with her. He could charm her as he had the other ranchers' daughters.

A wicked grin came to his face as he lay there in the dark thinking to himself that his dreams might be most exciting after tomorrow was over. His wildest dreams could become a reality!

As Karita sat at her dressing table brushing her hair after she'd put on her bright yellow blouse and dark brown twill riding skirt, Cara came into the room. "Hear you're going out for the afternoon with Ricardo Valdez."

"Yes, I'm going to ride over to their ranch to see their new colt." Karita told her as she continued to comb out her long curly tresses.

"That Ricardo! He'd try anything just to get you alone with him," Cara laughed. "You must know that he's been like a lovesick calf over you for months now, Karita. I'll swear I think you are blind, or perhaps it was that you could not see any other young man because you've set your sights on Vincent Navarro. Well, I haven't noticed him dashing over here."

Fury flared in Karita as she heard her sister's barbed remarks and she gave way to the impulse to whirl around on the stool and fling the hairbrush at her. Cara leaped up to move out of the way of the flying object.

"Karita—you—you bruja!" Cara shrieked.

"No Cara, *I'm* not the witch. It is you who are the little witch!" Karita snapped at her sister before turning back to the mirror so she could finish combing her hair and tying it back from her face with a bright yellow ribbon that matched her blouse.

She was happy to see Cara marching, belligerent and angry, from the room. She was glad to have peace and quiet to finish getting dressed, for Ricardo was due to arrive any minute now.

When she was satisfied with how she looked as she took the last glance at her reflection in the mirrow she left her bedroom to go into the parlor.

Yolanda was there, sitting in her favorite chair, mending one of her husband's shirts, and she looked up to see Karita coming through the door. "Well, nina— don't you look pretty! Yellow is a most attractive color on you, Karita."

"Thank you, mama."

"Ricardo will be coming any minute now, I imagine. Give my best regards to his mother when you get there, Karita."

"I will, mama. You and Ricardo's mother have been friends a long time, haven't you?"

"A very long time."

The two of them did not get to talk for very long because Ricardo promptly arrived at the hour he'd told Karita he would be there to meet her.

They immediately left Whispering Willows to ride over the countryside toward Ricardo's father's ranch. As she usually was when Ricardo had chanced to see her, Karita looked breathtakingly beautiful. Just being near her fired him with the wildest desires.

As the two of them galloped across the countryside, Ricardo told her how pleased his folks were about her visit.

With her black hair blowing back from her face and a lovely smile on her face, she replied to him, "I must remember to tell your mother that mama sends her best regards. It has just dawned on me how long they have been friends. Had you thought about that, Ricardo?"

"Guess I hadn't, Karita."

"Well, they have."

Ricardo found her a very exciting sight as she sat astride her little mare that could hardly keep up the pace with his larger horse.

All too soon to please Ricardo, they were approaching his father's ranch. He told himself that when he was escorting her back to Whispering Willows, the pace would be slower.

He realized that once they arrived at the ranch he would have no time alone with her. Ricardo was determined that this afternoon was not to be wasted. He'd waited too long for this to happen. He would not be cheated!

Before this day ended, Ricardo Valdez was going to taste the nectar of those honey-sweet lips of Karita Montera, he promised himself!

On the way back home he was going to collect the reward for all the time he'd waited for Karita Montera to come into his arms. God knows, he'd never been so patient for any other girl.

But he was tired of waiting!

Chapter 10

The gawky little fawn colored colt was as adorable as Ricardo had described him, and Karita was delighted that Ricardo had invited her to the ranch to see him. She had also enjoyed the warm hospitality of his parents when the four of them sat in the kitchen to savor Antonia's juicy fruit pie and steaming hot coffee. Their stone cottage was very similar to her own home and Karita knew that they were the same kind of hard working people as her own parents.

She knew that she should allow herself to be courted by a young man of a background similar to her own and not yearn for someone she could never hope to marry, like Vincent Navarro.

It was time that she announced to Ricardo that she should be getting back home, so she graciously thanked the Valdezes for the wonderful afternoon she'd spent at their ranch. "It was so nice, and I'm so happy that Ricardo invited me over here to see the darling colt. He is adorable. Your pie was delicious, señora. I'd say that you and mama must be the best cooks in the county."

Antonia smiled and told Karita, "Well I know Yolanda is, but I am glad you enjoyed it, Karita, and you must come again. Tell your mother that I will hope to see her soon."

Karita told Ricardo she must be leaving now. "If I am too late getting home, then they might not allow me to come again," she said.

Ricardo did not hesitate, for he was more than ready to have Karita all to himself again. From the house, José and Antonia watched the couple mount their horses to ride away. Both were thinking what a very handsome couple they made. Karita was such a sweet young girl.

José returned to the barn and Antonia turned her attention to her chores back in her kitchen as her thoughts dwelled on Karita and her son.

Once they were out of sight of the house, Ricardo slowed the pace of his horse. He knew his parents were probably watching until they rode out of sight.

When they were about halfway between the Valdez ranch and Whispering Willows, at a spot where he was going to suggest that they stop to talk for a moment before they rode the last half mile of the way, he spotted two riders coming quickly toward them. In another minute he recognized the riders as his compadres, Julio and Orlando. He cursed under his breath, and he was damned well going to let them know it tomorrow. He didn't appreciate their intruding into his afternoon, and he knew that they had plotted it, for he'd told them about his plans. Next time, he'd keep his damned mouth shut!

There was no friendly smile on his face as they rode up to him and Karita to greet them. "Hey, amigo— that's an awfully pretty lady there with you," Orlando said as he reined his horse up beside Karita's mare.

Julio came up on Ricardo's right side and all Ricardo had to do was look at his eyes to know that the two of them had been drinking again. He didn't like their attitudes and the look on their faces. There was no humor in the tone of his voice when he told both of them, "I've no time to talk to you two today. I've got to get Karita home. Her folks are expecting her back."

"Ohhh, come on Ricardo. We just want to visit with Karita awhile. You aren't going to deny us that privilege, are you?" Julio laughed.

"I don't want to talk with you, Julio," Karita curtly informed him. "As Ricardo told you, I'm due home. You'll have to excuse us."

She did not like the lecherous look on Orlando's face as he'd sided his horse so close to hers, and she instinctively felt that he was about to grab the reins of her horse.

Ricardo saw the apprehension on her pretty face and he, too was of the same opinion as Karita. He was convinced that the two of them had no good on their minds when Julio gave out a silly giggle, "Well, it wasn't exactly chatting we had in mind."

Swiftly, Ricardo leaned over to yank Julio's shirt and tell him, "Shut your filthy mouth, Julio." Just as swiftly his black eyes darted over to Karita and Orlando. "Ride for home, Karita. I've a score to settle with these two drunk idiots! You ride after her, Orlando and I'll kill you, I swear it!"

Karita did not hesitate doing as Ricardo ordered her to do. She spurred her little mare to go as fast as she could gallop. Not once did she look back to see what was going on behind her. The most welcome sight for her to see was her home just ahead. But as she was slowing up the mare's pace to go into the grounds of Whispering Willows, she was pondering whether she should or should not tell her folks. She did not wish to ignite a feud between her father and the father of Julio. She was a little perplexed about what had happened for she'd known Julio and Orlando all her life and they'd never acted the way they had this afternoon.

She knew that Orlando had been drinking for she had smelled the liquor from the few feet that divided them. Perhaps, this was what had made them crazy. Whatever it was she knew that the two of them had devilment on their minds!

Ricardo's gallant action had endeared him to her and she hoped he dealt with his friends soundly.

She would have been pleased to know that Ricardo Valdez's fierce temper exploded vehemently as soon as she galloped away.

"What the hell do you two bastards think you were going to do, eh?" His black eyes sparked with fire.

"Oh, come on, Ricardo. We just wanted to have ourselves a little fun. Haven't the three of us done that in the past?" Orlando reminded him.

"I had made no agreement with the two of you to share the favors of Karita Montera. Don't you dare to suggest that, Orlando! Don't you dare—damn you both!" Ricardo blasted the two of them.

Julio was far drunker than Orlando so he was not as aware of the fury seething within Ricardo. Orlando knew that Ricardo could be a mean man when he was riled, as he certainly was now. So he was backing up his horse to hightail it away. Julio could do whatever he wanted.

As he was preparing to leave, he heard Julio telling Valdez, "Hell, Ricardo—I thought she was just another girl to you. You know how you're always bragging about all the ladies you conquer. Guess we figured this one wrong."

"You figured it very wrong, Julio. Best you remember that in the future. Karita Montera is not just another girl to me!"

As Orlando had done, Julio went through the slow motions of veering his horse around to go in the opposite direction. There were no goodbyes said by the three of them as they parted this late afternoon.

Ricardo yanked the reins of his horse to turn back to ride toward home. He knew that Karita was safely home by now, but he wondered what she had told her parents as to why he had not properly escorted her home.

This was what was bothering him as he rode toward his own home. Those two drunk idiots had fouled up all his plans and it would be a long time before he would forget or forgive them.

He wasn't in the most pleasant mood when he arrived back home but he tried to mask his anger when he walked into the house, for he did not wish his parents to know what had happened. He could only pray that Karita did not tell her parents the truth for he could imagine what a furor all this could cause among the neighboring ranchers.

Something like this could cause a feud between ranchers that could last for years as it had many times in the past. Texans were an explosive breed of men and nothing could spark trouble more than a lady, be it a wife, daughter or ladylove.

Many a Texas feud had been ignited over a beautiful woman and Ricardo had heard the tales about such happenings all his life. Karita was capable of stirring up such a fever in any red blooded Texan.

He was glad to have the evening meal behind him and leave the presence of his parents to get to the privacy of his own room. Today had been a big disappointment to Ricardo, for things had not gone exactly as he'd planned. Next time, he would be more discreet and not announce anything to his stupid friends.

He had no one to blame but himself, he realized. When he finally went to bed he had decided that he was going to stay away from Julio and Orlando for awhile. They were nothing but trouble and a worthless lot if the truth were to be told.

So he did just that for the next few days. He worked diligently around the ranch beside his father and not once did he ride away from the ranch in the evening after supper.

José and Antonia were delighted that Ricardo was staying home in the evenings instead of carousing with his buddies as he often did during the week.

There was no doubt in the minds of Julio and Orlando that Ricardo considered himself their friend no longer, for he'd not come around for the last four days. Neither of them was brave enough to ride over to

102

the Valdez ranch to try to talk to him. They weren't too sure about how they would be received.

"Guess we went a little too far, eh Orlando?" Julio told his friend after Ricardo had not appeared the second day. "Guess he's damned serious about this one. I—I just thought he was playing his usual little tricks. Well, now we know that Karita Montera isn't just another girl as far as old Ricardo is concerned."

"That's for sure. Never saw such a mean look in his eyes as I did a couple of days ago," Orlando remarked.

"Si—there is a fever in Ricardo for this señorita and I'll remember that from now on," Julio decided and Orlando quickly agreed with him.

After Vincent had been at Silvercreek a week he found himself growing restless. It might be an idyllic place for his parents to spend the golden years of their life, but he was not quite ready for such peace and quiet day in and day out.

He wished that he'd offered his services to his grandmother ahead of Victor to take her back to El Paso and close down her house. It would have been exciting to see the place where the old Crystal Castle had once stood in the city of El Paso. He had heard the story about how it had burned to the ground some twenty odd years ago.

Quite different from him, his twin Victor had no talent as a gambler. Vincent figured he must have inherited a lot of his Grandmother Florine as well as his Grandmother Lucia, for he loved the challenge of a high stakes game.

One of the most enjoyable times he'd spent here at

Silvercreek was the evening after dinner when he and Lucia Navarro had sequestered themselves in the library to play cards for the entire evening. It was quite late when he finally escorted her upstairs to her bedroom. She, too, had enjoyed herself. She chuckled and declared to him, "I've not had so much fun in a long time, Vincent. We shall do this again—si?"

"Si, Grandmother. You've got some tricks to teach me, I've decided," he laughed.

"It would be my pleasure. Why shouldn't I teach my grandson the art of being an expert gambler? Neither of my sons was interested, and I guess if I had to be honest I was glad they weren't so inclined. My life as gambler was over the minute I married your grandfather. That part of my life was over forever."

Vincent's green eyes looked down warmly at the little elderly woman walking by his side. In a slow but very sincere voice he declared to her, "I find you a most fascinating woman, grandmother."

"You do, do you? Well, we have a mutual admiration society going here, for I find you a most intriguing young man who's going to reach out and grab for many things in life. I hope you will, Vincent, before you settle for something that you'd be discontented with years later."

"Glad to hear you say that, grandmother so I'll tell you something that I've not even spoke to father about. I'm going to go to Austin in a few days to seek out a gentleman I met back in Washington. I don't think I'm ready to stay here at Silvercreek to raise palominos. I'm going to leave that to father."

A sly grin came to Lucia's face, for she knew what Danton was hoping, but she said nothing to Vincent.

She'd realized long ago that she could not run her own sons' lives, and neither would her dear Danton be able to do it with his twin sons. That was just not the way life worked.

By the time they got to her bedroom door, her parting remark to him was, "A man has to do what he must, Vincent."

He bent down to kiss the tiny lady. "Thank you for saying that, grandmother. Your opinion means much to me."

She smiled and nodded her head as she disappeared through the door. She envisioned a glorious future for Vincent, for he had that quality about him that would make it happen. But when she thought of the future, she had to reflect on the past, and the past still haunted Lucia Navarro when she thought about her own twin sons!

She well remembered when Kristina had given birth to Danton's twin sons, how she'd felt a mixture of emotions flooding her. There was a part of her that was elated by the announcement of twin grandsons, but there was also that feeling of torment haunting her about her own past and her twin sons.

Danton had always been a wonderful son, but Damien had been so wicked that she'd pondered how he could have been sired by the very respected Victor Navarro and how she'd carried him in her womb.

Chapter 11

It did not please Danton Navarro when his son announced his plans to go to Austin for a few days. Vincent did not have to tell him why he was going to Austin. It was to seek out Adolfo Martinez whom he'd met back in the capital. Danton had to admit that Senator Martinez was a very impressive gentleman with his debonair airs. He was also a very wealthy, successful lawyer in the city of Austin so Danton knew what was going on in Vincent's head.

While she tried to soothe her husband's ruffled feathers, Kristina could not fault her son's desires to go to Austin. Besides, she'd chanced to meet Adolfo Martinez and he was a most imposing man with winning ways and a charming personality, which had obviously made an impact on Vincent.

She knew that her son had been impressed by the sophisticated, powerful Señor Martinez. He had squired some of the capital's most beautiful ladies when he came there for his short visits over the years. Kristina judged him to be in his mid forties and he'd never been married.

She knew that he had a reputation for having some of the grandest parties ever given in Austin and it was rumored that he was a very influential gentleman not only in the capital city of the state of Texas but in the capital of the nation.

She teased her husband gently, "You've got to recall, Danton, that you were not content here at Silvercreek either when you were young. I recall when you had your own little place in Austin and practiced law."

He could not argue with her, for what she said was true. "So you are saying that you don't think Vincent will be staying at Silvercreek?"

"That is a very good possibility, Danton."

"Well, then maybe Victor will be the one who will take some interest in Silvercreek. I would like to think that one of our sons would wish to take over the Navarro land."

Rarely did Kristina get vexed at Danton, but tonight was one of those times. How dare he speak about his sons and their interest in Silvercreek when he had been absent from Texas and Silvercreek Ranch for the last twenty years, pursuing his ambition in politics? He was not being fair with his sons. If she were to be absolutely honest, she would have to say that he was being selfish, and she didn't admire this.

As she prepared to leave his study, she remarked in a brusque tone, "Perhaps neither son will be interested in Silvercreek, Danton. Time changes things, as you must know at your age. Victor and Vincent have the right to make their own choices, as you did."

She turned sharply to make her exit, leaving Danton to mull over what she'd just said. He knew his lovely wife so well that he instantly realized that she was in a little bit of a temper. His auburn-haired lady was a spitfire and he'd experienced that from the first moment they'd met years ago.

But when he was alone he thought about what she had said and realized that she was right, as usual. He was just being selfish. He had to do nothing but think back to the time when he was their age to confess to himself that he had been just as self-absorbed as they were right now.

Never had Lucia Navarro tried to deny him what he wanted or persuade him to remain here at Silvercreek to take over the running of the ranch. She took charge. So he must do the same thing.

A few days later when Vincent left Silvercreek to go to Austin, Danton gave him a warm, friendly farewell and told him to give Senor Martinez his best regards.

Kristina was standing by his side and she gave him an affectionate smile and squeezed his arm to let him know she was glad he hadn't given their son an argument. Once again, she was very proud of her husband and loved him more dearly.

Vincent let Dorado break into a fast gallop as they left Silvercreek. Vincent could tell that the spirited palomino was enjoying himself as he was allowed the freedom to run wild as the wind as they sped over the country.

But a sudden impulse came over Vincent to veer off the main dirt road to take the side road along the river. If he was lucky he might happen to come upon Karita. That was enough to urge him to guide Dorado to take the side road. He would still easily make Austin before dark.

He had not traveled too far on the narrow road until he came to the Pedernales River. Another few minutes went by before he was rewarded by the sight that he yearned to see. The bright sun was shining down on her as she sat on the ground and her beautiful black hair looked so glossy with the sunshine reflecting on it.

That was exactly why she was sitting there in the bright sunshine, so she could allow her hair to dry, for she'd just washed it.

She'd come to the riverbank to get away from the house and her sister, Cara. Since the afternoon she'd returned from the Valdez ranch, Ricardo had not come around, and Cara had been taunting Karita constantly. She'd remarked two or three times a day about Ricardo having obviulsy lost interest in her older sister.

"I'd have thought he would have been coming over here almost daily like Alfredo does to see me," she'd remarked.

Karita had snapped back at her, "Alfredo is just a kid your age, Cara. Ricardo is a grown man with certain duties around the ranch. Until you know what you're talking about why don't you just keep that busy mouth of yours shut for a change!"

But later she had to admit that she'd wondered why Ricardo had not come over to see her and to know that she made it home safely that afternoon after he held Julio and Orlando at bay back in the woods.

She was beginning to question young men in general. Vincent Navarro had disappointed her, since he had made no effort to come to Whispering Willows after the fiesta as she would have expected him to do.

Ricardo Valdez had been so anxious to be with her and she had known that he was attracted to her for a long time. When she had finally agreed to his invitation to spend the afternoon with him, she found it was very perplexing to her that he'd not come over, especially after what had happened on the way back home.

Sitting in the sun and gazing out over the waters of the river, she was consumed with a feeling of discontent. There was a sad look in her black eyes as they stared off in space. But Vincent could not see this as he rode up, for all he could see was the delicate features of her profile and shapely figure.

Her lovely head turned with a jerk as she heard the pounding hooves of Dorado coming toward her. Immediately a pleased smile came to her face when she recognized Vincent. She should have acted with more reserve, she knew.

A handsome smile was on his face as he greeted her, "You make a most beautiful sight, Karita, sitting there in the sunlight."

She stood up by the time he had come to the spot where she'd been sitting. "I didn't expect to see you, Vincent."

"Well, I was hoping to see you. I'm on my way to Austin," he declared as he leaped off Dorado and came to stand beside her. "I was hoping very much to see you."

"You—you are going to Austin?" Her black eyes pierced him as she questioned what he'd just told her.

"I am. Just a visit with a friend of mine that I met back in Washington. I'll be coming back to Silvercreek. Will you miss me, little Rita?" He took her hand and urged her to a spot where the shade of the trees would provide a cool spot for them to sit down.

Karita had no answer to give him as she sank to the

ground. He sat beside her. His green eyes were dancing over her face as they sat so close together. "I'd like to think that you would miss me just a little," he grinned.

"Then I shall tell you that I will miss you, Vincent. But we've not been together that much, have we?"

It was not exactly the words the self-assured Vincent Navarro expected to hear from the sweet, naive Karita. It took him a moment to gain his composure before he replied to her question. "We've not known one another or been with one another very much, but I was assuming that the moments we were together were very special times. I considered them to be so."

"And so did I, Vincent," she admitted to him. "I also know that I am no daughter of a wealthy family. You are the son of a wealthy man, so I could hardly expect to see you too often, could I?"

A strange look came on Vincent's face as he listened to her talk. "What would make you say that, vida mia? I don't live by any rules but my own. It's good that you know this. The conventional ways of the past are not for me. They never have been!" His strong hands were holding her shoulders so that she had to look directly at him.

"I said what I did because I've had time to think about things that happened at the fiesta. I . . . I don't blame you, Vincent. I blame myself."

A skeptical brow rose up. "You've nothing to blame yourself for, Karita. My, you are a most serious young lady this afternoon."

"Perhaps I am, Vincent. But I can't change the way I am."

A smile came to his face as he leaned closer to her to murmur softly to her, "And I wouldn't want you to change, Karita mia. You're too perfect just the way you are. Promise me that you'll never change!"

Before she realized what was happening, his sensuous lips were capturing hers with a kiss. But this time she fought desperately, determined not to surrender to him as eagerly as she had during the fiesta. But the heat of his lips was so persuasive that for a few brief moments she had to allow herself to enjoy the ecstasy he gave her.

When she found herself feeling breathless she placed her two hands against Vincent's broad chest and pushed with all the strength she could muster. Gasping, she mumbled in a faltering voice, "No, Vincent! No! Not this time!"

Vincent found her to be a little wildcat as she scrambled to release herself from his arms. As he looked at her face with that determined look in her black eyes he saw how firm she was that it was not going to go any farther than the one lingering kiss he'd just enjoyed.

Slowly, he released her from his strong, muscled arms but he was in a quandary as to what was bothering the beautiful Karita. But he knew he would not find out today what it was.

"I'd never force my attentions on you, querida. I swear this to you. Next time, you will have to come to me and tell me that you are ready for me to love you as I did the day after the fiesta. It was a time I shall never forget, Karita. But now I think I must be on my way." He rose up off the ground giving her his hand to help her to her feet.

She stood close to him with those doelike black eyes staring up at him so innocently that Vincent wanted nothing more than to put his arms around her to enclose her and assure her that he cared very much for her. "Karita, you can always depend on me if you need me, and I hope you'll always remember that."

Reluctantly, he released her and walked over to mount Dorado.

She stood watching him swing his long leg over the saddle. Just as he spurred Dorado into moving, he grinned down at her. "Miss me just a little, eh, little Rita?"

She returned his smile as he started to ride away, thinking to herself that she would miss him very much and she wished she was riding away with him this afternoon.

Never could she feel about any other man as she did about Vincent Navarro!

Chapter 12

Senor Adolfo Martinez was pleasantly surprised by the arrival of Vincent Navarro in Austin and he would not allow Vincent to go to the hotel as he'd planned to do. "I would be insulted if you did not agree to be my guest in my home while you are here, Vincent. I well remember the gracious hospitality I received from the Navarro family when I was back east."

So Vincent accepted his invitation and went back to the lavish two story mansion at the edge of the city. It was the kind of home Vincent would have expected Adolfo to own. The furnishings were luxurious and showed the pride he felt about his Spanish heritage, as well as all the prized objects he'd acquired during his travels all over the world.

The debonair bachelor was a very refined, fastidious gentleman of forty. Vincent could understand why he had never married for it would take a lady of perfection to please this very demanding man. He had only to glance around at the rooms of this palatial home to know that Adolfo had chosen the furnishings and works of art with a very precise idea in mind as to how he wanted the rooms to look.

After they arrived, he ushered Vincent into his study, suggesting that they enjoy a drink before they went upstairs. "I have a lady who will be joining us at dinner. I would have arranged that differently if I had known you were going to be arriving, Vincent," he laughed.

"I'm sorry, Adolfo," Vincent replied to him.

"I'm not, and Paulina will be delighted. Handsome gentlemen always please her. This meeting was not just a night of pleasure, shall we say. It was an appointment to discuss some of her business affairs as well as sharing dinner."

Pouring Vincent a drink and then pouring himself one, he invited Vincent to sit down in one of the overstuffed black leather chairs. He sat down in the other one.

"So you and your family are back in Texas to stay now?"

"Been back here a little over a week now and yes, I would say that we're settled in at Silvercreek." He told Adolfo about his father's plans to start breeding palominos on the vast acres of the ranch. "He's very excited about it, I think."

"From the handsome beast you were riding, I must assume you will take an active part in his project," Adolfo remarked as he sat back in the chair relaxing and sipping his drink. As he often did when he talked, he made lazy little strokes on his mustache.

"Not necessarily, Adolfo. I own one palomino, but I can't say that the breeding of them would interest me as it seems to intrigue my father."

Martinez did not hesitate for a minute telling

116

Vincent what he had told him a few months ago back in the capital. "I can always use a smart young man in my law firm here in Austin. My offer still holds."

In just as candid a manner, Vincent admitted to him that this was why he'd come to Austin. "I've been thinking about what you said since I've been back so I thought I'd come here to see you and look over your city. I don't know much about Austin. I've only been here for brief visits."

"Well, Señora Castillo will be arriving in about an hour so we better get upstairs so we'll be ready to meet her," he smiled. "My house is yours, so stay a few days, think about my offer and look Austin over, Vincent."

The two of them mounted the stairway that spiraled from the first floor to the second. They walked down the plush carpeted hallway. Adolfo laughed and told him that he had given names to all his bedrooms. "Being a bachelor, I can give way to certain little eccentricities. I've named them for various countries. I guess I got the idea when I brought back so many things from each of the places I went. So I'll allow you to take your pick, Vincent. What shall it be Italy, France, England or Mexico? I already have Spain," he laughed. Vincent was to see a side of this very dignified gentleman that was simple and childlike along with his sophisticated airs.

"I think I'll take Italy," Vincent laughed and Adolfo directed him to the room directly across the hall from his own.

"I'll send my man, Rollo, to your room if you need anything pressed. He will have it back to you quickly. See you in an hour," he told Vincent as he turned to go across the hallway.

Vincent walked into the room and for a minute, he allowed himself to savor the luxury of this room as he had the other rooms he'd been in. On the walls were paintings by artists depicting the Italian countryside and street scenes. A magnificent five foot statue stood in one corner of the room, flanked with greenery.

Dark, highly polished furniture had been selected for this room and the coverlet and drapes were a vivid, brilliant color. Just outside the bedroom was a small private balcony encircled with a wrought iron railing. Huge urns sat on either corner of the balcony with brilliantly colored flowers in full bloom. Two comfortable chairs and a small table were there for the guest to enjoy the comfort of the balcony.

After Vincent had enjoyed a bath to wash away the dust of traveling from Silvercreek to Austin and got dressed, it was the small balcony he sought to enjoy before joining Adolfo downstairs. He felt he could have been in a villa in Italy.

He found Rollo to be a magnificent manservant. His pants and coat were brushed and pressed and back in the room by the time he'd finished his bath. By the time he was dressed, Rollo was there with a refreshing drink on a silver tray.

Since he wanted to be sure that Adolfo would be in the parlor when he went downstairs, Vincent leisurely enjoyed his drink and the gentle breeze blowing across the balcony. From the balcony, he saw the carriage arrive in the drive, bringing Adolfo's guest, Señora Castillo. When she got out of the carriage he saw that she was very pretty. He lingered on the balcony for a while longer before making any attempt to leave his room. It would allow Adolfo to have a few moments with her before he joined them.

When he did make his appearance in the luxurious parlor and met the stunning Señora Paulina Castillo he thought she was awfully young to be a widow. Later, he learned from Adolfo that she had been married to a much older man.

Paulina Castillo's curiosity was keenly whetted about Adolfo's young guest. She found him to be a very striking looking young man with the most devastating green eyes she'd ever seen. The night had become interesting and exciting for Paulina.

She had never fooled herself about Adolfo. He was a most charming man and she'd always accepted his invitations to social affairs in Austin. She'd realized that ladies envied her when she entered a room by the side of the debonair Adolfo Martinez. But Paulina also knew that he enjoyed his status as a bachelor and she rather doubted if Adolfo would ever marry. In fact, she was sure he wouldn't!

She had never considered that marriage was in the offering and truthfully, she was not interested. When she married again it was going to be a younger man than her first husband, and it would certainly not be a man as self-centered as Adolfo was. She wanted a man who would be willing to cater to her wishes and desires. Adolfo would never do that for any woman!

When Adolfo had introduced Paulina to Vincent he'd seen the sparks in her black eyes and he had anticipated this. He was also watching Vincent's green eyes appraising her and her voluptuous figure looked very alluring tonight in a brilliant blue gown and sapphire and diamond earrings. Her black hair was piled high atop her head.

"It is a pleasure to meet you, señor. Texas is very proud of your father, Señor Danton Navarro. I shall hope that you are going to be here in Austin for awhile," she said as she took the glass of wine Adolfo handed her.

"Well, I plan to be here a few days at least. I want to see your city. So far, I like what I've seen, señora," Vincent told her.

Adolfo saw qualities in young Vincent that would make him a great asset to his law firm. Just the family name, Navarro, would be worth its weight in gold. But the young man himself was a gallant charmer with a winning way about him. There was no question about it—he was devilishly handsome.

It was a most interesting hour as the three of them dined together and enjoyed Adolfo's fine wines and his cook's delectable meal.

After dinner the three of them went back into the parlor. Vincent shared an after dinner liqueur with them while they enjoyed pleasant conversation. But he also remembered that Adolfo had told him she had some business matters to discuss, so he set his glass aside to announce that he was going to retire.

"Señora, it has been a pleasure to meet you and I will hope to see you again before I leave. But I've had a long ride today from Silvercreek so I must excuse myself. I will say goodnight to you and Adolfo."

When he had disappeared into the hallway, Adolfo told Paulina, "He is being gracious because I mentioned to him that we had some business to discuss tonight."

"Gracious he is, but he's more than that, Adolfo. He is very handsome!" At this moment Paulina cared not about the business affairs she was going to consult Adolfo about, though they concerned her husband's vast estate.

An amused smile was on Adolfo's face as he said to her, "Well, between the two of us maybe we can entice him to remain in Austin. I've offered him a position in my law firm. I did that months ago, back in the capital."

"Well, I will certainly try!" she told Adolfo. The wicked twinkle in her eyes left no doubt in his mind that she certainly would do just that!

An hour later they had completed their business discussion and Señora Paulina Castillo boarded her carriage to return to her home. The only intimacy between them had been a goodnight kiss planted on her cheek by Adolfo before he turned to walk back up the steps and go inside.

This was usually the way it was between the two of them but Paulina knew that her friends and Adolfo's acquaintances thought of them as lovers. The longer she knew him, the more she wondered if any woman had ever shared his bed.

It was common knowledge that he liked to see and be with attractive women wherever he traveled, as he did back here in Austin. Adolfo had never been anything but the perfect gentleman anytime they were together but the very perceptive Paulina had come to some very definite conclusions about the dashing forty year old bachelor in recent months. She sensed there was another side to this meticulous man. With all his wealth and charm, this impeccable señor was a very lonely man with a dark side to his character.

What it was Paulina did not know yet and she wasn't

so sure that she wanted to find out. They were good companions, and he filled a void in her life as she obviously did in his. He was the best lawyer in the state of Texas , and so this was all that concerned her at this time.

What she did care about as she was traveling toward her own home was how she might lure that good looking Vincent Navarro to her boudoir. She planned to work on that over the next few days.

He was the most exciting man she'd seen in a long, long time!

Chapter 13

Adolfo climbed the stairs to his room, for the hour was late, but he was one of those people who did not require a lot of sleep. Six hours were enough for him to put in a full eighteen hour day.

No lamp was burning in Vincent's room so he had obviously came upstairs to go to bed as he'd announced an hour ago.

He saw that Rollo had laid out his attire for the morning as he'd instructed him to do. Adolfo undressed and prepared to retire. As he lay there in the darkened room he considered that the next few days were going to be very interesting. He felt quite sure that the beautiful Señora Castillo was going to be conjuring excuses to visit his home in hopes that she would encounter his handsome young friend, Vincent.

That cunning mind of his was far too active for him to go to sleep for a while, so he lay there for another half hour thinking about this evening. Finally, sleep came.

*   *   *

It would have done Paulina Castillo no good to have tried to get in touch with Vincent Navarro the next day for he was gone until the late afternoon. He took a grand tour of the city and he came to the conclusion by the time he returned to Adolfo's home that it was a very fine city that seemed to be thriving and growing tremendously since the capital was restored there after being moved to Houston in 1842, due to the incursions by the Mexicans.

The city was located on the Colorado River with rolling hills to the west. To the east were the plains. Vincent observed several magnificent palatial homes like the one Adolfo owned. He was unaware that he was going by the huge two story mansion where Paulina Castillo lived.

At the end of the day when he turned down one of the side streets to go back to Adolfo's home he chanced to pass a smaller two story house enclosed with a stone wall. He saw the poster there by the wall announcing that it was for sale. He gave a quick yank on the reins ordering Dorado to halt. Leaping off the palomino, he marched through the grilled iron gate and walked into the small courtyard area surrounding the entrance of the house.

Numerous trees provided a cool shade from the afternoon sun and nearby he heard soft rippling sounds from the waters of a fountain situated a few feet away, with grilled iron benches placed around it.

There was no way to compare this small little courtyard to the vast courtyard of Adolfo Martinez's elaborate gardens, but to Vincent it was just as beautiful.

When Vincent knocked on the door, an elderly gray-haired man answered. He informed Vincent that he was the caretaker and his name was Jules. "Señora Aquirre is no longer living here. She became too ill, so she is with her daughter. But I can show you the house and grounds if you would like to see them."

Vincent told him he would like to see the house and grounds and Jules invited him to enter the tiled hallway. Jules led him through the parlor and adjoining dining room. There was a rather large kitchen area very brightly decorated and a small room Vincent figured was a servant's quarters. Upstairs there were four nice sized bedrooms.

Vincent had sensed, as he'd roamed through the rooms, that happiness had dwelled within the walls of this house. All the furnishings were still in the rooms. He was sure that the Aquirres were a very happy pair and had loved this little place very dearly.

He asked Jules as they went around the back of the grounds toward the small stable, "Has Señora Aquirre been a widow and in ill health very long, Jules?"

"No, señor—just this last year since her husband died. They say she no longer has the will to live. She wishes to die."

"I see," Vincent said. He asked Jules what she was seeking to sell the property for, because he had already seen enough to know that he wanted to own this house.

When Jules told him what the señora was asking, Vincent asked him to take a message to her stating he was interested in buying her home.

"I will go to her this evening, señor."

Vincent told Jules that he would come by again the next afternoon to see what the señora had said about his offer.

He said farewell to Jules and went down the pathway toward the iron gate where he had Dorado tethered. He mounted and rode away. A strange exhilaration swelled within him as he went toward Adolfo's and he could not explain why acquiring this little house was so important to him. So he didn't try to reason it out, but he knew he wanted to own it. He had no doubt about it. He would own it!

Adolfo was not home when he arrived, so he went directly upstairs to his room. He proceeded to rid himself of his coat and boots as he sat down on the bed. It felt good just to roam around the room in his stocking feet. He had thought he had entered the house without any of the servants seeing him, but obviously Rollo had seen him arrive.

Vincent found him amazing and he could see why Adolfo had him as his manservant. He seemed to know exactly when his services were needed. When Vincent opened the door, Rollo greeted him, "Good evening, señor. Shall I prepare your bath? Perhaps, you would enjoy a drink until it is ready?"

"That would be fine, Rollo. Is Señor Martinez home yet?"

"No, señor—he is late tonight. This often happens with the señor. He is a very hardworking man."

"I have no doubt about that, Rollo. Señor Martinez is one of the most admired, respected lawyers I know."

Rollo nodded, agreeing with Vincent. Then he turned to leave the room to get on with his duties. Shortly he returned with Vincent's drink and turned his attentions to preparing the warm bath for him.

An hour later, Vincent had bathed and dressed. Since Adolfo had told him to make himself at home, he left his room to go downstairs. He figured if he didn't find his host in the parlor, then it would be a nice evening to take a stroll in the garden and enjoy one of his cigarillos.

As it would happen, Adolfo was not in the parlor so he walked on out into the gardens. He was anxious to tell Adolfo about the house he'd made an offer on today. He thought about the little garden area there and how pleasant it could be at night with the sound of the waters and spray of the fountain. He already had some very definite ideas of how he wanted to furnish the rooms and the changes he would make to the grounds.

He sat down on one of the benches in Adolfo's garden to enjoy the cigarillo and he was suddenly thinking not of the little house but of Karita Montera. He was thinking of every feature of her face and all the beautiful curves of her sensuous figure. There in the quiet serenity of the garden, he found himself yearning to see this enchanting little señorita again.

This was baffling to Vincent, for he could not recall ever reflecting about some lady in this way before in his entire life. What would make him think so intensely about Karita as he was doing? There was no doubt that she was beautiful, but he'd admired many beautiful ladies in his lifetime. When he was touring Europe, he'd spent time with the fair-haired lovelies in England and he'd spent many nights with the little French coquettes, but he'd never ever thought of them after he'd left them.

But Karita was like a fever in his blood, for the longer he thought about her the flame of passion rose with mounting desire.

Reluctantly, he left the bench in the moonlight

dappled garden to return to the house since he figured that Adolfo would probably be in the parlor ready to have his evening meal.

When he returned, he did find him there enjoying his favorite brandy, obviously relaxed as he leaned back against the high-backed velvet chair. He heard Vincent enter his parlor and turned to greet him.

"Good evening, Adolfo. You must have had a very busy day," Vincent remarked as he sauntered on into the parlor.

"Ah, but this is the way I like it, Vincent. I love the constant challenge I meet. I would find life very dull without it. Each day I wake up wondering what will happen that will test my wit and wisdom."

"I find that very interesting, Adolfo. I would hope to feel that way about life," Vincent declared as he sank down in the chair opposite him.

"Come into my office and work with me Vincent, and I shall teach you the secret to guide you to find that kind of life. I'll assure you that you'll never be sorry, amigo. It is such a simple formula—but you can't learn it from books. It must be experienced."

Needless to say, Vincent Navarro was whetted with curiosity about this power that Adolfo Martinez obviously seemed to possess to make things happen for him.

When they dined that evening, Vincent told him about the house he'd found a short distance away and that he had made an offer for it. Adolfo knew exactly the place he spoke about and about the family who'd lived there for many years. "Fine people! The price seems very fair to me, Vincent. I am sure that Señora Aquirre will accept your offer. Am I to assume that you

128

are thinking about settling here in Austin and accepting my offer?" A sly grin was on his face as he spoke.

"I think I am, Adolfo."

"I am delighted, Vincent! Truly delighted! You see, I have been looking for a young man like you for the last few years to bring into my firm. When we met in Washington, I had a very definite feeling about you. You were exactly what I had been looking for. You have a smart, clever mind which I admire and respect. But there was something else that you represent—that cavalier, noble air that is most important when you deal with the people I deal with. You can be a great asset to me and I can give you the knowledge of my lifetime, Vincent."

Vincent noticed a definite change on his aristocratic face when he added, "I've no son to pass this on to, Vincent, and the chances are I never will. I'd like for it to be you."

"I'd be most beholden to you, Adolfo, for such a great privilege of working with you," Vincent said. By the time the evening was over and Vincent was back in his own bedroom he realized, as Pauline Castillo had a long time ago, that for all his flamboyance Adolfo Martinez was a lonely man. He'd wager that few people really knew the real Adolfo, for he wore a mask to hide his true self.

He found himself curious about the man hidden behind that mask!

Part Two

A Desperate Journey

Chapter 14

A week later, Vincent was the owner of the Aquirre property and had started working for Adolfo Martinez. No one was more elated about the turn of events than Paulina Castillo. She had already offered Vincent her services in helping him decorate his new house.

It did not come as any surprise to Adolfo that Paulina was planning a dinner party to introduce Vincent to their circle of friends. He'd seen the flashing excitement in her black eyes when she'd told him about her plans.

What Adolfo found so amusing was that Vincent did not seem all that impressed by the sensuous Paulina. It was going to be interesting to observe the two of them in the weeks to come.

He was delighted to see that Vincent was enthusiastic about his work in the law firm. He could not have asked for a more eager worker. Now, he knew that he had made the right decision.

When the time came for him to step down, Vincent would be able to fill his shoes.

As strange as this might seem to a lot of the people in Austin who knew Adolfo Martinez, it was very important to him. The prestige of his profession and law firm meant everything to Adolfo Martinez. It had been the wife and family that he never had.

There had never been a time in his life that he'd felt happier than he did right now!

It was a most festive occasion for the Montera family. The Navarro family had come to Whispering Willows to share the evening and dine on the barbequed pork that Abeja had cooked all day. Victor had accompanied his parents to Whispering Willows. He couldn't wait to see pretty little Karita again.

The ordeal of spending all that time in El Paso with his grandmother, closing down her home and getting her settled back at Silvercreek, had involved far more time than he'd anticipated and his nerves were frayed by the time he'd returned. He'd come to the conclusion that Florine Whelan was the most determined, stubborn woman he'd ever encountered so he knew where his mother had inherited that stubborn streak. Vincent had been the smart one, not to have offered to escort Grandmother Florine back to El Paso. But then Victor had realized that Vincent would have enjoyed all her constant chatter about the days when her Crystal Castle was the liveliest place in old El Paso. He was not all that excited or impressed about it.

He was glad that his twin brother had gone to Austin and had not been around to ride over to Whispering Willows that evening. This way he could have beautiful Karita all to himself. Vincent had always possessed the ability to dominate the situation when the two of them were in the same group. It had been that way when they were just lads and it had continued as they'd grown. The distracting force of Vincent would not be there tonight.

Karita seemed to be very happy to see him when they arrived, and this was encouraging to Victor. The only thing that kept irritating him as the evening went on was Karita's youngest sister, Cara. She had made it utterly impossible for him to get Karita alone.

Just as twilight was falling around the countryside, the two families gathered around the long table the Monteras had constructed out of sawhorses and long planks. Señora Montera had draped a tablecloth over it and placed her plates and platters of baked bread and roasted ears of corn. A cast iron pot of beans simmered over hot coals. The aroma coming from the pit where a young pig had been cooking over mesquite chunks for hours whetted Victor's appetite.

Lanterns at either end of the table were lit, and when the meal was finished they all sought to linger, with such a beautiful starlit sky above them.

"Oh, Yolanda—you and Abeja outdid yourselves. I've never eaten such wonderful barbeque in all my life," Señora Navarro declared. "And it was such a marvelous idea to dine out here instead of inside."

Señor Navarro agreed with his wife and chuckled, "Think you might help me up from the table, Abeja, so the two of us can stretch our legs and have ourselves a smoke?"

Abeja laughed, assuring him that he thought he might be able to manage that. Slowly the two of them rose from the makeshift table and walked away.

Yolanda had noticed that Victor wanted a few

moments alone with Karita, but Cara had tagged along all evening. She knew what a little pest her youngest daughter could be at times. "Cara, dear" she suggested, "I'd appreciate it if you would gather up the dishes and take them inside while I visit with Señora Navarro."

Cara got up with a disgruntled look on her face. "Can't Karita help me?"

An amused smile came to her mother's face. "Karita set the table. I don't believe you helped her." Yolanda and Kristina exchanged glances and smiles.

Cara said nothing more as she started moving around the table, and Victor invited Karita to join him in a stroll around the grounds. He blessed Señora Montera for putting Cara to work gathering up the dishes.

Karita had a smile on her face as the two of them began a leisurely walk in the dark. She laughed, "I love my little sister dearly, but she has to be the laziest person I know."

"I gather she wasn't too happy about what your mother asked her to do. I've got to confess that I am happy to have some time with you alone. I would have liked to spend more time with you the night of the fiesta but my brother monopolized you that night."

All evening Karita had thought about Vincent; in many ways he and Victor looked so much alike. Being by Victor's side during the evening and sitting beside him at the table, she could almost swear that it was Vincent whom she was near.

"It was certainly a wonderful evening. I had a marvelous time, I must say," Karita told him.

"I would suspect that you did, for you were the prettiest girl there. I can appreciate why my brother

134

kept you cornered all night. He always does that for he has an eye for beautiful ladies wherever he goes. I was surprised to learn that he had already left Silvercreek to go to Austin to see his friend, Adolfo Martinez. Should have known that Vincent would be restless here after a week."

Karita was listening to everything he was saying about his brother. He had said enough already to set forth a flurry of troubling thoughts in Karita's mind. She knew that he did not realize that.

"Will Vincent not come back to Silvercreek? Will he live in Austin instead?" she asked, hoping that she was not showing the concern that was plaguing her.

"Who can tell about Vincent, Karita? I don't know what to tell you." He gave a shrug of his shoulders. It was enough to make Karita wonder if Victor was trying to tell her something about his twin brother.

"And what about you, Victor? Will you remain at Silvercreek?"

"I feel I owe my father and the family something after all they've done for me, so yes, I will stay here."

Karita found herself very impressed by the depth of loyalty Victor felt for his family. She was also wondering if she'd allowed herself to fall hopelessly in love with the wrong handsome Navarro twin. As she strolled here in the dark with Victor and gazed up at his fine-chiseled features, she had to admit that he was just as handsome as Vincent. He certainly seemed to be just as nice.

The strong hand holding her arm gave her the impression that he could be just as forceful and masterful as the man to whom she'd so willingly surrendered herself that day after the fiesta.

135

Victor sensed that he had accomplished exactly what he'd intended to do. He had planted a seed of doubt in the pretty little señorita who he knew was attracted to his brother. He had known that ever since the night of the fiesta.

But while he had the chance he wanted to give her more to think about the next few days. He laughed, "I just imagine that old Vincent is probably having himself a gay old time in Austin tonight. Señor Adolfo Martinez is known for his fabulous parties and all the most beautiful ladies in Austin attend his social galas."

All the things Victor was saying had upset her so that she lost her footing and stumbled. But for his hand holding her arm she would have fallen. He quickly lifted her to a standing position. To do this his other hand clasped her waist and as he raised her up, she leaned against him. The touch of her soft body against him was enough to spark a fire in Victor that he'd never known before. He found himself wanting to explore that soft body that felt so excitingly warm against him.

"Are you all right, Karita?" His head bent so that his lips were lightly touching her cheek.

"I—I am fine, Victor," she stammered, for she was feeling embarrassed that she'd been so clumsy. But she felt the nearness of his lips and gazed up to see the passion in his black eyes. "I—I guess we should start back toward the house, Victor. My ankle must have turned on me a little." She had not realized before that she could lie so easily but she was disturbed by the emotions flooding through her. Right now, she didn't trust herself.

Victor's arm was now resting around the back of her waist and his hand was clasping her waistline. She knew that he was merely giving her support he felt that she should have after she'd almost fallen. But it was her own feelings that were bothering her.

"I'm glad you are all right but we must check that ankle when we get back to the house so we can see it under lamplight," Victor told her. He walked her slowly back toward the house.

When they arrived back at the house, the presence of the others around them was a comfort to Karita for she had not trusted herself around Victor alone. She had only to remember what had happened between her and Vincent. The Navarro men seemed to have a strange effect on her. Vincent had completely bewitched her, and tonight she realized that Victor also had an overwhelming power to render her very receptive to his charm.

By the time they had finally boarded their buggy to travel back to Silvercreek and she had told her family goodnight to go to her bedroom, she was a very confused young woman. She paid no attention to Cara's endless ramblings until she'd had to hear them for a half hour. Her patience came to an end and she told her younger sister, "Will you please go to sleep, Cara! I am tired!"

But as she had expected, this didn't stop Cara, so she put the pillow over her head, hoping it would block out her sister's chattering.

Finally a blessed silence came to the room and Karita fell asleep quickly. But her sleep was restless and her dreams were not pleasant, for she dreamed about Vincent and all the beautiful women she saw surrounding him.

Oh, she wished that Victor had not been so honest

with her tonight! He would never know how he'd set off a torment of fury within her by being so honest.

What she could not know was that Victor had not been that honest with her. He had purposely set out to put Vincent in a bad light, and he had done so quite successfully.

When they had left Whispering Willows, he felt very smug about everything that had come about during the evening. Karita was such a sweet, naive girl possessing such simple honesty that he knew exactly the anxiety he'd stirred up in her. She was such a trusting little creature!

Now he was ready to make his next move to win her affection while Vincent was away!

Knowing that he could never compete with Vincent when he was around, he knew that he must use every precious moment that Vincent was gone if he wanted to win Karita away from his twin brother. He cared not what devious means he had to use to do it. Tonight he'd managed to plant some seeds of doubt in the beautiful Karita's mind.

This was exactly what he had intended to do!

Chapter 15

Victor was the one in his father's good graces, now that Danton was out of sorts with Vincent. Victor gloried in his brother's absence to build up this esteem, as he had done with his grandmother. He had had very selfish reasons for offering to accompany her and her quadroon servant, Solitaire back to El Paso. He had deliberately sought to win her favor.

None of his family realized the private tormenting thoughts that had haunted Victor all of his adult life. He could not voice them to anyone. Perhaps it was only natural for twins to share so much and yet be such opposites. Such had been the case with his own father and his twin brother Damien.

Damien had come to a sad, tragic end and Danton had lived a grand, glorious life. Victor had heard the tales of Damien's black moods and evil deeds. In the end, he had destroyed himself by his own wickedness. Would it be that way with him and Vincent? He was not the happy-go-lucky hombre that Vincent was. He was far too serious and found it hard to be gregarious like

Vincent. Everyone warmed to Vincent as they had since the two of them were young boys. The pattern had not changed as they'd reached their teens. By the time they'd reached their twentieth birthday, Victor had developed a very resentful feeling against his brother. This gnawing feeling was enough to make him feel guilty and Victor tried to fight it. He envied him as he had all his life. It was like a festering wound that grew more painful. Vincent had never done anything to make him feel this way, yet he always walked in Vincent's shadow.

When his family was back in the capital and his father was a senator, he found himself very depressed much of the time because of Vincent. All the beautiful young daughters of the other senators seemed to be drawn to Vincent instead of to him. Oh, he had his fair share of pretty ladies but they were always Vincent's leftovers.

That was why he was now obsessed with possessing the beautiful Karita Montera. Knowing that his brother was attracted to this enchanting young girl was enough to challenge Victor. All he had to do was recall the look in Vincent's eyes the night of the fiesta to know what he was thinking when he looked at the lovely dark-eyed beauty.

Nothing could give him a grander feeling of victory than to know that he had won the affections of Karita Montera and that she would choose him over Vincent.

Victor could not think of anything that would give him a greater feeling of power.

Solitaire was glad that her beloved mam'selle,

Madame Florine, was at Silvercreek with her daughter, and she had no complaints about the luxurious quarters that Kristina had prepared for them. There was an atmosphere of privacy which Kristina knew her mother would desire if she chose to live there. There were nights when Florine did not wish to join the rest of the Navarro family in the dining room, so trays were sent up to the room for her and Solitaire.

Kristina was a very understanding daughter so she allowed her mother to do as she wished. Most of the time Solitaire found that they lived much as they'd lived on the ranch at El Paso. There was only one disturbing thing here at Silvercreek that bothered Solitaire and she didn't quite understand it yet. There was an evil force brewing here and she felt it was within the young Señor Victor, for it was when she was near him that the feeling became so strong. She sensed it so strongly that she tried to stay constantly with her mam'selle. In all her life she had never doubted her bayou instincts, so she didn't doubt them now.

Solitaire did not trust Victor and she did not like the way he constantly tried to ingratiate himself and gain her favor. But she also knew that Florine Whelan was a very shrewd woman, so she would surely see what he was up to.

Solitaire was never more sure of her instincts being right than she was when Victor brought the pretty little señorita from Whispering Willows over to Silvercreek. She observed them during the young girl's stay at the ranch and during the lunch they shared out on the veranda with his parents and Señora Lucia. Florine did not wish to join them for she was not feeling well that day, so she had her lunch brought to her room.

Solitaire had observed the group from the private balcony.

She found it interesting when she saw Señora Lucia take the young girl away from the veranda to accompany her inside the house and she was curious as to what that was all about.

Victor was not to see Karita until two hours later, for his grandmother was instructing the curious young lady about the games played with cards, in which Karita had voiced an interest. Señora Lucia took her to her special little corner of the parlor where a teakwood table was placed.

Victor had to display a good-natured attitude about his grandmother stealing away the pretty young lady he'd brought to Silvercreek for the afternoon. What else could he do? But he was seething inside and paced on the veranda.

When the two of them emerged from the parlor, Victor realized that Karita had endeared herself to his grandmother by her avid interest in playing cards. He was pleased, for this fit in with his plans. It no longer mattered that he had been deprived of her company for two hours.

When Victor was escorting Karita back to Whispering Willows she told him excitedly, "Your Grandmother Lucia is the nicest lady, Victor. I couldn't believe it when she asked me to share an afternoon with her when she found out I liked to play cards."

"Oh, if you like to play cards it is no wonder why you got along so well. She'd rather play cards than eat," Victor laughed.

"Well, I spent a lot of time last summer doing

just that."

Victor could not imagine the hard working Yolanda or Abeja taking off an entire afternoon to indulge in a card game and she quickly informed him, "Oh, no—it was not mama or papa. One of my papa's hired hands, old Joel, injured his leg and couldn't work for a few weeks so we'd sit out on the front porch and he taught me how to play."

Victor teased her, "Well you just might find youself spending this summer entertaining Grandmother Lucia if you're not careful."

"I would not mind spending an afternoon every now and then with her, Victor. She's very sweet. I appreciate her invitation."

"Well, she has more time on her hands now that my mother has taken charge of running the house and servants," Victor explained.

Victor suddenly realized that they were quickly approaching Whispering Willows and all they'd done was talk about his grandmother. Somehow, when he was alone with Karita there was never enough time to become amorous with her. He could not just grab her and kiss her honeyed lips, although he ached to do so. With some women, he would not have denied himself that pleasure for so long. With Karita, he wanted it to be a romantic, tender moment, for it was much more than a kiss that he intended to have.

If he was wagering, he would bet money that she had never been with a man. No, she had to be a virgin, sweet and innocent!

Had he known that his twin brother, Vincent had changed all that the afternoon after the fiesta, Victor would not have been patient at all. He would have had his way with her one way or the other.

By the time he was helping Karita down from her horse and had walked her to the front porch, he was thinking to himself that his grandmother had probably done him a great favor. When she did come over to Silvercreek to share afternoons with her, he would find the opportunity to be with her too.

After Victor told her goodbye and walked back down the pathway to his horse, Karita dashed into the house to tell her mother about the wonderful time she'd had at Silvercreek. "Can you believe, Mama, that Señora Lucia invited me over to play cards with her?" Karita told Yolanda, and that night as they were gathered at the dinner table, Karita told her father the exciting news. Like Yolanda, Abeja had an amused smile on his face as he glanced over at his wife. "I think that's wonderful, Karita. I'm sure you will accept the señora's invitation—si?"

"Oh, si, Papa!"

"Can't see anything exciting about just sitting all afternoon to play cards," Cara muttered as she munched on a piece of her mother's fresh baked bread.

Karita gave her sister an insolent look. "Well, Cara, I would not expect you to enjoy a card game for you'd work your little brain too much."

"Karita!" Yolanda drawled to gently admonish her. She could not be too harsh knowing how Cara was constantly irritating Karita about something, it seemed.

"I'm sorry, Mama, but Cara is impossible!" She rose from her chair to clean the empty plates.

Yolanda and Abeja got up from the table to leave Cara sitting by herself to finish eating. Since doing the dinner dishes was a chore assigned to Cara and Karita, their parents left the two of them alone. Squeezing his wife's arm, Abeja smiled at her, "I hope there are no dishes broken in there with the two of them in such a foul mood."

"It is hard to figure out your children sometimes, Abeja. Cara always got along with Kristina when she was home and so did Karita. But never have those two seemed to get along with each other. I doubt that they ever will."

"There is a jealousy there, Yolanda. Our Cara was not jealous of Kristina but she is very jealous of Karita. That is why she's been such a little imp the last two years. That is when it came to a head!" Abeja pointed out to his wife.

Yolanda knew he spoke the truth for it wasn't this way when they were younger. It all started when Cara was about thirteen and Karita was fifteen. Abeja did not have to tell her what it was that stirred resentment in Cara. It was Karita's beauty that Cara envied, and at times, Yolanda felt sorry for her younger daughter. She loved Cara just as much as she did Karita but she could not deny that her middle daughter was the more beautiful.

But Karita did not seem to be aware of just how breathtakingly beautiful she was!

Chapter 16

During the next two weeks Karita made two trips to Silvercreek and she spent three hours in the company of Señora Lucia both afternoons. The two of them laughed and talked as they played cards and enjoyed refreshments out on the balcony outside Lucia's bedroom

Lucia developed a genuine fondness for the pretty daughter of Yolanda and Abeja Montera. Not only was she beautiful, but she was well mannered and very smart, Lucia decided.

She told Karita of her humble beginnings and how she'd turned to being a lady gambler because she was tired of being poor. "I just happened to meet the wealthy Victor Navarro, and he fell as madly in love with me as I did with him," she told Karita. As she was talking, Karita was thinking to herself that perhaps the same would come true for her. Señora Lucia's tale about her past drew her closer to the elderly lady, now that she knew that there was a time that she did not dwell in the spacious home surrounded with all the luxury she had now.

When Karita prepared to take her leave the last afternoon, Señora Lucia gave her a gift. When Karita opened the little velvet pouch she found a delicate gold cross on a chain. "Señora! Oh, it is lovely!" she declared as she pulled it out of the pouch and fastened it around her neck. Her fingers caressed the cross resting at her throat. She gave the elderly señora a warm, loving smile as she bent down to kiss her cheek. "You are so kind, señora, and I shall treasure this all my life." The truth was she'd never owned any jewelry at all, and it was a most thrilling thing for her.

"Well, Karita, you have given me two very wonderful afternoons. To be around someone like you, so young and full of life, is a far better tonic for me than being around someone as old as I am. I like being around young people like you and my grandsons."

"Oh, Señora— I don't look upon you as being old! Why, we've talked and laughed all afternoon. I think you are the most interesting lady I've ever met."

"Well, I am very flattered, Karita—truly I am! May I expect that you might enjoy another afternoon next week?"

"Oh, I would love to if I could," Karita quickly responded to her invitation.

"I would be delighted as long as your parents don't object," Señora Lucia said as she rose up from her chair to accompany Karita downstairs as she prepared to leave.

When they arrived at the entrance, it was not a hired hand sitting in the buggy seat but Lucia's grandson, Victor. He greeted them with a broad grin. "Buenos tardes, Grandmother Lucia. I shall see Karita home this afternoon."

A smile came to Lucia Navarro's face as she cautioned him, "Well, see that you get her home safely, Victor. She is very precious to me, nieto!"

"I will." He jumped down so he could help Karita into the buggy. They both waved back to Lucia as Victor urged the horse to move forward.

That last remark by his grandmother was enough to haunt Victor as the buggy traveled toward Whispering Willows. He was no longer sure that he wanted to pursue what he'd planned to do when he'd told the hired hand that he would be taking Señorita Montera home. Those piercing black eyes of his grandmother's had seemed to warn him to do exactly as she'd ordered—and that was to see Karita home safely. So he could not bring himself to stop the buggy there in the woods between Silvercreek and Whispering Willows to make love to her as he ached to do.

When once again he had walked her to the front door of the Montera house and said farewell without the reward of a kiss, Victor swore he was surely hexed where Karita Montera was concerned.

But as he turned on his booted heel to leave, he paused and turned around. "Oh, we've had word from Vincent. I almost forgot to tell you. He's planning on remaining in Austin and practicing law with Señor Martinez. Can you believe it—Vincent has even bought himself a house! Sounds like some pretty lady in Austin has got him thinking about settling down. Sure wouldn't have believed that of old Vincent. Well, goodbye, Karita!" he called out to her as he went on down the path, a smug look on his face.

His words wounded Karita deeply and turned a

wonderful afternoon into an evening of disturbing thoughts that haunted her all during dinner and long after she went to bed.

Damn him, she thought to herself as she lay in her bed tossing and turning. She wished Victor had not told her what he had. She realized that he could not know what a torment his words would cause.

The more she was around Victor, the more she realized that he was more serious than his twin brother. He was probably more responsible and considerate than Vincent with his happy-go-lucky ways. From various things Victor had mentioned, his brother possessed a restless heart where the ladies were concerned, and it was evident that he preferred the excitement of the city to the quiet life of Silvercreek.

Victor would have been happy to know that tonight he had planted even more doubts in Karita's mind about Vincent. That was his intention, but he did not know how successful he had been.

In the privacy of their bedroom, Abeja was remarking to Yolanda how nice it had been for Señora Lucia to give Karita the dainty gold cross.

"From what I've heard about her, I think she must have taken an instant liking to our Karita. To have someone like the señora fond of you can mean much to a young girl. Karita probably does not realize this, as young as she is, but I know how much it can mean. Señor Navarro took a liking to me."

Yolanda understood exactly what he was saying and agreed with him. "But, Abeja, Karita has thoroughly enjoyed her time with Señora Lucia. It was not just a matter of her being kind to an old lady," she told her husband.

"Señora Lucia knows this, and that is what is so satisfying to her. This is what has endeared Karita to her in the brief encounters the two have had," Abeja told his wife. He kissed her goodnight, thinking about the early hour he had to get up in the morning to start his chores.

Once the deal was made on the Aquirre property, Vincent told Jules that he would like for him to remain there if he would like. "I'd like for you to oversee things around here, Jules. You could be a great help to me. I know nothing about the care of gardens and the courtyard. Since you are already quartered upstairs in the stable, why don't you just stay there and work for me?"

Nothing could have been greater news for Jules. He had worried about what he was going to do once the property was sold, and he never expected the new owner to want him to stay around.

Vincent saw the surprised excitement on the man's face and noticed how his voice cracked when he did speak. "Señor—Señor Navarro, I would be most happy to stay here. I am a good gardener and a carpenter as well."

"You see, I can ask your help in many ways," Vincent grinned. "Shall we say the matter is settled? As of now, you are in charge of getting the grounds in order. Whatever you need to buy you just let me know—all right?"

"Si, señor. I shall start tomorrow." Vincent could have sworn he saw the old fellow's chest swell with pride about the authority Vincent had just given him.

He was very impressed that he was given a month's wages in advance for Vincent figured that he was in need of funds for living expenses.

Giving Jules a vote of confidence was to be well rewarded, for five days later, Vincent viewed his perfectly manicured gardens and courtyard. It was more beautiful than he'd imagined it would be when he'd walked through the iron gate that first afternoon. All the shrubs had been pruned and shaped and urns now were planted with flowers. The front door of the house had been freshly painted. No weeds grew anywhere. The lawn looked like a plush carpet of green and no weeds grew between the cracks in the flagstone walks.

Vincent was well pleased and praised Jules for the many hours he knew he'd toiled making everything look so nice.

Since his purchase price included all the señora's furnishings, Vincent left Adolfo's house to move into his own new house. The first room he sought to refurbish was his bedroom. None of the old furnishings did he wish to keep. The ruffled curtains would never do. Massive pieces of dark rich wood were what he wanted, pieces that were a reflection of a man's room. Since the house had no library or study, he purchased a large mahogany desk and lined one wall with shelves for his collection of books. He bought himself an oversized leather chair like the one in his father's study back at Silvercreek so he could sit comfortably to read over the many documents and papers he would be studying at night after he left Adolfo's office.

The other side of the room was engulfed by the huge bed and nightstands. The drapes at the windows and the spread on his bed were the rich earthy colors of gold, rust and brown.

With Jules's help, the next project was getting the kitchen in order and hiring a cook and housekeeper to live in the small quarters at the back of the kitchen. Jules found a nice Mexican lady who was delighted to be a housekeeper and cook since she was a widow with no children at home. The offer to have her quarters furnished and a small salary sounded wonderful to Aspasia Cerventes. She eagerly accepted Señor Navarro's offer.

With the two loyal servants he'd employed, Vincent found that his new home was functioning quite nicely after the first two weeks.

After he put in a full day at Adolfo's law office, he was ready to retreat to his new home to enjoy Aspasia's good dinner then go upstairs to plan the next project for his new home and look over papers to take to the office. So he had no time to accept Paulina Castillo's constant dinner invitations.

Paulina was becoming exasperated and perplexed as to how to lure Vincent over to her house in the evening. The next time she and Adolfo dined together, she told him with a pretty pout on her lips, "Doesn't he ever relax and just enjoy himself? I wanted to have a party for him so I could introduce him to our friends, but I find it impossible to catch him."

It was obvious to Adolfo that the beautiful Paulina was out of patience. For all her charm, she'd been unable to work her wiles on Vincent.

"Vincent is a very intense young man, very conscientious about being a good lawyer, and he will be a good one. He's very occupied with getting the house he's purchased in order, Paulina," Adolfo attempted to soothe her.

"Well, I'm beginning to think he's too honorable and scrupulous for my liking."

Adolfo laughed, "Oh, Paulina! Paulina!"

"Don't you think that it would be to his advantage to meet certain important people here in Austin?" she asked him.

"Oh, I agree, mi cara Paulina! We shall do it. When would you like to have your party?" Adolfo asked her, trying desperately not to display the amusement he was feeling. He knew that she was interested in his young friend and that Vincent had chosen to ignore her overtures. Paulina was not used to anyone refusing her. Obviously, Vincent had refused her more than once or twice. This was enough to gall haughty, conceited Paulina Castillo.

Privately he was applauding young Vincent Navarro. This young man was not one to be influenced by just another pretty face and figure. The woman who would intrigue Vincent would have to be that rare young lady, set apart from all the others. She would have to be very special.

Having met the Navarro family, Adolfo concluded that the woman who would capture Vincent's heart would have to have the grace and charm that his beautiful mother possessed. Adolfo considered Señor Kristina Navarro one of the most beautiful ladies he'd ever met. Danton Navarro was a lucky man, Adolfo mused.

In fact, Kristina Whelan Navarro was one of the few ladies Adolfo had met who'd caught his interest, but she was married already. Few ladies had ever intrigued him. Paulina Castillo was delightful to escort to social affairs, but she was nothing like the vision of feminine perfection Adolfo had dreamed about finding.

He had begun to wonder if it was a damnation for a man to seek such a goddess as he wanted to find. That woman had to be the rare exquisite jewel which only one man possessed and greedily cherished; one no other had touched or tarnished.

Adolfo was still seeking such a jewel, but he was now doubting that he would ever fulfill his desire. He had visions about how she should look and the delicate features she should have. He had always known that the minute he gazed on the face of such loveliness he would know it, and nothing would stop him from possessing her!

Chapter 17

Adolfo Martinez was certainly convinced, when a few more days went by, that Vincent was not going to be lured into Pualina Castillo's little trap. When he'd been with Vincent on a couple of occasions and Paulina had just conveniently happened to appear, Vincent was always gracious and friendly, but Adolfo sensed that he wasn't that attracted or interested in the worldly lady. But Vincent did accept Paulina's invitation to her dinner party, and he thanked her when she told him she thought it was the perfect way to introduce him to all of her friends in Austin.

"This is very generous of you, señora, and I truly appreciate your thoughtfulness," Vincent told her.

"Ah, it is my pleasure, Vincent." She smiled sweetly up at him, for he towered over her. Paulina was a petite lady who barely measured five feet tall.

"And it shall be my pleasure to be there, Señora Castillo."

"Oh, Vincent—you make me feel like an old lady. I insist that you call me Paulina as Adolfo and all my friends do. We are going to be friends—si?"

"Of course, we are, se—Paulina," he grinned. Adolfo was also grinning, for he was intrigued just watching her turn on all her charm on Navarro.

When the two men departed to go back to the office and Paulina boarded her carriage, Vincent turned to Adolfo to remark, "That is very kind of her, Adolfo."

"Oh, Paulina can be a very generous lady when she likes someone. She can also be a witch when something or someone rubs her the wrong way. The lady has a very explosive temper. I've witnessed it," Adolfo laughed, thinking that he should give his young friend a gentle warning for the future.

"I would have expected this to be true. I've met a few spitfires in my lifetime," Vincent replied.

The two of them put in a long afternoon at the office and it was almost six when they left for the night. Vincent expected that Aspasia would be fuming that he was late to enjoy her evening meal at its best. But Vincent was beginning to realize that there would be many evenings he would not be getting home at a regular hour. Adolfo did not let the hands of the clock rule him at the office.

When he stepped inside the front door, he smelled the fine aroma coming from her kitchen, for she now truly considered it her kitchen. The happy-go-lucky Vincent enjoyed teasing the little Mexican woman and she enjoyed every bit of his boyish clowning. Actually, Aspasia hoped that this would be her home for many years to come and that she could work for Señor Vincent as long as she was able. She found him so kind and friendly.

Like Aspasia, Jules had a sense of belonging so he

tried to give the señor a full measure of his services each and every day. At his age, he could not ask for a better opportunity than the one he had been given by the señor. He had comfortable quarters and while he didn't take his meals at the main house, Aspasia always gave him a part of the meal she'd prepared for Señor Vincent.

He spent little of the wages Vincent paid him for he knew that he should try to save all he could for that time when he could no longer work for the señor, or anyone.

Having all the grounds in perfect order, he had spent the last few days helping Aspasia wash down the walls of the extra bedrooms upstairs. The large dining room and parlor downstairs were ready for the señor to furnish when he wished. For the time being Señora Aquirre's furniture remained there, polished and cleaned. Aspasia had gathered flowers which gave a pleasant fragrance to the parlor and dining room where she'd placed the vases.

It was nice for Jules to see the little stone house come alive after all the weeks that it had been vacant. A feeling of sadness had always come over him when he'd made his daily tour of the house for Señora Aquirre after she'd gone to live at her daughter's home.

One afternoon he'd walked the distance to pay a visit to her and tell her about the young gentleman who'd bought her home, and that he was to remain there with him.

The ailing lady had managed to smile when he spoke about Vincent Navarro. "I am very happy to hear this, Jules. This is the kind of young man I would wish to have our home. I hope he will know the happiness that my husband and I enjoyed there for so many years."

"That is why I wanted to come and tell you this, Señora Aquirre. But now I must be starting back. I will try to come back again to see how you are," Jules told her as he picked up his straw hat to prepare to leave.

"I thank you, Jules. I thank you for being so thoughtful. You come anytime you can," she told him in a weak voice.

Jules nodded his head and left the room. As he left to start his long walk home, Jules thought to himself that the next time he came to visit Señora Aquirre she might not be there to see. He was glad he'd come this afternoon. At least his news today had brought her some happiness: knowing her old home was in good hands.

Victor had appointed himself to come to Whispering Willows to escort Karita over to Silvercreek on her last two visits. By now, Karita was feeling very much at home when she went to spend her afternoons with Señora Lucia. She always wore the little gold cross around her neck which told Lucia how much she appreciated it.

Lucia was also beginning to realize that her grandson was very attracted by the enchanting Montera girl. As much as she adored her grandson, she had no intention of permitting him to misuse or take advantage of the young lady. So she always made a point of impressing on her hot-blooded young grandson the protective attitude she had about Karita Montera. Victor knew exactly what she was trying to tell him.

But Victor had forgotten all her admonishments the last time he escorted Karita back to Whispering Willows. He finally found that one magical moment to take a kiss from her lips—lips as sweet as new wine. He yearned to seek another kiss but he sensed a frightened reluctance on Karita's part, so he did not force the issue.

More than ever he was convinced that not only was she a virgin, she'd probably never been kissed by a man before, so he was feeling exhilarated that he was surely the first one.

"Ah please, Karita—I shall not press you for another kiss but I could not help myself. I've wanted to do that every time I've been around you. Please don't be angry," he had pleaded with her.

"I'm not angry, Victor. I—I just . . ."

"I understand, Karita. Really I do. I will respect your wishes."

Karita said nothing as she gave him a warm smile which was enough to please Victor. As they went the last mile toward her home, Karita found herself comparing the Navarro brothers. They were nothing alike. The irresistible, compelling charm of Vincent was not Victor's way, and she should find this admirable. She would be wiser if she gave her attention and affections to Victor, she privately thought to herself.

God knows when she would ever lay eyes on Vincent Navarro again! If he felt about her as he'd told her he did, why had he not written a letter to her, as he had to his family. She was beginning to wonder if her younger sister was right when she had taunted that Vincent Navarro had considered her a passing fancy. "You don't really think he'd marry you, do you Karita?" Cara had smirked a few days ago.

Deep in her heart Karita knew that she had believed that Vincent could have cared enough for her to marry her, or she would never have surrendered to him as she had that day after the fiesta.

She was no wanton! She'd heard the gossip about the neighboring ranchers' daughters who allowed themselves to frolic in the haylofts with one hombre after another. She had never been like that! She was eighteen and Vincent was the first man she'd ever lain with. She suspected Cara had already experienced making love with a man, and she was only sixteen. Her older sister, Kristina, had married the one and only man she'd ever courted, and Karita felt sure she was a virgin when she and Juan married.

Long after she'd bid Victor goodbye and he'd turned the buggy to go back to Silvercreek, she wondered what he was thinking about her and the way she'd acted when he'd kissed her. He seemed to accept her wishes not to kiss her again, but she had to wonder about herself and her reaction toward him.

She doubted if any other ranchers' daughters around these parts would have refused him. He would make most of the young girls' hearts pound with excitement with those handsome good looks and his tall, trim physique.

She knew what the answer was. It was very simple, really—he wasn't Vincent. He didn't have dancing green eyes or the power to make her flame with a fever of passion and desire at a mere touch.

But what had happened this afternoon with Victor had an effect on her, and Yolanda noticed her very

162

quiet mood during dinner. She hoped that there had been no discord between Karita and Señora Lucia for she knew that would surely pain her daughter very much. She knew Karita had been in a cheerful mood when she'd left to go to Silvercreek.

The other possibility had to be Victor, and Yolanda noticed that he had been the one escorting her home the last two visits.

Was it possible that young Navarro had made some improper advances toward her daughter and Karita was too ashamed to say anything to her and Abeja? Yolanda decided that after the meal was over and her kitchen was in order, she was going to have a motherly talk with Karita. She always wanted her daughters to know that they could come to her to talk about anything without shame or embarrassment.

She was glad that Cara was not home this evening. They had had a visit this afternoon while Karita was gone with their oldest daughter and her husband, and Cara had gone to stay with them for the next three days.

After their evening meal was over and Abeja left the two of them in the kitchen, Yolanda tried to sound casual when she asked Karita, "Did you and the señora have a nice afternoon?"

"Oh, yes mama—but then we always do. She raves about my skill at cards. She swears that I could deal at a gaming table like she did when she was young."

"Well, thank goodness you don't have to do that, dear." Her mother smiled gently and brushed a stray lock of hair from her face.

"I still find myself fascinated by her past, though, and that she was the famous Lolita at the Palace

163

Gaming Hall in San Antonio, don't you?" Karita asked her mother.

Yolanda laughed, "Yes, I do. I also feel the same about Señora Florine running the same sort of establishment called the Crystal Castle."

"Life is really crazy, isn't it mama?" Karita sighed deeply.

Yolanda smiled as she glanced over at her daughter. She dried the last dish and placed it in her cupboard. "So you are beginning to find that out—si?"

"I suppose I am." For a brief moment Karita's mood had been lighthearted when she'd been talking about the señora but now she seemed preoccupied as though something was on her mind.

"Karita, dear—I think something has you bothered since you've returned from Silvercreek. Mothers can help their daughters at times, you know. We've lived alot of experiences by the time our children come along."

Karita never was able to hide her feelings from her mother. Yolanda had always sensed when she was bothered about something.

"Karita, you are a beautiful young girl, so I must ask you if Victor Navarro has made any improper advances toward you. You don't have to be shy with me, dear."

"Oh, absolutely not, mama! Victor has been the perfect gentleman. Please ease your mind on that," she quickly declared to her mother.

Yolanda was satisfied that she was telling her the truth. Karita had never been a convincing liar even as a child.

Karita could see the relieved look on her mother's

face. She thought to herself that it was the other Navarro twin that was causing her the torment.

But she could not bring herself to go to her dear mother about things bothering her lately. There was no one she could go to about this except Vincent Navarro, and he was many miles away in Austin.

She might just be forced to go to Austin and seek him out!

Chapter 18

By the time Karita paid her next visit to Silvercreek to spend three hours at the teakwood table playing cards with Señora Lucia, she was certain she must be pregnant with Vincent Navarro's baby. So as she and Señora Lucia had their little chat during the card game, she asked very casual questions about Vincent.

"Victor tells me that Vincent is practicing law in Austin and has bought himself a house there," she remarked to the lady sitting across from her.

"That's what he said in his letter to his father. I had not exactly expected him to leave Silvercreek so soon after arriving here, but I must say that he couldn't work for a more successful lawyer anywhere than Adolfo Martinez."

Karita absorbed the name so she would not forget it. That name could be very important to her, she realized.

When she told Señora Lucia farewell this afternoon and went to join Victor standing by the side of the buggy, there was a wave of sadness washing over her for she felt that she would not be seeing the dear elderly lady for a long, long time. Oh, she had promised to pay a visit a week from today, but Karita also knew that she was probably not going to keep that promise, as much as she hated not to do it.

Victor noticed the rather sad look on her lovely face as he helped her up to the buggy seat. When he went around the buggy and got up to sit beside her, he put the bay in motion and asked her, "You look unhappy, Karita. Was my grandmother in one of her foul moods this afternoon? She can be cantankerous at times."

"Oh, no, Victor! Madre de Dios, she is always a joy to be around. My visits with her have been such a wonderful experience. I always look forward to coming here to see her," she declared with such sincerity that Victor knew she spoke the truth.

"For my grandmother to know you feel this way would mean very much to her, Karita. You are a most unusual young lady," he told her. His dark eyes looked at her affectionately.

"She has become very dear to me, Victor. But then I don't think I have to tell you how the Montera family feels about the Navarro family. As you know, it was your generous father who bought and later gave Whispering Willows to my father and mother. As you must also know about my mother working for your mother as her maid, it explains why they are so devoted to one another."

"I know all this, Karita. I have always found all their young lives very exciting. I'd like to think that my own life would create such a bounty of memories when I am their age."

She smiled and gave Victor's hand a gentle pat. "Oh, Victor, you will have many wonderful memories to think about when you are the age of your parents."

He suddenly yanked up on the reins and the bay came to an abrupt stop. When he looked at her the look in his black eyes was very intense. "You must know that I care for you, Karita. You would have surely sensed it for you are not like most silly young girls I've met the last few years back in Washington. There is a serious side to you, too. I think you are the most beautiful girl I've ever met and I've traveled around the world."

"Oh, Victor—you are going to make me blush! I could not possibly be the most beautiful."

"Ah, you see—that is what makes you so exceptional! You do not seem to realize this and you are so delightfully unpretentious."

She gave him a shy smile as she asked, "And is that good, Victor?"

"I think it is remarkable, Karita. Most young ladies I've known that were pretty—but not half as beautiful as you—were usually conceited."

"But maybe all men would not look at me and see me as beautiful, Victor. Maybe they would see me as a plain and simple girl," she told him. Perhaps this was now how Vincent was remembering her now that he was in a city of many lovely ladies. He was most likely moving in a social circle quite different than the one here at Silvercreek or Whispering Willows. Having never been in a city like Austin she could not imagine what it would be like.

Victor laughed and gave her hand an affectionate pat before he brought it up to his lips to kiss it. "Never has a man lived that would not gaze upon you, Karita, and think that you were beautiful!"

Her eyes darted down to her lap. Victor was so dear

169

and sweet to her and she was very much in need of the praise that he was showering on her this afternoon.

Perhaps this was why she was more willing to linger in his arms when he pressed her close to him and bent his head down to capture her lips in a kiss. This time she did not stiffen immediately as his lips joined with hers.

When he finally released her, he gave a low moan. "Oh, God, Karita! You can't imagine how you affect me. I find you so intriguing." She saw fierce passion in his black eyes, as it had been in Vincent's the afternoon they'd made love by the little waterfall. But she also knew she could not allow that to happen with Victor. She simply could not!

Breathlessly, she stammered, "Oh, Victor—please. I must not—I cannot allow us to do something that we'd both later regret. I—I must get home, Victor!"

She sensed the tenseness in his broad chest as he reluctantly freed her slightly, but his arms were still encircling her waist.

In a husky voice, he told her, "I can't promise you, Karita, that I'll always be satisfied with only one kiss. But for this time I'll abide by your wishes."

"I must be getting home, Victor," she insisted. Something about the look in his eyes urged her to linger there no longer. Something told her that he was annoyed with her even though there was a smile on his face. She felt it was a forced one.

Flippantly, he said with a grin on his face, "Your wish is my command, my pretty Karita. But I want you to remember what I said."

Now it was Karita who forced a little laughter. Both of them put on a false front for the rest of the way to Whispering Willows. Both were dwelling in their own private musings as the buggy rolled along.

When he told Karita goodbye, he had no idea of the desperate plot she was anticipating. She'd asked him to tell the señora that she would hope to see her this time next week. That was no lie, for she did hope to see her, but Karita knew she probably wouldn't be seeing her.

But she knew nothing else to do but carry through with the plan she'd gone over and over for several nights as she'd lain in her bed thinking about the dilemma she had gotten herself into by one moment of reckless romantic folly.

She would not shame her hardworking parents by announcing to them that she thought she was pregnant. She would not stir up a feud between the Navarro and the Montera families and destroy a lifelong friendship just because she had been foolish.

There were only two individuals responsible— Vincent Navarro and herself. The rest of the Navarro family were not guilty. She had to go to Austin and tell Vincent the truth, and the rest was up to him. She would find out just how much of a man he was and if he was willing to assume the responsibility that was his.

But since she was no longer that wide-eyed innocent, she asked herself what she would do if he was not willing to do the right thing by her. She would stay in Austin and find work. She would pray that she could make enough to take care of herself and the baby for the weeks she would not be able to work after the baby was born.

She already had her plans worked out that she would leave the house in the early morning hours when the rest of her family were fast asleep. By the time they were waking up she'd be close to Austin. Once she arrived in

171

Austin she would seek out this Señor Adolfo Martinez, and he would be able to direct her to Vincent.

Karita had spent many hours during the last week thinking about these plans of hers. She was convinced that she was pregnant.

Tomorrow, she was going to make her final plans and write the letter she felt that she must write to her beloved mother. In the early morning hours, she would leave the house to slip to the barn and saddle up the mare that her father had given to her on her sixteenth birthday. She and Bonita would steal away from Whispering Willows to travel to Austin.

She tried very hard to be as gay as she could possibly be all evening, for it was a very precious evening to her as she thought about the fact that it would be the last one she'd share with her parents for a long time.

Thank God, Cara was not here. She would have never been able to pack the few belongings that she intended to take with her if that nosey Cara had been home.

When she went to her own bedroom to retire she was convinced that she was doing the right thing. This eased any qualms she might have been harboring.

Karita had done a marvelous job of convincing her mother that she was in the highest of spirits that evening. When she and Abeja retired to their own room, she remarked to her husband, "It is so wonderful to me to see Karita so happy as she was tonight."

"Her face glows when she is happy, doesn't it, Yolanda? She is a beautiful girl! You see—I told you long ago that the two of us would have beautiful children, and we have!" he teased her.

"Oh, Abeja—everything you promised me has come

true. I am a most happy woman and you have made it happen. Our Kristina is soon to present us with our first grandchild. We are to be grandparents, Abeja! I find it hard to believe!"

"Does it make you feel old, querida?"

"Not at all. I am excited about it and it makes me feel glad that I had my children while I was so young," Yolanda told her husband.

"Well, you will be the most beautiful grandmother I know, Yolanda. To me, you were always the most beautiful woman I'd ever seen," her husband told her. His arms reached out to enclose her and draw her next to him. He forgot the long hours of the day he'd put in around Whispering Willows.

Yolanda also forgot that she had been working since sunrise around the house and her garden as she began to yield to her husband's amorous caresses. The years had never dimmed the flame of their passion, for they were among those who had discovered the secret of making that splendor continue to glow now that they were no longer young.

Yolanda knew that she was not the little black-eyed señorita that Abeja had met and fallen in love with some twenty years ago, but he constantly told her that she *was* that beautiful girl.

That meant everything to Yolanda!

Chapter 19

Her room had been dark for hours but Karita had dared not lay her head on the pillow for fear that she would fall asleep and not wake up when she needed to. She had to leave the ranch long before her parents got up.

But it was boring to sit there and wait out the time. Just sitting there in the quiet of the night, she thought about what the future held for her, and many dubious thoughts paraded through her mind. She had very little money to take with her but she tried to comfort herself by thinking that she'd have her little mare to ride back home if it became necessary.

Finally the hands on the clock told her it was time to get up and get dressed. She'd just been lying there on her bed with her undergarments on. Slipping into the dark divided riding skirt, she slipped a cotton tunic over her head and tucked it inside her skirt. She did not intend to put her boots on until she was outside. The few belongings she was taking with her were folded and stuffed in a pillow case, as she did not possess a valise.

Dear Lord, she was glad Cara was away!

For a moment she hesitated and placed her note on the kitchen table as she went into the kitchen. Deciding that there was nothing else left for her to do, she went quietly to the door and opened it. Her heart was beating erratically and she felt that she could hardly breathe as she went toward the kitchen. It was only when she was outside that she took a deep breath of the night air. By the time she was in the barn preparing Bonita for their journey she finally began to relax.

While Abeja and Yolanda slept in the early hours of the morning, their daughter was galloping toward Austin. With the cool breeze whipping at her face and blowing her long hair back, Karita found that she was enjoying the ride through the darkened countryside. Her young heart was now pounding with exhilaration and excitement. She never considered the dangers she might encounter traveling alone.

She knew that she was making good time, and Bonita kept up a fast, even pace. The small hamlet of Driftwood was quiet, with everyone still sleeping, when she rode down its one main street and soon she was on the outskirts of the town, heading for the countryside again.

Time had passed so fast that Karita did not realize she had already been on the road two hours. So many random thoughts were rushing through her pretty head that she had not been aware that the skies above her had changed from a starlit darkness to complete darkness.

It took her completely by surprise when she felt giant raindrops pelting her face for she'd seen no lightning, nor heard any rumble of thunder. She spurred Bonita to go faster in hopes that she could find the shelter of a grove of trees to protect her and Bonita should the rain get heavier. Now she was in open country and all she could see was the blacklands. There were no farmhouses in sight as far as she could see in the darkness, and the sun was not coming up yet.

So she kept riding, for it would have done no good just to stop without the cover of a tree. The rains did come down harder but there was no lightning for which she was grateful. Bonita would have gotten panicky.

She could feel the dampness of her blouse pressing against her flesh. But right now she could not be worried about her appearance. By the time she'd ridden another few minutes she knew that her hair was also damp from the rains as small wisps fanned against her face.

If she'd been familiar with the countryside, she would have known how close she was to Austin. But she did the only thing she could do and that was to go on.

About the same moment she noticed that the sky was a little lighter, she spotted the first house she'd seen for a long time. She also noticed that the rains seemed to easing up. By the time she and Bonita galloped past the little farmhouse another house was right ahead of her.

She suddenly realized that she was at the outskirts of Austin, and dawn was also breaking. Back at Whispering Willows her parents would be getting up and they would find her note.

By the time she realized she was in the main part of Austin, she found that a few people were beginning to move on the streets. She realized that she might have to ask several people before she found out how to get to Señor Martinez's house. So she reined Bonita up to the edge of the street where a shopkeeper was preparing to unlock the door of his tobacco shop.

"Señor, may I ask you if you'd know how to direct me to the home of Señor Adolfo Martinez?"

The man turned around to look at her and shook his head. "I do not know the man."

So Karita urged Bonita on up the street and when she spied a fellow sweeping the walkway in front of his leather goods store she asked him the same question, but he did not know Señor Martinez either.

Karita was becoming a little discouraged. Victor, as well as Señor Navarro, had remarked that Martinez was such a fine lawyer, she'd assumed everyone in Austin would know him. Feeling a little dejected, she urged Bonita into a slow pace as they moved up the street.

When she spied a very fancy lady alighting from her buggy and going to the door of a hat shop, she urged Bonita to move along. Karita had never seen such a frock as the lady was wearing. Swishing flounces were around the bottom of the skirt and the material was a shining rich scarlet taffeta. In her hand she carried a dainty parasol of the same color.

Karita pulled up on the reins and called out to her, "Could you please help me—direct me to where Señor Adolfo Martinez lives?"

A pair of flashing green eyes turned in Karita's direction and a smile broke on her face as she drawled, "Ah, that one! Oui, I know where he lives. I've delivered a few of my chapeaus there over the years." The lady told her the directions to get to the palatial mansion where Adolfo lived.

Karita thanked her and spurred Bonita instantly into motion. Back down the street the owner of shop, was curious about the very beautiful black-eyed miss with the long black hair.

Karita had no trouble following the directions given her but she was a little taken aback by the grandeur of the place. As she moved Bonita on up the drive toward the entrance, another sudden downpour of rain began and she figured it was the one she'd just ridden out of a few miles back.

There was a ghostly quiet around the vast grounds of the house, and Karita concluded that life did not begin stirring around the grand house like this one in the city as early as it did back at Whispering Willows or Silvercreek Ranch. So when she dismounted from Bonita and slowly walked up the two steps to the porch, she was hesitant about knocking on the door for she heard no sounds or movement in the house.

The rains were coming down but she had a roof over her head and she sought to sit down on the grilled iron bench on the porch, for she felt very weary. For over three hours she had ridden Bonita and had no sleep, and it was suddenly taking a toll on her.

So she sat down and cozily lifted her legs up on the bench to rest them. Bowing her head, she closed her eyes.

This was the strange sight to greet Rollo, Adolfo's manservant, when he went out on the porch, as he did in the early morning, to survey the plants in the huge urns on either side of the doorway. He was so startled that he said not a word to the sleeping little stranger on the bench but rushed back into the house to summon the señor.

179

As it would happen Adolfo was descending the stairway attired in his maroon silk dressing robe to go into his study to enjoy his coffee and look over the papers he wanted to take back to his office. He planned to leave the house in an hour or so.

"Señor, we have a little urchin out on our porch," Rollo announced. There were few times that Adolfo had observed Rollo as flustered as he was now.

"An urchin, you say?" Adolfo raised a skeptical brow.

"Yes, señor! A little miss no bigger than a mite all curled up in a knot out there on the bench."

"Well, then, we shall go see just who she is." Adolfo took the lead as Rollo trailed behind him toward the front door.

But when Adolfo went out to the porch he found himself as affected as Rollo had been. His black eyes stared at the petite little figure all curled up with her legs pulled up to her breasts and her head slumped on her knees. The thick mane of black hair fell around her shoulders. He saw the signs of the naturally curly texture of it for it was damp but beginning to dry, so there was a curl and wave to it.

He pondered why this little señorita would take refuge on his front porch. He wasted no time in finding out. Something about the sight of her brought out compassion in Adolfo. So his touch was gentle as he touched her small shoulder to awaken her.

"Señorita! Señorita!" His voice awakened Karita and she came alive immediately. Adolfo was rewarded with a weak smile, but he thought it was such a beautiful smile as he gazed down at her. Never had he seen a more beautiful face.

180

In a soft voice, she apologized for going to sleep on his porch. "But I did not wish to disturb you since I arrived so early. I was afraid everyone in the house was still asleep."

"So you came here to see me, señorita?"

"Yes, señor, I did," she told him as she straightened up on the bench.

Needless to say, Adolfo's mind was whirling and his interest was whetted keenly. But Adolfo found himself mesmerized by the enchanting beauty of this girl. She was like the image of the goddess he'd always envisioned in his dreams but had yet to meet.

"Well, please, let us go inside where it is more comfortable. I'm sure you will join me in a cup of coffee." Adolfo's eyes had danced from the top of her lovely head down to the dainty tips of her black leather boots. His eyes had not missed the damp blouse she had on and how it clung to the sensuous curves of her rounded breasts.

She laughed softly and sighed, "Ah, a cup of coffee sounds wonderful to me, señor."

Adolfo offered her his hand and she took it. As she allowed him to guide her through the door, Adolfo told Rollo to see to her horse being quartered in the stable and out of the rain.

Karita was already forming an opinion about this very nice gentleman and the consideration he showed for her little mare, Bonita.

As she followed him inside, she was convinced that this was what castles looked like. Never had she expected to see one. Up until now, Silvercreek was the grandest house she'd ever seen, but the grandeur there was nothing compared to the splendor of this place.

Adolfo saw how impressed and awestruck she was by his lavish furnishings. Feeling she might be a little more relaxed in his study than the spacious parlor, he led her down the long hall.

But when they entered the room and Adolfo had taken her over to the long leather sofa to sit down, he saw that she was really in need of getting out of the wet clothes she had on.

With a kindly, warm smile on his face he told her in a fatherly tone, "I think just as important as a hot coffee is some dry clothing, señorita. So I'm going to suggest that I have Rollo show you to one of my guest rooms upstairs. I think I've an extra robe you might wear while your own clothing is drying. Then Rollo can bring you some coffee and perhaps some breakfast."

He had such an authoritative air about him that Karita gave him no protest whatsoever. "I still see a very tired young lady. It might be wise for you to get some rest. When I return home from my office the two of us can talk. By the way, since you seem to know who I am, may I ask what is *your* name, señorita?"

"My name is Karita Montera, señor."

"Such a very beautiful name. There is almost a musical sound to it. Yes, I like that name. Well, now you've found me as you said you were seeking to do. You must rest. I will be back by the time you have rested. I shall be at your service."

He escorted her and Rollo upstairs for he had to get dressed to go to the office, so he bid them goodbye to go to his own room.

As he dressed he kept repeating her name over and over for he thought it was as beautiful as she was.

Chapter 20

During the day as he worked at his desk, Adolfo found his thoughts drifting away from his papers and documents to the lovely little creature back at his house. He could sit there now and envision those lovely black eyes of hers fringed so thickly with black lashes gazing up at him with such a trusting look—as if she'd known him all his life.

It stirred a pleased feeling within him that was new and strange. He could never remember feeling that way before and if he had it had to be many, many years ago.

He said nothing to Vincent about the little stranger he'd found on his front porch when the two of them shared lunch at a nearby little tearoom near his office.

Usually, Adolfo spent the afternoon completely engrossed in his work, not caring what the hands of the clock were saying the time was. But this afternoon he found himself watching the clock and when it chimed four, he decided to do no more work that afternoon and get home early. He wondered all day long what pretty Karita Montera was seeking him out about. He had to find out for he was a curious man.

He ambled into Vincent's office to announce his intentions to leave early. "I've a client to see at his home so I thought I'd better leave now if I want to get home by the dinner hour."

Vincent had been going over a case that Adolfo had turned over to him yesterday and glanced up to see what the time was. He said nothing to Adolfo but he, too, was going to leave a little earlier today. Furnishings he'd purchased for his parlor were going to be brought to his house at four thirty.

"I'll close the office, Adolfo," he told him.

"See you in the morning then. Have a good evening, Vincent," Adolfo told him as he turned to go back to his own office. He filled his leather case with the papers he wished to take home with him and he left.

He made a hasty retreat from the office and boarded his buggy to head homeward.

As soon as he arrived home the first thing he did was seek out Rollo. "Well, how is our little gamin?" he asked his manservant.

Rollo laughed. "You were right, señor. She was very weary for she'd ridden all night to get to Austin and been caught in the rain showers twice. But I've got her clothes all dry—the ones on her back as well as the ones she'd brought in a pillow case. I fixed her a tray and gave her one of your robes. I guess she must have slept the rest of the morning and afternoon. She woke up only a few minutes ago."

Rollo also told him that she was upstairs now enjoying a warm bath. Adolfo saw the amused grin in Rollo's face. "What is it, Rollo? What brings that grin to your face?"

"The young girl, señor. She is so—shall we say . . . she is so unpretentious—so refreshing. She greeted me as if she'd known me forever and she looked like a gamin as you said in that oversized robe of yours."

Adolfo laughed. He could tell from the way Rollo was talking about her that he, too, was taken with the black-haired beauty.

"Well, I think I shall go up and prepare for dinner, Rollo. What are we having tonight for dinner?" Adolfo asked him. Perhaps it was the anticipation of sharing the dinner with the delightful little creature upstairs but Adolfo found himself famished and eager to dine tonight.

"Cook fixed a roast chicken with that stuffing you like so much. Your favorite white wine is cooling for you, señor."

"Ah, Rollo—that sounds wonderful to me!" He turned to go to the stairway.

While Adolfo was in his room changing his clothes to the more casual attire that he enjoyed wearing when he was not having guests, it happened that Vincent's buggy was going past Adolfo's mansion. He found it a little surprising to see Adolfo's buggy in the driveway. He could not figure out how he'd already spent time with his client. Maybe it was not a client at all who was urging Adolfo to leave the office early, Vincent thought to himself as he guided his buggy on to his own home.

When Adolfo had refreshed himself with a bath he put on one of the soft silk shirts he'd purchased in the Orient last year. He paired the pale yellow shirt with a pair of rich brown pants he'd bought in London. He was always fastidiously dressed whether he was in his office, at home, or at some gala social affair.

Most of his friends considered him the best dressed gent in the city of Austin, and so did Adolfo. As he did in his home, he took a great pride in his appearance. He could not tolerate imperfection in anything.

While Adolfo was taking his bath and dressing, Karita was doing the same thing a short distance down the long hallway. Since Rollo had dried out the things she brought in the pillow case and pressed all the garments this afternoon, she chose the simple little sprigged muslin dress to wear tonight when she joined Señor Martinez for dinner.

Rollo had told her that dinner was served at a certain time and the señor was usually in his parlor before that to enjoy his usual glass of wine.

Wearing the deep green dress sprinkled with white flowers and leather sandals on her feet, she sat at the dressing table to brush out her long hair. Her fingers caressed the little gold cross at her throat. She thought of Señora Lucia and how she was going to miss seeing her this next week.

Everything about this room had intrigued her since the moment Rollo had left her this morning. She'd loved the softness of the silk robe she'd worn most of the day. She knew the vivid blue silk robe had to be Señor Adolfo's. Here on the dressing table were the silver brush, comb and mirror. There was a little trinket box of silver. Small cut crystal bottles were there, and one was Lilies of the Valley and the other one was Carnation. The aroma of each of them was so sweet and fragrant that she took the bottle containing the Lilies of the Valley toilet water and dabbed her throat and behind her ears.

She looked at the clock on the nightstand and remembering what Rollo had told her, she felt certain that she would find Senor Adolfo in his parlor now. She took one last glance in the mirror at herself and felt quite pleased with the reflection. She left the guest room thinking that by now, she had hoped to have been directed to where she could find Vincent, for that was what this venture was all about.

Adolfo was sitting in the parlor enjoying his glass of wine when the petite figure emerged through the large arched entrance of his parlor. Everything about her appearance impressed Adolfo. Her simple frock was basic with no frills, but it molded to her curvy body perfectly and was most flattering. In fact, the simplicity of it enhanced her gorgeous figure. The only adornment was the gold cross around her throat.

There were no fancy upswept curls or fashionable coiffures. Her glorious crown of black hair looked like glossy black satin. It fell free and loose around her shoulders, swaying to and fro as she walked up to greet him. "Good evening, Señor Martinez," she smiled.

As she met with him and he was there so close to her he admired her flawless deep golden complexion. Here was a face that had no blemish and looked like smooth silk.

"Good evening to you, Karita. Rollo tells me you enjoyed a good rest and I am happy."

"Oh, I did, but I must apologize to you for I never intended to intrude into your household like this. I merely sought you out so you could tell me where I could find Vincent—Vincent Navarro."

By now, Adolfo had taken her hand and led her to the brocade covered chair next to his.

187

"So it is young Navarro you truly seek? Is this so?" Adolfo had turned to serve her a glass of his white wine.

"Si, señor. I was told by his brother that he was working in your office here in Austin. You see, I live in Blanco County."

"But you obviously know the Navarro family?"

"Si—our families have known each other for years."

"I see, and Vincent's twin brother told you about me?"

"Si, he told me this."

Adolfo's keen brain was already whirling with many thoughts as to why she had been urged to come to Austin to find Vincent. He considered her that rare beautiful female that a man never hopes to find. "Do your mother and father know you have come to Austin, Karita?"

Something about this older man drew from her a trust and faith that demanded she be truthful with him, so she could not lie. "No, señor, and they are probably worried about me tonight, but I had to come here."

This was enough to tell Adolfo that she was a desperate young lady and he was damned well going to help her in any way he could.

"Karita, everything is going to be just fine whatever it is troubling you. I can take you to Vincent, but I'm selfish and I want you all to myself tonight," he laughed lightheartedly.

"And I would like to enjoy this evening with you, señor. You and Rollo have been so kind to me. I am very grateful to both of you."

"Well, you are a very special young lady so it makes it easy to be nice to you, Karita. I hope you like roast chicken with stuffing?"

"Oh, I love it. My mother makes it all the time," she told him.

"Ah, then your mother is probably an excellent cook."

"She is the best, señor!"

The dinner he shared with this unsophisticated girl was the most entertaining evening he'd had in a long, long time. He found himself entranced as she told him about her home, Whispering Willows, and how her family and the wealthy Navarro family had been connected for so many years.

"So you are telling me that there was a time when your mother, Yolanda, served as Señora Kristina Navarro's maid and your father, Abeja, was Señor Danton Navarro's manservant. So their young romance brought your parents together?"

"Si, señor. This is how they met. I have always found it very romantic how my parents met when they were young and were both working for Señor and Señora Navarro."

"I, too, find it so, Karita. I have known the Navarro family for a few years and I have always found them most fascinating."

When the two of them had finished the delicious meal Adolfo was certainly not willing to call a halt to the evening so he took her back to the parlor so he could hear the interesting stories she had to tell him about her family as well as the Navarro family.

Adolfo was a smart man and he had already figured out that this young lady was enamored with the handsome Vincent Navarro. That was why she'd made this desperate journey from Blanco County. Adolfo had already decided if Vincent did not come to her to do what he should, then *he* would.

By the time the two of them mounted the stairway to retire, Adolfo told her that he would take her to Vincent's house. "It is only a short distance from here, Karita,"

"Thank you, Señor Martinez! Thank you for so much! How can I tell you what just spending this one evening with such a gentleman as you has meant to me. I shall never forget it!" She gave way to the impulse to reach up and kiss his cheek.

The dapper Adolfo was overcome with an emotion that Karita could not possible know. What he appreciated so much were her honesty and genuine feelings, and that was rare.

Ah, yes, she was truly the woman Adolfo had dreamed about as a young man and as a man who had reached middle age, but had never found. Now that he had reached forty he had finally found her, but he knew that her heart belonged to Vincent Navarro.

Should Vincent not be the man he thought he was and do right by this beautiful young lady then Adolfo was prepared to do it, and so willingly!

A Karita Montera did not come into a man's life that often, Adolfo knew. He had searched a lifetime!

Chapter 21

Adolfo had been gone from his house for over two hours when Karita roused from sleep. She lay there in no hurry to get up from the comfortable bed which was so wide and massive—so unlike her own narrow bed back at Whispering Willows. She loved all the bright, vivid colors in the room. Her mother would never have put such an array of bold colors in any of her bedrooms for she loved the soft pastels of pink, blues, and yellows. But if she could see this room she would have to admit that it was a magnificent combination when it was done with the expertise that the señor had decorated it.

She had come to some very definite conclusions about the señor even though she'd only met him yesterday. Everything he said or every move he made was done with such an air of self-assurance. She thought how wonderful this must be to feel about himself as he obviously did.

Just being around him was stimulating to Karita and she was not as apprehensive about her dilemma as she had been when she had arrived here. Just being there in his fine house and with him had been very inspiring to her. She was ready to face Vincent Navarro and tell him the truth and demand of him that he save her from the shame she would face if he didn't assume the responsibility that was his.

She dressed with special care before she left her room, for she remembered that the señor told her that he would take her to Vincent today.

As she was descending the stairs, Rollo was coming down the hall and saw her. "Ah, señorita—you are up. I did not wish to knock on your door to see if you wanted me to bring up a breakfast tray for fear that you were still sleeping."

"I'm not used to being waited on, Rollo. At Whispering Willows, there are no breakfast trays." She gave a merry little laugh.

Rollo grinned, "Nor where I was brought up, señorita."

They agreed to share a cup of coffee in the sunny tiled kitchen together. There, with the bright morning sunshine streaming through the east windows, Karita told him about her home and family, and Rollo told her about his family.

When they were having an enjoyable chat, Karita gave a sudden gasp, and with a painful grimace on her face put the coffee cup down on the saucer.

"What it it, child?" Rollo anxiously asked her as he rushed from his chair and around the table. She had turned so ghostly pale.

"I—I don't know, Rollo. I don't see how it could be anything I ate for that was hours ago, and coffee would surely not cause such a pain as this."

"Let's get you up to the room, eh?" he suggested as he gave her support out of the chair. For a few moments Karita felt no discomfort. Holding tight to Rollo's arm, she mounted the stairs and turned to Rollo to declare, "I feel all right now, Rollo."

But no sooner had she said it when another spasm of pain jarred her petite body and she bent over and moaned. Rollo took his other arm to support her as the two of them struggled through the bedroom door.

"Oh, señorita—I think I'd better get Doctor Cortez over here to see about you. Something is wrong," Rollo told her as they got to the edge of the bed and Karita sank down on it. Karita could not understand what demon was suddenly invading her body for she had felt so wonderful when she first got up. She was rarely ever sick.

"Let me just lie back here on the bed a minute and let's see what happens, Rollo," she insisted as she took off her sandals and raised her legs up on the bed. But she, too knew that something was very wrong for she felt flushed and fevered. As she pushed herself back on the bed to prop herself up on the pillows, she knew that she was about to have another round of pain. She tried to bear it without moaning so poor, frightened Rollo would not know it.

"Señorita, you need a doctor and I'm not waiting any longer. Now you lie right there and I'm going downstairs to send little Concho for the doctor."

By now, Karita was in too much pain to argue with him so she said nothing as he went out the door. For the next hour she knew very little about what went on as she came in and out of the maze of pain she was experiencing. By the time the elderly white-haired doctor arrived to examine the young girl lying there on the bed, tossing and turning, his knowing eyes spied the small pool of blood on the back of the gown she was wearing, he knew immediately what was happening.

He requested Rollo's assistance to help him do what he must do, and informed the manservant what was happening with the young guest of Señor Martinez.

An hour later, Karita had been changed from her blood-stained gown to a clean nightgown. The doctor had administered all the things necessary when a lady miscarried as Karita had. He had given her a mild sedative just before he prepared to leave the room. But knowing that she was in a dazed state, he told Rollo what she should and should not do.

"Never fear, Doctor Cortez—I'll see that she does everything you've said," Rollo assured him.

"Oh, she will bounce back in a day or two, Rollo. She was only a few weeks pregnant. If I was to guess I'd say about two or two and a half months at the most. She will be fine, I assure you."

"I thank you, doctor, for getting here so fast, and Señor Martinez will appreciate it too. We had no idea and I'll admit that I was scared stiff."

"Well, you can rest easy now, Rollo. She will probably sleep for a few hours now. So you just relax, eh?" Doctor Cortez grinned as he gave Rollo's shoulder an assuring pat.

"Yes sir, I will now." Rollo escorted him from the room and to the front entrance of the house to stand on the porch until the doctor's buggy pulled away to travel down the drive.

Returning to Karita's room to see that she was asleep, Rollo pondered what he should do about telling

194

the señor. The señor would be furious with him if he came home in the evening to learn that he was not immediately informed about what had gone on this morning. Rollo did not wish to face that fury. So was he to leave Karita here to go to the office and tell Señor Adolfo? If he stayed here at the house, he could write a message and have young Concho take it to Señor Adolfo. This would be better, Rollo decided. The truth was he did not wish to leave the house and Karita after what had happened.

So he hastily wrote a note to the señor and summoned young Concho. "Take this to Señor Adolfo at his office and give it to no one but him. Do you understand me, Concho? This is to be given to no one but the señor!"

"Si, señor. I give it to no one but Señor Adolfo," the young lad declared and nodded his head. He took the message and flung the straw hat back on his head before he turned to leave.

Rollo turned to attend to the duties that he had not been able to address earlier with the unexpected event that had happened. He did take the time to check in on Karita once to find that she was still sleeping peacefully. So he went back downstairs. He said nothing to ease the curious stares of the housekeeper and the cook. He did give the menu to the cook that Señor Adolfo had requested for the evening meal that night.

When Rollo chanced to see the señor's buggy speeding up the drive, he realized Señor Adolfo's genuine feelings had caused him grave concern, for him to have left his law office so early in the day to come home was most unusual.

When he had leaped out of the buggy and come rushing through the door to meet Rollo there in the hall, his manservant could never recall seeing a more serious, uneasy look on his face. "Madre de Dios, Rollo—she had a miscarriage?"

"Si, señor. We were laughing and talking as we had coffee and the next thing I knew she was doubled up with pain. But Doctor Cortez says she will be fine. She was not far along, he said. She has slept ever since he left, señor."

This news seemed to ease Adolfo's concern, Rollo noticed instantly. Adolfo told Rollo that he would be in his study for awhile. Rollo turned to go about his duties as Adolfo went on down the hallway.

A fury seethed in Martinez, for he now knew why this beautiful young lady, so sweet and innocent, had come seeking him to find Vincent—what her desperation was. She had found herself pregnant and she knew not where to turn if she could not seek out Vincent who was responsible. Adolfo knew one thing for certain: Vincent would do for this young lady what he should do, or he'd kick him out of his law firm promptly. It mattered not to Adolfo that he was a Navarro!

Adolfo made his way to the liquor chest as soon as he got to his study and poured himself a strong, stiff drink. As he sipped on the liquor Adolfo was asking himself what it was about the little girl up there in his guest bedroom that brought out such violent emotions in him. Right now, he was feeling the deepest compassion for that poor little girl upstairs, and he was also feeling disfavor with his young associate, Vincent Navarro, whom he'd always admired and respected.

Adolfo could never remember a time when his emotions had been in such tremendous turmoil as they were right now.

When he left his study to go upstairs, he had to see for himself that Karita was all right, so he quietly slipped into her room to see her sleeping peacefully. Her glossy black hair fanned out on the pillows. He had never seen a lovelier face on any woman. As quietly as he'd entered, he left the room.

Rollo was to know the senor's devotion to this young girl when he requested that he share a tray for his dinner so he could keep her company while she ate her evening meal.

Adolfo was encouraged to see that she ate with relish and that she could smile and laugh as they shared the roast beef and vegetables the cook had prepared.

Karita shared a glass of his favorite red wine and when she told him how good it was this pleased him, for it was his favorite. "You have a good taste for fine wines, Karita. This is my favorite."

"Señor, I never intended to do this to you and I apologize. I can't believe that I have been so blessed as to have met you. I don't know what to say."

"You do not have to say anything. Can I tell you something—I've had two of the most wonderful evenings in your company that I can remember in a long, long time."

"Oh, Señor Martinez! An important man like you must surely be around interesting people all the time. I cannot imagine a person like me could be as exciting or interesting. But I thank you for saying that."

"Karita, may I tell you something? I am much older than you so I speak with some authority. A lot of so-

197

called interesting people I have found to be the biggest bores. You, my dear, are so refreshing and so unspoiled. This is what makes you a delight to sit and talk to."

Karita turned her face away from the kind man. "Well, now you know why I was seeking you out. I found myself expecting Vincent's child and I could not bring shame to my family. They did not deserve that so I knew that I must leave Whispering Willows to come to Austin."

"Well, Vincent will hear from me about this, and you *shall* see him," Adolfo told her.

"No, señor!" she pleaded with him in a very adamant voice. "I have no reason to see him. Today changed all that. I would like to stay here long enough to be able to travel back to Whispering Willows. I want to go home."

"Karita, you can stay here as long as you like, but when you do feel like leaving I'm going to see that you get back home safely and that means you don't need to be riding alone—not a pretty young lady like you," he told her.

This wealthy middle-aged man had been so kind and generous to her that Karita was overcome with emotion. She could not restrain the tears from flowing. Adolfo was so affected by her crying that he rushed over to console and comfort her.

"It is all right. Cry if you feel like it for it has not been a very good day for you, little Karita. Just know that I will do anything to help you, and all you have to do is ask me." He held her in his arms until her crying ceased and she was breathing evenly.

"Oh, señor, you . . . you didn't deserve to have all

this dumped in your lap and I'm truly sorry for that," she stammered, rubbing the tears from her cheek. Her black eyes looked at him with embarrassment and grief.

Just holding her like that with his arms around her, gave Adolfo a strange feeling of such wonderful contentment. It made him want to plead with her to stay there with him and not return to Whispering Willows.

Chapter 22

Vincent figured that the reason he'd seen Adolfo's buggy in the drive yesterday was because he'd stopped by his house to pick up some papers before paying his call on his client, as he'd told Vincent he was going to do. He'd given it no more thought when he arrived home for his time was occupied seeing that the new furnishings were arranged in a proper order.

But today Vincent was in a quandary when Adolfo dashed out of the office without saying anything to him. He had stayed there until six before he finally decided that Señor Martinez was not returning for the rest of the day. He was puzzled about his behavior, for it just didn't seem to be his usual routine.

Perhaps Adolfo would explain it all to him tomorrow, Vincent thought as he went toward his own home.

But tomorrow came and Vincent was given no explanation. The truth was he was greeted by a very cool, aloof Señor Martinez, and Vincent wondered if he'd displeased him some way. If his work wasn't satisfactory then Vincent would prefer that he just say so instead of acting this way.

He'd been under the impression that Adolfo was more than pleased with his services here at the office. How could things have changed in two days' time?

He knew how conscientiously he had worked to prove himself to Adolfo, so his attitude this morning had not left him in the best of moods. That afternoon, he had chanced to glance up from his desk to spy the debonair figure of the señor going toward the exit, to leave the office. But he did not glance Vincent's way nor did he take the time to say anything.

Vincent worked on for another hour before he moved away from his desk to leave for the day. But he knew one thing for certain and that was he would approach Adolfo if this continued for another day or two.

He was certainly not feeling in a festive mood for Señora Castillo's party tomorrow night. He suddenly was wondering if this had something to do with Adolfo's changed mood the last two days.

He found himself especially happy that night to enter the front door of his house and walk inside the small hallway. His small parlor looked very inviting. The new furnishings and the colorful bouquets Aspasia had placed in vases lent a warmth and charm to the old room. Jules had taken one of the tropical plants from the garden and potted it in a huge piece of pottery. It sat in the corner where the sunlight would make it thrive and grow. His two servants were endearing themselves more and more to Vincent for they worked so hard for him around the house. He had come to the conclusion that they considered this was their home, too, since as far as he knew, neither of them had any family.

He mounted the stairway slowly, for his mood was a thoughtful one. Adolfo's strange behavior was still weighing heavily on his mind. Once he had dropped his coat and leather case on the bed, he sauntered over to the liquor chest and poured himself a drink. Sinking down in one of the chairs by the window where he could look out over the small courtyard he decided he was doing no work for Adolfo this evening. In fact, he was wondering if he had made a wrong decision in accepting Adolfo's offer. He did not *have* to work for him for he had a rather nice inheritance from his Grandfather Navarro, which he and Victor had inherited when they reached twenty-one.

For the first time since he'd arrived in Austin, and because he'd been so busy, he found his thoughts drifting back to the Silvercreek Ranch and the people there. But it wasn't only the people at Silvercreek he thought about. There was that beautiful little Karita over at Whispering Willows!

All kinds of frivolous thoughts paraded through his mind as he enjoyed his evening meal and strolled through his gardens to enjoy a smoke after he'd eaten.

Would Karita like his little house here in Austin? Somehow, he felt that she would, and he knew that she would love his garden so fragrant with the night-blooming flowers. The bubbling fountain with benches on either side provided a quiet place to rest and enjoy the garden's tranquility. Recalling how he'd found her sitting on the bank of the river, that early spring day some weeks ago, he knew she would find this a place as enchanting as she had when he first came here.

203

As he took a seat by the fountain, Vincent came to the decision that it didn't matter whether he continued to work for Adolfo or not, he was not sorry he'd purchased this property.

When he finally left his garden to go up to the house, all the cares and worries of the day were behind him. The thoughts occupying his mind were about the beautiful Karita and not Adolfo.

His sleep was deep and peaceful. His dreams were about the little black-eyes señorita back at Whispering Willows.

Sleep had not been peaceful for Yolanda and Abeja since the morning they'd awakened to find their daughter's note on the kitchen table. They were both distraught! That first day they moved as people in a daze, trying to perform their chores around the ranch. Both were glad that their daughter Cara was at her sister's house.

That night they sat and talked, trying to figure out what had caused Karita to do such a thing. It was Abeja who came up with the idea that they should go over to Silvercreek to have a talk with Victor. Perhaps she had said something to him that afternoon when he'd brought her back home that would give them a clue as to where she had fled.

Yolanda was willing to do anything in hopes of finding out something that would ease her worried mind. Karita had never been any further than Silvercreek Ranch on her own, and the thought of her riding alone through the Texas countryside petrified her mother. More than ever Yolanda realized how her daughters had been so protected from the evils of the world, compared to her own life at sixteen when she was out in the world on her own. Thank God, she had managed to get under the protective wing of Señora Kristina!

The two of them wasted no time the next morning and immediately boarded their buggy to go to talk to the Navarro family. Danton and Kristina were stunned by the news the Monteras told them.

"And she gave you no hint as to why she was leaving or where she had headed, Yolanda?" Kristina asked.

"Nothing, señora. She just wrote that she must leave and vowed to return home when she could. She urged us not to worry about her," Yolanda told her. "But Karita is not the sort to do something like this unless she was desperate. That is why we thought maybe she might have dropped some hints to Victor. You know how it is with young people. They sometimes find it easier to talk to another young person than their parents. I recall how the two of us were always talking."

Kristina smiled and nodded her head, recalling how she would have talked to Yolanda about certain things much quicker than she would have with her mother, Florine.

"We'll summon Victor to join us. Maybe he knows something," Danton told them. A servant was sent immediately to ask Victor to join them out on the east veranda.

The minute Victor strolled out on the veranda he knew instinctively that something was wrong from the grave look on the faces of his parents and Karita's parents.

He greeted the Monteras and they returned his

greeting. Danton urged his son to have a seat and told him the reason he'd been called to join them.

"Karita has left Whispering Willows all alone?"

"That's right, Victor and we hoped—well, we hoped that maybe she'd said something to you the afternoon you'd brought her home. Did she indicate that she was worried about something—something that would force her to want to run away from home?" Yolanda asked him.

"She seemed very happy as far as I can remember, Señora Montera. I—I am as confused as the two of you must be. I can't imagine her doing such a thing." He inquired about relatives she might have gone to but the Monteras knew of no one she would have gone to except Kristina, her sister. Her sister Cara was visiting there so they doubted that very seriously.

Dejectedly, they said goodbye to the Navarro family and realized the futility of their journey to Silvercreek. They had learned nothing.

After the Monteras had gone, Victor's cunning mind began searching for an answer. Why had the pretty Karita slipped away in the middle of the night? She wasn't the type of girl to act so recklessly or irresponsibly, and Victor was very shocked by this news the Monteras had told him.

His grandmother was very distressed about the news and he realized this that evening when she called him aside after dinner. Was he sure there was not something he could remember that might help? "Think, Victor. It might be just the slightest little thing, dear," she insisted.

"I can't think of a thing, grandmother. I've thought about the afternoon when I was taking her home and

206

she seemed in the best of spirits and was laughing about the delightful time she'd had with you. Now that I think of it, she even mentioned to me that she would be seeing you this week. So she gave me no hint that she didn't intend to come here this week as she had been doing."

Lucia Navarro shook her head in despair and puzzlement for she was very upset. Many frightening things raced through her mind when she thought about a beautiful girl like Karita Montera out on her own when she'd been as sheltered as she knew she had been. Lucia had seen and experienced the sordid side of life.

Lucia just prayed that the lovely little señorita had a guardian angel riding on her shoulder, as she was sure she had had when she was Karita's age.

Often Karita thought about Señora Lucia as she lay in bed regaining her strength those next two days. Her fingers played with the little cross around her throat. She realized that had she been back at Whispering Willows she would have been making the trip over to Silvercreek to spend this afternoon with Lucia Navarro. A part of her was telling her that she could not go back.

How could she possibly face her parents or confess that she'd suffered a miscarriage? What would she tell them was the reason for leaving if she did not tell them the truth? She remembered Señor Adolfo's remarks that he was going to see that she was escorted safely home and that he was not going to let her travel alone. So what was she to do?

The rest of that day and that night she pondered what the answer was for her. Lucia had told her that she was very good at cards. Could she earn a living as the señora had, dealing cards at one of the gaming halls here in Austin? She could not accept Senor Adolfo's generosity much longer. It would not be right.

Karita knew there was only one solution once she had regained her strength. She would have to slip out of this palatial mansion in the still of the night as she had when she'd left her own home back at Whispering Willows.

She'd find a job somewhere in Austin until she could sort out the tormenting thoughts plaguing her right now. All she knew was that she wasn't ready to return to her parents. Right now, she had no interest in Vincent Navarro. He had done nothing but cause her trouble. Right now, she did not care whether she ever saw him again.

The pleasures he'd given her had only caused her pain that would last much longer than that moment of pleasure! No man was worth that kind of heartache, she'd decided, after what she'd been through.

That carefree world of sweet innocence was left behind when Vincent Navarro carried her through that threshold, initiating her into a new world she'd never known before. Now she knew about the world. She was a woman who'd felt the pleasure and the pain of loving a man!

Chapter 23

Señora Paulina Castillo's party was like her; it was a flamboyant, showy affair. Paulina was a very striking hostess as she greeted her guests in a brilliant emerald green satin gown. An emerald necklace hung around her throat and exquisite emeralds dangled from her ears.

Flambeaus lit the long drive going up to the front entrance of her house. Young men in a livery of green and black were at the entrance to take charge of the carriages as they arrived.

The first thought entering Vincent's mind as he entered the front door and saw all the servants scurrying at the back of the hall was that Adolfo's home reflected a quiet opulence. Paulina's reflected her vivacious personality. But he had little time to dwell on any private musings for soon he was facing his very beautiful hostess, Paulina.

"Ah, señora—you look absolutely stunning!" Vincent said as he took the hand she had extended.

"And you look very handsome. All my friends are

going to be happy to meet you. So many already know your father and mother. I've never met them but I've heard that your mother is a most beautiful woman."

"She is," Vincent told her but this was all he was allowed to say for the guests were arriving in a constant stream. Vincent moved on, but since he knew none of the guests he searched the room for Adolfo. Paulina's parlor was a very spacious room and he was met by a sea of faces, none of whom were known to him.

Suddenly he found Paulina's hand clasping his and she urged him to stand with her in the line to greet her guests. "After all, this party is for you, Vincent," she said gaily.

He readily accepted her invitation since he knew no one there. He had expected that he and Adolfo would come to this affair together since he was a stranger here in Austin. Adolfo's behavior remained strange to him.

He saw Adolfo enter the door and his impressive figure, impeccably attired, was enough to make an impression on anyone seeing the dapper gentleman.

Vincent would have expected a warmer greeting than he received from Adolfo. It was enough to catch the eye of Paulina and she turned to Vincent to ask, "What is the matter with Adolfo tonight? Was it a bad day at the office, Vincent?"

"No, it wasn't, but Adolfo has been in a strange mood for the last three days," Vincent told her. He was wounded enough to decide that he was going to bring this thing to a head tomorrow.

Paulina tossed her head back and laughed, "Well, we don't need Adolfo, Vincent. We shall have a good time tonight. Adolfo is a very complex man and I've known him for many, many years."

Vincent could certainly believe that after the last three days around him. He played the escort to Paulina as she moved around the room greeting the guests, and when they moved into her elegant dining room to sit down for the delectable feast her cook had prepared, he remained with her.

Vincent found himself by Paulina's side most of the evening. From time to time he glanced around and saw Adolfo's black eyes on him. He wondered if he was jealous that Paulina was paying so much attention to him. Was it that Adolfo was used to being the center of attraction at Paulina's parties?

Vincent had found it amazing that so many of the guests knew his mother and father and the great esteem they felt for Danton and Kristina Navarro. As their son, he felt an overwhelming pride.

No longer did it matter to him that Adolfo was in a foul mood so he began to enjoy Paulina's party. It proved to be a gala affair. At the stroke of midnight, most of the guests were still there.

By midnight, Vincent had consumed enough champagne that he arrogantly walked over to Adolfo and said, "Well, Adolfo—I thought before the party was over I'd better come over here to speak to you since you've made no effort to speak to me. You haven't seemed to be enjoying yourself tonight."

"Well, Vincent, *you* obviously are," Adolfo retorted in a tone of distaste.

"Don't know any reason why I shouldn't, do you?" Vincent asked.

Adolfo said nothing but he was thinking about his little house guest, Karita.

By now, Adolfo's demeanor was offensive to Vincent. He worked for the man standing there beside him and this man had anxiously wanted him in his office, so why was he acting so obnoxious toward him tonight?

"What the devil is bothering you, Adolfo? I don't play stupid games and I don't like them played with me," Vincent said heatedly. His patience had reached its limit.

Adolfo saw heads turning in their direction. "We'll speak about it tomorrow, Vincent, when champagne is not being drunk," he told Vincent as he turned sharply on his heels to walk away into the sea of guests milling around the parlor. He heard Vincent mutter, "Damned right we will!"

As soon as Adolfo spotted Paulina he politely and graciously told her that he was going to have to leave for he had an early hour client to see. "It was a magnificent party my dear, as all your parties are, and I'm sorry that I can't linger any longer."

"Oh, Adolfo!" she gave him a pretty pout. "I think you are being a meany."

He forced a smile on his face and gave her a peck on the cheek. "You'll forgive me, won't you?"

"Si, Adolfo—you know I will. I am delighted that our young friend is making such a fine impression. Everyone is charmed by him."

"Ah, Vincent has a winning way about him. There is no doubt about that," Adolfo forced himself to remark before he gave her a final farewell. But there was a chill in his voice.

Paulina slowly turned around to see if she could spot the handsome Navarro in the crowd. It didn't take her too long for he towered over most of them.

She should have known he would be in the company of one of her lady guests. Pretty, blue-eyed Ashley Morgan had him cornered and as he had all evening he wore a devilishly handsome grin on his face. A sly smile came to Paulina's face as she slowly managed to move in their direction but she was delayed by various guests wishing to chat with her. By the time she was only a few feet away from the spot where he and Ashley had been standing, he was no longer there.

She wondered if Ashley had urged him to take a stroll out on the terrace. This was exactly what Paulina's intention had been when she was making her way to join him. So now that he had disappeared, her black eyes began to scan the spacious parlor, and once again she spied him back at the archway. He looked like he was searching around the room and she dared to hope that he was looking for her. So she rushed through the crowd as hastily as she could.

When she was just a few feet away she called out to him, "Vincent, I've been wondering where you were."

He smiled. "Well, I was looking for you, Paulina. In this huge crowd it's not so easy to find you when you are so petite."

He took her hand as she finally came to stand by his side. He drew her hand up to his lips to gently kiss it. Paulina's black eyes flashed brightly and wild anticipation engulfed her. But when he spoke she was crestfallen.

"I've got to take my leave from the fabulous party, Paulina. I have to meet Adolfo in the morning with a clear head and I won't be able to do that if I stay here and drink any more champagne. He's got a burr in his butt, if I may be so blunt with you, and I don't know what about."

"Adolfo is out of sorts with you, Vincent?" she stammered, shocked to hear that, for Adolfo had nothing but praise for Vincent when they spoke together. But she *had* noticed that he was not his usual gregarious self tonight. Adolfo was a man who could sink into a black, ugly mood. Tonight happened to be one of those times.

"Oh, is he out of sorts! But damned if I know why. I've worked my tail off in that office but he's acted strange for a couple of days. So I'm going to tell you goodnight and thank you from the bottom of my heart for the wonderful evening. I liked all your friends, Paulina."

"And they adored you, too. I'm disappointed that you have to leave but I do understand, Vincent. Besides, there will be other evenings—si?" she said, tossing her head coquettishly.

"Si, Paulina," he assured her. Saying goodnight, he turned to go. Paulina moved to get herself another glass of champagne for the party was over as far as she was concerned. Under her breath, she was cussing Adolfo Martinez for ruining it for her.

Paulina figured she knew Adolfo as well as anyone here in Austin, and yet she knew she didn't truly know him at all. He was a very secretive individual that allowed no one to invade his privacy. Paulina had realized very soon after they'd become acquainted and he'd escorted her to social affairs and elegant dinner parties that Adolfo would never share his life with any woman. She did not insist on entering his private world, and it was the only reason that they had continued to see each other throughout the years.

But she was as puzzled as Vincent about Adolfo's behavior.

Karita had been surprised to see Adolfo's buggy coming up the drive so early and she quickly dimmed the lamp so he would think she was asleep when he came upstairs. All evening after he'd left for the elegant dinner party, she'd moved around the room, testing herself to see how strong she was.

She had considered that while he was gone it would be the perfect time to slip out of the house and leave. There was no way she could return to Whispering Willows so there was nothing left for her to do but leave when he was not around to stop her.

So determined was she about the plans that she'd made earlier that she'd spent the last four hours walking around the room and packing her belongings. She was dressed and was about to slip out of the room when she happened to hear his buggy rolling up the drive.

Had Adolfo chanced to glance up at her bedroom there on the second landing he would have seen the sudden darkening at her window, but he didn't. He was thinking of other things as he pulled up the drive.

When he entered the front door, Rollo had already retired. The house was ghostly quiet as Adolfo mounted the stairs. When he reached the second landing he saw the darkness under the threshold of the bedroom Karita occupied so he went on into his own bedroom.

Adolfo was not a happy man tonight, for he realized

that he was probably going to lose a young law partner about whom he had such great hopes. What was really troubling him more than anything was his own emotions, for he'd never allowed emotions to play on him as they had the last few days. He had always been a cool, calculating man who had allowed nothing to stand in the way of his ambition.

To find himself vulnerable now was very startling. To admit that it was all about a lady young enough to be his daughter was even more alarming.

Long after he'd undressed and sat in his robe in the chair by his window, Adolfo was doing a lot of soul searching as to why his little world was being shaken to the core over the beautiful Karita Montera.

As intelligent and clever as he was, Adolfo could not come up with the answer. At least, he was not yet ready to admit to the truth.

Chapter 24

Black, ominous clouds shrouded the city of Austin as Adolfo left his house to go to his office. The weather seemed to reflect his own black mood as he knew he was going to have his talk with Vincent Navarro this morning as soon as he got to the office.

Vincent was feeling very much like Adolfo as he left his own house to go to the office. He felt like it was a bad omen that the morning was so dismal and dark with the threat of storms moving in at any minute.

Dressed in the same divided skirt and blouse she'd worn the day she arrived there, Karita went downstairs for the first time in two days to be greeted warmly by Rollo. "Ah, señorita—it is nice to see you looking so well. Obviously you are feeling much better."

"Oh, I am, Rollo! I am ready to get out of the bedroom. I don't like lying around as I've been doing."

"Well, you were a sick little lady, señorita. You needed to be in bed for a day or two."

A warm smile came to her face as she recalled how Rollo had taken charge of her in her moment of

217

helplessness and she knew how he'd assisted Doctor Cortez. "I appreciate what you did for me, Rollo. You are a kind man and I shall never forget you as long as I live."

"Oh, Señorita Karita—I didn't do that much really." Rollo gently urged her to accompany him to the kitchen so that they could share a cup of coffee at the little table in the kitchen.

There was no bright sunlight beaming through the window as there usually was at this time of the morning and Rollo told her that he was going to be leaving shortly to run some errands for Señor Martinez. "But I can leave now that I know you are doing so well, señorita. I won't be gone long. I should be back in an hour."

"I will be fine, Rollo," she assured him.

When the two of them had finished the coffee, Rollo prepared to leave and Karita left to go back upstairs, knowing that this was the perfect time for her to make her departure. By the time Rollo was guiding his buggy down the long drive, Karita was gathering her belongings and going back down the stairs.

A few minutes later, she and Bonita were galloping down the drive. She knew not what her destination was to be. But she sought the center of the city, so she spurred Bonita out of the residential district to the business area of the capital of Texas.

As she was riding down the street her eyes saw a huge two-story white frame building. The sign out front said, "White Palace," and for whatever reason she yanked up on the reins. She urged Bonita to move closer and as she did two gentlemen came out the door to give her a most admiring stare.

At the same moment that the men had come out the door, a rumble of thunder broke in the sky above her and she cast her eyes up. Billowing black clouds were hanging there. Karita had not noticed the threatening skies in her haste to leave Adolfo's house.

A shrill female voice was calling her attention suddenly, "Honey, get yourself inside! Don't you know that we've got ourselves a cyclone coming down on us!"

Karita turned to see a full-figured woman standing in the doorway. Her hands were motioning to Karita to get off her horse and come inside.

Karita sensed the danger, so she did not hesitate when she saw the bolts of lightning going from the sky to the ground. She did not take the time to tie Bonita to the hitching post as she dashed to the doorway.

The terrifying atmosphere surrounding her made her give way to panic. So quickly the sky had become black as night.

By the time she stood beside the woman Karita felt she could hardly breathe. "See what I mean? There is a quietness just before those devils wiggle down from the sky. Now you come with me and we'll take cover until this thing passes over or lands somewhere."

The woman led her behind the massive bar counter and urged her to join her on the floor. "You hear a roar, you stick yourself as far under this counter as you can manage cause that's what I'm going to do," the red-haired woman told her.

"I will," Karita assured her, her black eyes flashing with concern. She was still too scared to think about Bonita.

The two of them sat on the floor saying nothing for a minute or two, as if they were listening for that roar

219

to come. The woman told her, "My name's Margie— Margie McClure. Wasn't thinking about introductions. What's your name, honey?"

"Karita—Karita Montera. I thank you for the shelter."

"Your folks are probably fretting that you aren't home right now." The girl was so young and pretty and she'd obviously left her house before this storm started brewing.

"My folks don't live here in Austin."

"Are you here alone?"

"Yes, ma'am—I am," Karita told her. "My home is back in Blanco County."

But before Margie could ask her any more questions a torrent of rain began to fall and strong gusting winds were slamming the frame building. "Here it comes!" Margie said tensely. She stood up for a second to see the sheets of rain pelting the front of her saloon coming right out of the southwest.

She sat down on the floor and found herself curious about a girl as pretty and young as Karita up here in Austin if her folks lived down in Blanco County. "Here to visit relatives, Karita?"

"No, I have no relatives here in Austin." Karita saw the inquisitive look in her green eyes as Margie McClure looked at her. "I was trying to find a job this morning. At least, that was what I had intended to do until this thing struck."

"I see," Margie commented. "What kind of work do you do, Karita? Where have you worked?" She would wager that this young miss had never worked anywhere besides around her own home.

By now, Karita knew that this was a cantina, for all

the bottles of liquor and the glasses lining the shelf there behind the counter bar. But she'd never seen the inside of such an establishment before.

But she could not tell Margie McClure this. She desperately needed to find work, and perhaps she could be hired to work in the cantina.

"I can deal cards. The truth is I play a fine hand of poker, ma'am," Karita boasted.

"Oh, how could that be for one so young?" Margie was trying to keep an amused grin from coming to her face.

"Just a natural talent, I suppose, but I've played cards with the famous Lolita and she tells me I am very good."

"Are you talking about the well-known lady gambler back in San Antonio who worked the Palace in San Antonio? How could this be?"

Karita knew that she'd caught her attention. "Yes, that is the same lady I'm speaking about. She is elderly now but she still loves to play cards. I just happened to live nearby so I visited her regularly."

Margie knew the girl was telling her the truth. Whatever dilemma she was in Margie knew she could not turn her down.

"I've no need for a card dealer, Karita, but there are other things I might hire you to do here at the White Palace, and I furnish a bedroom to the girls who work here. Salary isn't much unless you prove to be worth more."

Karita did not inquire what the job would be for she had no bed to sleep in tonight if she didn't accept Margie's offer. She seemed like a nice enough woman and she'd called her in out of the storm. Right now she

221

could have been drenched to the skin but for Margie McClure offering her shelter.

"Well, I'm willing to try to prove my worth to you, Señora McClure."

Margie smiled at her, "And I'm willing to give you that chance." All the turbulence outside seemed to have subsided and Margie rose up from the floor. A gale of laughter came out as she spied the intruder in her saloon. Karita rose to see what she was laughing about. It seemed that Bonita had also sought shelter from the storm and was standing there in the saloon.

"Madre de Dios, I am sorry, señora." She quickly moved to her little mare and took hold of the reins. But Karita did not scold the mare; she apologized to her for forgetting about her. This told Margie a lot about this young lady.

"There's a shed out in back. Why don't you put her in there? When you get her taken care of then you and I will talk some more, eh?"

"Si, señora," she said as she started to lead Bonita out the opened door. Margie was left to ponder what she could assign Karita to do and the wages she would pay her. She did not want to see that sweet innocent girl being exposed to some of gents that frequented her establishment. Girls like Gertie, Estelle and Maria were a different breed than this one. Her head was whirling as to how she could fit her into the White Palace but anything she could think of would expose her to the lecherous eyes of the fellows who came here to enjoy their drinks and the company of her girls.

Margie decided that for the first few nights the safest place for Karita was to keep her back in the kitchen with her cook, Rosco. She could assist him in making

222

the sandwiches she furnished her patrons at the bar when they were drinking. Yes, that might be the best solution and Rosco could assist her bartender at the bar on their busy nights when he could use some help.

There were not many problems that Margie couldn't solve when she tried. For the last fifteen years she'd run the White Palace without the help of her husband, Gus. One winter he'd got pneumonia and died, and it had not been an easy life for Margie without Gus by her side, but she'd survived. This had amazed her when she took the time to think about it.

When Karita came back she had a pillow case in her hand. She laughed, "My belongings. They're a little damp. Guess Bonita didn't decide to come in for a while."

"Well, let's get you settled in, honey. I'll talk to you later about what you're to do here," Margie told her as she motioned to follow her up the stairs. She guided Karita down the full length of the hallway and opened the door to the last bedroom. "This will be your room, Karita."

Karita could not help thinking what a contrast this room was to the one that she had slept in last night. But this did not matter to her right now. She had a roof over her head and a job. It was only the middle of the day. She thought to herself that Adolfo would not realize that she was gone from his house. Rollo would have returned to the house by now but he would not have any reason to come upstairs to check on her.

"Now, honey, you just get settled in cause I've got some things to attend to. I'll see you a little later. We all eat at different times around the White Palace. Our hours aren't the conventional ones so you might as well know that right now."

"That won't bother me, señora," she assured her.

"Well, you just sashay down to the kitchen and tell Rosco you're my new girl and you're hungry and he'll feed you." Margie laughed as she turned to go back out the door.

"I will."

"Now, you do it—all right?" Margie closed the door and went back down the hall to tell Rosco about her new employee. She also wanted to tell him why she was going to assign Karita to him. She knew that Rosco would understand when she told him about the girl.

Upstairs, Karita was busy taking her clothing out of the pillow case, hanging it on the pegs and across the chairs to dry out the dampness.

She suddenly realized that she wasn't as strong as she thought she was early this morning. The miscarriage had drained her more than she'd suspected.

She lay across the bed to rest and before she knew it, she was sleeping peacefully. Mid-afternoon this was where Margie found her. The kindhearted Margie decided that she was not going to insist that she work tonight. The girl was exhausted and weary. She did not know what had happened to her but she suspected that it was not pleasant.

Tonight, she would invite Karita to join her for dinner in her room before she went downstairs to work in the saloon and tomorrow Karita could start working with Rosco.

The red-haired saloon keeper was very curious about this very beautiful girl who'd come into her life!

Part Three

A Fury of Vengeance

Chapter 25

Rollo was caught in the fury of the storm that came down on the city of Austin. He managed to finish his errands for Señor Martinez, then struggled with the bay to get him back home. He heaved a deep sigh of relief when he turned the buggy over to the stable boy and dashed into the house.

It was a fierce-looking sky out there this morning and it was as dark as twilight, even though it was not yet noon.

It felt good to be within the walls of the strong stone structure as the galelike winds blasted against the house. He watched the branches of the tall trees in the courtyard twisted and bent by the power and force of the wind.

Thinking that Karita might be frightened, he rushed upstairs to check on her. He wanted her to know that he was back at the house. Perhaps, if she was frightened, it would be a comfort for her to know this.

But Rollo got no response to his knock on the dor and he knocked again and called out to Karita.

Something told him he should go inside the room; perhaps she had fainted due to her weak condition. Maybe coming down the stairs and returning to her room had been too much for her.

But she wasn't on the floor or on the bed. The next thing he did was check the armoire; all her belongings were gone. The little señorita had taken her leave, he had to conclude. He searched the room for some farewell message to the señor, but there was none.

He rushed back downstairs and to the stable. Finding her mare gone left no doubt that she had fled while he was out. His heart was pounding with fear and indecision. Should he ride immediately to Señor Martinez's office to tell him or wait until he came in this evening?

The rains were still coming down steadily so Rollo paced back and forth in the kitchen delaying his departure for Señor Martinez's office. When the winds calmed and the rains started to decrease, he went back to the stable to hitch up to the buggy and left the house to tell Adolfo that their guest was gone. Rollo was surprised and a little hurt that she had left like that, without a farewell to the señor or to him.

The air was thick with tension that morning when Vincent Navarro strode through the door of Adolfo's office. Before he made the effort to open the first folder on his desk, he decided that he and Adolfo should talk as Adolfo had suggested last night. As far as he was concerned there was no reason to prolong the agony any longer.

"Good morning, Adolfo," he said. "I'm here to have

that talk we need to have."

"Sit down, Vincent," Adolfo curtly told him. Vincent did as he requested. When Vincent was seated in the leather chair at the front of his desk, Adolfo stared at him across the desk before he spoke one word. "Tell me about Karita Montera. Being a lawyer, I like to know both sides of the story."

Angrily, Vincent reared up out of the chair. "For Christ's sake! What—what has Karita Montera to do with the way you've been acting? How the hell does she enter into the association I have here in your office? Can you fault my work?" Vincent's green eyes glared down at Adolfo.

"It wouldn't have if the young lady had not landed on my front porch a few days ago. Then it became my business, Vincent."

"Karita is here . . . in Austin?" he slowly whispered. He sank back down in the chair. "Why did she come to your house to seek you?"

Adolfo detected the shock of his news on Vincent. "She came to me in her desperation to find you. Obviously."

"I'm sorry, Adolfo—I still don't understand," Vincent told him, shaking his head.

"I'll make this very simple, Vincent. She was a very desperate young girl because she found herself pregnant after you left Silvercreek. She came here to find you. Is that clear enough?"

A play of emotions reflected on Vincent's face before he spoke. "So why did you not bring her to me and why wasn't I told immediately?" His voice was choked and he was breathing hard.

Adolfo's glare never wavered. "I intended to do just

227

that, but something happened that prevented it. She had a miscarriage, Vincent. She is no longer carrying your child. After that she told me she had no reason or wish to see you."

Vincent gave a moan of anguish, "Oh, God! Little Karita!" He looked over at Adolfo and there was pain in his eyes as he muttered, "Well, I want to see her for I care for her and I would not want her to think otherwise. If only I had known this, things could have been different. Is she still at your house, Adolfo?"

"She is."

"Then may I have your permission to go there right now? I've a lot to make up to her."

Adolfo knew that he had not been wrong about this young man for he saw the sincerity on his face as he spoke. He had been too harsh on Vincent, he realized.

"I can't promise you how she'll react to you, Vincent, but you have my permission to take the entire day off if you'd like. She is a charming young lady that I've become very fond of in the few days I've known her."

Adolfo knew how this young señorita could get under the skin of a man, for she'd bewitched him with her simple charms. There was something refreshing and exciting about Karita Montera . . . something that he found so lacking in most of the women he encountered.

None of them was more breathtakingly beautiful than Karita, or as guileless!

Vincent got up out of his chair. "Thank you, Adolfo. I have to let her know that I do care very much, and if she will let me I'll certainly assume responsibility for her. If she does not wish this then I shall see that she gets back safely to Whispering Willows."

228

"Go to her, Vincent. She needs to know this, I think," Adolfo told him.

Vincent moved quickly to leave the room, but the carved oak door suddenly swung open, almost slamming Vincent. It was a very distraught Rollo rushing into the office to tell them that Karita was gone.

"Calm down, Rollo. What do you mean she is gone?" Adolfo inquired, standing up from his desk.

"Just what I said, señor. She came downstairs and she seemed just fine. We sat in the kitchen and shared some coffee. I left the house to do the errands, and she went back upstairs. When I got home in the middle of the storm, I went upstairs to check in on her and the room was empty and her clothes gone. I went to check on her horse and it is also gone. She left while I was away from the house."

Adolfo and Vincent exchanged glances; both of them were shaken by Rollo's news. It was Adolfo who spoke first, inquiring if she knew anyone else here in Austin.

"I would doubt that, Adolfo. Surely she decided to go back to Whispering Willows."

Both of the men were thinking to themselves that they were not going to be able to concentrate on their work this day. Maybe the storm had been a bad omen.

Adolfo sank back down in his chair and told Rollo to go home. "I'll see you later. Thank you for coming here, Rollo. I'm glad you came immediately to tell me."

Vincent sat down in the chair, pondering if he should ride to Whispering Willows to see she had returned home safely.

Vincent suggested this to Adolfo. "Damned if I know what to tell you!" Adolfo muttered. *Why did she do this foolish thing,* he wondered? He had let her know that she was welcome at his home in every way that he possibly could. It made him realize how very naive this young girl was to travel around the countryside as she was doing. She was a headstrong young lady!

He also had to ask himself this: if she had not left Austin, where would she have gone, here in the city?

Dejectedly, Vincent told Adolfo that he did not know where to look for her here in Austin. "I know nothing to do but go to Whispering Willows. I would hate to think that I would arrive there and she would not be there. I would only compound the worry her parents are already feeling."

"I'm going to leave this in your hands, Vincent, for you know Karita much better than I do."

"Right now, I am thinking that I don't know little Rita at all. Right now, I'm thinking about a lot of things, I must confess to you. Only my parents knew that I had taken the position with you and bought my house. I'd not written to Karita. Oh, I had intended to write her but I'd been so busy getting the house in order and trying to prove to you that I was worthy that I never took the time to write to her. I would have later."

"So how would she have known about me?" Adolfo asked him.

"This is what I am asking. The Montera family does not come to Silvercreek that often, nor does my family visit them at Whispering Willows."

Adolfo walked around the desk and extended his hand to the young man. "Vincent, I have a suggestion that we declare the rest of this day a holiday. Neither one of us would be worth a damn and we both know it.

If you decide to ride back to Blanco County and you don't show up tomorrow, I will know if I don't see you here at the office what you're about. I—I must say one thing before we part company. I believe in you, and that is the most important thing to me."

"And I must tell you that I value that very much, Adolfo. That was troubling me greatly the last few days."

The two shook hands and left the office together, both of them feeling much better about their relationship and the new understanding they had.

The sight of his house and his garden courtyard gave Vincent a feeling of repose he found himself needing this early afternoon. In a way it was strange, for he'd never expected that being the owner of a home would kindle such pride in him. It would not have a year ago when his father was a senator and he was living in Washington. Many things had changed for him when his father returned to Texas to live at Silvercreek.

A week at Silvercreek had convinced him that he would not be content to live there the rest of his life. Silvercreek was the empire that his grandfather had created in his lifetime. He was always sorry that he'd never got the opportunity to know him but his Grandmother Lucia gave him an idea as to what kind of gentleman he was.

Unlike his father, he had no desire to be a politician or a rancher. It didn't interest him. But he did love the law and always admired shrewd, clever lawyers like Adolfo. He'd met many of them in the capital while he was growing up during those years when his father was a senator from Texas.

That was why Adolfo's offer was so appealing to

him. So he was arriving home a much happier man today now that the barrier between him and Adolfo was removed.

He entered his front door and was taken by surprise to see his twin brother Victor sitting in the parlor. "Victor—this is a surprise!"

"Well, I hope it is a nice one?" Victor asked.

"Oh, you know it is! I'm sorry that I wasn't here to welcome you when you came through the door."

"Well, Aspasia gave me a very warm welcome when I told her I was your twin," Victor laughed.

"She is priceless! So how do you like my little house?" Vincent asked him.

"Well, it isn't exactly Silvercreek," Victor grinned.

"But Silvercreek isn't mine, Victor, and this is all mine."

"And this is very important to you, Vincent?" Victor asked him.

"It is very important to me!" he replied warmly.

For the next few minutes they talked about Silvercreek and Vincent asked about his parents and grandmothers. Finally, Victor brought up the subject of Karita Montera. "She ran away from home and her parents are worried about her. They haven't heard a word from her."

"Were you around her before she left, Victor?" Vincent's eyes grew in intensity as he stared at his brother.

"Why did you ask that, Vincent?" his brother asked him. His voice held a certain degree of indignation.

Giving a shrug to his shoulders, Vincent told him, "I thought maybe she might have given you some hint that she was planning to run away."

"No, we spoke about many things the last afternoon I took her back home after she and grandmother had played cards. They'd been doing so weekly since shortly after you left Silvercreek."

"Ah, that Grandmother Lucia and her cards. I find it hard to imagine her and little Rita playing cards together," Vincent laughed.

Victor told him that he'd told Karita the news about him and his plans to stay in Austin. Now, Vincent knew how Karita had found out about him working for Adolfo, but he decided not to mention to Victor that Karita had come to Austin. Of course, after Adolfo's talk with him today, he knew why it was so urgent for her to come here, but this was none of Victor's affair!

Chapter 26

Vincent was not very good company that evening and excused it to Victor as a busy time in the office the last few days.

"We're brothers, Vincent—remember?" he laughed. "You don't have to consider me company. I just found myself curious about your house so I decided to ride up here for a couple of days."

By the time the two of them said goodnight and went to their separate bedrooms Victor had to admit that he'd guessed wrong about something—one of the reasons he'd decided to come to Austin. Had he found Karita here with Vincent as he suspected, he could have returned to Silvercreek to be lauded for finding the missing girl. Everyone at Silvercreek and Whispering Willows would have been singing his praises.

Had he found the pretty Karita in the company of Vincent, his twin brother could have had a devilish bad time explaining that to his family or the Monteras.

But now that he was alone in the room he thought about their discussion of Karita's disappearance, and

Vincent did not show the stunned reaction he would have expected to see.

Tomorrow, he was going to come right out and ask Vincent if he'd seen the girl. He was still convinced that Karita was headed for Austin when she left Whispering Willows.

As Victor was pondering various things in the privacy of his room, Vincent was still absorbed with his thoughts about Karita and where she could be. He had been thinking very seriously about getting up at sunrise to ride to Whispering Willows to see if she went back home. But there was also some argument going on within him, for to do that would mean he'd have to confess to her parents that she had been in Austin.

One question would surely bring on another one, and how could he possibly tell them that their daughter had run off to find him in Austin and that she'd had a miscarriage? He knew what that would do to the Montera family.

For the longest time after he stretched out on the bed, he lay in the dark thinking what would be the best thing to do for everyone concerned. Something told him that she was still right there in Austin. After all, Victor had traveled over the same road she would have been riding southward if she was going back home. Remembering the time Rollo had rushed into the office today, he could fairly well pinpoint the time she'd slipped away from Adolfo's house.

Logic told him that Victor's path and hers would have crossed today if she had headed home. But there was another thing that Vincent was convinced about the more he thought about it.

236

With everything that had happened to her, he doubted that Karita was ready to return home to face her parents. This made him feel very guilty. He'd taken the sweet innocent love she'd willingly given and then he'd left Silvercreek with no thought about her.

With some women, he would have had no qualm of conscience. Karita was different, for he knew that he was the first man to make love to her. When she'd found herself pregnant, he could imagine the panic she must have felt, and the need to run away. She must have known the tremendous worry she would put her parents through. Ah, yes, he was feeling an over-whelming burden of guilt!

By the time he closed his eyes and gave way to sleep, Vincent had decided against going to Blanco County. Instead, he was going to search every inch of the city.

He'd start tomorrow under the guise of showing his twin brother the sights, but as they roamed around the city, his eyes would be scanning every street corner they passed.

The next morning, he got up early and asked Aspasia to tell his brother that he was going to the office to ask Señor Martinez for the day off. Adolfo had already told him to take the day off but Vincent wanted to tell him the theory he'd come up with about Karita.

Adolfo felt he just might be right. "As you pointed out it would seem that your brother traveling north would have met her on the way as she was going south to get back to Blanco County. I think you may be right, Vincent. You take the day off and take your brother on a tour of the city. Between the two of us, if she's here in the city we'll track her down. I've two fellows I've used in the past to do some snooping around for me and I

237

will hire the two of them today."

Vincent turned to leave telling Adolfo that he would see him tomorrow morning. Adolfo nodded his head and wished him good luck.

Vincent went back to his house, where he found Victor enjoying Aspasia's hearty breakfast. Victor had no inkling of the heavy heart Vincent was carrying, as he forced a happy-go-lucky expression onto his face and greeted him, "Well, eat hearty, brother, because we're going to put the day in seeing all the sights of Austin since you will be leaving tomorrow."

Victor grinned and gave him a nod of his head for his mouth was too full to try to speak.

A few minutes later, the two of them left Vincent's house. Instead of taking the buggy, Vincent rode his palomino, Dorado, and Victor rode his horse. The two Navarro twins made a handsome pair as they galloped down the streets of Austin.

Rosco was not going to forget this night at the White Palace for a long, long time, and he wondered what Miss Margie, as he called Margie McClure, had let herself in for by taking this sweet, wide-eyed child under her wing. She was not for the likes of those here at the saloon.

Oh, he could not fault her for not being a hard working little miss. But he watched the shocked expression all night as she labored beside him as her ears heard some of the foul language and raucous remarks just outside the kitchen door. He dared not let her carry the trays of food out to the bar. "I'll take the tray, little miss. It's too heavy for you," he'd told her.

"But I want to earn my keep, Rosco. I owe Señora Margie a lot for giving me this job."

"You're earning it, miss. You're a big help to me," the husky, ruddy-faced Rosco told her.

Karita's curious nature had urged her to peep through the kitchen door a couple of times that first night she worked in the kitchen. The world she saw out there in the saloon was like nothing she had ever known before. She saw three women dressed in very revealing gowns that displayed an abundance of cleavage. She'd never seen ladies wear so much makeup on their faces as these ladies did.

The gents seemed to take generous liberties with the women as they stood together at the bar or sat at the table. She watched one man patting Gerta's hips as she stood with him at the bar. Karita was suddenly glad that she was not out there, but safe in the seclusion of the kitchen.

There was one sight that did not make Karita gasp and this caught her interest. She stood at the door while Rosco was gone from the kitchen to observe four men sitting at a table playing cards.

The hour was late when Rosco told her to go on upstairs, for the crowd was thinning out and there was no need to make any more sandwiches that night.

Karita gave him no argument for she was tired and more than eager to seek the comfort of her bed. She did just that as soon as she could get undressed. Sleep came quickly as her head lay on the pillow.

After she had worked in the kitchen with Rosco for three evenings, he noticed that she was getting accustomed to the White Palace. She seemed to ignore the sounds outside the door where they worked. It was

239

obvious to Rosco that Miss Margie was genuinely fond of the little black-eyed girl when she came sashaying into the kitchen during the evening. She'd help herself to one of the sandwiches on the tray they were filling and talk to Karita.

More than once, she would tell the girl what a fine job she was doing. Rosco saw that this pleased Karita and he found himself very curious about the background of such a well-mannered young lady who was here in Austin all alone.

As they worked together longer, Rosco became bold enough to ask her one night if she was an orphan. She smiled up at him, "Oh, no. I have two very wonderful parents." But this perplexed the robust Rosco all the more as to why the girl was here in the city alone. She should be with them and not in a place like this.

By the time the week was ending, Rosco knew that she had parents and she had lived in a place called Whispering Willows.

"That sounds like a wonderful place—Whispering Willows," he smiled at her.

She told him that it was named that because of all the willow trees that grew by the river bank, and before she realized it she was telling Rosco how she loved to sit on the bank of the river to enjoy the serenity and peace she always found there.

His eyes were warm with the genuine feeling of concern he felt for her. "Then, honey—why don't you get yourself back to that beautiful place. You don't need to be here, Karita. This isn't for you."

Her doelike black eyes looked up at him and he saw a hint of sadness there as she softly declared, "Oh, I shall someday, Rosco, but right now I can't."

Rosco said no more on the subject but more than ever he wondered what had brought this beautiful young lady to a place like this. Oh, he didn't look down his nose at Miss Margie, for he'd worked for her and her husband, Gus, before he'd died. He admired the courage of the woman to have continued to operate this place without the help of her husband. More than once he'd dashed out of the kitchen to toss some rowdy dude out the front door. If little Karita stayed long enough she would see this happen.

Of the three women working for Margie, Karita found she had most in common with the twenty year old Maria who was also of Mexican descent.

Karita was a fine seamstress so she'd offered to mend the frock one of the fellows had torn the night before and Maria was very grateful.

"That asno! He wasn't worth the price of a drink!" she'd declared to Karita. Karita was to learn that this was the part she, Estelle and Gerta played here at the White Palace—to encourage the patrons to drink more liquor. Maria had told her if the fellow they were drinking with wished their company for the evening he must pay a price for it.

Now, Karita understood what Rosco was trying to tell her. For awhile she was appalled until she thought about what she had done, and she had charged no fee to Vincent Navarro. She had willingly surrendered to his overpowering charm because of love. She could not imagine lying with a man for a fee as Maria, Estelle and Gerta did here at the White Palace. But neither could she bring herself to blame them, for they were so kind to her.

She never would forget the kind-hearted Margie

McClure taking her in as she had. There would be those who would not have such a high opinion of a lady saloon keeper, but Karita did.

She would always be grateful to her for her generous act that stormy day when she'd left Adolfo's house. But there was not one person she'd met at the White Palace that had not opened their arms to her. That big bear, Rosco, might look like a fierce individual but he was as gentle and kind as a lamb.

After Karita had been with her about a week, Margie McClure could not forget what she had told her . . . that she played a wicked card game. Had it been anyone other than Karita, Margie might not have believed the fantastic story she'd told about knowing and playing cards with the renowned Lolita.

But when she'd invited the girl to play cards with her one afternoon, Margie became convinced that she was a very skilled player. An idea was born that afternoon. She would not wish sweet Karita to be out there in the saloon where Gerta, Maria and Estelle were nightly, but in one of the private backrooms where certain gentlemen came to play cards. These men were of a higher caliber than her customers in the saloon. Karita would be safe sitting in one of those games.

It could certainly allow her more freedom if Karita took her place at the tables some of the nights. She could well imagine what a beautiful vision the girl would make in a fancy gown with her lovely black hair piled atop her head. She could imagine how those gents would be entranced when she brought Karita into the room and told them that Señorita Karita Montera would be sitting in for her that evening.

A smile came to Margie's face knowing how the word would spread about the beautiful señorita at the White Palace. Why, she'd have that room occupied every night of the week!

Tomorrow, she would take Karita shopping for the most stunning gown her pocketbook could afford. The money would be well spent, Margie figured. She'd get it back tenfold in the first week, she was sure.

Karita Montera was going to bring her good luck.

Chapter 27

The next day Margie announced her plans to Karita and they sounded very exciting to her. She thought about Señora Lucia. Karita saw herself living the same life that Lucia Navarro had lived when she was her age.

"Do you really think I'm good enough, Señora Margie?" she asked with excitement flashing in her black eyes.

"I know you are! If I didn't, honey, I would not be spending my hard earned money on a pretty gown for you." She gave a hearty laugh.

"Well, I'll try to earn the price of that gown back for you the first week," Karita giggled.

"Oh, you will. I've no doubt about that."

A short time later, Karita was ready to go shopping. She rushed back down the steps to join Margie in the saloon. Margie looked up from the ledger she'd been going over. "Ready, honey?"

"I'm ready!"

Margie put the ledger on a shelf under the bar and they left the saloon. As they traveled down the street in

Margie's buggy they drew stares, for they were such a contrast; Margie with her frizzy bright red hair and the younger Karita with hair as black as a raven's wing.

It seemed that Margie McClure knew everyone for she was constantly waving to someone as the buggy went up the street.

They stopped in front of a small shop; the sign read Francine's Frocks. Margie told Karita, "My old friend Francine will find something pretty for you."

They got out of the buggy and entered the little shop. A lady about the age of Margie came rushing out to greet them. She and Margie gave one another a warm embrace, then Margie introduced Karita to Francine.

"We want to see something that would be most attractive for Karita."

"Well, Karita would enhance any gown I have in my shop," Francine declared.

"Oh, you are very kind, Señora Francine," Karita smiled warmly at her.

"I am just being honest. But I have a gown that I think is just perfect for you with that tawny skin of yours and those black eyes and hair. Come and let us see if I am right." She took Karita's hand to lead her to the back of the shop, all the time wondering if this was a new girl Margie had hired to work with the other three. This one was not like the others.

She took Margie and Karita to her small private office and bid them to have a seat. "I shall get the gown I am thinking about for you, señorita."

When she returned, Francine was holding a gorgeous emerald green gown of soft shimmering satin. It had puffed sleeves and a gentle dipping neckline. The lines of the gown were simple and basic and there were no frills or flounces. This was why Francine chose this gown for Karita, for her sensuous figure would provide all this gown needed when it molded to her lovely curves.

"Here, dear—go across the hall and try this on and let us see what it looks like on you. I think I already know but I want Margie to see it on you," Francine said, handing the gown to Karita.

Karita took the gown and left the room. Only when she had left did Francine turn to Margie to ask, "She is not going to work the saloon, is she?"

Margie saw the look on her old friend's face and knew exactly what she was thinking and why the idea offended her. "No, no, no, Francine! Rest assured—I would not put this sweetie in my saloon. She is to sit in my place in the back room at the table. She is a whiz at cards. You know some of the gentlemen who grace my back room so Karita would be safe, as well as a magnificent drawing card to the White Palace."

"She looks so young, Margie, that I was just curious. But there is also an air about her that tells you that she's not—well, she's . . ." Francine found herself stammering to find the words she wanted to use. But Margie came to her rescue. "You're saying that she's no Saloon Sally, right?"

"Oh, don't be offended, Margie. I know it was Gus who dragged you into that saloon when you married him. You know that we go back a lot of years," Francine quickly responded to her.

Margie laughed goodnaturedly, "I know that, Francine. I'm not offended. I know exactly what you mean, and I agree with you. The truth is I'm as curious about the girl as you are and I don't know that much

247

about her background. She came to me on a stormy day and I urged her to come in to take shelter against that fierce storm about a week ago. So far I've had her working in my kitchen with Rosco and I can tell you that she's a hard little worker."

Neither of them had a chance to speak further for Karita was coming into the room looking absolutely ravishing in the emerald green gown.

"Ah, I was right!" Francine excitedly exclaimed. "You are stunning, my dear. Isn't she, Margie?"

"She is absolutely gorgeous! That gown has to be hers!" Margie told Francine that it was exactly what she was looking for and they would take it. So Karita returned to the room across the hall to change back into her own clothes.

Karita had never had such a beautiful gown. It was startling to see herself so elegantly dressed. What a difference it made! Looking in the mirror, she saw herself as just as grand a lady as Señora Kristina Navarro or Señora Lucia.

She thought about this all the time she and Margie were riding back to the White Palace. What Margie was proposing that she do was not like what Gertie or Maria was doing. So if she could make some money for herself as well as for Margie, what would be wrong with it? Señora Lucia had done it and Karita considered her a very grand lady.

Karita found herself anxious to get started in this new venture!

Suddenly Karita understood that there was an excitement here in Austin that she'd never known existed when she was back at Whispering Willows. It made her realize what a very cloistered life she'd led for

248

the first eighteen years of her life. In less than a month's time she'd suffered a miscarriage, lived in the home of Señor Adolfo Martinez, and now she was working in a saloon. She could imagine the shocked expression on her parents' faces if she went home and told them all this.

But she could not do this to her two beloved parents. Not now. Some time had to pass before she could be reunited with them, and now that she'd had a taste of the outside world, she seriously doubted that she could ever find the contentment she'd once known back at Whispering Willows.

She and Margie were in a lighthearted, gay mood. It was only as they were getting out of the buggy that Margie moaned, "Oh, darn it, Karita!"

"What, Señora Margie—what is it?" Karita inquired.

"I forgot slippers for you! Maybe mine or Maria's will fit you. That Gerta and Estelle have big feet so I know theirs wouldn't work."

"I'm pretty sure that Maria's slippers might fit me . . . if she wouldn't mind me wearing them with the gown," Karita told her as they went on into the saloon. Everything was quiet and no one was moving around the place as they mounted the stairs.

When they got to the second landing and were about to part company, Margie told her that she wanted her to sit in with her tonight in the private room where some men would be playing poker. "This way you will see what's going on before you actually sit at the table. Check with Maria about some slippers and be all pretty and ready to go with me at nine this evening. Forget about helping Rosco in the kitchen."

"All right, señora. I will be ready." Karita went on down the hall to her own room.

As soon as she'd hung up the lovely emerald gown, she dashed down the hall to Maria's room and told her about the señora's plans for her here at the White Palace. "You should see the gown she got for me to wear! It is the most beautiful thing I've ever seen but she forgot about the slippers. She suggested that I see if you had a pair I might borrow for tonight."

"Well, little princess—let us see what we can find for you, si?" She looked over the many pairs of slippers lined up in a neat row. There were a variety of colors. "Try these, honey." She handed Karita a dainty pair.

The slippers proved to be a perfect fit. She gave Maria a pleased smile and a nod of her head.

"Well, it seems you're all fixed up for tonight." The expression on the prostitute's face was warm and generous. "I will be anxious to hear how your night goes. Old Rosco is going to have to work harder tonight without you in the kitchen," Maria laughed.

She thanked Maria and started back to her room. An hour later she enjoyed the luxury of a warm, perfumed-scented bath. Putting on her wrapper after she got out of the tub, she padded down the long hallway to seek the advice of Estelle as to what she could do with her hair to fashion it in a sophisticated style. She thought Estelle's fancy upswept hairdo was most attractive.

Just as Maria had accommodated Karita by lending her slippers, the auburn-haired Estelle fashioned her black hair into an elegant upswept hairdo that was very flattering to Karita. It did give her a most sophisticated look. "Ah, chickie—you are going to knock those guys

250

out tonight when you walk in that room with Margie! They aren't going to have their minds on their cards, I'm thinking."

The two of them laughed as Karita thanked her and prepared to go back to her own room. She was appraising herself in the mirror when there was a knock on her door and she heard Gerta calling to her.

"Come in, Gerta!" Karita hurried to open the door.

Gerta came bouncing into the room with a big smile on her face. "Got something for you to wear, Rita honey. They ought to be perfect for the gown Maria told me about." She handed Karita a pair of earrings with a brilliant green stone encrusted in gold. "They sure aren't emeralds. Wish to hell they were for my worries would be over, I can tell you!"

"Well, it doesn't matter. They are beautiful and they will match my gown perfectly. Look at it, Gertie. Isn't it gorgeous?"

"Lord, it sure is that, little Rita!"

"Why did you call me that, Gerta?" Karita asked her, for this was what Vincent Navarro had always called her and she could never recall anyone else calling her that until now.

"I guess cause it seemed right. You are a tiny little thing you know. At least, you are when I compare you to me." The tall willowy Gerta smiled, brushing back her blonde hair.

Karita smiled up at her, "I guess I am sorta small." Gerta could not possibly know the painful memories of Vincent that were brought back to her by the use of that name. But she had no time to dwell on thoughts of Vincent. As soon as Gerta left her room she saw that it was time for her to get ready to join Margie.

When she was dressed in the lovely satin gown, she put on the earrings and they were most attractive. She had never felt so beautiful or grand in her entire life. She found herself wishing Vincent could see her right now. The fancy ladies here in Austin that Victor had remarked about to her, the ones that Vincent was probably squiring, were no more attractive than she was tonight, she'd wager.

There was an air of self-assurance about her as she left her room to join Margie McClure. When they met, Margie heightened her confidence when she declared with fervor, "Damn, honey—you are a *knockout!*"

"Well, I have you to thank for it!" Karita told her. An unexpected blush rose in her cheeks, making her lovely face even more radiant.

"Oh, no, honey—a gown never made a woman this beautiful, but a beautiful woman can sure make a gown look stunning. Tonight *you* look stunning, Karita Montera."

The four gentlemen they joined in the private room of the White Palace would certainly have agreed with Margie as she came sashaying into the room with Karita by her side. "Gentlemen, may I present my new assistant. She will be sitting in my place some evenings. Gentlemen, I'd like you to meet Señorita Karita Montera. Karita, this is Mister Slater and Señor Lucas Lorenzo. Over here, this is Ralph Gerard and Zack Martin."

All the gentlemen gave Karita a smile and a nod of their head and all were thinking how it was going to be very hard to keep their eyes on their cards. Such a breathtakingly beautiful temptress!

Needless to say, the enchanting vision of Karita

Montera had added a spice and zest to the gentlemen's evening already, and it had only just begun.

Adolfo had invited Vincent and his twin brother Victor to be his guests for dinner that evening. He was most anxious to hear any report that Vincent might have to give him, as he'd taken his brother all around the city that day.

As of this afternoon, the two men he'd hired were searching the city of Austin for the young girl. At this point, it was all Adolfo could think of doing.

When the Navarro brothers arrived at his home that evening, he found himself thinking how different they were. He had not noticed this when he had met the two of them back in Washington.

He greeted them and ushered them into his parlor, for Rollo was assisting the cook in the kitchen tonight. Adolfo told Victor what a pleasure it was to see him again and have him here in his home in Austin.

"And I must say that it is a great pleasure for me. I'm very impressed by your magnificent home. It is a beautiful place, Señor Martinez."

"Well, I'm glad you like it, Victor. This house is my castle," Adolfo told him.

By the time the trio went into Adolfo's elegant dining room, his keen lawyer's mind was already forming an opinion of Vincent's twin brother. They both had tall, trim bodies with firm hips and trim waists, along with broad muscled shoulders. They had the same black hair and tawny skin but it was the eyes, and the reflection in the eyes, that Adolfo found revealing about these two.

253

Vincent's bright green eyes looked directly at you but Victor's eyes were always shifting. Adolfo never trusted a man with shifting eyes. There was no mention about Karita Montera and Adolfo sensed that Vincent did not wish to have discussion about her.

The three of them enjoyed the fine wine and the delicious feast Adolfo's cook had prepared. They lingered at the table after the meal was over to enjoy more conversation. Adolfo enjoyed his cheroot and Vincent smoked his favorite long slender cigarillo as did Victor. All of them sipped another glass of the excellent wine Rollo served them.

Adolfo inquired of Victor, "So, you plan to return to Silvercreek in the morning? Please give your dear parents my best regards."

"I will, señor. Since Vincent seems to be settling here in Austin I'm sure the Navarro family will be coming here more often."

"Well, I don't think I have to tell you how the people of Austin and Texas feel about your father, Senator Navarro," Adolfo told Victor. This evening he had suddenly remembered something Karita had said to him when she was at his house: It had been Vincent's twin brother who'd told her about Vincent working for him. That was why she had sought him out when she'd made her desperate journey here.

Something else gnawed at the cunning Adolfo and that was why Victor had so suddenly appeared at Vincent's house. He didn't believe for a minute Victor's remarks about his curiosity to see the house Vincent had purchased, nor would he wager that Vincent had accepted that for the truth.

No, there was another reason why Victor Navarro

had made this trip to Austin! There was not a shadow of doubt about this in Adolfo's mind.

Adolfo was also certain that the cool reserve and expressionless face was a mask Victor Navarro wore. He felt the urge to warn Vincent of this when the time was right.

Chapter 28

Vincent had to admit that he was glad to see Victor leaving Austin to go back to Silvercreek. It had nothing to do with him, but it had to do with what he'd just learned from Adolfo the day Victor had happened to arrive.

"Tell mother and father that I will get back there before too long, and give Grandmother Lucia and Grandmother Florine a kiss for me."

"I will, Vincent. My only regret is that I can't take any news back to Whispering Willows about Karita. I thought I might find out that you had seen her," Victor said as his dark eyes surveyed his brother's face as he spoke. He was still not unconvinced that Vincent had not seen Karita.

"Sorry, Victor but I've not seen her."

It was only after Victor had ridden out of his drive that Vincent began to question just why his brother had come here to Austin. He was very doubtful that it was any interest in his house. No, there was another reason why Victor had come to Austin. He didn't have it figured out yet but he would, he told himself.

As it had been in the past, Victor had tried his hand at outfoxing him, but Vincent was convinced that he had failed in whatever it was he was attempting to do.

Now Victor was gone and Vincent prepared to go to his law office. But he knew that his mind was not going to be on his work today; he was too haunted by Karita and the guilt he was feeling. If he had not come into her simple life at Whispering Willows none of this would have happened. She would never have had any reason to leave her family. He could not easily dismiss all this and turn his back on it.

Adolfo realized that his young partner was troubled and preoccupied as he tried to put in his day at the office. This increased the respect Adolfo had for the young man he'd hired to work for him. Vincent Navarro was not a disappointment, and he had made the right choice in offering him a position.

Margie was elated about the first evening that she'd introduced Karita to her special patrons who came to her private room to play poker.

After an hour, she had excused herself to allow Karita to take her chair. The pretty señorita was a natural. The moment she'd slipped into the chair where Margie had been sitting and brightly announced, "Gentlemen, shall we play cards?" Margie knew she had nothing to be concerned about for she saw all the smiles on the fellows' faces.

Karita found that she was as much at ease playing with these men as she had been when she and Señora

Lucia played, for none of them had expertise. In fact, Margie was so pleased with Karita's performance that she decided to leave Karita to carry on on her own.

As she made the rounds of the saloon, she passed the news on to her girls that the little Karita was doing magnificently. Smiles broke on all their faces. It was only in the kitchen that she found a disgruntled Rosco, because he was having to work much harder tonight without Karita there to help him.

"So you miss her tonight, eh Rosco?" Margie laughed.

"Didn't realize how much that little imp was doing until tonight, ma'am," he confessed.

"Well, she's doing very well in that back room tonight too, Rosco," Margie informed him.

"That little lady is something else, isn't she, Miss Margie? She sure isn't afraid of hard work," Rosco declared.

"No, she isn't, and that is enough to make me feel good about hiring her. She's earning her pay," Margie told him as she prepared to return to the private back room to see how Karita was doing. But she realized that she had no reason for concern, for she heard Karita's soft, lilting laugh as she spoke to the very wealthy Lucas Lorenzo. As she listened to them talking, Margie realized that Karita had a special charm that she herself had never had, nor ever would.

It was evident to Margie that he had been praising Karita's skill at poker. She was about to open the door when she heard Karita's soft accented voice telling him, "I had a excellent teacher, señor. She was one of the few lady gamblers who made a name for herself and was very much respected by any gentleman who sat at her table."

This was enough to intrigue Lucas Lorenzo, and Karita sensed this as she watched his face light up with interest. After the experience of the last few hours, she could understand why Lucia Navarro had found that time in the Palace in San Antonio so exciting and exhilarating. She had felt that way tonight and she had enjoyed the power she'd felt as she'd played cards with these older, affluent businessmen.

She had no idea how much the money this particular game had added to the coffers of Margie McClure, but Margie did. The gown was bought and paid for, and she still had a generous profit. She knew that this was where she should keep Karita. They would have to make another trip to Francine's shop for another gown very soon, for it would never do to have her regular patrons see Karita in the same dress night after night.

By the time the White Palace was shutting down for the night, Karita found herself the center of attraction with everyone singing her praises. It was very gratifying to Karita, for she felt that she had finally given something back to Margie McClure for all the generous things that had been given to her in the last weeks. This meant a lot to Karita.

The second night, she sat in Margie's place for the entire evening. Margie came to the room only once during the evening, for she saw no reason to look in on her after last night. She found it very interesting that Lucas Lorenzo had come again, for he rarely gambled two nights in a row. Being a very prosperous businessman in Austin, he usually came about once a week to try his luck at the poker games in her backroom.

Margie suspected that it was the beautiful Karita who'd been the incentive drawing him here again tonight for Lucas was a middle-aged bachelor. Karita was obviously the reason.

She did go to the kitchen two or three times during the evening to try to soothe Rosco's ruffled feathers, for he'd not expected to be without his little helper again tonight. Scrambling to get the tray of sandwiches ready to go to the bar, he'd given a good slice to his finger, and that had not helped his mood.

Margie took pity on him and worked with him for the next few minutes. It reminded her of the time she worked the kitchen while Gus carried out the duty she was now doing. She recalled how weary she was by the time she climbed the steps to go to bed. That was why she could feel sorry for Rosco tonight. But Rosco would have to attend to the kitchen without Karita's services from now on, for she was far more valuable to Margie in the private card room.

Margie would have been thrilled to know how the word was floating around Austin in certain circles about her place, thanks to Lucas Lorenzo. He had told two or three of his acquaintances about the new attraction at the White Palace.

The day after he'd visited the White Palace, he was having lunch in the dining room of the Ambassador Hotel when he saw his old bachelor friend, Adolfo Martinez, walk into the room. He motioned to Adolfo to join him at his table and Adolfo accepted. As the two of them enjoyed their lunch, Lucas told him, "You'll have to go with me next week, Adolfo, for a little cards and see this fantastic little dealer Margie McClure has just hired. She is absolutely stunning!"

Adolfo smiled, fidgeting with his mustache, "A real beauty—si?"

"Prettiest little señorita these eyes have looked on in a long, long time. You want to go with me next week when I go?"

"I'll think about it, Lucas, for now you've got me curious to see this beautiful lady."

"Well, you won't be disappointed. It isn't just her beauty. She's a very skilled poker player for one so young. She is amazing."

"And what is the name of this enchanting creature that you are raving so about?"

Lucas sat thoughtfully, trying to recall her name, but he could not think of it. Helplessly he shook his head for the name would not come to him. "Just can't recall it. I do recall the last name was of Spanish origin but I can't recall that either . . . but I know she kept me watching my cards. She's ruthless at the table—never misses a trick."

"Well, you really are making me interested in seeing Margie's new dealer. I think I must accept your invitation here and now. What night do you go to the White Palace, Lucas? I'll arrange my plans so I can accompany you."

"I'll be going there next Friday night and I'll look forward to having you join me, Adolfo. It was nice having lunch with you but I'm going to have to leave. I have an appointment in thirty minutes."

Adolfo told him goodbye but he was going to linger

there to enjoy the rest of his wine before returning to his law office.

As he slowly sipped the last of his wine, he dwelled in his private musings about another beautiful young lady and he only hoped that she was all right. If only she had not been so impulsive and left his house that stormy morning. He had already decided to be her protector if Vincent had been unwilling to assume that responsibility, but he had not let her know that. Now he wished that he had, because he had decided that the very day she miscarried Vincent's child.

As Victor rode along the countryside, going back to Silvercreek, he questioned whether Vincent had told him the truth about not seeing Karita. Vincent could be a most convincing liar. He could look you straight in the eyes and never blink an eyelash.

There was something abut the dapper Austin lawyer, Martinez, that he did not like. He had such piercing black eyes. Victor sensed that he did not warm up to him, and all evening while he was at his house, Victor felt like he was being analyzed and examined by the señor.

Victor was not in the best of spirits as he was finally approaching the rolling countryside of the Blacklands by the Pedernales River. He was in a black mood. He knew once he walked into the house everyone was going to want to ask questions about his twin brother.

He was not going to be able to tell them the startling news that he'd anticipated telling them—that he had found Karita and she was in the company of his brother, Vincent. He had not found her in Austin. If she wasn't with Vincent, and she had not returned to Whispering Willows, then where was she?

He was already dreading the evening facing him as he would be dining with his family. The conversation was going to be centered on Vincent. His family would be asking about the new house Vincent had purchased in Austin and how he was doing in his new position with Adolfo Martinez. His well laid plans to go to Austin and come back to Silvercreek as the knight in shining armor who had rescued Karita and brought her back to her home had been for naught. He had accomplished nothing that he could crow about.

More and more over the last two years, Victor had been comparing himself to his self-destructive uncle, Damien Navarro. Like him and Vincent, Damien had been the twin brother to his father, Danton. During their lifetime, it seemed that his father had been the one with the bright shining halo over his head while Damien was the black, brooding one.

Something which his parents had not realized, and only he knew, was that he sought solace when he was alone by drinking himself into a drunken stupor. From all the stories he'd heard about his Uncle Damien, this was also his way of dealing with unhappiness.

Victor remembered when it all started with him. It was back in the capital when Vincent caught the eye of a young lady in whom he was very interested. But Victor did not exist once she met Vincent.

After that, the pattern repeated itself over and over again and Vincent seemed to accomplish it so effortlessly. Victor seethed with a galling resentment.

The same thing had happened once they arrived here in Silvercreek. He had been entranced by the beautiful Karita Montera but it was obvious to him that it was Vincent who'd attracted her the night of the fiesta.

Had he been able to come back to Silvercreek with the news that Vincent had sorely used the girl and that was why she'd left Whispering Willows, he could have finally been the hero and champion. But once again, he had failed!

He asked *"Is history repeating itself? Am I cursed by the same fate as Damien Navarro?"*

He was beginning to think that he was.

Chapter 29

Victor received a warm welcome from his family when he walked in the front door of the sprawling hacienda but as he suspected, all of them were anxious to hear the news about his twin. All the time he told them about Vincent's new home and his life in Austin, he was wearing a mask to hide his true feelings.

He told them about having dinner with Señor Adolfo Martinez the night before his return home. His mother expressed her great admiration for the man. "Vincent could not be associated with a better lawyer. I admire him tremendously."

"Well, I think the feeling is mutual, mother. He finds you a most admirable lady and he told me so," Victor told his mother.

Before he left to go upstairs to his room, he made a point of inquiring about the Montera family.

His mother told him that they still had no word from Karita and they were distraught about their daughter. "They are convinced that Karita went to Austin, Victor. Is this not interesting?" his auburned-hair mother remarked. "Cara found an old map in their bedroom with the route marked. It was lying under Karita's bed. But the only thing puzzling them is why the child would have gone to Austin."

Victor said nothing but he was now convinced that Vincent could have been lying to him. "I wish I had known this, mother for I would have searched the city of Austin for her before I came back home."

"Well, dear you didn't." Kristina Navarro told her son.

"Yes, but a nice girl like Karita should not be in a place like Austin by herself," he told her.

"No, she shouldn't, and that is why this is such a nightmare to poor Yolanda and Abeja," she sighed. Victor knew how his mother and father were obviously affected by this tragic ordeal their old friends were going through right now.

Victor took his leave to go upstairs. Performing as the dutiful grandson should, he gave each grandmother a kiss on the cheek before he left the room, but he noted a curious look in his Grandmother Florine's brilliant blue eyes as he kissed her.

Both of his grandmothers might be getting frail and aging but their minds were just as sharp and keen as ever, Victor knew. Neither he nor anyone else should sell them short. He never underestimated the wisdom they possessed. Both were such worldly old dames for they'd known both sides of life. They'd known how it was to be poor and they'd both enjoyed the luxury of being wealthy. He found both of them a little intimidating, for they were so worldly-wise.

Florine Whelan was not finding it the easiest thing to adjust to life here at Silvercreek after being the mistress

268

of her own home back in El Paso, and she knew that Lucia Navarro was going through the same struggle. It had been Lucia's idea that she appoint her daughter-in-law, Kristina the new mistress after she and Danton had returned to the ranch to make their home.

Florine could certainly not criticize her daughter about anything, for she had done everything to make her rooms comfortable and attractive. But it was still not like having that spacious ranch house to roam around any time of the day or night with all the things she loved there for her to enjoy. So many of those keepsakes and memories had to be packed away. She was missing her past.

There were times when she felt like cussing this body of hers that had urged her to accept Kristina's suggestion to come live with her so she could look after her. She saw the wisdom of it but she didn't like it.

At least she still had her devoted Solitaire with her, and that was wonderful. Solitaire represented and shared so much of that exciting past, as well as those times of pain and heartbreak. God, she was so glad to have her!

As the quadroon had always been, she was still Florine's confidante. Her most intimate thoughts had always been voiced to Solitaire and no one knew Florine better than her old maid—not even her beloved daughter, Kristina.

The two of them had gone to Florine's private suite leaving the rest of the family downstairs shortly after Victor left the parlor and soon they were sequestered in their own little private world. Solitaire was very perceptive to her mistress's mood. She noted the quiet thoughtful air as she went over by the windows to sit in a floral chintz chair, laying her walking cane on the floor.

"What is troubling mam'selle?" Solitaire's soft voice inquired.

Florine's blue eyes turned to look at Solitaire in that direct, straightforward way of hers. "My grandson, Victor. There is something about that young man that disturbs me, and I can't put my finger on it, Solitaire. I see it every now and then when I look into his eyes. It was there just a moment ago and I've seen it a couple of other times since they've returned from Washington."

"I know, mam'selle," she said.

"You know? Are you saying that you see something too?" Florine inquired as she saw the sad look in Solitaire's dark eyes.

"I see a smoldering devil within the young man, but I don't know what it could be, mam'selle."

If it had been anyone other than Solitaire saying this to her she might have been offended, but Solitaire with her uncanny instincts was merely speaking the truth as she felt it. Florine knew her background back in New Orleans before she'd run away and ended up in El Paso. Her mother was a black woman and she'd been sired by a white man, a planter.

Solitaire had told her of her early memories as a child and how her mother practiced the black magic of voodoo. How she'd ever managed to leave New Orleans and finally end up in El Paso, Florine had never figured out when she was only sixteen. Florine had taken her in and the two of them had been together ever since.

Florine might not have said it was a smoldering devil she saw in Victor's eyes; she would have called it a fury.

She could not understand it for she knew that Danton and her daughter, Kristina had loved their twin sons dearly. But there had always been a difference in the personality of each of them. They were as different as day and night.

Two hours later, Señora Florine and Solitaire went back down the stairs to join the rest of the Navarro family for dinner. It was one of the stipulations of Florine living here at Silvercreek that Solitaire would be joining her at dinner as she did back in El Paso. She was no longer considered a maid, but a companion. Kristina had readily agreed to that for she too felt that Solitaire was a part of her family and her past.

The statuesque quadroon with the colorful kerchief tied around her head led the petite Señora Florine down the stairs to join the family in the parlor. There they gathered to converse before going to the spacious dining room for the evening meal.

Victor was not overjoyed to be back at Silvercreek and gathering with the family again for dinner. He'd never taken too fondly to that black woman his grandmother was so devoted to. He wasn't too sure that she wasn't capable of casting a spell on a person if she sought to. Those black almond-shaped eyes could have a hypnotic effect and that was why he chose to ignore her as much as possible when he was around her. Solitaire sensed his wariness of her.

He'd sensed that she had not liked him from the first time they'd met and he damn well didn't like her!

It was a miserable time for Victor as the group sat at the table dining, for his Grandmother Lucia had not been downstairs when he arrived in the afternoon, so he had to go over all the many questions she was asking

271

about Vincent. He could tell by the delighted sparkle of her eyes that she was pleased to hear about Vincent working with Adolfo Martinez and about the house he'd purchased.

"Ah, that Vincent is doing all right for himself, I would say," she exclaimed. She knew her grandson had to show great promise as a lawyer for the esteemed Martinez to take him into his office. She took no notice of Victor's face.

Once again, Victor was witnessing his twin prevailing in the eyes of his grandmother. As it had always been, Vincent had the power, it seemed, to dominate.

If only he could have gathered the evidence to blacken Vincent's image when he'd gone to Austin, he would have been a very happy man tonight. But he had failed, as he usually did where Vincent was concerned. His twin was obviously charmed and he was surely hexed!

During the dinner, Florine chatted with the family so she was not concentrating on Victor as Solitaire was. Those all-knowing eyes of hers watched him as he replied to the numerous questions his Grandmother Lucia asked him. That evening the quadroon found the answer she'd been searching for about young Victor.

She was also aware that he did not like looking in her direction and tried not to if he could possibly avoid it.

Later when she and Señora Florine were back in their rooms, she told Florine, "I think I have the answer to the question that has been troubling both of us, mam'selle."

"Tell me, Solitaire. Tell me what the fury is that I see."

272

Florine saw the emotion on the quadroon's face as she started to speak. "The fury, mam'selle—the fury is his twin brother, Vincent."

Dejectedly, Florine shook her head in agreement for this had been her own private thought. She knew the story about the two other Navarro twins, Danton and Damien. Her heart was heavy for the pain her dear daughter would suffer if this were true, for she knew how much Kristina loved her sons. Was there damnation in being a Navarro twin, Florine wondered?

After five nights of working in the private room, Karita was enjoying herself as she had never imagined that she might. She and Margie had made another trip to Francine's shop and she now had two beautiful gowns to wear in the evening. Karita had never possessed as much money as Margie had paid her last night for the first five nights of her labor in the back room. But when she'd tried to protest that it was too much, Margie had assured her that she'd earned the price of the gowns and salary she'd paid her. "This is for you, Karita, honey. Believe me, you're worth every cent of it!"

It was a grand feeling to Karita to feel that she could earn so much money and enjoy earning it so much.

She tucked the money into a little leather pouch she had. She thought that if she could keep adding to this little stash she could return to Whispering Willows with her head held high and she would not have to feel ashamed of what had happened to her.

She had come to terms with her miscarriage and she figured that it was God's way of punishing her for the wrong that she had done. But what then, was Vincent's punishment? Was it hers to bear alone? She had certainly borne all the pain.

Karita had found the last few nights in the back room at the White Palace to be an exciting experience for a girl like her who'd never known anything but the quiet peaceful countryside of Whispering Willows. She realized, quite suddenly, that her beauty could have a devastating effect on men. In her innocence she had never been aware of this power a woman could have over a man. She knew the force and power of a man like Vincent Navarro, and she knew what it had done to her, but she now realized that as a woman, she possessed the same power.

She now had a new assurance and confidence in herself that she would have never known had she not left Whispering Willows. She knew that as much as she must have hurt her parents by running away, she had done the right thing.

Always, she wore the little gold cross around her neck that Señora Lucia gave her and she swore it had brought her luck. She remembered with fondness the gracious old woman who had dared to be different in her own youth. Karita drew strength from her example and faced each new day with the hope of great success.

The only thing she bought for herself from the salary Margie McClure had given to her was a pair of etched hooped gold earrings. The large hoops of gold that dangled from her ears were very attractive, and she thought that they would certainly enhance her beautiful purple gown.

Karita felt very excited as she dressed that evening in the new gown with its low-scooped neckline which displayed Señora Lucia's dainty gold cross. On her ears were the gold earrings she had purchased for herself and it was gratifying to her that she could buy her own jewelry. She had no way of knowing that there would be more exquisite jewels adorning her ears and throat before the next year was over. A woman of such rare beauty frequently received admiring gentlemen's gifts as a tribute to them. But Karita had much to learn about the ardor of such men.

But she was to find out very soon that the men sitting in that room with her were beguiled by her charm. She had no idea how the name of Karita Montera was being touted in certain circles of Austin. Never in her wildest imagination would she have expected to receive such attention. It was overwhelming when bouquets of flowers were sent to her after the poker games. She was elated!

Chapter 30

Adolfo saw how dejected Vincent was when he sank down in the chair by his desk to report that he had not uncovered one clue as to where Karita might be. By now, he'd checked every hotel and inn he'd come upon as he'd traveled up and down the streets.

"I'm beginning to believe that she left Austin, Adolfo. She'd have to be staying somewhere if she were here and I swear I've hit every darn place like that this last week."

"I think that you are right, for neither of the two men I hired have come up with anything either. Maybe she and your brother did not cross paths. While they were traveling the same road but in opposite directions they could have missed one another," Adolfo pointed out to him.

"It's just not knowing that is driving me crazy, Adolfo, and I can't get her off my mind. Might as well confess to you that the little minx means more to me than I realized until just lately. But when you told me about her coming here to find me and that she was carrying my child it made me love her more dearly. I've much to make up to her when I can find her."

Vincent's working in the office the last month had lightened Adolfo's work load, and he was ahead of his usual heavy schedule because of it. He could afford to give Vincent a week off if he wished to return to Silvercreek to see if he could learn any news about Karita Montera. If she were back at her home, Whispering Willows, he would have the opportunity to ease his guilty conscience.

"Take a week off, Vincent, and go to Silvercreek. That way you'll satisfy yourself if she did go home. I'll still keep my men looking here in Austin."

"Are you sure, Adolfo? I've hardly been working for you long enough to take that much time off," Vincent told him.

"We're in fine shape thanks to your hard work so I can spare you now. In a few more weeks I might not be able to do so. Leave tomorrow and I'll see you back here next Tuesday."

"Thanks Adolfo—thanks a lot. I'll see you next Tuesday then," Vincent gave him a warm handshake as he turned to leave the room.

Adolfo watched his tall figure leave the room and truly hoped he would return free from the misery plaguing his soul. Guilt was a destroying force, the lawyer knew.

Victor mentioned nothing to anyone about his plans to ride over to Whispering Willows that morning. Once and for all he had to satisfy himself that she was not at home, for he was still convinced that she was back in

Austin. He'd concluded that Vincent, as well as Adolfo Martinez, could have been lying to him.

But when he arrived at the little stone house near the river, he found no one but Cara at home. He quickly found out that Karita was not home, nor had they had any word from her.

"Right now I hate her for all the worry she's causing papa and mama," Cara declared to him venomously.

Very solicitously Victor told her that he understood how she was feeling. "Well, just as long as she has come to no harm then I would think your family would soon be getting a letter from her."

"Oh, I don't think she wants us to know where she is. Well, I have my own ideas about Karita and where she is but I won't tell my folks, for it would hurt them too much."

Victor smiled down at the sixteen year old girl. "Well, what is preventing you from telling me, little Cara? Why don't you tell me?"

"You'd probably think I was loco," Cara told him.

"Try me," Victor challenged her.

"All right, I think Karita followed your brother to Austin. Maybe you don't know it, but then you *couldn't* have known that she's been lovestruck for two or three years. Vincent Navarro was the only man that Karita ever thought about. Do you know that she has constantly refused the fellows around here who came to court her? Ricardo has tried time and time again, and most of the girls find him very handsome. But Karita gave him a cold shoulder."

Karita's little sister was being quite a chatterbox and Victor was intensely listening to everything she was revealing to him.

"Then there was something that makes me think she's gone to Austin. I found an old map under her bed after she left and a route was marked which I'm sure she was planning on taking. I did not show this to mama."

"Looks like you might be right, Cara. So you see I don't think you're loco at all. In fact, I think you're a smart young lady."

A pleased smile came to Cara's face. She could not figure out why Karita found Vincent more appealing than Victor. She certainly felt attracted to him as they sat on the porch together and his black piercing eyes were upon her.

"Well, I'm sorry to hear that your sister feels so devoted to Vincent, for I fear my brother has a fickle, restless heart where beautiful ladies are concerned. She could find herself with a broken heart," Victor cunningly told her.

"I told her this myself. I told her that your brother would never marry the likes of her. His wife would be the daughter of one of your family's wealthy friends."

When Victor decided that he was going to learn nothing more from Cara he prepared to leave and told her to give her folks his best regards.

Inside the house, Yolanda had been listening to the last few minutes of the conversation going on between her daughter and Victor Navarro. She sought not to let her presence be known when she heard the two of them discussing Karita. Since she returned to the house along the back trail and came from the barn after leaving the buggy out in the back of the house, they'd not seen or heard her.

Victor rode home more convinced than ever that Karita was in Austin and she was with Vincent. Adolfo

280

Martnez had been in league with the two of them so this made him Victor's enemy too. Somehow, they'd all just managed to outsmart him. This made him angry.

When Cara came into the house, she saw the weary look on her mother's face but it was the sad look in her dark eyes that made Cara uneasy. She had evidently heard what she had told Victor and what he had said to her. "I—I didn't know that you were back, mama."

"I know you didn't, Cara. I found your conversation with Victor very interesting. Your Papa and I will go to Austin and confront Vincent about Karita." Yolanda got up and quietly prepared to leave the room.

"And I will be going too?" Cara asked, trying to tone down the excitement in her voice at the prospect of going to the city.

"No, Cara—you will be taken to your sister Kristina to stay until we return." Yolanda turned to go to her bedroom to freshen up before she attended to her own chores before supper. Abruptly she stopped to declare, "You talk too much, Cara!"

Later that evening Yolanda discussed this with her husband, and he could not refuse her request to go search for their daughter. He would have done anything to find Karita and bring a happy smile back to his lovely wife's face.

He promised her that he would make arrangements with old Gomez to come over to do the chores around the barn for him while they were away. "I'll go over there tomorrow, Yolanda, and we will go to Austin the next morning bright and early."

Yolanda gave him a weak smile and an approving nod of her head. For the first time in a few weeks her sleep was a little more peaceful. Abeja was grateful for

281

that, for it pained him to see her looking so drained.

Vincent left Austin as the dawn was breaking. He dressed in black twill pants and white open neck shirt to be comfortable when he rode Dorado, for the days were getting warmer now than when he'd first come to Austin. He traveled light; there were plenty of clothes back at Silvercreek, for he'd not taken that much with him to Austin.

Dorado was enjoying the wide open countryside where he could break into a swift gallop as he was eager to do. Vincent suspected that Dorado was not happy with his confined quarters and brief rides in Austin.

After they had traveled about an hour, Vincent was thinking that he might just leave Dorado back at Silvercreek when he returned to Austin. If his father was now involved with the project of raising palomino horses, Dorado could certainly sire some fine young colts for him.

The farther they traveled, the more Vincent's mind was made up about Dorado. It was unfair to the spirited golden beast that he couldn't enjoy the freedom of the countryside. Many days Vincent did not have the time to take him out for a run as he'd like to do.

He had already decided that he was stopping by Whispering Willows before he rode for another hour to Silvercreek Ranch.

When he stopped for a minute to see the river in the distance he knew he was not far from Whispering Willows. Seeing the river reminded him of the beautiful Karita sitting on that river bank with her soft black eyes staring at the river as she'd been doing the day he'd come this way, a few months ago.

God, he prayed he'd find her sitting there again today. He'd convince her very quickly that he loved her and she'd never have to run away again!

But fate didn't deem this to happen when he came to the spot. So he rode up to the little cottage situated a short distance away.

Dismounting quickly, Vincent walked up the pathway to the front porch. The wooden door was open so he gave a rap on the screen door and called out. It was Yolanda who heard his call and came from her kitchen to greet him.

"Vincent!" she exclaimed with a quizzical look on her face.

"Señora Montera, it's good to see you again," he said as he strolled through the door. Vincent could see the lines of worry etched on her face, and knew instantly that he was not going to find Karita back here at Whispering Willows.

"You—you are on your way to Silvercreek, Vincent?" she asked in a stammering voice for she was feeling very awkward and tense as to how to speak to this young man after what she'd overheard yesterday being discussed by Cara and Victor. She wasn't feeling exactly friendly toward him.

"Yes, señora, but I had to stop by here first to see if you'd had any word of Karita. Victor was in Austin last week and told me about her leaving Whispering Willows."

"So you have not seen her in Austin? She has not been with you, then?"

Her words were enough for Vincent to raise a

skeptical brow, wondering why she'd said that. He firmly replied, "No señora—I have not seen Karita, but I wish to God she had come to me. I—I just wish I could ease your concern, but I can't."

Yolanda knew sincerity when she heard it or saw it in a person's eyes, and young Vincent was speaking the truth. She meant it when she told him, "I wish she had come to you too, Vincent. But where can she be?"

"I don't know, señora. I wish I did. I swear to you that when I return to Austin I will search for her. I was hoping I would find her back here with you. Now that I know she isn't here I will not be staying long at Silvercreek."

"Are you saying that this is why you came from Austin, Vincent?"

"Yes, Señora Montera. It was my only reason," he confessed to her.

A few minutes later he told her goodbye and prepared to ride on to Silvercreek. Yolanda watched him ride away and she knew that there was no reason for her and Abjea to make the trip to Austin now.

Vincent Navarro had not lied to her. She was sure of that!

Chapter 31

When Abeja returned from seeing his friend Gomez, Yolanda told him, "We have no need to go to Austin now."

"You are telling me that Karita came home?" he asked with excitement flashing in his eyes as he clasped his wife's shoulders.

"No, dear. Vincent came by here this morning on his way to Silvercreek. He stopped by to see if she was back here. He swore to me that he had not seen her and I believe him, Abeja. For all that talking between Cara and Victor yesterday that I overheard, I am convinced that it was not right."

"And you do not wish to go to Austin now, querida?"

"Where would we go, Abeja, when we arrived there? We were going to seek out Vincent but he is here. What could we do once we got there? We could not just camp out for days, Abeja."

She spoke wisely so Abeja said no more, and he turned to wash his hands and face in the basin. He told her that he would ride back over to tell Gomez early in the morning that their plans had changed.

Cara had a strange look on her face as her parents continued to talk about Vincent's returning, and she noticed her mother's dark eyes glancing in her direction every now and then. She realized that she was in her disfavor right now because of what her mother heard her tell Victor, so she did not linger around her parents after she'd helped her mother clean the kitchen.

Once she was in her bedroom, she unpacked the clothes she was planning to take to her sister's, now that she would not be going there.

As Yolanda had been surprised to see Vincent standing outside her door that late morning, Kristina Navarro was so overjoyed to see her handsome son riding into the walled courtyard that she flung aside the basket filled with flowers she'd just cut.

"Vincent! Oh, Vincent—what a nice surprise!" she declared as she rushed across her gardens to greet him.

A broad grin creased Vincent's face as he opened his arms to greet her. She was still a damned attractive woman and he'd always taken a great deal of pride in the fact that the beautiful Kristina Whelan Navarro was his mother.

"Good to see you, Mother, and may I say you look awfully pretty."

"Oh, it seems like you have been gone for so much longer than just a few weeks, Vincent. Your father will be so happy to see you."

The next question she asked him as the two of them walked back to the spot where she'd flung her basket of colorful dahlias was how long he'd be able to stay.

"Just a day or two, Mother," he lied, which he usually didn't do to his mother. He felt it was necessary right then.

Vincent bent down to help her gather up the pretty pink flowers. Then they went into the house. "Your father will be in his study. Come, let's go there so you can surprise him as you did me."

Danton turned from his desk to see Vincent standing beside his mother. He leaped up from his desk as enthusiastically as Kristina had back in the garden.

Kristina left the two men in the study to take her basket to the kitchen and give the cook some changes to make in the evening meal now that Vincent had arrived.

Neither of the grandmothers was stirring around downstairs yet, and Kristina had no idea where Victor was.

So she rejoined her husband and son in the study and announced to them that the cook would be bringing in a carafe of coffee for them in just a few minutes. She knew that Vincent had just told his father that he could only stay for a day or two because Danton was saying, "Well, I'm amazed that you were given this much time off, for I hear Martinez is quite a hard-working man."

"You're right, Father, although Adolfo asks of me no more than he is willing to give, and I admire him tremendously. I am gaining experience that no law books could ever provide. So yes, I'm delighted to have a couple of days off." He added that the distance between Silvercreek and Austin was not that vast.

For the next hour they all spent a pleasant time while Vincent described his new house and small courtyard. It reminded Danton of the home he'd owned in Austin

287

when he was practicing law before he'd married Vincent's mother.

Danton was very receptive to Vincent's suggestion to leave Dorado at Silvercreek when he went back to Austin. "He's not for city living. He needs the wide open countryside to be free to run. I'll take one of your less spirited horses back to Austin."

"I'd be happy to make a swap like that with you, Vincent," Danton chuckled.

When he excused himself to go upstairs, Vincent laughed, "We have a deal, father. Now I'm going to rid myself of some of the dust before I greet my grandmothers." He turned to go and stopped long enough to inquire about Victor.

"I don't really know, Vincent," his mother replied. "I saw him riding away from the barn when I came out of the door to work in my garden."

"Well, I'll see him later too," he told her as he turned to go out the door of the study.

While Danton and his wife sat in the study, he boasted to his wife that he was very proud of their son. "Vincent seems to know where he wants to go with his life. I liked what I heard from him, Kristina."

"Yes, he certainly does seem excited about his life in Austin," she smiled at him.

"I wish our other one would give me some inkling of what he plans for his future," Danton declared with a note of consternation in his voice.

"Has Victor done something to disturb you, Danton?" She also had some concern about Victor lately that she had not voiced to Danton for she thought it might be merely the imaginings of a doting mother.

"No, Kristina—it is more that he is not doing

anything. He takes no interest in the running of the ranch and I've tried to encourage him to do so. He's not the least bit interested in my idea about breeding the palomino and this I can accept. Now forgetting all this, I am asking myself what is to occupy his time. I'd prefer that he left Silvercreek to go search for his future as Vincent is doing than to just lie around here idling away his time."

"Oh, I agree with you, Danton. But I don't know what it is Victor is seeking. I wish I did," Kristina sighed.

Danton's dark eyes looked across at her and his deep voice told her, "That is the problem, querida—Victor doesn't really know either, and we can't do it for him. He has to do that for himself. Navarro wealth won't provide the answer either." What he didn't tell her, for he did not wish to disturb his wife, was what was worrying him lately about Victor: he reminded him of his own twin, Damien.

The moment Victor returned from his ride and spotted Dorado in the barn he knew that Vincent was at Silvercreek. He lingered in the barn for a moment before he went toward the house. What the hell was he doing here?

All kinds of crazy thoughts were parading through Victor's mind as he sat on a bale of hay to think and ponder this unexpected visit from his brother.

With Vincent's luck, he had probably found Karita and brought her safely home. Oh, what a hero that was going to make him! He'd be the golden boy of the Navarro family, and the Montera family as well.

289

By the time he left the barn to go to the house he had decided to go to the back entrance. He did not want to encounter the gathering of the family where Vincent was sitting, holding court like a young prince.

The cook and her helpers paid no attention to him as he came through the door and mounted the back stairs that led to the second landing. Obviously, they were working in the kitchen to prepare a gala feast for Vincent's homecoming.

Luck was with him, and he met no one as he went down the hallway toward his own rooms. Once he got to the second landing he closed the door, securing the lock. He went directly to the chest to get his favorite liquor and took a generous gulp. He sank down in the chair with a sullen look on his face. When he finished the first glass, he filled it once again. He figured he was going to need to be numbed to meet that miserable crowd tonight for the evening meal.

By the time he had taken a bath and changed his clothes, he was feeling bold enough to go through the parlor door to meet with his family as they always did before going into the elegant dining room for the evening meal.

Gay laughter was resounding as he descended the stairway. He knew that he was going to be the exception tonight for he was in no festive mood.

He heaved a deep sigh before he sauntered through the parlor door and his family turned to see him. Vincent greeted him with one of those happy-go-lucky smiles of his, "About time you came down, brother. I was just about ready to come up to get you."

"I had no idea you were home, Vincent. You made no mention about plans to come home when I was with you," Victor pointed out to him.

"I didn't know myself," Vincent answered as Victor gave both of his grandmothers and then his mother a kiss on the cheek.

He took a glass of wine like the others were enjoying before dinner was announced. Danton was sitting there observing his sons now that Victor had joined the gathering. He suspected that Victor had already had a few drinks before dinner.

It was his Grandmother Lucia who remarked that it was nice to have her two grandsons there with her tonight. "Your vacant chair will be occupied tonight, and this pleases me, Vincent."

"Look at it this way, Grandmother. When it is empty, I'm always here in spirit," Vincent soothed her.

"That's nice, Vincent. That is very nice and I'll try to remember that when you are back in Austin."

It was hard for Victor to restrain a scowl from coming to his face. That Vincent and his silken tongue! He seemed to always know just the right thing to say.

So it went throughout the evening meal. His mother glanced over to see the quiet mood of Victor and her eyes darted over to see that Danton was also observing him.

She wondered if her husband was thinking what she was thinking: Victor was not pleased to have his twin brother back home.

All she had to do was look at Victor's face to know this!

Chapter 32

Twin brothers they might well be, but Vincent had always known that he shared very little with Victor, for they were so different in temperament. As young boys they'd not been the best of playmates so each of them had gone his own way, doing the particular things they enjoyed doing. As they'd gotten older, each had had his own friends. Rarely had they warmed to any mutual friends.

Vincent had found himself interested in young ladies at a much earlier age than his twin. So it had gone after they had their twenty first birthday. It was about that time when Vincent had developed a keen interest in the law.

To this very day, Vincent had no idea what his brother wanted to do with his life. Once, back in Washington, when the two of them had been talking about the time when his father would be leaving the capital, Vincent had asked him what he was going to do after the two of them returned from the grand tour of Europe that their parents had promised them. Victor had made a reply that, being the son of a senator and wealthy Texas rancher, he didn't consider that he was pressed to make a quick decision about it.

Vincent had never brought up the subject again. But they'd had the tour and now they were twenty-five. While it was true that their Grandfather Navarro had left them a nice little inheritance, Vincent found it disturbing that Victor was so lacking in ambition.

Tonight he had sensed a very definite feeling of cool reserve in Victor. Vincent had just been amused by it and it didn't cramp his lightheartedness as he'd visited with his grandmothers and parents. But he had no pity for Victor for he made himself look like the outsider in the family sometimes. It seemed that was the way he wanted it. He thought to himself that he would put Victor out of his misery tomorrow, for he was going to leave early enough so that he could get back to Austin before dark.

It was time he turned his energy back to his job for there was nothing more he could accomplish here. Karita was not at Whispering Willows. Far better he get back to Austin and hunt for Karita. He retired to his room before midnight so he could get up early in the morning.

By the time the sun was rising, so was Vincent. He shared an early morning breakfast with his father and they enjoyed a nice talk. His mother was always absent from breakfast for she enjoyed sleeping an extra two hours.

Victor made no appearance. So Vincent had a private visit with his Grandmother Lucia and then he was going to go to his other grandmother's suite to chat with her a while. But it was while he was visiting with

Lucia Navarro that she remarked about a possibility he'd not considered in his search for Karita Montera. As he was about to take his leave, she told him, "I became quite fond of her, Vincent. The child is a whiz at cards—darn good! Go to some of the gambling halls when you get back to Austin. It might be there that you'll find her."

"I shall, Grandmother. I'll do that," he told her with his bright green eyes sparkling for she might have just made a brilliant suggestion. He'd checked on none of those establishments.

While he could not picture little Karita working in one of those places, he had to remind himself that both of his grandmothers had when they were Karita's age.

After he had visited with his Grandmother Florine and his mother, who gently protested about him leaving so soon, Vincent went to the barn to say farewell to his palomino. In Dorado's place, he mounted up on one of his father's horses and rode out of the barn.

By the time Victor came downstairs he would find his brother gone. But he did not know about the deal Vincent had struck with his father to leave the palomino at Silvercreek until he went to the barn that afternoon.

A devious grin came to his face when the young hired hand told him that Dorado was to remain here and that Vincent had taken another horse to ride back to Austin.

"Well, saddle up Dorado for me and I'll take him out for a ride, Pedro," Victor ordered the young Mexican boy.

"Si, señor." Young Pedro got busy throwing the

295

saddle on Dorado's back as Victor paced in the barn.

As if Dorado sensed that it was not Vincent who was going to be the rider, he became rambunctious and Pedro had a difficult time getting him ready for Señor Victor.

"Dorado is not himself today, señor," Pedro told Victor. He had a perplexed look on his face as he turned over the reins to him. Dorado had never given him this kind of trouble.

Victor mounted the fiery palomino and spurred him to action but Dorado did not like the man atop him. Victor sensed that the horse was fighting him.

By the time they were galloping down the long drive, Victor was determined that he would show this firebrand who was the master before they returned to the corral. When they had gone about a couple of miles, Dorado shook his head and mane in defiance. As if to challenge his rider and rid himself of him, he reared up in a frenzy and Victor had to hang on with all his strength to remain in the saddle. He put the quirt to Dorado's rump with four sharp blows, and the palomino had never felt the sting of a quirt before.

He became as wild and untamed as a bucking bronco and there was no way that Victor could ride out his fury. He landed on the ground, stunned and dazed. Dorado galloped back in the direction they'd just traveled, heading back toward Silvercreek Ranch.

When Pedro spotted Dorado by the corral fence with Señor Victor not on him, he hastily jumped over the fence to take the reins and saw the panic in the palomino's eyes. At that minute, Señor Danton came dashing toward the corral to inquire of Pedro who had had that palomino out.

296

"Señor Victor," Pedro told him. By now he spied the evidence of the quirt lashes on the palomino. Now Danton Navarro spotted them too. He could not recall when he had been as angry as he was right now and Pedro saw the fire in his black eyes. "You have orders, Pedro that no one—absolutely no one—is to ride this horse but me. Is that understood? Señor Victor has his own horse and if he ever tries to take this horse out of that barn again you are to come immediately to me."

He told Pedro to go minister to the horse. Young Pedro gave him a nod of his head and started to walk away with the palomino. Suddenly he stopped and asked Señor Danton, "Do you wish me to ride out to see about your son after I doctor Dorado, señor?"

"No, Pedro—let him walk home. He deserves the long walk," Danton Navarro said as he angrily turned on his heel to march back to the house.

Pedro took Dorado to his stall and gently applied a healing ointment to the ugly marks on his golden coat. All the time he was going about it he thought about Señor Vincent. It was good that he was not here at Silvercreek for there could have been a killing over this. Señor Vincent loved this horse and would think anyone doing this would deserve to be killed.

Pedro did not envy Victor Navarro right now for when he did return home he was going to be facing a very riled father. It was not going to be a very good afternoon at Silvercreek, he thought to himself.

After Señor Victor had walked back home from wherever it was that he was thrown off Dorado, he was going to be in a devil of a temper, and the young Mexican boy only prayed that he would go straight to the house and would not come to the barn.

Every so often as he went about his chores, Pedro searched the long drive for sight of Victor. Inside the spacious house, Danton sequestered himself in his study until he could gain some control of his raging temper. He fired hired hands right on the spot when he discovered them being cruel to any of his animals. and he would not tolerate it in his son. Victor had damned well better take heed of the stern admonishment he would be getting as soon as he returned home.

Having no idea how far out Victor had ridden, he could not know when he would be getting back on foot but he did not care if he had to walk the entire afternoon.

If Vincent ever found out what what had happened, there was going to be the devil to pay. That was why Danton was so angry that this had come about the first day that Dorado had been left in his care.

To Victor, it seemed like the spacious, red-tiled roof house was never going to come in sight. It seemed like he had been walking for hours in the hot Texas sun. His white linen shirt was damp as if he'd been walking in the rain. The dampness extended to his pants. His fine black leather boots felt tighter and tighter on his feet and he had no doubt that he was going to have a crop of blisters by the time he took them off.

His black felt flat-crowned hat was flung off his head to rest on his back so that he could mop off his damp face and hair with his neckerchief.

He was going to see that that devil of a horse paid and paid dearly before he was through with him. He cussed the horse as his feet grew heavier and his legs felt weaker.

When he finally saw the house in the distance and the long drive just ahead, he tried to hurry his pace but it was impossible.

Pedro spotted him coming up the drive and the young Mexican boy scrambled up to the hayloft so he could hide. Up there he could observe him through a small opening as Victor came slowly closer and closer all the time. He was a sorry looking sight to behold.

For a moment, Pedro thought Victor was going to come into the barn when he hesitated for a minute, but then he went on toward the house and Pedro heaved a grateful sigh.

Pedro was not the only one observing Victor's return. After he'd calmed down, Danton had sought the comfort of the quiet, cool patio in the garden courtyard that gave him a view of the gate which he knew Victor would have to come through.

If it had not been for his act against Dorado Danton could have felt sorry for him, but he deserved to be hurting. So there was no pity for him.

He did not stop him as he moved down the walkway and to the door to go inside the house. Today had been a shaking experience for him for he'd never felt such anger toward either of his sons during their entire lifetimes.

It was there that his wife came upon Danton and she was taken by surprise to find him quietly sitting there so deep in thought. "I thought you were in your study working, Danton," she exclaimed.

"Sit down, Kristina. Sit down with me," he requested. Kristina took the chair next to him and she had only to look at his troubled black eyes to know he was disturbed.

As it had always been, there were no secrets between them. He told her what had happened and why he was very upset with Victor. Now the happy smile on Kristina's face had disappeared and in its place was a look of distress.

"How could he be that cruel, Danton? How could a son of ours be that way to such a beautiful beast as Dorado? Dear God, Vincent would feel like killing him, Danton. Pray he never finds out!"

"I have thought about it and when I go upstairs to talk to Victor I want you to know what I'm going to tell him. It will be a stern ultimatum and one I will carry out if he ever again tries to ride that palomino. He has his own fine thoroughbred and there was no reason for him to take Vincent's horse. Nobody rides Dorado but Vincent and Victor knows this."

"And what is it you will say to him, Danton?" his wife asked. She was recalling her two sons as tots and how both of them could have the same exact toy but Victor was always grabbing for Vincent's toy. She would slap Victor's hands and tell him to go get his own. It had always seemed that he was never satisfied with his own things.

"I shall tell him that if he were a hired hand he would have been booted off Silvercreek. I will tell him that one warning is all I'll allow him—son or not. He is never to ride that horse again or he will be asked to leave this ranch."

Kristina saw the firm determination in Danton's black eyes and knew that he meant every word he'd said. She could only pray that Victor would abide by his wishes but she knew how defiant he could be. Years ago, she'd had to do battle with Victor's belligerent ways.

Looking over to see the frown on her lovely face, his hand reached over to clasp her hand and bring it to his lips. "It will be all right, querida. Don't you worry!"

Chapter 33

The feisty little black mare that Vincent had ridden back to Austin did not have strong long legs like Dorado, so she didn't make the trip back as fast. But he knew that he'd done the right thing leaving Dorado at the ranch so he could roam the lush green pasturelands and not be confined to a stall, as he was in Austin. Time did not permit Vincent to put him through the paces daily when he put long hours in at the law office.

It was a quiet pleasure for Vincent to get back to his own house and turn the mare over to Jules and walk through the kitchen door to greet Aspasia.

"Ah, señor—this is a nice surprise."

"Well, thank you, Aspasia. Everything gone all right while I was gone?"

"Everything is just fine, señor. Jules went fishing with his friend Marcos bright and early this morning so we shall have a nice fish dinner if this pleases you."

"That pleases me very much. Hmmm, a big platter of fried fish all crisp and golden can be some mighty fine eating, and it's been a long time since I've had any. I'll be looking forward to dinner, Aspasia."

"You wish to dine at seven, señor?"

"That is fine, Aspasia."

He mounted the stairway ready to have a bath and put on a fresh shirt and pants before he went downstairs to enjoy the feast of fish.

As he flung away the small bag he carried with him and sank down on his bed to remove his boots, he was thinking how funny life was. All his life Silvercreek had represented the family's home. Even when his family had resided in the elegant townhouse most of the year, it was always Silvercreek that was called home. Vincent was calling this place his home now. He owned it and he was the master here.

Maybe that was why he felt as he did. He couldn't explain it except to say that this was where he felt more comfortable and at ease.

A few hours later, after he'd enjoyed Aspasia's fish dinner, he was ready to go back upstairs. He wished to retire early after the long day he'd put in so he could get to the office early the next morning. Adolfo was going to be surprised to see him back so soon.

Now that he knew that Karita was not back in Whispering Willows, he felt that she was surely here in Austin. His grandmother's suggestion that he check out the gambling halls was going to be the next search he made in his spare time.

His troubled soul was not going to rest until he found that little black-eyed enchantress.

He would find her, he vowed!

*　　*　　*

Karita loved the new gown Margie had purchased for her at Francine's shop and she anxiously dressed in the gown of scarlet trimmed with black braid around each of the flounces. Around her neck she wore some jet beads and matching earrings she had purchased for herself. Each night she put her earrings in a little pouch in her drawer and she found it got fatter and fatter all the time. This was a thrilling feeling for her.

It was an exhilarating sensation to be so pampered by the other employees of the White Palace. Margie was constantly heaping praise on her for what she was doing for her establishment.

Karita received many baskets of flowers from the various gentlemen who played at her table, and she always shared these with Maria, Estelle and Gerta.

All this adoration and attention had changed Karita. She was no longer as shy and unsure of herself as she had been. She had no awareness of the air of sophistication she had taken on but it showed in the way she walked and the way she held her pretty head high and proud.

There was a very self-assured attitude about her when she made her grand entrance into the private room where the gentlemen were already gathered.

She always gave them a very warm welcome as she greeted them. "Gentlemen, good evening," she would say. "Shall we play cards?" A lovely smile always was on her face as she took her seat at the table. Whether the gentlemen won or lost, they always found it an exciting evening with the exquisitely lovely Karita Montera.

Friday night was usually the night that Margie's wealthier patrons came to her back room. Margie had told her as she prepared to go downstairs that she was surely going to knock their eyes tonight out with that gorgeous scarlet gown.

"Just hope I'll make enough to pay for it, Margie," Karita laughed.

"You already have, honey," Margie answered with a smile.

The two parted company at the base of the stairs when Margie went one direction and Karita went another.

She entered the room as she usually did. There was a smile on her face and a twinkle in her black eyes as she swayed through the door with her gown swishing back and forth.

"Good evening, gentlemen. "Shall we play . . . cards," she said in hesitation as she suddenly recognized Adolfo Martinez sitting in one of the chairs. It took all the will power she possessed to try to at least appear calm. She wondered how he had happened to come here tonight.

Slowly she took her seat and once she was seated and her legs didn't feel like they were turning to jelly she dared to look back in his direction, realizing that he was in a state of shock equal to hers. Somehow, this had a calming effect on her and she smiled at him, "It is an unexpected pleasure to see you, señor."

Adolfo stared at her in amazement for she seemed to have changed from the young frightened girl he'd last seen back at his home. Could just a few weeks do this?

"My pleasure as well, señorita." He was thinking to himself that Vincent was going to be in for a shock when he told him how he'd found Karita by chance here at the White Palace. He'd never thought of

306

searching out a gambling hall when he'd been scurrying around Austin that first week after she'd disappeared from his house.

Lucas was leaning over to ask Adolfo, "You didn't tell me you knew her. How come?"

"You did not mention the young lady's name, Lucas," Adolfo whispered to him as Karita was making lighthearted conversation with the two other gentlemen at the table.

"That's right, I didn't. Well, now you know why I was raving so much about her," Lucas remarked to his friend.

Now that she'd had her usual brief conversation with the gents at her table, Karita was ready to play cards. The game began.

Adolfo compared this young woman to the magnificent tapestry hanging on his parlor wall with its many brilliant colors. She was colorful and exciting and he saw so many sides of her.

She was a fantastic poker player and he could not recall playing with anyone better. There was no doubt in his mind why Margie McClure had hired her, but he found himself curious about who had taught her since she was so very young. As he recalled, she'd told him that she was eighteen. He also remembered her telling him that she had never been away from Whispering Willows until she'd left there to come here to Austin to see Vincent Navarro.

He watched her nimble, dainty hands deal the cards with expertise. There was a masterful air about the young beauty sitting there in her scarlet gown, and he envisioned how striking she could look when adorned with expensive jewels and elegant gowns. She was a stunning creature, and Adolfo thought to himself that he would proudly take her to any elegant social function he attended in Austin or anywhere else. She made the voluptuous Paulina Castillo look pale in comparison.

When the evening came to an end and all the gentlemen were saying farewell to Karita, Adolfo purposely lingered behind the rest of them so he might have a private word with her. He asked Lucas to excuse him for a moment for he wished a private word with Señorita Montera.

As soon as Lucas was gone it was Karita who spoke. "I owe you an apology, señor, and I am sorry, but I could think of nothing else to do for I could not return home then. I can't now."

"You owe me nothing, Karita. I wish you to come dine with me before you go to work some evening. Would you do me the honor?"

She wasn't expecting an invitation like the one he'd just extended to her. In a stammering voice, she told him, "I would be delighted, señor, if you would really like for me to come."

"I would like it very much, Karita. I find you absolutely fascinating and I had no idea you were such an expert at cards."

She gave a lilting little laugh, "I love it!"

"I would too if I could play as well as you do," he smiled. "When can you come for dinner, my dear?"

"Just about any night, señor, but I will have to be back here by nine, if that is all right?"

"I'll arrange it. How about tomorrow night? I could pick you up at six. Would that be all right?"

She gave him a smile and nodded her head. "I shall

be ready at six, señor."

They said goodnight and Adolfo left her to join his friend Lucas, feeling in the highest of spirits which Lucas could tell the minute he came up to him.

"Damned, Adolfo—I think you must know everyone! If that wasn't the damnest thing tonight. You knew her already!" Lucas grinned and shook his head.

When the two of them parted company at the late night hour, Lucas taunted Adolfo, "I have a feeling I won't have to be asking you to go to the White Palace. You'll be wanting to go whether I ask you or not."

Adolfo gave him no reply. He only gave him a smile.

Neither of the elderly ladies at Silvercreek realized the undercurrent of emotions washing over their family, for Danton sought not to say anything to them as they dined that evening. But they were both curious as to why Victor was not at the table. Danton had made some feeble excuse and shrugged it aside by changing the subject. It had not been a pleasant day for him and he felt drained after confronting Victor up in his room. He saw no reason to say anything to his mother or Kristina's mother. There was no point in upsetting them.

Victor had never seen his father so riled and he knew that his father was furious with him when he'd marched into his room without knocking first as he customarily would have done.

Victor was lying across the bed with his boots off and puffy blisters were on his feet for Danton to see. His father's deep stern voice declared, "That is why we put so much importance on the fine horses we ride, Victor.

That is why we show them the respect they deserve."

"That Dorado is wild and crazy. There was no handling him!" Victor declared defensively.

"He is not yours to handle and you had no right to try what you did, and so you pay the price. You have your own horse. Dorado is Vincent's horse."

A sullen look broke on Victor's face as he lay there, making no reply. Danton walked on over to the side of the bed and his piercing black eyes glared down at his son. "That you took the horse without my permission is not what riles me as much as you daring to use the quirt on him. That is revolting to me, Victor! As I told your mother, if you were a hired hand you would have been kicked off this ranch hours ago. But son or not, I tell you this and I will say it only once. If you ever take that palomino out again or do what you did this afternoon you will leave Silvercreek Ranch. I will see to that!"

Victor still had nothing to say but he knew that his father meant every word he'd just spoken. Danton could not fathom what was going on behind that stonelike face of his son. He made no effort to apologize for anything he'd done, but that was Victor.

Danton had said what he'd come to the room to say so the rest was up to Victor. He turned to walk out of the room and hesitated only for a minute at the door to tell his son, "I meant what I said, Victor!"

So it had not surprised Danton Navarro that his son had asked for a dinner tray instead of joining the family for dinner this evening.

Chapter 34

Sharing dinner with the beautiful Karita Montera was everything Adolfo had anticipated. Just being around her made him feel like a young caballero in his twenties again. If he'd thought she looked stunning the night before in her gown of scarlet, she was breathtakingly lovely tonight in emerald green. One as beautiful as she was should have had emeralds dangling from those dainty ears and draping her throat, he thought as he gazed at her in the candlelight while they dined.

It pleased him that she seemed so perfectly at ease with him. Her lighthearted laughter told him that she was enjoying his companionship. Adolfo could not help thinking what a magnificent pair the two of them could make. He, being a very successful wealthy lawyer, could lavish on her the luxury her beauty deserved. Such exquisite loveliness would be an asset to any man, especially to a forty year old man like Adolfo, who moved in the circle of wealthy and influential people.

He could do more for her than Vincent could ever do, he thought to himself. Why, she could be his "queen" here in his luxurious "castle". Never would he cause her the heartbreak and pain that young Vincent had already caused her.

As he did with most of the precious treasures accumulated in his palatial mansion, he stood back and admired her. He was beginning to feel the same way about this lovely little goddess. She was the woman he'd dreamed of finding for years.

He suddenly found himself glad that Vincent was going to be away from Austin for a week. Many things could happen in a week.

By the time he had escorted her back to the White Palace and returned home, he had convinced himself that he had to try to win her love even if it meant sacrificing a most promising young law partner. The only disappointment of the evening was that she could not dine with him the next night, for the card game was to start an hour earlier.

But he did have her promise to join him the next night, and this was enough to make him happy. When he retired his dreams were of Karita and how she might soon be his.

The next morning he woke up feeling more alive and full of zest than he had in a long, long time, and he gave the credit to the little black-eyed señorita, Karita.

Adolfo was already planning to purchase an impressive gem to present to her when she next dined with him. Anticipating the pleasure of that night, Adolfo told himself that he'd endure dining in solitude for one evening.

He hurried to his office and immediately immersed

himself in the paperwork on his desk. Concentrating so intensely on what he was reading, Adolfo did not hear Vincent entering the outer office door or his footsteps in the hallway. But as soon as Vincent had laid his leather case on his desk, he turned to go into Adolfo's office.

Adolfo still had not heard him. "Good morning, Adolfo," Vincent greeted him.

Adolfo looked up, startled. "Vincent! You—you've not been gone a week."

"I know, Adolfo. Only three days. There was no reason to linger so I thought I'd best get back to help you. Karita has not returned to Whispering Willows."

Adolfo could have told him that he knew this and that he was with her last night, but he did not want to tell Vincent that. So he remained silent.

"I trust you had a nice visit then with your family?" Adolfo said.

"A very nice visit, Adolfo, but I was ready to get back. Strange as it might seem I find this house I've bought seems more like home to me now than Silvercreek. After I found out that Karita was not at Whispering Willows I found I had no reason to tarry there."

"I think I can understand that, Vincent. Well, it is good to have you back." Adolfo knew that he was lying. He saw that his plans could go awry now that Vincent was back and he didn't know how long he could continue to lie to him about Karita.

As the day went on, Adolfo was ridden with guilt that he'd not told him that he knew where Karita was and what she was doing. When they'd shared lunch together he'd been tempted to tell him, but something held him back.

Suddenly the afternoon was gone and it was time to close the office and go home. Vincent had not mentioned his plans to Adolfo to start searching out the gambling halls in Austin as his Grandmother Lucia had suggested. This he intended to do in his free time from the office. He considered that Adolfo had been very understanding about him taking time off for things that did not pertain to the law office.

So the two of them left the office to travel to their homes that late afternoon. Adolfo was resigned to having a quiet dinner tonight and retiring early, but this was not Vincent's plan at all.

When he arrived home a little after five, he requested that dinner be served earlier than seven and Aspasia assured him that she could serve his dinner by six thirty if he wished it.

"Thank you, Aspasia." He left the kitchen to go up to his room and rid himself of his coat so he could get comfortable for a brief moment before he dined. It had been a busy day for Vincent but he was glad to be back in the law office. He took off his fine-tailored gray coat and pants and dressed in more casual attire. After he was dressed in black pants that molded to his firm muscled body and a clean white linen shirt left open at the neck, he felt very relaxed and comfortable. He flung on the bed the black leather vest that he would wear later when he left the house to go for his search of the city at the gambling halls.

By the time he'd enjoyed Aspasia's dinner and had a couple of drinks he was feeling very relaxed and ready to spend several hours searching the gambling halls. He owed the Montera family that much, and more important to Vincent, he owed it to Karita.

He rode the little black mare out of the courtyard as the clock was striking nine. He rode down the street that went past Adolfo's home, which was a short distance from his. He could not know that the street he rode down beyond Adolfo's house was the same route Karita had taken that morning as the fierce storm was ready to assault Austin.

It was as if destiny were taking him by the hand and leading him toward the lady he loved and was seeking so desperately. Soon he came to the two story white frame building with a large sign out in front alerting the passers-by that it was the White Palace Gambling Hall. He immediately dismounted and led the horse to the hitching post, then moved to climb the plank steps to go in the front door.

As he went through the door, he saw a lively crowd sitting around the tables. He could not imagine that this was a place he'd find the beautiful Karita.

As good looking as Vincent Navarro was, he was soon noticed by Gerta, Estelle and Maria, but it was Maria who broke away from the fellow with whom she had been laughing and talking. She sauntered up to the end of the bar where Vincent was standing. It was not often that Maria's eyes had seen such a handsome devil as this.

"Good evening. Welcome to the White Palace," Maria purred with a provocative look in her black eyes. "Your first visit to the White Palace, señor?" Maria knew if he'd ever been here before she would have recognized him instantly.

"Si, señorita—it is my first time here." Without asking her he told the man behind the bar to serve her a

315

drink. He realized that this was her job but he also hoped to question her about Karita.

Maria gave him a big smile and thanked him for the drink he'd just bought her. This might be a lucky night for her. Just maybe she'd found herself a generous hombre. Some of the fellows expected her company and time without spending their money on a drink for her.

Glancing over his shoulder he saw that some men were at the back of the tavern playing cards. Two of the tables were occupied.

"It says out front that this is a gambling hall so that must be back behind those closed doors, eh?"

"Si, señor, but it is a busy night back there tonight. So it is gambling that you are interested in?" Maria asked him.

"Maybe. What is your name, señorita?" Vincent's green eyes stared down at her for she was a very tiny woman.

"Maria. You like?"

"Maria is a pretty name. You worked here long?"

"Ah, si—a long time. Señora Margie is a good lady to work for," Maria told him.

Vincent saw that she had already emptied her glass and he was well aware of the little game she played, for his glass was still half full. He motioned to the man tending the bar to bring her another.

"I imagine that it is Señora Margie back there in the back room where the real gambling is done. Am I right?"

"Tonight she is, for it was a busy night and it started early."

"Full rooms, eh?" Vincent inquired.

Maria laughed, "A very good night at the White Palace."

Vincent asked her if he might look in on the games going on. "I might like to sit in on some of those games now that I've found the White Palace. I might just want to come back here again to see you, Maria." He gave her a charming smile that Maria found very over-whelming.

"I don't know if I can take you back there without talking to Señora Margie, señor. She has very strict rules about that. I—I could try, I suppose."

He gave her an affectionate pat on the waist. "Why don't you do that, and I'll wait right here for you to return."

Maria was reluctant to leave his side for she knew that Gerta or Estelle would certainly try to move in on him while she was gone. She did as he'd requested but she moved very hastily so she would not have to be gone too long.

When she entered the back room where Margie McClure was dealing cards to the three gentlemen that Karita Montera could not accommodate at her table in the adjoining room, she bent down to whisper in Margie's ear. "Sure, bring him in," Margie told her for she always welcomed a new patron.

Once out the door, Maria dashed back into the tavern to join the handsome stranger at the bar. She hoped to find him alone and much to her surprise he was there alone. But he had had to tell Estelle that he was waiting for Maria to return. The minute Maria had gone through the door, Estelle had come over to the bar.

"It is all right, señor. Come with me," Maria invited

317

him and Vincent picked up his unfinished drink to follow her.

He followed her toward the back door of the tavern. As the two of them entered the room, the men sitting at the table looked up to give Vincent a quick nod of their heads but Margie McClure took a long, appraising look at the tall, handsome man standing beside Maria. He gave her one of his winning smiles and Margie returned a smile as she invited him to have a seat. His eyes were like a pair of matched emeralds as they glanced down at Margie. Those all-knowing eyes of hers saw the fine cut of his tailored pants and fine linen shirt and told her that he was a man of means and wealth. The next question she asked herself was who this devilishly handsome dude was!

She knew one thing and that was that she'd never seen him before in the White Palace. A woman never forgot a man who looked like this one!

Margie wasn't so old that a good-looking dude like this one couldn't excite her still!

Chapter 35

As Margie was dealing the cards, she made a fast introduction of the men sitting at the table with her and Vincent introduced himself. The minute he said it, Margie recognized the name, for it was a very prestigious one. As she sat there playing her cards the name kept hammering away at her and then it came to her that there was a Senator Navarro. Was it possible that this was a relative of his?

After they had been in the back room awhile, Vincent nudged Maria that he was ready to leave. He bent down to whisper his thanks to Margie before he made his exit. The hour was growing late and he had to get to the office early in the morning.

The two of them slipped quietly out the door. Maria told him, "The real game is in here. Señora Margie rarely plays at the tables anymore."

"Well, shall we slip in here for a minute, Maria?" he smiled at her.

But Maria had suddenly realized that she was making no money for herself and hadn't for almost an hour. "Shall I go get you a drink, señor?"

"Si, Maria and one for you, too," he said with a grin coming to his face as she whirled around to go through the door leading into the tavern.

He moved toward the door and when he opened it he saw an alluring lady sitting at the table in an emerald green gown with her black hair swept high atop her head. He knew even before he saw her face why Maria had told him that this was where the real game was going on, for he recognized a couple of the gentlemen at the gaming table. He had met them at Paulina's elegant party. They looked up from their cards to see Vincent Navarro walking slowly through the door. Karita turned to look up and Vincent's eyes locked with hers.

A queasy feeling washed over her and she felt like she would faint as they stared at one another. Vincent realized that she was as shocked by the sight of him as he was to see her sitting there at the poker table. He saw how her long lashes were fluttering nervously. Her lovely sensuous lips were parted as though she was ready to gasp.

But he was amazed at how quickly she regained her composure and greeted him, "How nice to see you, Vincent!" She introduced him to the players except for the gentlemen he obviously already knew.

For a moment the high stakes poker game was interrupted but Karita was determined that Vincent would not distract her. She was not going to allow him to do that. She owed too much to Margie McClure to allow that to happen. There was too much money on this table tonight!

320

She gathered her forces to proceed with the game and with determination pounding fiercely within her, she found that Vincent did not prove to be the distraction she feared he would be as he sat over in the corner. In fact, she was concentrating so intensely on the game that she did not even know when Maria entered the room with a drink in her hand to give to Vincent.

She did not know when Vincent had graciously dismissed Maria by telling her that he was going to stay in the room a while. But he more than pleased her when he took her hand and placed a roll of bills there for the time she'd spent with him tonight. Maria could not be offended that he was dismissing her for she knew from the feel of the roll that he was being most generous. She quietly left the room.

It was not until the last gentlemen had said their farewell to Señorita Montera that Vincent made his move. Only he and Karita were in the room when he moved out of the chair back in the corner to stand there before her and declare, "Little Rita, we've some talking to do, and talking we are going to do right now. Are you through for the night?"

Her doelike eyes looked up at him as she pleaded with him, "Please, Vincent—don't make any trouble here. Let me turn this money over to Margie and I will come back here if you will wait right here."

"I will wait, Karita, but it is not here we will talk."

"All right, Vincent. I will be back in just a minute." She rose from the chair with the huge pile of bills in her hand and started for the door. "Just sit over there and wait for me," she suggested as she prepared to leave the room.

"Only so long," he told her as he watched her go out the door. While she was gone, Vincent had time to reflect on this evening and this new beautiful young woman he'd observed tonight. She was not the same sweet innocent he'd made love to by the little waterfall. But then he had to assume responsibility for some of that change. There was an assurance about her now that had not been there in the past.

But he had no time to dwell on his private musings any longer, for she came back to the room. "All right, Vincent, I am free to talk now." Her black eyes seemed cool and indifferent as they gazed up at him. He now stood, towering over her.

Wiser than she had been when they were last together, Karita sensed confusion in Vincent's green eyes as he slowly searched her face. "Does it have to be here?"

"I suppose it doesn't," she drawled slowly.

He took her arm and invited her to come with him. She allowed him to lead her out of the backroom. They walked through the tavern that was now quiet with only a few lingering patrons.

She heard a familiar voice calling out to her, "Goodnight, Karita!" She turned to see the husky Rosco hanging out of the kitchen door to wave to her and she flashed him a warm friendly smile as she waved back at him.

All the girls had gone upstairs so they had not seen her leaving with Vincent as they walked out of the swinging doors to the plank floor outside.

"Are you hungry after the busy night you've just put

322

in?" he asked her as they stood just outside the door.

"I did have a busy one back there, I have to admit," she said. She did find herself famished, for she usually went into Rosco's kitchen after work to get a tray of food for herself to take upstairs to enjoy before she retired.

He did not tell her where he intended to take her. Instead, he scooped down to lift her up in his arms and walked over to where his horse was tethered and swung her up on the mare's back.

Giggling, she exclaimed, "Vincent! Wh-what are you doing?" He leaped up behind her and declared that he was going to see that she got fed. Karita felt his strong arms encircling her waist as he held the reins and she could not shrug the feelings aside as though they weren't there.

But she insisted on knowing where he was taking her. "It is so late all the dining rooms in the hotels will be closed, Vincent. It's well after midnight."

"Ah, chiquita—I know a kitchen that is still open with the most delicious food in all of Austin," he grinned. He was feeling the soft warmth of her body there so close to him and he was suddenly aware of how very tiny her waist was with his arms snaked around her.

As they rode along she recognized the street they were riding down for it appeared to be the route she had traveled when she left Adolfo's mansion. It suddenly dawned on her that it must have been Adolfo who'd told Vincent where she was working.

As they continued to ride down a residential street, she wondered if he was taking her to Adolfo's house.

323

She asked him, "Where is this kitchen you are talking about, Vincent?"

"My home, Karita. I am taking you to my house," he replied.

Suddenly Vincent had reined the horse through the small archway into the privacy of an enclosed area off the main street. Bringing the horse to a halt, he leaped down and held up his hands to help her down to the ground.

"This is my new home, Karita," he told her as he led her through the grilled iron gate which opened into the small walled courtyard. They had only gone a few steps when she heard bubbling sounds and spraying mist of the fountain there in the courtyard. Vincent felt her suddenly hesitate as she'd been walking by his side. "Oh, Vincent—how beautiful your garden is!"

"I like it. That is my favorite spot here in the garden day or night. I like to just come out here to sit on that bench at night. It's so peaceful and quiet except for a nightbird singing."

Karita stood there absorbing the intoxicating aroma of the night blooming flowers. But she was also seeing a side of this handsome young man who had stolen her heart some time ago—a side that he'd not shown her before. Karita had to remind herself that theirs had never been a courtship, it had been a very brief romantic interlude.

He led her up to the kitchen door and they went into the dark room. Vincent lit the lamp and urged her to sit down at the little table.

"Aspasia is a fantastic cook and I'm lucky to have her. She attends to my house very well, I must say."

Scouring through the cupboards he found some pie left over from the supper he'd enjoyed earlier and by the time he was through he presented Karita with a plate of cold roast chicken, fresh baked bread and some relishes. She pleaded with him that she needed no more.

So he poured two glasses of his favorite white wine and sat down at the table with her, sipping his wine as she devoured the food with pleasure.

When she had finished the last bit, Vincent smiled, "Feel better?"

"Much better, thank you," she declared. She did not know what she had expected when she'd left with Vincent tonight but he was being very gracious. Maybe she was expecting anger from him or perhaps she was expecting him to ridicule her for working at a place like White Palace. But he'd done none of these things.

He took her from the kitchen through the rest of the downstairs of his home and she could see the pride on his face as they strolled through the parlor and dining room and he told her all the changes he'd made. He told her how his garden was full of kneehigh weeds when he first saw it. He told her of Jules, and Karita suddenly realized that those first weeks in Austin were busy ones for Vincent. She was rather doubting that he'd had much time to be escorting all the lovely Austin lovelies around as Victor had hinted to her. Now she found herself doubting a lot of things Victor had told her.

Now that she was not so naive about men as she had been a few months ago, she believed that Victor was jealous because he knew that she was attracted to Vincent and not to him. She could recall those times

325

when he escorted her back to Whispering Willows, and she'd seen the fiery desire in his dark eyes and his amorous attempts with her.

She was convinced that Victor was trying to plant little seeds of suspicion about his twin brother. She also recalled his brooding black eyes the night of the fiesta when he watched her and Vincent dancing together.

"Would you like to see the upstairs, Karita?" he asked her with a boyish enthusiasm.

She was tempted to say no and tell him that she could not stay too much longer. They had still not had their talk. But she found it too hard to refuse him when he was looking at her as he was. Vincent had the most devastating eyes of any man she'd ever seen. She'd seen them display such a gamut of emotions. Right now they were brilliant and shining with the excitement he was feeling about showing off his new house, but she could recall the warm, dreamy look they took on when she was lying in his strong arms. Then there was that twinkling sparkle of the carefree Vincent she knew. For a moment tonight, when he'd first walked into the room at the White Palace, she'd seen for a brief moment the green fire of anger in his eyes.

When they got to the second landing, he told her he had two bedrooms yet to furnish and only one guest room was completely furnished.

"Now, this is my room." A lamp was burning in this room for Vincent had not dimmed it when he'd left tonight.

Karita stepped inside to see the haven he'd created for himself. It was a spacious room, warm and inviting, and more than just a man's bedroom. It was an office

326

and very cozy sitting room. He led her over to one of the overstuffed settees and urged her to sit down beside him.

"Oh, Karita—it is nice to have you right here with me but I must know why you didn't get here sooner. I won't rest until you tell me that. Adolfo told me about your miscarriage, but why did you not come to me instead of running away from Adolfo's?"

Her black eyes looked up at him as she declared, "I had no reason to come to you then, Vincent. Your baby was gone." There was a pained look on her face and Vincent lowered his eyes and shook his head dejectedly. "I never meant to bring hurt to you, Karita. I . . . I never thought about the fact that I might have left you carrying my child when I left Silvercreek. I really didn't, but damn it, I should have!"

But a couple of things prodded Vincent, and he wanted the answers to them so he asked her how she knew to seek out Adolfo Martinez here in Austin. He wanted the answer to why Adolfo had not told him that she had arrived at his home that day.

While she might have taken on a more sophisticated air about her the last few months, Karita was still that very honest, unpretentious girl he'd fallen in love with.

"I learned of Señor Adolfo from your brother, Victor, when he was escorting me home after I'd spent the afternoons with your Grandmother Lucia. That was how I learned about him, Vincent, so when I was convinced I was pregnant I knew I must come to Austin to find you and tell you. I could not shame my family— or yours. I don't have to tell you how our families think of such a thing. I was so scared!"

327

He clasped her hand tighter and it made his guilt heighten as he listened to her tell him how she'd been caught in a storm and was drenched to the skin by the time she'd made Austin.

But luck had been with her when a lady owning a hat shop had known Adolfo and directed her to his house. The ride, storm, and her two months of pregnancy had exhausted her, so when she arrived at Adolfo's she'd curled up on one of the benches on his front porch. "This is where he and Rollo found me and took me in."

"Did you tell Adolfo why you'd come to Austin and to him?" Vincent asked.

"I did before I collapsed once I was taken to one of his guest rooms."

This really baffled Vincent. Why hadn't Adolfo told him this, that morning when he arrived at the office? If only he'd been told he could have come to Karita at Adolfo's. For whatever reasons, Adolfo had chosen not to tell him.

"I can only say I wish Adolfo had told me, Karita, for it would have saved you and a lot of other people some grave concerns."

Maybe it was because the hour was late but many thoughts were whirling through her mind. The same was true for Vincent as he sat there, savoring the sight of her.

"I've much to make up to you, Karita, if you will let me. I would never have neglected you if only I'd known." His eyes were so intense and the expression on his face was so sincere that she had to believe that he spoke the truth.

She said nothing but just looked up at him.

Somehow, Vincent felt that she did not believe him. God, he knew he loved this lovely creature sitting beside him! It seemed only right and natural that his arms should claim her and draw her close to his broad chest that was throbbing so with yearning to feel the warmth of her next to him.

Like the force of a powerful magnet she felt herself being pulled closer and closer. She could not resist such a force, so she did not try to pull away.

She would have been helpless and she knew it!

Chapter 36

How swiftly it had all happened Karita would never know but she suddenly found Vincent's heated lips caressing her and the flames of wild desire were completely consuming her body. All reason left her. Nothing mattered to her now that their bodies were touching and his hands were playing that certain magic that stirred her soaring heights of ecstasy.

His deep voice was whispering in her ear, "Oh, querida—querida I love you so very much. Quiero hacer el amor contigo!"

She sighed breathlessly, "Si Vincent, querido!" She knew how hungry she was for his all-consuming love to fill and sate the longing she was now feeling. His firm muscled body sank down to burrow between her soft, velvety thighs as his lips continued to kiss her.

She felt the powerful force of him suddenly fill her and she gave a gasp of delight. Arching her supple body, she heard the husky moan of pleasure coming from Vincent.

Together they ascended to that height of passion

where only true lovers ever go. When they soared to that summit they both shuddered with the wild exultation exploding within them.

Vincent had never known such a fever to consume him as it had tonight with his beautiful Karita and he knew that he would do whatever he must to keep her by his side.

He continued to hold her lovingly in his arms and his deep voice whispered in her ear, "I'll never let you go, Karita. Now that I've found you nothing, or no one, will ever take you from me again."

She said nothing but she snuggled closer to him and Vincent needed no other answer from her. He planted little featherlike kisses on her eyelids and his finger removed the straying wisp of hair from her lovely face.

It felt right that she was lying there by his side. He had no intention of taking her back to the White Palace.

"Sleep, little Rita, and so shall I," he murmured as a feeling of serene exhaustion swept over him. It mattered not to Vincent that he might be late getting to the office for he was not feeling too kindly toward Adolfo Martinez right now.

When he reluctantly left Karita's side about five hours later to get dressed, he took the time to write her a message urging her to stay until he returned to the house at five that afternoon. He wrote that he had informed Aspasia that she was his guest, which was what he intended to do when he went downstairs.

He liked the sight of her in his bed with her lovely black hair fanned out over the pillows. She slept so peacefully, like a sweet innocent child, and he guessed that he would always see her as childlike because she was so much younger than he was.

Very quietly, he made his exit from the room and went downstairs. He had not had too much sleep but he was in the highest of spirits when he greeted Aspasia puttering around the kitchen. Quickly, he gulped down two cups of coffee before making his departure.

"I've an overnight guest, Aspasia. Señorita Karita Montera's family and my family are very close and dear to one another. See that she is taken care of until I can get back home at five."

"Si, señor—I'll take care of the young lady," Aspasia told him as he dashed out the door. After he was gone, a sly smile brightened her face for she'd never seen Señor Vincent as excited and happy as he seemed this morning. That fancy Señora Paulina Castillo had not brought out this air in him when she had visited here, Aspasia thought to herself as she watched him jauntily race out the back door to board his buggy to go to his office.

Aspasia puttered around the kitchen with her curiosity whetted about the young woman the senor told her was upstairs.

Since she had been working the tables at the White Palace, Karita usually woke up by noon, but it was well past one by the time she began to open her eyes. She stretched her petite body with lazy, slow motions and a smile came to her face as she recalled the tender caresses of Vincent's hands and lips from the night before. Right now she couldn't care less what time it was, for she was free until nine this evening when she would once again go into the back room at the gambling hall.

But when she finally left Vincent's bed and slipped

333

into her undergarments, she found Vincent's message and saw no reason why she could not wait for his return. That still gave her four hours before she was due for duty. So she did not rush to get back into the fancy green gown she had been wearing last evening when she'd come here with Vincent.

She roamed around the room surveying everything most carefully and she found it to her liking. It was not a lavish showplace like Adolfo's but then she realized that Vincent was not trying to impress. He was merely interested in pleasing himself—he was not concerned with how it would be praised by the guests who entered the portals of his home.

Only one thing urged Karita to leave the cozy comfort of Vincent's bedroom and that was the need for some coffee to make her alert before he got back home. So she slipped into her gown and descended the stairs to make her way to the kitchen.

She found no one in the kitchen but she did find the coffee pot sitting at the back of the stove, so she helped herself to a cup and went over to have a seat at the little table where she'd had her late night snack the night before.

When Aspasia came through the back door with the bouquet she'd gathered she saw the fetching creature in her green gown sitting at the table sipping coffee. For a moment, Aspasia said nothing to alert the young lady of her presence, for she had never seen a more beautiful young woman.

At the moment that Aspasia was going to greet her, Karita looked up in her direction. She gave the little Mexican woman a warm smile and said, "You must be Aspasia. I am Karita Montera, and as you can see I've helped myself to a cup of coffee."

"Oh, Señor Vincent left orders for me to take care of you while he was gone, and here you have had to do for yourself." Aspasia laid the huge bouquet down on the counter and asked her if she would like something to eat.

"Oh, no Aspasia—just the coffee. I've not been used to someone waiting on me anyway. I am fine!" But Aspasia refilled her empty coffee cup before she went to attend to the flowers.

"Can I do anything else for you, señorita?" Aspasia asked her. She put the flowers in a huge pan of water until she could fill the vases in the parlor with the freshly cut flowers from Vincent's garden.

Karita's request was only for a refreshing bath before Vincent arrived at five. Aspasia summoned Jules immediately to see to that since she had the dinner to prepare. Karita was enjoying the luxury of a warm bath in the bronze tub that had been brought to the guest room. Karita smiled, for she realized that Jules and Aspasia had assumed that this was the room she'd spent the night in instead of Vincent's.

It mattered not to Karita where she bathed so she allowed them to think this as she enjoyed the refreshing bath in the guest room.

But she did slip back across the hall into Vincent's room once she had bathed and dressed and she was sure that Jules had gone back downstairs and the second landing of the house was quiet except for her.

With her curls all neatly in place and some of the gardenia toilet water dabbed behind her ears, she was ready to greet Vincent when he came into the room at five as he'd promised.

She had forgotten completely about the invitation from Adolfo to have dinner with him that night, as she'd promised him the night before last. But that was before Vincent had entered her life again.

Right now, Karita was realizing what she'd dreamed and yearned for since she'd left Whispering Willows to come here to Austin to find Vincent. Many things had happened contrary to those hopes but last night it did happen when Vincent came into the back room of the White Palace. The world stood still and Karita was carried back to that magical afternoon by the little waterfall where she'd surrendered to Vincent Navarro. She'd never forgotten the intriguing legend of that place. That had been where his grandmother Lucia had stood as a young bride with her husband, and they'd decided to call their ranch Silvercreek because they gazed at the silvery moonbeams shimmering on the little creek below the waterfall. Karita had thought it was a most romantic story, and she still did.

She had no way of knowing that the spot where she had surrendered to Vincent had been the same grassy spot where his own mother had made love the first time to Danton Navarro, his father.

It was an interesting day for Vincent at the office with Adolfo, and he found it taxing to play the role he had to play especially since Adolfo mentioned not one word to him that he knew that Karita was working at the White Palace.

Adolfo could not bring himself to do it when he was anticipating Karita's visit to his house tonight to have dinner with him. He wanted nothing to destroy the evening he'd planned with the lovely Karita and he could not wait to see the spark in her black eyes when she saw the emerald teardrop earrings he'd purchased for her. He planned to present them to her tonight when they dined together.

He was as eager as Vincent was to be out of the office by five and be on his way home. But as Vincent traveled in his buggy toward his house he was convinced that Adolfo Martinez was enamored of his beautiful Karita.

He entered his house a few minutes after five and was greeted by Aspasia's colorful bouquets in his parlor and an exciting aroma of food cooking in his kitchen. He went directly to the kitchen to ask Aspasia about his guest. "Is Señorita Montera still here?" All day he'd had doubts that he would come home this evening and find her not there waiting for him. All day these apprehensions had gnawed at him, for she was not the same Karita Montera he'd known back at Silvercreek and Whispering Willows. But he found her far more exciting and intriguing and he could not deny this.

He had thought of many things today as he'd tried to concentrate on the papers he was going over there at his desk. He could not imagine any woman more perfect to share with him the life he sought to live in Austin. With the beautiful Karita by his side, life would be wonderful! She had miscarried their first child but there would be others. Never had he thought about having his own sons and daughters but now he did, and he wanted them to be the children that Karita would give him. This told him just how deep his love was for her. What magnificent sons and daughters they would have!

When he arrived home and Aspasia told him that the

señorita was still there, it was enough to make him make a hasty dash upstairs. He left a smiling Aspasia in the kitchen as she watched him rush to leave.

It was a glorious sight for Vincent to see. He entered his bedroom, and there she sat in her gorgeous emerald green gown in the sitting room alcove of his bedroom suite. There was an elegant air about her as she sat there sipping on a glass of sherry as he had so often seen his Grandmother Lucia do in the late afternoon. He was suddenly to realize the parallel of their lives, and maybe that was why his grandmother had developed such a fondness for the girl. Lucia's origin had been a humble one until she chanced to meet the wealthy young Mexican rancher, Victor Navarro. It was obvious that his grandfather had lost his heart to Lucia just as quickly as he'd lost his own heart to Karita Montera.

When Vincent came through the door, Karita set her wine glass down on the table and went to meet him with a lovely smile on her face. He loved that instant impulse of hers to greet him. His hands reached out to her as he took her to encircle her with his arms. "Chiquita, I hoped that you would be here when I came home. You are here!"

Her dark eyes gazed up to look at his handsome face as she declared, "You did not know that I would be waiting here for you after last night?"

"I only hoped, Karita. I've come to realize you are a most unpredictable young lady." he told her with a teasing grin on his face.

An impish smile came to her face as she tilted her head to the side. "Oh, Vincent—I'm not so unpredictable! You know better than that."

By now Vincent had gone about getting comfortable

by removing his coat and unbuttoning the top three buttons of his shirt. He sauntered over to where she was sitting and tilted her chin up so he might kiss her honey lips. Softly he murmured, "I'm just glad you're here, querida. That is all that matters to me."

When his warm lips touched hers, she was glad she was there too. She had completely forgotten that she had promised Adolfo she would dine with him that evening.

But she had sent a message to the White Palace by old Jules to let Margie know that she was all right and would be at work promptly at nine. Knowing that Margie was going to be curious about her absence last night, she informed Margie that she had been the guest of an old family friend.

She figured that was all Margie needed to know! For now, she was going to enjoy these precious moments with Vincent.

Chapter 37

It was not until Vincent was taking her back to the White Palace that Karita remembered that she had promised Adolfo Martinez that she would dine with him. Just being with Vincent had made her forget all about that appointment.

They were not too far away from the gaming hall when she declared to Vincent, "Lord, Vincent—Señor Martinez is going to be so angry with me. I forgot all about his invitation to dinner."

"Don't worry about it, chiquita. I'll explain to him that it was my fault," he smiled at her. Now he knew why Adolfo had been so eager to leave at five this afternoon. It served him right for playing his little game of deception. There was no question in Vincent's mind now that Adolfo was smitten by Karita, and a score would have to be settled.

"Karita, we've many things to talk about. Our time went by too fast. You know I am reluctantly bringing you back here only because you insisted."

"I know, Vincent, but I owe Margie. I could not

leave her without anyone to sit in for me. That would not be right," she declared.

"I appreciate that and I admire you for feeling that way, but that is why we must talk about many things. There are your parents to consider. They need not endure more days and nights of worry."

"I know this too, but they would not approve of what I'm doing," she said with a tone of bewilderment in her soft voice.

By now the buggy was pulling up at the front entrance and Karita had assumed that he would just leave her there at the door but the tavern was already crowded with patrons. Possessively, he held her arm and led her through the room toward the back. It was at the base of the stairway that he told her goodbye and gave her a final kiss. "Remember, we must talk, chiquita. What about tomorrow afternoon? Shall I come by here after I leave the office?"

"No, Vincent, I'll ride Bonita over to your house. I"ll . . . I'll come over about six," she promised him as she turned to dash up the steps for she had to change her gown and straighten up her hair.

Halfway up the stairs she heard him call out to her and she turned to look down at him standing there with a warm smile on his handsome face. "I adore you, Karita!"

"And I adore you too, Vincent Navarro!" She rushed on up the steps with her heart racing madly for she'd never been happier in her entire life than she was at that moment.

*   *   *

Most people considered Adolfo Martinez a most placid, impassive man who was always in control of his emotions. He was aware of the violence that could rage in him at certain times but none of the people closest to him had ever seen such a display.

Tonight such a rage consumed him as he sat alone in his dining room to have his dinner. Rollo sensed his angry mood when he'd returned from the White Palace—without Señorita Montera accompanying him, as Adolfo had expected.

Of course, Rollo had not known of the exquisite emerald earrings Adolfo had purchased and had intended to present to her tonight. But the look on Adolfo Martinez's face when Rollo returned to the mansion to tell him that Señorita Karita Montera was not at the White Palace and was not expected back until later that evening, was as hard and cold as granite. Rollo would never forget the look in those fierce black eyes.

He'd quickly dismissed Rollo, and his manservant had been grateful for that.

Karita Montera had done something that no other woman had ever done to the arrogant Adolfo and he could never forgive her for the embarrassment she had caused him. How dare she insult him? Adolfo found it difficult to accept such an indignity.

Once he was in his bedroom and the huge carved oak door was closed, he marched over to the long chest where the velvet case with the emerald earrings inside lay. With a raging thrust, he flung the case against the wall as he went into his dressing room. Señorita Montera would regret that she'd not showed up to dine with him this evening as she'd promised. Adolfo had had few people cross him and all of them had lived to regret it. Karita Montera would too!

He would have been far more riled if he had known that the distraction had been his young law partner, Vincent Navarro.

After dinner, he left the dining room to sequester himself in his bedroom so he might give way to the black mood engulfing him. Sitting in a chair with a brandy, he sipped and thought of the shame Karita had caused him. His keen, devious mind knew exactly what he was going to do to get the gratification he sought.

Walking over to his desk, he began to compose a poisonous letter. An hour later, his face wore a smug look as the letter was finished and placed in an envelope. He would mail it tomorrow, before he went to his office. When Señorita Montera's parents received his letter and read it, they would know where she was and exactly what she was doing. He spared them no details about her having a miscarriage and that it was Vincent Navarro's baby she had been carrying.

Seething with the angry rage that was within him tonight, it mattered not that he was going to lose Vincent once the young man found out what he had done. This didn't matter to Adolfo tonight.

Only one thing obsessed Adolfo and that was that Karita had to pay for the insult she'd given him.

Two men who had admired one another so very much until Karita Montera came to Austin were now feeling pangs of disillusionment and distaste, each for the other.

Vincent was not willing to play the sly games that Adolfo had often played in his lifetime as a lawyer or a gentleman. It was not his way, for there was too much of Danton Navarro in his breeding. While he had tremendously admired the clever, keen mind of Adolfo, their technique and methods in a courtroom were different.

That night, after he'd left Karita at the White Palace, Vincent had decided that he was going to let Adolfo know he had found Karita there. If Adolfo was as smart as he'd given him credit to be, then he would know that Karita had told him about seeing him and dining with him. Adolfo would also realize that Vincent knew he had not informed him of this the first morning he returned from Silvercreek, as Vincent would have expected him to do.

He didn't know what kind of attitude Adolfo would have about being found out, for he was a proud man. But there was nothing to keep Vincent from opening his own law offices here in Austin if he wished. He, too, was a very proud man and not even Adolfo Martinez would play him for a fool! But that was exactly what he'd tried to do.

By the time Vincent went to bed, he had accepted all these possibilities and was ready to meet them head on in the morning.

As he was getting up the next morning to prepare to go to his office, Karita had just gotten to her room to go to her bed because Greta, Maria and Estelle were eager to ask her a million questions about the devastatingly handsome stranger with whom she'd left last night and not returned until this evening.

There was no question about Maria's feelings as to how she'd been impressed by the handsome Navarro. "Ah, Karita—that is mucho hombre you have for yourself!"

There was a lot of laughter and chatter and Vincent Navarro was the main topic of their conversation.

But Karita sought only to tell them so much, for the things between her and Vincent were very private and special. She knew that she left the three still very curious and that was how she wanted it.

"We'll talk tomorrow—all right? I'm exhausted and ready to go to bed," she declared, preparing to leave Gerta's room.

She hastily left to go to her own room, for she was thinking about her promise to meet Vincent tomorrow evening at six. But something else was troubling Karita tonight, and it had been all evening, ever since Vincent had said what he did to her just before they'd parted company.

He was absolutely right about her letting her parents know where she was and that she was all right. What she'd done to them had been very cruel, and they had not deserved this pain and suffering.

She also owed Señor Martinez an apology, but what could she say to him? How could she say that she simply forgot their dinner engagement? He would never understand this and she could hardly fault him for that.

The long day and the busy night made sleep come quickly to Karita the minute her head hit the pillow. She slept deeply. When her thick lashes fluttered and she began to rouse, the hands of the clock were at two in the afternoon.

She felt refreshed and was ready to get up. She still had four hours before she was to meet Vincent at six.

When she dressed, she put on the divided skirt and sheer batiste tunic blouse so that she would be comfortable riding her little mare, Bonita, over to Vincent's house later. After she had gone downstairs to help herself to a pot of coffee from Rosco's kitchen, she went back to her room to do what Vincent had suggested—to write a letter to her parents.

Before she rode toward Vincent's house that late afternoon, she mailed the letter to Blanco County. There was certainly no mention of her miscarriage, but she did tell the truth about how she was earning a living. Karita could not see anything to be ashamed of in what she was doing when she thought about Senora Lucia doing the same thing at her age. She only prayed that her family would understand. Never would she want to hurt them, for her love was deep and devoted.

Her spirits were lighthearted and gay as she mounted Bonita to ride to Vincent's house and enjoy a few brief hours before returning to the White Palace.

She was anticipating the evening meal they would share at his house. Aspasia was a fantastic cook and she liked her and Jules very much.

She looked more like the young, innocent girl from Whispering Willows when she rode up the long drive to dismount at the grilled gate to enter Vincent's courtyard.

Vincent watched her as he stood by the wide window in his parlor. He was thinking, as he watched her, how many different ladies there were in that petite

347

being. Last night in her elegant emerald gown she'd looked so very sophisticated and blasé, for he'd seen her sitting at that gaming table earlier, playing cards with gents much older than she. Now, here she came riding her little mare that she'd ridden to Austin from Whispering Willows, and he was seeing the girl who'd enchanted him back in Blanco County. He watched her dismount and secure Bonita before she came through the grilled gate.

Her glossy black hair was flowing down around her shoulders and she looked far too young to have lost a baby sired by him. A new wave of guilt washed over him as he thought about this. He knew for certain that it was with Karita Montera that he wanted to have his sons and daughters. This time they would live, for he would not forsake her as he had in the past.

The sight of her was enough to make him forget the unpleasant day he'd put in at the office and the very strained atmosphere around Adolfo Martinez. Right now, he could not have cared less if he ever worked another day for Adolfo.

Today he had seen a side of Adolfo that he'd never known existed, and he didn't like what he saw. He walked out of his office late in the afternoon realizing that he viewed a very complex man.

Looking him straight in the eye, Adolfo had still not admitted to him that he'd known where Karita was. He had allowed Vincent to tell him that he had discovered her at the White Palace and they had dined together last night, but Adolfo had not confessed that he had known her whereabouts two nights ago.

That cold, granitelike face of Martinez's never

flinched when Vincent mentioned that he and Karita had dined together last night. Adolfo knew why Karita had forgotten about their dinner engagement, and this made him even more furious.

Now Adolfo Martinez felt the need to seek his revenge against his young law partner as well as the pretty Karita. He knew not yet how he would do it or what he would do.

What Vincent could not know was the length to which this man was prepared to go to seek his revenge!

Chapter 38

The Mexican housekeeper, Aspasia, thought that the two young people sitting at the table eating the special meal she'd prepared made a handsome pair. The dining room was a very romantic setting, with the candlelight glowing on their faces and her lovely bouquet in the center of the table.

But as soon as she served them she made a hasty exit back to her kitchen so they could be alone, as she knew they wished to be. No one had to tell her that they were very much in love. It was obvious from the way they looked at one another.

It had pleased Vincent to hear that she had written a letter to her parents and mailed it on her way to his house. "They'll be so happy to hear from you, Karita."

"I know, Vincent, and I'm sorry I waited so long," she admitted to him.

They took a moonlight stroll in Vincent's gardens after dinner. The time went by so swiftly as they walked and talked about so many things that Karita knew she was soon going to have to take her leave so she could get back to the White Palace.

"You don't have to leave yet, do you?" Vincent was distressed at the thought of her leaving him so soon.

She reached over to kiss the side of his face and laughed, "It takes a lady much longer to dress than it does a man, Vincent."

But he urged her to come with him to sit on the bench for a minute. "There is something I must know, Karita, for both our sakes. I work with Adolfo, as you know, so I must know what your feelings are for him."

For a moment his words puzzled her. "Adolfo is a very nice man who was kind to me. I—I guess that is the best answer I can give you. May I ask why you ask me that?"

"Adolfo could have told me that he had seen you and knew where you were working, but he elected not to do that. I happened to come to the White Palace because of my grandmother Lucia's suggestion that I search out the gambling halls. So I have to ask myself why he tried to keep your whereabouts a secret from me. I think I know why, so that is why I wanted to know how you felt about him."

"I don't exactly understand what you're talking about, Vincent. I can't understand why Adolfo would not tell you. He, like you, was surprised to find me at the White Palace. He came with one of the regular players, Lucas, but I was as shocked to see him as he was to see me."

Vincent realized that she had no inkling that Adolfo was enamored of her, so he thought it best for her sake that he enlighten her. "Well, Karita . . . I think Adolfo is infatuated with you. That is why he didn't want me to know where you were, since he knows how *I* feel

352

about you."

"Señor Martinez? Madre de Dios, I can't imagine that, Vincent!"

"You are a very attractive young lady. Any man would be attracted to you, my sweet Karita. I am."

"But Vincent, Señor Martinez is so much older than me," she protested softly.

"He's not that old, chiquita," Vincent grinned.

Karita shook her head in disbelief of what Vincent had told her, for she had certainly never felt romantic where the dapper Adolfo was concerned.

"Why are you telling me this tonight, Vincent?" Her black eyes gazed up at him for she knew that there had to be some reason for it.

"You need to be aware of it, should Adolfo come again to the White Palace. He is a very powerful force, Karita."

The intense look in his green eyes was very serious as he looked down at her. "You—you are frightening me, Vincent, by the way you are acting."

"Perhaps, I want to, in a way, for I know you've never known such a man as Adolfo and I rather doubt that I have. But I saw a different side of the man I had so admired in the past for his forceful, masterful ways. I'm not so sure I liked it," he told her truthfully.

"He must be angry with me. I did not keep my dinner engagement with him and I do owe him an apology for that. So now he must know that it was because I was with you that I forgot all about it. I am sorry, Vincent, that this has caused trouble for you."

His arms went around her and pulled her close to him. "I'm not sorry, Karita. I'm not sorry at all. I don't want you to be sorry, either."

As he finally released her after a long, lingering kiss, Karita leaped up from the bench to shriek, "Oh, Lord, Vincent, I forget everything when I'm around you. I've got to get to my job. I'm going to be late." She immediately broke into a mad rush to go to Bonita. Vincent quickly went in pursuit to catch up with her.

As she was mounting with his assistance, he told her that the job was something else they had to talk about.

"Not now, Vincent. Another time," she said as she spurred the little mare into a hasty pace.

Vincent watched her go, and once again he was wishing that she had not had to leave him or his home. This was where she belonged, not at the White Palace.

When they were together the next time, he intended to tell her this. As he went back through the dark gardens toward the front door, he knew it was time to ask Karita to be his wife. He didn't want her to remain at the White Palace.

The many weeks of not knowing where her beautiful daughter was had taken a toll on Yolanda Montera, and her husband saw it nightly when he came in from his chores to spend the rest of the evening with her.

The only good thing that had come out of this horrible time in their life was that his youngest daughter, Cara, had been better about helping her mother with the chores at the house since Karita was not there. No longer was she so spoiled and lazy, because her older sister was not there to do the jobs that Cara did not get done.

But fate was to play a cruel trick on the Montera

family when Adolfo Martinez's letter arrived a day earlier than the one they would have received from Karita. Yolanda read Señor Martinez's letter telling them about what had been happening to her daughter since she'd left their home. It was more than she could endure in her weakened state. When his letter stated that her beloved Señora Kristina Navarro's son had been responsible for this, it was enough to make her give way and collapse. Cara rushed out to the field to fetch her father.

Abeja had come to the house to find his wife so lifeless that he feared she would die. But he and Cara administered to her and she revived enough to tell him about the letter. He soothed her by telling her, "Yolanda, Yolanda—it can not be so bad that there is not a solution. You just rest. Nothing matters as much to me as you do—not even my daughters! Do you hear me, querida?"

She managed a weak smile and nodded her head. Abeja ordered Cara to sit with her mother while he went over to pick up the letter which had been dropped on the floor. After he read it he understood why his beloved Yolanda had given way to such news as this. But Abeja was not as deeply stabbed by the news in the letter as Yolanda had been. He was grateful to know that his daughter was alive, for he'd dwelled in the fear that something far worse had been her fate. At least, he knew that this was not the case. Abeja's worry right now was for the one and only woman he'd loved all his life. His concern was for Yolanda.

As a doting father, he was not thrilled to know that his unwed daughter had had a miscarriage and that she had been carrying a baby sired by young Vincent, but this was not the end of the world. The end of Abeja's world would have been to lose his Yolanda!

For the moment, this was his only concern. As soon as he'd read the letter he went back to her bedside and asked Cara to leave the room to attend to some chores while he stayed with her mother.

Abeja quietly talked to his wife and soothed her pain and hurt. By the time he had talked to her for half an hour, Yolanda had begun to realize the wisdom of her husband's words. He was right and she realized that she, too, had feared that their beautiful Karita had met with foul play and that was not true.

"You see, we have much to be grateful about, Yolanda," he told her in that special soothing tone of his. "Our Karita is alive!"

"Oh, Abeja . . . what would I do without you? You are so right! The rest does not matter, does it? Not really!" A bright, alive look came to her dark eyes that encouraged Abeja very much. She reached up her arms to encircle his neck and he came down to kiss her tenderly.

"No, Yolanda, the rest does not matter. We can face all that. We shall face that later. Right now, I'm concerned with getting you on your feet again. That is what is important to me. I love our daughters, Yolanda, but never as much as I love you, vida mia."

Yolanda lay there looking at the intensity on his face and that was enough to make her want to be her old self again for her husband's sake. Nothing should ever make her forsake her devoted husband, Abeja—not even a daughter!

"I will be fine, Abeja. Do not worry about me as I know you have for all these weeks. I will be all right,

356

I promise!"

"I know you will, for I shall see that you are, but the rest of this day you will rest and Cara will fix our dinner—si?"

"Si, Abeja." She gave him the brightest smile that he'd seen in a long, long time. When Abeja left the room so she could rest he knew what he was going to do but he had no intention of mentioning that to her today or this evening.

He helped Cara put together their meal and finished up the chores at the barn that his youngest daughter had not done. He was happy to see that Yolanda had been sleeping all this time.

It was very encouraging to Abeja to see the difference in Yolanda after her few hours' rest and a hearty meal. She was already more like the old Yolanda and this was enough to soothe the concern in Abeja.

Adolfo Martinez had accomplished the first assault of pain and hurt that he sought but he hadn't reckoned on the Montera family. They were as strong and powerful as he was! His power was in his wealth and influence, but theirs was rich in their love for one another, and that was all-consuming.

His letter did not do to them what he had expected it to do, nor did it dent the unrelenting spirit that thrived at Whispering Willows. Adolfo found that hard to understand.

Abeja's sleep was far more peaceful tonight than it had been for many a night and Adolfo would have taken no pleasure in knowing that. He was anticipating

357

a night of torment for the Montera family and an instant hatred for young Vincent Navarro. This was not the case.

In fact, as Abeja lay in the bed as his wife was sleeping peacefully, he started to ponder why this man Adolfo had written such a letter to them. He did not even know the Montera family, so why would he make an effort to write such a letter?

Abeja was not an educated man, but he had a lot of good common sense, so he asked himself a question: what was this man's motivation in informing them of all this? He had not done it out of the goodness in his heart.

Tomorrow, he was going to ride over to Silvercreek and seek the counsel of Señor Danton Navarro. He knew that he could trust him even if his own son was involved.

As soon as he got his chores done, Abeja rode to Silvercreek to seek out the counsel of Señor Danton, who'd never failed in the past to advise him wisely. There was something about Señor Adolfo's letter that disturbed him, and he had no way of knowing that he would be receiving a letter from his daughter the next day that would ease a lot of his concerns.

At least Abeja knew his daughter was alive. That was all that really mattered to him!

Part Four

Love's Eternal Flame

Chapter 39

Victor happened to see Abeja Montera riding up the long drive and he was curious as to why he would be coming to the ranch at this time of the day. He left his room to go down the stairs. He knew that his parents were sitting on the veranda as they often did this time of the morning. It was there they enjoyed a extra cup of coffee after Danton ate a hearty breakfast. His wife, Kristina never did.

Knowing that this was where Abeja would be joining them, Victor moved to a spot by the dining room doors leading out to the veranda so he could overhear their conversation.

He lingered back in the hallway until he saw Abeja being escorted by a house servant through the dining room and out to the veranda. After the servant had gone back into the hallway, Victor made his way to the opened double doors to stand behind the thick branches of a palm in the dining room.

Victor heard his parents greet Abeja and ask about Yolanda. He heard Abeja tell them that his wife was drained from all the weeks of worry about Karita. "But she is going to be better with a little time, I think," he told Danton.

"Yolanda and you have had a few miserable weeks and it is understandable that you should both be weary," Kristina declared as she motioned Abeja to sit down with them, offering him a cup of coffee which he politely refused.

"Well, at least we know now she is alive and that is why I came to Silvercreek. I've a letter I felt you should read, Señor Danton. I think you will see why I say this after you read it," Abeja told him. He handed Danton the letter from Adolfo Martinez.

Danton took the letter and carefully read it. Abeja saw the displeased look on his face as he was finishing it. Without saying a word, he handed it to Kristina and then sat with a solemn look on his face.

It took only a brief moment for her to read Señor Martinez's letter. She put herself in Yolanda's place and realized what a stunning blow this letter must have given her. She did not immediately pass harsh judgment on Vincent, for there were too many unanswered questions and her first question, before she condemned her son, would be to know if he had known that Karita was carrying his child. As a woman, and thinking like one, she questioned why this busy lawyer with his lucrative law practice in Austin had sought to take the time to write to the Montera family. With Vincent working for him, why would he wish to sully his name as he was obviously doing in this letter? She did not hesitate in stating this to her husband and Abeja.

Victor stood listening, a grimace on his face. It was

so like his mother to defend Vincent but then he had always known that she favored him. Listening to her now thoroughly convinced him of this.

He heard Abeja say to her, "This was my thought, Señora Kristina. I was a little confused by all of it."

"I do not excuse Vincent, Abeja, so please understand this, but as Kristina points out I would like to hear from Vincent and also from Karita. Let me say that I agree that they acted foolishly, as young people will, but they are both fine young people. We both know that."

"Then shall we allow them to live their own lives for a while and see what comes about, señor?"

"Karita is your daughter, Abeja, and I can't tell you what to do. For myself, I'm just grateful to know that she is alive and no real harm has come to her. You can rest assured I shall be speaking with Vincent about this."

Victor had no reason to remain any longer for he'd heard enough to know that he had been a fool to be so considerate of Karita Montera when he was escorting her back and forth from Silvercreek to Whispering Willows.

The little witch with that sweet innocent look on her pretty face was no virgin. Once again, Vincent had bested him and taken his pleasure with her. A rage smoldered in him similar to the one that had brewed in Adolfo Martinez, but Victor had no way of knowing about Adolfo's humiliation.

Like Adolfo, he was obsessed to seek revenge against not only Vincent but Karita as well. He immediately went back upstairs to make his preparations to leave Silvercreek just as soon as he could. When he bid his parents goodbye he told them he was going to Fredricksburg to see his old friend, Gunther.

"I forgot that Gunther's folks lived here in Texas. Give him our best regards," Danton told him, recalling the close friendship his son and the young German gentleman had had back when they were living in Washington.

Victor took his leave from the ranch but it was in the opposite direction that he intended to travel. He rode the thoroughbred unmercifully for he was a man on a mission—a mission of vengeance.

It was dusk when he rode into the outskirts of Austin but it was not to Vincent's house he went when he got to the city. He went to a hotel to seek lodging.

When he had refreshed himself from the ride and dined in the hotel dining room, he left to go to Señor Martinez's house.

Adolfo Martinez was dining, and not in the most cordial mood. He instructed Rollo to show Señor Victor Navarro to his parlor, saying that he would join him shortly.

His feelings for the Navarro family were not too favorable. He was puzzled as to why Vincent's twin brother was calling on him at this hour of the evening. Adolfo had noticed the strange, aloof demeanor about Vincent today. But he was no fool, and he knew the influence and power of the name, *Navarro,* here in Texas' capital. So he was reluctant to dismiss the son of the respected former senator although he knew that the association between Vincent and him was destined to come to an end. How it would happen he wasn't sure, but it was inevitable.

Unhurriedly, he finally rose up from the table and

sauntered toward the parlor.

It had not set well with Victor that he had been ushered to the parlor to wait for Adolfo Martinez to make an appearance.

When he saw the suave figure of Adolfo Martinez come into the parlor, he rose out of the chair to greet him. "Señor Martinez, I apologize for this unexpected visit but I've just ridden here from Silvercreek and Whispering Willows. I've been sent to fetch Karita Montera after her parents got your letter yesterday."

So his letter had arrived! This was enough to bring a pleased smile to Adolfo's face. "Well, it is nice to see you again, Victor." He changed his air to being more serious for Victor's benefit as he added, "It was not a letter I enjoyed writing but I felt I must, you understand?"

"Well, we all have to do things we don't wish to do at times," Victor declared.

Adolfo invited him to sit down and share a glass of wine with him. Victor accepted the offer. As the two of them drank their wine, Adolfo spoke of his remorse about having to tell Karita's parents about her. "But I was shocked to find the girl working at a place like the White Palace. After all, she is so young. I'd just chanced to go there with my friend, Lucas, so you can imagine how stunned I was to see her sitting at the poker table."

Adolfo had just filled in the missing information that Victor needed. Now he knew where Karita was.

Now that he knew this, he had no more time to waste with this pompous lawyer. He took a generous sip of the wine so he could say goodnight to Adolfo and be on his way to the White Palace.

Getting up from the chair, he thanked Adolfo for his gracious hospitality and told him that he had to leave. "I've much to do before this night is over. Karita's mother is very ill so I must get her back to Whispering Willows as soon as possible. That was my reason for coming to Austin," he convincingly lied to Adolfo.

That revelation was enough for Adolfo to know that his letter had accomplished exactly what he wanted it to do.

He spent the rest of the evening gloating with malicious pleasure about the hurt he'd caused and the pain he was going to cause Karita to feel about all this.

His sleep was never sweeter when he retired.

Sleep was restless for Vincent and he could not figure out why he was tossing and turning so much in his bed. He got up and got one of his cigarrillos to smoke and sat looking out on the darkness of his gardens below. He could not put his finger on the foreboding that was plaguing him, but it was there nevertheless.

Tomorrow evening he would see Karita and everything would be all right, he soothed himself.

That was the thought that finally settled the apprehensions prodding at him. But if he knew the devious plot of his twin brother, Victor, and how those evil plans were already set in motion he would have understood why his sleep had been so restless.

The White Palace had attracted a lively crowd of customers by the time Victor Navarro ambled through the swinging doors.

A roar of laughter greeted him as he stood inside for a moment before moving on over to the bar. Maria's busy black eyes saw him immediately and for a moment, she would have sworn that it was the gent Karita knew, but she saw that it wasn't when she got closer to him. Nevertheless, he was a tall, handsome fellow with the kind of sensuous looks that always made a woman's heart beat a little faster. She knew that hers was pounding faster as she sided up to him. "Good evening, señor," she purred with her dark eyes sparkling and her long lashes fluttering as he turned to look at her.

Victor gave her no immediate greeting. It wasn't for the company of the likes of her that he had come here. But this didn't stop Maria from chattering that it must be his first time here for she would have remembered him.

"I've not been here before," Victor remarked, thinking to himself that it would probably be his last time too.

Maria gathered right away that he was not the friendly sort. Maybe he was one of those men who enjoyed being alone when he drank, for he did not order her a drink when he told the bartender to bring him one.

She gave him a flippant goodbye and turned to wander around the room. "Enjoy yourself, señor," she said with a hint of snap to her voice.

Victor was glad to be without her and the very pungent fragrance she was wearing. He saw no sign of Karita, so it was obviously not in this part of the saloon that she worked. But he was not to be left alone for too long, for the flaming-haired Estelle came sashaying up to his side to greet him. The voluptuous Estelle was far bolder than Maria and she did not wait to be offered a drink. She gave him a big smile and said, "Hi, good looking! Buy a thirsty lady a drink?"

Victor could hardly refuse her when she put it this way, so he called out to the bartender to bring her a drink. "Ah, gracias, señor. I thought you were a true gentleman. What brings you to White Palace? I've not seen you here before. Estelle never forgets a handsome hombre like you."

"I am looking for a young lady who works here by the name of Karita Montera," Victor told her. He figured that he should not delay his real purpose any longer.

"It seems that all the handsome gentlemen want to see Señorita Karita lately." Estelle laughed.

"Well, my reason for seeking her out is a little more urgent than the gentlemen you are speaking about. I know Karita and have for several years. I've news she needs to know about her parents."

His sober, serious manner brought a look of concern to Estelle's face. "I trust it is not bad news, señor?"

"It is urgent that I see her. I was told she works here but I do not see her here in the room," Victor replied.

"She works in the back room. She plays the poker tables for Margie McClure, the owner. Right now she is working and will be for a few more hours."

Victor displayed a look of dismay at the thought of having to endure the atmosphere of this smoky, raucous saloon.

"Do you wish to wait in Karita's room or mine, señor?" Estelle asked him. "You rode far today?"

"It's been a long day and I've a long ride again the

first thing in the morning. Would it be all right if I waited in her room until she is through for the night?" Victor inquired of her.

"I can't see why not. Come on with me and I'll show you to her room. Why, you'll have time to stretch out for a nap before she's through for the night." She smiled at him. It was evident to Estelle that he was a man of class or she would never have dared to do what she was now doing. But as entranced as she was by his dark charm, she'd not asked his name and he had not offered to tell her.

When they got to Karita's room, she opened the door and ushered him inside. "I'll get word to Karita that you're up here waiting for her," she said.

Estelle suddenly realized that she had earned no money for the time she'd spent with this handsome man. It also dawned on her that she did not know the man's name. Estelle hoped she had not acted too impulsively. Margie would have her hide if she had!

Chapter 40

When Estelle slipped into the back room to whisper in Karita's ear that there was a gentleman waiting in her room, Karita assumed that it was Vincent. She wasted no time in idle conversation with Margie when she turned over to her the night's take at the poker table.

Hastily, she rushed away to climb the steps and go to her room. She didn't stop in Rosco's kitchen to fetch a snack even though she was famished.

As she rushed into the dimly lit room, she thought the sprawling figure on her bed was Vincent. She smiled as she moved toward the bed and sank down beside him. The sudden warmth of her nearness roused Victor and he sat up suddenly to see this ravishingly beautiful lady sitting beside him. This was not the Karita he knew. In her fancy gown, with her hair pulled high atop her head, this enchanting beauty was as exquisite and elegant as any he'd seen in the high society circles of the capital.

The smile on Karita's face changed to one of surprise when she realized it was Victor lying on her bed instead of Vincent. Quickly, she rose up and asked him what he was doing there.

"I felt you should know what's been going on back at Whispering Willows, Karita. I know you love your parents very much."

"What are you saying, Victor? Is something wrong with mama or papa?"

By now Victor had swung his long legs off the bed and sat on the edge. "Well, need I tell you that your disappearance has had them worried? But it was the letter that devastated your mother, Karita."

She stammered, "But—but I hoped that would ease her concern about me to know I was happy and what I was doing was no more than your own grandmother had done, Victor, when she was young."

"It is not *your* letter I speak about, Karita. No letter from you had been received when I left. It was the letter from Señor Martinez they received."

Karita shook her head in confusion. "I fear I am not understanding what you are talking about. Perhaps, I am just tired from working so many hours, Victor."

"Your parents received a letter explaining everything that had happened since you arrived here in Austin and why you had come here to find Vincent. They know now why you left Whispering Willows. Karita, need I say more?"

"No, Victor . . . you need to say no more," she sighed dejectedly. She had hoped to spare them the fact that she'd miscarried Vincent's baby but obviously she couldn't now. How cruel and vicious of Adolfo to do this! Never would she forgive him! Why had he done this? Now she understood Vincent's warning.

Victor watched her, sitting there on the stool at her

dressing table with her head bowed in despair. But it was more than despair Karita was feeling and she had never before felt hatred for any human being. Right now, she hated Adolfo Martinez for what he had done to her and her parents. She wondered why she had ever thought he was such a marvelous gentleman, for she no longer admired him.

"Karita, I came to Austin to tell you this. I hope you will want to leave with me in the morning to go back to Whispering Willows to be with your mother. She is not well. I think she needs you with her right now," Victor told her in a most convincing tone of voice.

She did not hesitate a minute in agreeing to go with him. He prepared to leave her room after he told her the hour he would come to meet her. "I'm not staying at Vincent's. I've got lodgings at a local hotel. I've got my own reasons for doing it this way, Karita. I can't explain all this tonight for the hour is late and you need to get some sleep if we are to leave early. I'm going back to the hotel and I will see you in the morning."

"I will be ready, Victor," she promised him.

After he had left her room she took the time to write Margie a short note explaining that she would have to be away for a few days in Blanco County because her mother was ill. After that was done she collapsed on the bed for a few hours' sleep.

In less than five hours she was pulling her weary body up from the bed to get dressed in her divided riding skirt and comfortable tunic—the same outfit she'd worn when she left Whispering Willows many, many weeks ago.

She saw no cause to take much with her for she had clothes back home, but she did pack the very pretty lace shawl she'd purchased so she could give it to her mother. She could always buy herself another one.

Before Victor got to the White Palace, she had gone downstairs after she'd slipped her letter under the threshold of Margie's bedroom. By the time Victor was galloping up to the White Palace, she was leading Bonita around the side of the building to tie her to the hitching post.

The few belongings she was going to take with her were already secured to the saddle. "Good morning Victor! I'm ready to travel if you are."

A pleased smile came to Victor's face as he watched her petite figure move with a graceful motion to mount her little mare.

She gave him a bright, warm smile as she spurred the mare into motion and the two of them left the White Palace toward the outskirts of the city. It was not until they were traveling along the open countryside that she suddenly realized that she had not had time to tell Vincent of her plans to leave Austin. Everything had happened so swiftly.

But right now her concerns were at Whispering Willows, for she adored her parents and they had suffered enough because of her. She had to right all this.

These things were occupying Karita's thoughts as she rode along with Victor Navarro. It was all right with Victor that she rode beside him silently, for he was preoccupied with his own plans. This day he would not allow her to protest when he sought to take his pleasure with her. This time he would not be denied what his twin brother had already enjoyed. How could she dare cause any trouble for him or point an accusing finger at him when she was a woman who'd already had a lover? A young woman who earned her wages playing poker nightly at a place like the White Palace was hardly considered a naive, innocent young maiden back in Blanco County, he knew. So there was nothing to stop him from doing what he was going to do when they reached a certain point along the trail. It was secluded and densely wooded, so Karita could scream and protest all she wanted but no one would hear her. It mattered not how she managed to get home after that. He would ride on to Silvercreek and announce his return from Fredricksburg to his family.

He rather doubted when Karita got to Whispering Willows that she'd say anything about what had happened, and if she should, Victor was prepared to call her a liar. Who could ever prove that she wasn't lying?

Karita was beginning to see the familiar sights of the countryside that told her they were getting closer to Whispering Willows. Another hard hour of riding was going to see them reaching their destination. She was very grateful to Victor for coming to Austin to tell her about her parents and what had happened.

Karita had also noticed something else that Victor had been too preoccupied to notice. Her father, Abeja, had taught her how to heed the signs in the skies and she'd noticed the tall thunderheads building and mounting over to the southwest. A turbulent summer storm could brew up quickly when the hot afternoon heat mingled with the abundant flow of moisture from the Texas gulf. So Karita spurred Bonita to move at a faster pace.

When they were just about at the point that Victor

was going to suggest to Karita that they take a brief break and cool themselves from the hot Texas sun, he noticed that she was riding slightly ahead of him. He called out to her to slow down, but she merely shook her pretty head to tell him that she did not intend to do that.

He spurred his horse up to catch up with her. When he was galloping by her side, he called over to her, "Why, Karita? We've run our mounts a good pace all the way from Austin."

"And I intend to keep doing it, Victor. Look to the southwest. You know what that means over the blacklands. We've got a good storm moving in. I'm not about to stop!"

Old Solitaire would have said that there was a guardian angel riding on Señorita Karita's shoulder that afternoon that would prevent Victor's evil plans from taking place as he'd eagerly anticipated.

He realized that nothing was going to make that little minx stop in the woods with him. She was hellbent on getting to Whispering Willows and nothing was going to stop her.

When he saw the futility of that, he gave up, and the two of them galloped over the countryside.

Karita knew she was home when she saw the banks of the Pedernales River but she did not feel like the young, wistful girl who used to sit by the riverbank to dream her dreams. Yearnings had been satisfied and some of her dreams had been realized. But she was still not ready to quit dreaming.

When the little two story stone cottage came in view, Victor knew that he did not wish to be a part of the scene of the reunion. This he had not bargained for, so he insisted that they stop for a minute to talk and Karita was agreeable to this.

"I think I should allow you to ride up to the house alone. You will be sharing a very private family reunion with your family and I should not be there. I leave it up to you if you wish to tell them that I escorted you back from Austin, but I think that it would be better that you tell them you came home on your own," he told her.

"I think you are right, Victor," Karita agreed with him and she appreciated his understanding of the situation. "I thank you from the bottom of my heart for making the trip to Austin, Victor. I shall never forget your thoughtfulness and concern for my family. They are most precious to me."

He forced a warm, compassionate smile, but the truth was Victor felt not one qualm of the guilt that most would have felt. All he felt was utter frustration that his plans had gone awry.

They parted company at the fork in the road; there Karita would take the road leading up to her home and Victor would follow the river road that would take him to Silvercreek.

Sitting in the swing on her front porch this afternoon watching the storm clouds build back in the southwest, Yolanda swung back and forth. She hoped Abeja was seeing them, so he could get to the house before the sharp lightning started to strike. But suddenly her dark eyes saw the sight of her daughter riding her little mare, galloping up the trail to the house. Her black hair was flowing back as she rode the little mare and tears started flowing down Yolanda's cheeks, for there was no sight more wonderful to see. She had prayed to see

375

what she was now seeing. Karita must have seen her mother sitting in the swing, for Yolanda saw the excited smile on her face as she rode up to the hitching post.

Yolanda knew not how to explain it, but the heavy burden pressing against her chest for so many weeks was now suddenly lifted and she could breathe. Her Karita was home! Never had she looked more beautiful than she did riding up to the hitching post! Yolanda jumped out of the swing to rush down the steps and dash down the path to the gate.

The two of them embraced and both allowed the tears to flow, giving way to the pain and anguish they had suffered over all these many weeks.

Whatever had taken her daughter away did not matter to Yolanda Montera right now for she was holding her in her arms and she was alive and well. Karita was saying to herself that she was home and her mother did not look too ill to her. She cared about nothing but making up to her for any hurt and pain she caused.

"Oh, mama—it's so good to be home!" she stammered as they finally broke the embrace. "I've so much to make up to you and papa. I—I never meant to hurt you."

Yolanda's dark eyes locked with hers. "You are home, Karita, and what you did you felt you had to do. It does not matter. Let us just be grateful that you are here at Whispering Willows. Oh, how happy your papa will be!"

Arm in arm, the two tiny ladies walked down the stone path to the front entrance of the house. Karita was pleasantly surprised when Cara rushed up to embrace her as they walked into the small parlor. All she could say was, "Oh, Karita! Karita, you're back home!" This meant a lot to Karita.

"I am home, Cara!" she smiled as she embraced her sister. It was a wonderful sight for Yolanda to witness her two daughters being so close and loving.

Cara's busy eyes noticed that her older sister was wearing one of her old riding ensembles—a divided skirt and loose drawstring tunic. But even Cara saw a different person than the sister she'd last seen here at Whispering Willows. Karita had certainly changed. There was a boldness and an air about her which was so different that Cara could not begin to understand. All she knew was that she saw a young lady who was very sure of herself. In the weeks that Karita had been gone, she'd become more beautiful, Cara thought.

As crazy as it might seem, Cara was suddenly looking up to her older sister with admiration. The sixteen year old was saying to herself that Karita had been in the capital city of Texas for all these weeks. She had obviously had Vincent Navarro as a lover if she suffered a miscarriage as the senor's letter stated, which made Karita far more exciting than her other sister, Kristina, who had married her first sweetheart and was living a very dull life on his ranch.

All Cara knew, after she'd spent some time with her oldest sister and her husband, was that she wanted more to happen to her before she settled down to be a housewife and a mother. She wanted to a free spirit, like Karita, before she married any of the ranchers' sons.

As Cara saw it, all her oldest sister would do for the rest of her life would be Juan's wife and have his babies.

377

That sure didn't seem too thrilling to Cara!

When Abeja came in from his chores to be greeted by his beautiful daughter, he did not try to restrain the tears which flowed down his cheeks. He held her protectively in his arms to declare his happiness that she had come home.

"I knew that you would, Karita, when you thought the time was right. I am so happy to have you back with us," Abeja told her. He held her in his arms, so close and secure, as a father who loved his daughter as dearly as he loved her.

"Whispering Willows is always home to me. I could never wander too far or be away too long. There would always be something beckoning me back. You must know that. I did what I had to do at the time, papa. I only pray that you understand." Her black eyes pleaded with him.

"I do understand, niña! You need to say no more, Karita. You are home and we are so very happy to have you back."

There was a most festive air at Whispering Willows this summer night! Yolanda and Abeja were the happiest people in Blanco County!

Chapter 41

Karita experienced a strange mixture of emotions. There was a comfort and warmth she felt to be back with her family in this little stone cottage that had been her home all her life, and yet it seemed strange not to be putting on one of her fancy gowns to go downstairs to sit at the poker table for the evening.

She lay in bed staring out at the night's darkness surrounding the countryside. She could not lie to herself and say that she was going to be content to stay here at Whispering Willows week after week and month after month. That had all changed now that she'd lived away from here during these last weeks. She wasn't the same girl who'd stolen away during the night to go to Austin, and she knew there was no going back to that same girl. Too much had happened to her.

At least, her absence from Whispering Willows seemed to have brought about a change in Cara. She was much nicer to be around and it was obvious to Karita that Cara was genuinely happy to have her back home.

Karita finally closed her eyes to give way to sleep for she could not sort out her life tonight. It was best she take one day at a time. But she also knew that her parents would furiously protest the idea of her returning to Austin if she decided to leave Whispering Willows in a few days.

As much as she would not like it, she might have to steal away at a late night hour when she decided to return to Austin. She knew already that she would be going back.

When the family gathered at the long dining room table at Silvercreek, Victor thought he was telling a superbly detailed story of his trip to Fredricksburg to see his old friend, Gunther. Danton and Kristina accepted his lies and Señora Lucia did too.

It was only when Florine Whelan and her maid Solitaire were back in the privacy of their quarters, sitting out on the little moonlit balcony, that Solitaire declared to Florine, "I think your grandson lies, mam'selle."

"Dear God Almighty, Solitaire—you are uncanny, I'll swear. You seem to be able to read my thoughts when I'm not even expressing them! I was thinking exactly the same thing."

"We know each other so well, mam'selle. That is why it is this way," Solitaire told her.

"I suppose you are right, Solitaire. I'd be curious to know just what the young man was up to the last couple of days and why he would lie to his father and mother."

"For him to lie about it would tell me that it was something he wanted to conceal the truth about.

Would you not consider that as a possibility, mam'-selle?"

"Exactly, Solitaire." Florine took the last sip of her favorite brandy. As she had done nightly when she was the owner of the Crystal Castle in El Paso, she enjoyed a brandy before she retired.

But tonight there was something else on Florine's mind and she had given it much thought since she had moved here to Silvercreek. Last week she'd discussed it with Kristina and Danton. Danton had carried out her wishes and made a new will, leaving everything to Solitaire. Her reasoning was that Solitaire had no one but her. Her daughter had a wealthy husband who would inherit all of Lucia's wealth. Her grandsons were already wealthy young men from their grandfather's inheritance. She felt that Solitaire was the one deserving anything she might leave.

Florine spoke to her old friend of the will she had drawn. After they came inside from the balcony, Solitaire helped her get undressed and comfortably settled in her bed.

"Oh, mam'selle! I don't like such talk. I can't imagine a life without you with me. We've been together for all these forty years."

"Nor can I, Solitaire, but I'm going to make sure that you will not go wanting. I saw to that last week," Florine declared to her as she moved over to her bed.

"And Mademoiselle Kristina approved of this, mam'selle?"

"She did wholeheartedly, Solitaire. Now you get to your bed too, eh?"

"Yes, I will," Solitaire told her as she prepared to dim the lamp on the nightstand. It meant very much to her that Kristina did not object to her mother doing this. Knowing Florine Whelan as well as she did, Solitaire knew when she made her mind up about something there was no changing it, so Solitaire accepted what Florine had told her. She felt that the luckiest day of her life was when she chanced to meet that pretty auburn-haired lady down in El Paso.

When Karita did not come to his house as she had the done the evening before, Vincent Navarro rode toward the White Palace to see why she had not come to him.

But when he arrived there he was told by the feisty little Maria that Margie McClure was working Karita's table in the back room because Karita would not be there tonight. Maria's information was very vague but she did tell Vincent that Karita had left with a gentleman. Vincent was certain the gentleman she was talking about was none other than Adolfo Martinez.

Margie could have told him that Karita had gone home to Whispering Willows to see her ailing mother, but with the information Maria had given to him, Vincent angrily left the White Palace to ride directly to Adolfo's house.

He figured as he rode there that this was going to be the moment that the storm which had been brewing for days would erupt in full force. He did not know what kind of ploy Adolfo had used to get Karita to accompany him away from the White Palace, but he did not trust the man where Karita was concerned. Damned if he was going to get by with whatever it was!

It had been an honor to work for such a renowned

lawyer as Adolfo Martinez, but nothing was worth the sacrifice of Karita. He'd failed her once but he vowed never again would that happen. He rode swiftly through the dark streets of Austin.

He went through the grilled iron entrance of Adolfo's estate. It was Rollo who answered the door.

"Is Señor Martinez home, Rollo?" Vincent inquired of him.

"Yes, Señor Navarro," Rollo told him but there was a quizzical look on his face, for the señor had not told him that his young law partner would be coming to dinner this evening as he usually did when there was to be a guest.

"May I see him? He is not expecting me if that is what you are wondering, Rollo," he stated as he noticed the expression on Rollo's face.

Apprehension about taking Vincent Navarro to the parlor plagued Rollo since the young señor had told him he was not expected. Señor Adolfo could react very strongly about intruders into his private world and he considered this house his castle. Unexpected visits riled him even when it was people he liked. This evening when he'd arrived home from the office Rollo had noticed that his mood had not improved since the night before.

Rollo had no way of knowing what had put his employer in such a foul mood, but he knew when it had started. That was the night he'd returned without the pretty little señorita. But he'd tried to shrug the thought away that any woman would have such an effect on Señor Adolfo. As long as he'd worked for Adolfo Martinez he'd never known that to happen.

A scowl creased Adolfo's face when he saw Vincent

entering his parlor, fury etched into every line of his face, looking like a thunderhead. Rollo wasted no time lingering there with them.

"What do you want, Navarro? I didn't invite you here this evening," Adolfo barked.

"I didn't come here to visit, Adolfo. I want Karita and damn it, don't you try to play any more of your stupid little games with me. Where is she?"

Adolfo threw back his head and gave a roar of laughter. Raising up from his chair and setting his glass on the table, he smirked, "So now she is not keeping an appointment with *you,* eh?" He was feeling a devious pleasure that Vincent was hunting for her and was distraught; he obviously did not know where she was. With a cocky swagger he moved a couple of steps closer to the towering Navarro to tell him, "I don't know where she is and I don't give a damn!"

"You're telling me that she didn't leave the White Palace with you?"

"No! She is no longer welcome here, for you see, I've come to the conclusion that Karita Montera is a tramp!"

The words were hardly out of Adolfo's mouth before he felt the mighty force of the backhand slam of Vincent's powerful hand against his face. For one startled minute Adolfo felt his body swaying from the blow. His black eyes glared at the young man standing before him, daring him to say anything else.

Vincent's green eyes were ablaze with fire as they glared down at the shorter Adolfo. "She is no tramp, Adolfo, and you damned well know it! But *you* are a bastardo!"

With his teeth clinched, Adolfo hissed, "You are through at my firm! I'll ruin you! Get out of my house!" Adolfo was trembling with the fury churning within him.

A broad grin came to Vincent's face as he took a couple of steps backward. "I've been through with your firm, Adolfo, since the night I found out that you knew where Karita was and you didn't tell me. I've only been curious about your motives and then I finally figured out that it was because you wanted Karita for yourself."

Like a wild man, Adolfo shrieked at him, "Get out of here! Get out of here right now!"

"Oh, I'm getting out of here, Adolfo. Never fear that. I'm leaving your house and your law firm, but damned if you'll ruin *me*. The name Navarro has far more influence in the state of Texas than the name Martinez. If you don't think so then I dare you to put it to the test."

With Vincent's laughter ringing in his ears, Adolfo stood in his parlor like a man in a stupor. But he was not too dazed to realize that every word Vincent had said was true. He did not have the influence and power of the respected Navarro family. He was not a fool and he would not dare try to test it for he would be a loser, and Adolfo had never been a loser!

When Vincent left Adolfo's house he rode directly to the law firm. When he left a half hour later, his desk was cleared of any of his personal belongings, for he knew that he would not be stepping inside the office again. By the time he returned to his own home the clock in the hallway was chiming ten. He was famished, for he'd missed Aspasia's dinner.

He made his way to the kitchen to see what he could find and he was not disappointed. There was a platter of fried chicken and a huge crock of those brown beans she made that tasted so delicious with the onions and chilis. He helped himself to some of the little cornbread cakes she had piled on a plate, a couple of drumsticks, and the cold beans, for it mattered not to him that the beans were now cold. He ate with relish.

But once he was in his room, his thoughts drifted back to Karita. Who was it that had taken her away?

Who could it have been to whisk her away from the White Palace, to persuade her to ride away with him and not keep her promise to come to Vincent's tonight?

He knew that he must return to the White Palace tomorrow so that he could talk with this Margie McClure. He had to believe that it was something very important to Karita for her not to have left him some kind of message. He had to! He was so sure of her love for him, for he knew the depth of his love for her.

She could not have made love with him as she had the night before if she didn't truly love him, Vincent was convinced. He could not think of anything that would have kept her from coming to him as she'd promised but the call of Whispering Willows.

No one had to tell Vincent of Karita's great, devoted love for her mother and father. He was firmly satisfied, by the time he lay down on his bed, that it must have been this. But there was still the unanswered question about the man with whom she'd left the White Palace.

Maybe Margie McClure could enlighten him about that and that was who he intended to seek out in the morning. He did not have to concern himself about going to the law office.

That was now in the past, but Vincent was not worried about his future. He'd be a better lawyer than Adolfo Martinez had ever been. Adolfo's threats did not intimidate him at all!

Chapter 42

Her daughter had only been back at Whispering Willows for some twenty four hours now, but Yolanda saw in that brief time that she was not the same young girl who'd left there only a few weeks ago. Karita was always meant to be different than the other two girls in the Montera family. Always, she had known this.

There were certain traits in Karita that reminded her of the young Kristina Whelan, Florine's daughter. Both of them were exceptionally beautiful women. That posed certain attitudes that the ladies with plain looks did not have to deal with. Yolanda could well recall the tempestuous love affair of the beautiful auburn-haired Kristina Whelan and Danton Navarro, for she'd been a part of that time in Kristina's life.

She should have known that of all her daughters, Karita would be the one whose life would be challenging and unusual. She would not be easygoing as the daughter she'd named for the mistress she loved so dearly, or her youngest daughter, Cara. It was Karita, her middle daughter, who would find life complicated and confusing.

It came as no surprise to Yolanda when Karita announced to her that she was going to pay a visit at Silvercreek to see Señora Lucia. She was pleased that Karita wished to see the elderly lady who'd been so kind to her.

"I never take off the little cross that she gave me, mama. I have come to think of it as a good luck charm," Karita told her mother.

"I rather think that it might have been, Karita, and I know that Señora Lucia would be very pleased to hear that you feel that way."

There was a plea in Karita's black eyes for her mother to understand her feelings as she began to speak, "Oh, mama, I never felt that I was degrading myself, or you and papa, by working at the White Palace. I was doing something I enjoyed and I knew I was good at because Señora Lucia told me I was. I felt if it was good enough for such a lady as she was then it was good enough for me. After all, she won the love of Señor Navarro, did she not?"

Yolanda agreed with a nod of her head. "That she did and from all I've heard, they were a most remarkable pair."

"And this is the legend I've heard all my life, so I felt no shame about what I've done in Austin. Tell me, mama, that I haven't."

Yolanda reached out to give her daughter a warm, loving embrace as she assured her, "You've never shamed me or your father, Karita. All I ask of you is never to let me worry about you again as I have these last miserable weeks, Karita. That was a terrible time for me."

"Oh, mama—I think I know, but I was so scared. I didn't know what to do. I was so desperate and frightened," Karita confessed to her mother.

"And what young girl would not have been? I would not have been as harsh on you as you probably thought I would have been."

It was a very special moment for Karita that she and her mother had had this talk, for she knew that whatever the future held for her, she would never feel restrained in talking any of her problems out with a very understanding mother. This meant so much to Karita for there was no lady she admired more than she did this dear little mother of hers.

"Thank you, mama—you—you don't know how much what you've said means to me," she told Yolanda with a misting of tears coming to her eyes.

"Oh, I think I do, Karita. I've no doubt that you have a wonderful life ahead of you. I felt this way about Señora Kristina when I worked for her, and I feel the same way about you. There is such a thing as fate and it is there for you as it was for her. Now, don't ask me to explain it for I can't do it. It is just something one knows."

Karita believed her mother's words of wisdom for she'd never told her anything that had not been the truth. She wanted to believe her now. She wanted to have a wonderful life.

She left her to go to the barn to get Bonita saddled to ride over to Silvercreek and visit Señora Lucia. When she and Bonita were riding away from Whispering Willows, Karita thought about all that had happened to her since the spring when she was just beginning to blossom with girlish, romantic ideas of what love was all about. For as long as she could remember, she had thought of Vincent Navarro as her knight in shining armor and the young man who represented all the things she'd envisioned in her romantic fantasies.

All of that had happened. She'd had all those dreams come true, for he had been her lover and she'd even carried his child for a few brief weeks. There was only one thing missing to complete Karita's romantic girlish dreams and this had not happened yet. Vincent had not asked her to be his wife, even though she had once again surrendered her heart and soul to him. Once again, she could find herself carrying his child as she had a few months earlier. But now that she thought about it, she had no more to count on for the future than she had many months ago. Vincent had not made any commitment to her yet!

But whatever happened Karita knew she would never again be that frightened young girl who'd left Whispering Willows. She could always return to the White Palace and Margie would allow her to work there as long as she wished. By now, she was well aware of how much she'd brought to Margie's coffers.

She had been so absorbed in all her musings that she suddenly found herself approaching the hacienda. It seemed that it had taken her a very short time to ride from Whispering Willows.

The first person she encountered as she was preparing to secure Bonita at the hitching post was the very dignified Señor Danton Navarro. He looked striking in his tailored black pants, open-necked white shirt and his black flat-crowned felt hat.

He gave her a warm friendly greeting, "Karita! How good to see you. I can't imagine a nicer sight than seeing you as I walk out my door."

"It is good to see you, señor. I thought I'd ride over to see Señora Lucia. I—I have missed her terribly," she told him. By now, he had taken her hand in his as the two of them had come together at the steps.

"Well, she has missed you too, Karita. She looked forward to those afternoons when you kept her company. Come, let me take you in the house before I go to meet the gentleman waiting for me out at the barn." He told her that he was getting ready to check out a fine palomino mare. "Vincent left Dorado here when he went back to Austin. Austin wasn't the place for this high-spirited fellow, Vincent felt. He needed the wide open countryside here at Silvercreek."

"I think he was right, señor. Dorado was surely not happy in the small confines at Vincent's place in Austin," Karita commented as they went back into the house.

"Well, I was delighted that he decided to do it and I shall sire many fine foals by him. But he must have the right lady to do this. She must be as special as Dorado, so I must pick the right one."

Karita gave a light gale of laughter, "Ah, señor—you shall pick the right lady!"

"Kristina just told me that same thing a moment ago. I have got to believe that you two pretty ladies are right." There was a twinkle in his eyes that reminded her of Vincent. He was about to lead her into the parlor so that he could summon one of the servants to announce to his mother that she had a guest. But it so happened that Señora Lucia was slowly descending the stairway and it was a wonderful sight for her to see Danton and Karita Montera there in the tiled hallway.

393

A spark fired in her eyes at the sight of the young lady she'd missed so much, and her voice reflected that when she called out to her as she was coming down the last four steps, "Ah, Karita! Karita, you are home!"

Danton immediately rushed to her, leaving Karita to stand alone for he worried constantly about her going up and down that winding stairway. But Señora Lucia was so stubborn that she would not hear of a companion for herself such as Florine had with Solitaire, constantly by her side when she went up and down the stairs to her private quarters.

Lucia was adamant about this, and Danton could not change her mind. Nevertheless, it constantly worried him as she became more feeble all the time. He could envision her tumbling down those steps but when he'd voiced these fears to Lucia, her retort to him had been, "Then so be it, Danton! When I should get to where I can't get around my home then I might as well be dead, for life would have no meaning for me."

While this did not quiet his concern, he understood what she was trying to tell him. How could he fault her for that, for he would surely feel the same way. Such a spirited, independent lady as Lucia Navarro could never abide being a helpless individual. He had nothing but admiration for this lady who was a true firebrand with a stubborn will of her own. No one was going to change that.

It was only when Danton had escorted his mother and Karita into the parlor that he took his leave. Lucia had only to observe the beautiful young girl for a few brief moments to know that she had changed very much since she'd last sat in this parlor. Lucia also noticed that she wore the little gold cross that she had given her.

Karita felt no shame in telling Lucia what she had been doing in Austin, and the two of them talked at length about her nights in the back room. Karita told her about the fancy gowns she wore and the mountain of money she turned over to Margie McClure every night. Karita watched the fire flashing in Lucia's eyes as she told her all this. She knew that she was recalling the days of her past.

"Oh, how I would like to be in that room for just one night to watch you at the table! What a thrill that would be! It becomes a fever in your blood, doesn't it?" Señora Lucia asked her.

"I shall find it hard to stop working there, Señora Lucia. I must confess to you that I will not be content back here at Whispering Willows after what I've been doing at the White Palace. But I know what I will face with my parents, and I do love them."

"Well, I think I know exactly how you must be feeling, dear. But what you are doing is nothing to be ashamed about, Karita. There was only one thing that ever made me give up my job in San Antonio, for I was proud to be Lolita, the lady gambler, and that was the powerful force of one Victor Navarro. But for him, I would have remained there much longer."

She quickly added that it was a decision that she never regretted.

For over an hour the two of them sat in the parlor and talked. Some might have thought it strange that this elderly lady and this eighteen year old girl could have formed such a camaraderie as they shared.

Neither of them knew that their conversation was being heard by Victor as he stood by the archway of the parlor, listening.

Their conversation about the interlude of the gambling hall did not bother Victor—it was when his grandmother asked Karita to tell her why she'd left Whispering Willows and Karita had confessed to her the truth. He listened to his grandmother saying to Karita, "Well, I consider that Vincent is a very lucky young man. I just hope he realizes what a gem he has in you."

"For as long as I can remember, Señora Lucia, Vincent has been the one in all my romantic dreams, so I guess that might explain how it all happened. All other men pale when I compared them to him."

Karita's words were like a knife stabbing into Victor's gut. As nice as she'd been to him on the occasions they'd been together and alone, he had never been any threat to his twin brother. Her heart had always belonged to Vincent. He'd never get a chance to woo or win her, Victor realized. Adolfo Martinez hadn't either, for all his wealth or prestige. None of this had impressed Karita Montera.

No man had a chance with Karita as long as Vincent was there to taunt and tempt her. When he finally slipped down the hallway, Victor realized that, as long as he lived, his twin brother would always be the thorn in his side. He always seemed to keep him from getting the things he wanted the most. It had been that way since they were children.

There was only one solution, as Victor saw it, and that was to rid himself of Vincent once and for all. If Vincent was no longer around things could go the way he wanted them to go, and he could find the satisfactions he'd always yearned for but never known. It was Vincent who had denied him this gratification, he was convinced.

Vincent was the devil plaguing him. Vincent was his torment!

Chapter 43

Slipping out the back hallway and out the back entrance of the house, Victor went to the stables to get his horse ready. But he had no intention of riding very far. He was going to ride far enough to waylay Karita when she was riding back to Whispering Willows. This afternoon there were no storm clouds brewing. There were only clear blue skies.

Today, he was going to be there, in that grove of trees, when she rode over the countryside on her return to Whispering Willows. Today nothing was going to stop him from doing what he'd yearned to do since the first time he'd gazed on her sensuous loveliness when they'd returned to Silvercreek back in the spring.

He mounted his fine thoroughbred and galloped down the drive out to the main road leading away from Silvercreek. It was only a few minutes' ride to the grove of pines where he intended to wait for Karita to come galloping along the trail.

He halted his horse and lit up one of his cigarillos as he sat there waiting for her. But the wait was longer than he had anticipated, for he expected her to appear within an hour after he'd left the ranch.

Impatience gnawed at him after almost an hour had gone by and still she did not come down the road. It was tiresome just sitting in the saddle staring at the road. So he got off the horse and sank down on the ground, leaning against the trunk of a large pine tree.

What Victor could not know, and why Karita had lingered longer than she had intended, was that when she was preparing to leave after her pleasant visit with Señora Lucia, Danton Navarro had insisted that she go to the back corral to see the golden palomino mare he'd just purchased. He was as excited as a young boy about the purchase.

"I think Dorado will be very happy with his new mate. She is a beauty, Karita. You must help me think of the right name for her," he told her.

When they reached the back corral and Karita saw the magnificent golden horse with its creme colored tail swishing and long silky mane of the same color, she gave a sigh of admiration. "Dorado will be very happy, señor!"

After the two of them had stood there at the railing for a while, talking and watching the feisty mare prance spiritedly around, trying to get acquainted with her surroundings, Karita told Señor Danton, "I am glad you brought me here to see her and I will give some thought about the name, señor, but I must be getting home."

"Take the back lane over there, Karita. It will be a much cooler ride and cut off about two miles rather than the going on the main road. I always go that way when I ride over to Whispering Willows," he told her.

A smile broke on her face and she declared that she

400

would take the lane. "I never knew of this lane, I must say."

"Few do, but all the shade of the trees sure helps when that hot sun is shining the way it is today. By the way, young lady, I think it was awfully thoughtful of you to come to visit my mother. I know it pleased her, Karita."

"It has always been a pleasure for me to spend time with Señora Lucia. I find her a delight to be around," she told him.

"Well, come anytime you can and give your folks my regards," he told her as she mounted Bonita and urged the little mare toward the narrow lane.

She could certainly see what Señor Navarro was talking about when he said it was a shortcut, for she arrived at the edge of Whispering Willows property much earlier than she would have if she'd taken the usual country road between her folks' ranch and Silvercreek.

Victor Navarro was utterly befuddled, for he damned well knew that his eyes had not missed the sight of her coming down that road. He'd sat there for well over an hour and it was late in the afternoon when he decided to admit defeat. He found it unlikely that she would have remained at the ranch this long.

When he mounted his horse to ride back to the ranch he was in a disgruntled mood for it seemed once again fate had worked against him. But then that seemed to always be his fate, Victor was convinced.

When he arrived back home he met his father coming from the back corral, and Danton anxiously insisted that he come with him to show off his new mare.

"I showed her to Karita just before she left and she

thought she was a real beauty," Danton declared to his son.

"Did Karita just leave?"

"Oh, no, she's probably home by now. I urged her to take the lane over there so she could get home quicker."

Victor knew now why he'd not seen her passing by the spot where he'd been watching. He had never thought about that little back lane that was so rarely used. He had his father to thank for messing up his plans.

Victor went through the motions of admiring his father's new horse, even though it was of no interest to him if he'd have bought a dozen palomino mares. But he knew now that his father was sincere about his plan to breed the animals.

After today, Victor was once again convinced that he must surely be like his ill-fated Uncle Damien who was always unlucky during his short life. He did not live to enjoy his thirtieth birthday. Would that be his fate? It seemed that there was a parallel to their lives. That, Victor could not dismiss.

Kristina Navarro had not known of Karita's visit to the ranch until Danton told her as they were dressing to go downstairs for dinner. "Oh, I would have liked to see her. But I was with mother most of the afternoon."

"Well, she will be back before too long, I'm sure, if my mother has her way. They had a nice visit and I got to show her my new mare before she left."

"Well, Danton Navarro—I haven't even had that privilege yet." She pretended to pout.

"I told Karita to start thinking of a name for this

beautiful lady but I guess I better let you do that, to stay in your good graces." He smiled as he strolled over to plant a kiss on her cheek.

"I was only jesting, querido! I think that was very sweet of you. I—I can't forget what Adolfo's letter stated about her carrying Vincent's baby. She carried our grandchild, Danton. I can't forget that."

Danton's black eyes were very tender as he looked down at her. "Nor can I," he declared. He turned and moved slowly across the room to gaze out the window into the gardens below that were now shrouded in darkness. His deep voice was soft and thoughtful as he spoke. "I've a feeling so deep within me that I know it must be the truth, mia vida, and I must share it with you. Karita will give us a grandchild. When Navarro men get a fever in their blood for a certain lady it seems to last forever and ever. Karita is even more beautiful now."

Kristina moved away from the stool at her dressing table and quietly moved to stand behind her husband. Her slender arms wrapped around his waist as she softly whispered to him. "Oh, I pray you are right, Danton. I hope Vincent does take Karita for his bride. From the first minute I saw the two of them together I thought how they reminded me of us. They had that same love on their face and that glow in their eyes. I knew that they were meant to be together."

Slowly, Danton turned around to look down at her and his dark eyes danced over her face as feverishly as they had years ago. "It will happen, querida. Vincent, like me, will be helpless to resist such an enchanting creature as Karita. Could I cast off the spell you put on me?"

The two of them joined in a warm embrace as they broke into a gale of laughter. When Danton finally released her, his eyes warmed with adoration as he told her, "It has been a wonderful life we've shared, chiquita. I think I'd like to live it all over again even though you were certainly a little hellcat!"

"Thank goodness I was, Danton Navarro, for you were not exactly a paragon!"

Kristina moved back over to the dressing table to finish placing a jeweled comb in her auburn hair that was now beginning to be sprinkled with gray.

She was then ready to accompany her husband down to dinner but it was strange that their sentimental reminiscing had also stirred up another memory. It was not a happy one, for she kept thinking about what he'd said about the Navarro men having a fever in their blood. She remembered the evil fever in Damien's soul when he was determined to possess her when he knew that it was Danton she loved.

Her all-knowing eyes had seen both of her twin sons when they'd been around Karita Montera, and it was like history repeating itself, for Kristina saw the lusty longing in Victor's eyes.

She'd also seen the glowing love in Karita's eyes—only for Vincent—the night of the fiesta. Oh, there had never been any doubt in Kristina's mind which one of her twin sons Karita was in love with. So she was a lady dwelling on bittersweet memories this evening as she sat at the long dining table with her husband and the rest of the family.

Abeja could not have been a happier man as he sat in

404

his kitchen sharing the evening meal with the ones he loved so dearly. His lovely Yolanda was no longer sad-eyed and weary looking. The miracle had been Karita's return to Whispering Willows.

As they ate Karita told them about her visit to Silvercreek and the pleasant time she spent with Señora Lucia. She told her father about the señor taking her to see his new palomino mare.

Abeja commented, "Then he must be serious about raising the breed."

"Oh, papa—he must be, for he was so thrilled about buying this mare today," she told her father.

When the meal was over Abeja went outside to stroll in the yard while his wife and daughters washed the dishes and put the kitchen in order. Karita happened to look at the clock on the kitchen mantel, and the hands were at seven. She found her thoughts wandering across the miles dividing her from Whispering Willows and the White Palace.

She felt a yearning to get dressed up in one of her pretty gowns and go down to that back room at the White Palace. There was no where to go here except her room or the parlor. As much as she adored her family, it was not going to fill the void within her.

An hour in the parlor with her mother and Cara was enough to urge her to seek escape, and the only place that seemed to offer her the solitude she needed was the bank of the Pedernales River.

She announced to her mother and Cara that she was going to take a walk down by the river. Yolanda could not resist urging her to be careful since it was late. Karita gave her a warm smile as she reminded her that she was to used to going to bed by nine or ten.

After Karita had left the parlor, Cara told her mother, "Karita told me that she didn't even start to work at night in Austin until eight or nine, mama. She lived a different kind of life there, and you are going to have to remember that."

"I know it, Cara, but I guess I just forget." Yolanda smiled at her youngest daughter.

Cara had been tempted to suggest that she accompany Karita down to the river, but she sensed that her older sister needed to be alone. Of all of her family, Cara was the one who'd sensed and noticed Karita's restless spirit since she'd arrived back home. Cara also felt that this was only going to be a visit, for Karita was going to return to Austin sooner or later.

Cara was exactly right, for this was what was on Karita's mind as she roamed down by the riverbank. She was ready to leave now that she had visited with her family and seen Señora Lucia, but she did not know how they would react to such an announcement. She did not want to leave as she had before if she didn't have to.

She lay back on the grassy carpet of grass and gazed up at the starry sky above her and she knew she had to live her life in her own way. She had some thinking to do.

The bright full moon seemed to be shining directly down on her and it was a most sensuous silhouette she made there on the riverbank.

A pair of lecherous eyes were devouring her!

Chapter 44

Dappled moonlight played through the thick branches of the tall old oaks where Karita stretched out on the grass. It mattered not to her that she was swallowed up by the blackness. She found herself aching for the touch of Vincent's warm body beside her. That would have made everything perfect.

He was the most urgent reason for her to get back to Austin for nothing must ever destroy their love again. But since they'd once again shared that ecstasy after he'd found her at the White Palace, Karita was sure that Vincent Navarro did care for her. That was all she needed to know. Her only regret was that she'd not sent word to him before she left so hastily with Victor.

Victor had certainly over-exaggerated the seriousness of her mother's illness. She knew that now. Such a hasty departure from Austin had not been necessary.

The more she was around Victor, the more he puzzled her. There was a strange side of him that made her not exactly trust him. He and Vincent might be twin brothers, but she did not believe there was any closeness. There never seemed to be any warmth in Victor's voice when he made a remark about Vincent. The truth was, there was usually an undertone of coolness.

So deep were her thoughts that she did not sense or hear the stalking figure until he was upon on her, pinning her helplessly on the ground. One hand covered her mouth so that a scream was impossible. The other hand was fondling her in a lascivious, disgusting way that made Karita shudder.

When she felt his hand move away from her mouth she tried to open her lips to let out a scream, but his mouth was covering her lips. His kiss was cruel and her lips felt bruised from his roughness.

Fiercely, she tried to struggle to be rid of his powerful thighs. There was no doubt that this beast of a man was enjoying the agony and pain he was inflicting on her, for she heard his deep, husky chuckle even though he'd not spoken a word.

In her anguish, she prayed for the moonlight to shine down so she might see the face of this devil attacking her. But complete darkness concealed that.

Now, she felt the ripping of her sheer batiste tunic as his strong hand yanked at it and once again the lewd touch of his hand pinched the tip of her exposed breast. But his other hand muzzled her mouth so her moan sounded like some wounded creature of the woods.

The man's frenzied desires were now so enflamed that he was unaware of the shifting of his own body. It was enough to allow Karita's right arm and leg to be freed. She was guided only by instinct to protect herself and flee to the safety of her home. With all the power she could manage she doubled up her fist and swung it to the side of the man's face. At the same time, she bent her leg and thrust it upward as hard as she could.

The slam to his face and thrust at his groin caused Victor to cuss and groan at the pain she'd inflicted on him, and at just that moment the moonlight did come down through the trees' branches. Karita was to know her attacker.

"My God, you—you bastard!" The fury of seeing who it was turned her into a wild hellcat. Karita was so determined that Victor Navarro was not to have his way with her that she fought him like a mountain lion.

There was no way Victor could manage to get her pinned on the ground the way he'd once had her, for they were rolling over and over. The more desperate he got to conquer her, the more furiously she fought to prove to him that he would not.

Suddenly, in the distance, came a voice calling, "Karita—where are you? Karita, do you hear me?" Never had the sound of Cara's voice been so sweet to her older sister. She managed to give a scream before Victor's hand slammed over her mouth.

Victor was no fool; he knew he couldn't fight two Montera hellcats. He leaped up and dashed back to where he'd left his horse to gallop hastily away.

Cara rushed to the sound of her sister's voice and heard the galloping hooves of a horse fleeing into the darkness. But she could not recognize the rider.

When she came upon Karita trying to rise up from the ground, with her tunic torn and her hair all tousled around her face, she sank to the ground and embraced her. "Oh, Karita! who did this to you?" Cara brushed her hair away from her face.

Karita gasped, "I—I—let me . . . get my breath."

For a few minutes Cara just sat there holding her sister, waiting for Karita to gain control of herself. Karita took off her torn blouse and gave it to Cara. "Go down to the river and wet this so I can wash my face. I'll never wear it again anyway."

Cara left her long enough to do as she'd requested. Karita told her that she was now able to talk. "You've got to help me get to the house without mama and papa hearing us. They must not know about this, you hear me?"

"I hear you, Karita, and I will. They're both sound asleep anyway. I came out looking for you because it was getting so late."

"Thank God you did, Cara! Thank God you did!"

"I want to know who did this to you, Karita. Tell me," Cara insisted on knowing.

"Only if you swear to me it will be our secret. You have got to swear, Cara," Karita demanded of her.

"I swear to you, Karita. You can trust me."

"I must, for there would be bloodshed over this and I want nothing happening to papa. It is over and he didn't get his way with me, but he could have if you'd not yelled out when you did, for I was exhausted from fighting him."

Cara reached over to kiss her sister on the cheek. "I'm glad I saved you, Karita. I love you very much even though I might not always have acted like it."

"That was the past, Cara. Forget it. When I tell you who it was you'll understand why I've said what I did and why we must keep this to ourselves. The man was Victor Navarro."

"Madre de Dios! Karita!" Cara gasped and her body stiffened from the shock of what her sister had told her.

"I know. I am still stunned."

With her damp blouse clutched in her hand, Karita held her sister's arm as they slowly walked toward the house. They managed to slip into the house and to their bedroom without rousing their parents. Karita realized that she would probably find the marks of Victor's vicious attack on her body in the morning. But tonight she wanted only to get into her nightgown and go to bed.

But more than ever, she knew now that she had to leave Whispering Willows. She could not possibly stay here after what had happened tonight.

In fact, she was going to tell her parents that she would be leaving for Austin early the next morning.

To get an audience with Margie McClure proved to be difficult for Vincent Navarro, but once he did, there was no doubt who it had been that had left with Karita. But what did perplex him was why she'd not let him know of her plans. He could understand why she would be upset about the news that her mother was ailing, but, still, she would have found a way to let him know.

If he were to wager on it, he'd bet it was Victor who'd insisted that they must leave Austin immediately. Knowing all the underhanded tricks Victor was capable of, Vincent was sure his brother had insisted that they head for Blanco County and take no time to leave a message at Vincent's house.

After he left Margie, he decided there was no reason for him to delay his own departure for Blanco County. He had no law office to go to now that he was no longer a partner with Adolfo. There was no reason to delay something else that had been on his mind since the night he'd gone to the White Palace to find Karita there. He'd be the biggest fool in the world to try to deny that he didn't love her, because he did, and more than he'd realized. There was no need for him to delay asking her to be his bride and what better place to propose to her than in Blanco County where he'd first fallen in love with her? He found himself eager to get there to see her.

Vincent was sure that both families would be delighted by their announcement. As soon as he arrived home, he announced his plans to Jules, then went on into the kitchen to tell Aspasia.

After dinner, Vincent did not linger in his parlor, but immediately went upstairs to retire so that he could ride out at daybreak to Blanco County to claim the woman he loved for his bride.

He would not have slept so peacefully had he known what was happening to Karita. There was no sleep for Victor this night, either. He rode away from Whispering Willows as if demons were chasing him, for he knew that he could not remain at Silvercreek. By the time he got home, the cool night air had cleared his head enough to make him ponder the madness that had urged him to do such a thing. But it was too late now for him to feel sorry for what he had done. How could he ever explain such insanity to his family or to the Montera family?

He knew he must have hurt Karita as they fought like two vicious dogs there on the ground. There was only one course open to him and that was to get as far away from Silvercreek as he could to prevent bloodshed in the Navarro family. Vincent would not hesitate a minute to seek revenge when he learned what had happened.

It was late when he rode into the ranch grounds and entered the house quietly to go directly to his room. The articles he started to gather and put in a leather bag were not clothing but the valuables he owned. He was glad to have the money he'd put away in a leather pouch.

He took a few extra moments to scribble his parents a note. For one brief moment in Victor's life he spoke the truth for he hoped they would try to understand what he was trying to tell them. He stated quite simply that he was going to Mexico to find his roots and rid himself of the torment in his life. His Grandfather, Victor Navarro, had been born there and came to Texas to make his fortune. Victor thought this might be the answer for him, too.

As quietly as he'd entered the house, he left it to get back on his horse to travel southward. By the time dawn was breaking over the Texas skies, Victor had traveled many miles toward the Mexican border.

When his parents woke up they would find the note he'd slipped under their bedroom door. By the time they read it, he would be approaching the outskirts of San Antonio.

It would have been welcome news for Karita to know that Victor was many miles away. When she woke up and started to move out of the bed, she realized the beating her small body had endured last night. Slowly, she sought to stand up. The first thing she surveyed was her face in the mirror; by some miracle, her face had been spared. There were bruised spots on her arms so she made a careful survey of the rest of her body. There

413

was an ugly redness on the upper part of her chest and on her thighs. But she was happy to see that she could conceal all this from the eyes of her family, and she immediately went through the ordeal of dressing.

But as she was dressing, she found herself wanting more and more to be away from here. For her own and everyone's sake, Karita had made up her mind that it was best she leave today for Austin. She was glad that she had woken up as early as she had. Cara was still sleeping soundly. Karita knew that out of all the bad had come some good, for there was a bond between the two sisters that had never been there before. She and Cara now shared a sisterly closeness that would endure for the rest of their lives. She was happy about this. Cara had saved her last night and she would never forget that.

But she knew she had to get away from Blanco County as soon as possible!

Chapter 45

Karita told Cara about her plan to return to Austin. "I must, Cara, and I know you can understand. I think it's for everyone's best interest. But don't you fret that I'll be away too long this time. Besides, now you know where I am."

It was her mother she confronted next with her plan to return to her job in Austin. "I owe the lady, mama. She's been good to me and I earn very nice wages. Besides, I'm no child anymore, as you must know. I'll not be away too long."

Yolanda was not surprised by her daughter's announcement, for she'd sensed it almost from the first day she'd been home. Whispering Willows was not going to satisfy her any longer. "You must do what you think is right for you. I realize you're a young lady with a mind and will of your own. You know you have my blessing, Karita, if this is your wish."

"Thank you, mama. This means very much to me."

The last to know of her plans was Abeja, and he gave her a little more protest, but he saw that she was determined to leave so he said no more. "Come home often, Karita. We miss you," he told her, and she saw a hint of mist in his dark eyes.

She gave him a warm embrace as she assured him. "Oh, papa I'll be back very soon. I promise you that! You and mama know where you can find me, so there is no longer a reason for you to worry about me."

"That is a good feeling, niña."

Knowing that the afternoon was going to be a hot one, Karita decided to delay her departure no longer. At least, she could have an hour's ride behind her before the mid-day sun began bearing down on her. With any luck she could beat the hottest hour of the summer days which were in the late afternoon.

The departure from Whispering Willows had been much easier than she'd expected and she was grateful that her parents had given her no objections, for then she would have felt guilty. But it took all her will power not to cry out in pain when her father gave her a strong embrace. The pain was excruciating! A soreness had settled in her chest and waist.

After she'd ridden about an hour she was glad that she had left when she did, for the afternoon's ride was going to be a miserable one. The sun was already beating down on the countryside.

She rode through the rolling hillside country which lay west of Austin and took a few moments to rest in the shade of the thick grove of trees she came upon before riding on toward Austin. It was a welcome sight to see the Colorado River, for she knew she was approaching Austin.

She knew that she was going to arrive in the city at an hour that would allow her to rest for a while before she had to go to work. She could tell from how high in the sky the sun was that it was not yet five in the afternoon.

She rode through the heart of the city, and passed by the impressive capitol building which had just recently been built, to go to the other part of the city where the White Palace was located.

She hoped that her absence had not put too much of a load on Margie McClure, but she planned to make it up to her. Tonight, she would start to do just that.

It was a good feeling when she led Bonita up to the gambling hall. Leaping off the little mare, she led her around to the back of the two story building to get her to the little stall and quarters where she had a small area to exercise. When she had taken off the saddle and attended to Bonita's needs, she left to go inside the saloon.

It was Rosco she first encountered and she received a warm welcome back to White Palace. "Place ain't been the same with you gone, Karita," the husky Rosco declared.

"Well, I'm glad to be back, Rosco," she told him, trying not to linger too long for she felt the need of a warm, refreshing bath to wash away the dust from the trail.

So she told Rosco goodbye and turned to go toward the stairway. She did not check in with Gerta, Estelle or Maria until she got to her room and had a bath. Her blouse was clinging to her with a dampness caused by the heat of the afternoon.

Later, after she'd requested the bronze tub filled with warm water and the perfumed bath oils were permeating the room, she sank down in it and languished there. It gave a soothing comfort to her bruised upper chest

417

and arm. Weary from her long ride, she had not taken the time to lock her door and Margie McClure came bursting through it as she sat in the tub.

"Well, you're back and it's a damned good sight for me to see. I've lost money by you being gone, Karita," she smiled impishly.

Karita broke into a smile as she flippantly retorted, "I shall make up for it tonight, I promise you, Margie."

"I know you will, honey. I hope your mother is better."

"She was never that bad, Margie. I'll tell you about that later," Karita promised her.

Margie's keen eyes had just taken notice of the bruise on Karita's arm. "You are all right, aren't you, honey?"

"I am fine, Margie. Believe me!" Karita told her, noticing that Margie had spied the bruise.

"Tell me, Karita—tell me that it was not the young man I talked to who did this to you. He seemed so nice when he was inquiring about you. But he came to me after you'd left and seemed very concerned that you had not contacted him, so I told him about your message to me."

"No, no, Margie—that was Vincent. He did not do this. It was his twin brother, Victor, that I left with because he told me my mother was so ill. He lied."

"The bastard! Oh, Karita—I'm so sorry. You don't have to work tonight if you don't feel up to it," Margie told her.

"But I want to, Margie. I am fine. Everything was pleasant on my visit back to Whispering Willows. I made my peace with my family and I got to see the dear Señora Lucia. So it was all worth it."

"You saw the famous Lolita?"

418

"I did, and I told her about you and what I was doing, and she was very excited about it, especially when I told her that your gambling hall was called the White Palace. She is in her seventies now but you'd never believe it if you saw her or talked to her. She is so vibrant and alive."

"Dear God, I'd love to meet her," Margie exclaimed.

"Maybe you will, Margie," Karita told her.

"Well, I better get out of here so you can get your bath and get pretty."

Karita gave her a smile as Margie turned to leave the room.

Vincent arrived at Silvercreek long before Karita got back to Austin, but he had started out much earlier that morning. It was not exactly a happy atmosphere greeting him when he entered the spacious house. He encountered his father first and his father's manner told him something was wrong.

"That is an awfully serious look on your face, father. I wouldn't like to think it's my arriving home that caused you to look so sober," Vincent laughed.

Danton shook his head as he told his son, "No, quite the contrary. I'm glad you're home and it will do a lot of good for your mother to find you're back home. Come to my study so we can have a little talk before you see the rest of the family."

"Mother isn't ill, is she?" An anxious look broke on Vincent's face, for rarely was she ill.

"No, Vincent, she is well," Danton told him as they entered the study and shut the door behind them. Striding over to the desk, he urged Vincent to have a seat. "Read this and you will see what is troubling me and your mother. We found this when we woke this morning. Victor had pushed it under our bedroom door before he left, sometime late last night or early this morning."

By now Vincent had read the brief message and his first question to his father was to ask if Victor had got himself in any kind of trouble. "Could that have been the reason he hightailed it out of here to go to Mexico, father?"

"I'd thought about that, I'll admit. But there has been no trouble that I've heard about so far. I just don't know what to make of him. I've even told myself that it was a thing of impulse, of a young man wanting to go for a little roaming, but that would be something I'd have expected of you more than Victor."

"But I would have come to you, father, and told you what I was planning."

"True—you would have done that. By the way, only you and your mother know about this. I've not had an opportunity to tell either of your grandparents yet. Both of the ladies have got to where they don't come downstairs until the late afternoon."

Danton told his son that he had been aware of Victor's discontent since they'd returned to the ranch. "Funny, really, that he's seemed bored, because I thought he was eager to get back to Silvercreek. I guess I was wrong."

"Well, that is Victor's problem, not yours, father. You know as I do that Victor's a moody person. When he is in one of his moods no one can reach him. I'd venture to say that one of his dark moods urged him to leave last night." Sadly, Danton Navarro gave an agreeing nod of his head.

The two of them talked a while longer before Vincent left the study to go to his room to freshen up before he saw his mother and the rest of the family.

Danton left the study to go for a stroll in the courtyard gardens, for it was always peaceful there. Just to roam down the stone path and feel the cool shade of all the trees brought a kind of serenity to him. The flowers had never been so beautiful as they were this summer, and butterflies were there to take the bountiful nectar in the blossoms. They too were bright and colorful. Danton always enjoyed the sweet trilling of the songbirds. Vincent's arrival had lightened the gloom that had hung so heavily since he'd found Victor's message. He knew it would have the same effect on Kristina.

But he was still faced with telling the two grand-mothers, and as he was walking there in the gardens, he decided that he would go to each of them before they came downstairs this afternoon. With this in mind, he turned there on the path to go back to the house and get it done immediately.

He went to his mother's room first. He took Victor's note with him and allowed her to read it as he had with Vincent.

She read the note and handed it back to her son. She did not seem disturbed by the news as she told Danton in a very calm voice, "Perhaps Victor will come back a better man, Danton. We shall hope so. Whatever happens from here on, my son, you just remember he and Vincent are their own men now. You and Kristina did a fine job of raising them."

Danton reached down and kissed her on the cheek.

"Thank you, mother. I'd like to think so."

He left her to go to Florine's room. Once again, he found himself amazed that she took the news with the same calm as his mother had. A very pleased expression came to her face when he told her about Vincent's arrival.

When he left Florine's room, he went to seek out his wife to announce to her that her other son was home. That would surely help the confusion she was feeling about Victor leaving Silvercreek without telling her goodbye.

That evening the gloomy atmosphere that Danton Navarro had expected to find during the evening meal was not present. Vincent's happy-go-lucky air and his usual charm played on his mother and grandmothers and was exactly the tonic they all needed. Danton was very grateful that he was making it such a happy evening for his family.

When the meal was finished, Vincent requested that all the wine glasses be filled, for he had a toast to propose.

"I've an announcement to make to my family. I had another reason to come back home today. I intend to ask Karita Montera to be my wife tomorrow," he told them. "Shall we drink a toast that she will accept my proposal?"

Vincent heard the murmurs and sighs of excitement his announcement had created, and he knew from the happy look on his parents' faces that they were pleased by his choice.

His lovely mother tilted her head with a smile on her face, asking her handsome son, "And you've said nothing to Karita yet, Vincent?"

"No, so I will have to hope she doesn't turn me down, for I will be one embarrassed fellow, won't I?"

Everyone broke into laughter. The dignified Danton Navarro confessed, "You're braver than I would have been to dare make such a statement, son."

But Kristina Navarro had always known that there was a self-assurance about Vincent as there had been in Danton. She had always admired that. She didn't doubt for a minute that Karita's answer to Vincent would be yes.

Nothing could have made her happier than the prospect of having the daughter of Yolanda and Abeja for a daughter-in-law!

No one sitting around the table was more thrilled by Vincent's news than Señora Lucia Navarro. It would have been the young lady she would have picked for him if the choice had been hers to make.

Florine Whelan was grateful that one of Kristina's twins could give her such a happy evening. She could see that Kristina was extremely pleased about young Vincent's news. This was enough to make Florine happy.

Solitaire sat beside her mam'selle saying not a word, but her black almond-shaped eyes were slowly surveying everyone at the table and she was absorbing the pleasant atmosphere here in the dining room this evening. Under her breath she was saying to herself, "The evil is now gone from this place and there will now be happiness here."

She was pleased to have that shroud lifted away.

Chapter 46

Lucia Navarro asked her grandson to come to her room before he left the next morning for Whispering Willows. Vincent assured her that he would, and kissed her goodnight.

When there was only he and his parents alone in the parlor, Vincent made another announcement. "I am no longer associated with Adolfo Martinez. I can't work for a man I can't trust, and I came to not trust him." He explained to them how Adolfo had known where Karita was working but that he sought not to reveal that to him when he'd returned to Austin.

"It baffled me, because he knew that I had made the trip back here to see if she'd come home when she disappeared from Austin. I questioned his motives and I saw a different side of Adolfo. I saw a different side of the man I'd admired so tremendously. So I cleaned out my desk and walked out of that office. I will not return there."

"And what are your plans now, Vincent?" his mother wanted to know.

"I shall open my own law office," he told her in a bold confident voice.

"As you know, Vincent, your father had his own law offices in Austin. Your practicing law does not depend on Adolfo Martinez," Kristina declared.

"That was the conclusion I came to, mother. Now, I am going to bid the two of you goodnight. I plan to ride to Whispering Willows the first thing in the morning." He went over to kiss his mother goodnight and his father gave him a warm embrace. "Good to have you home, son." Vincent smiled and nodded his head.

For a while after Vincent got to his room and undressed to stretch out across his bed, he gave a lot of thought to his twin brother's abrupt departure. He only hoped that there was sincerity in the message he'd written but he could not dismiss the suspicion that it was Victor who'd brought Karita back here. It was a long ride from Austin to Whispering Willows.

For Victor's sake, Vincent only hoped that he'd treated her like a lady, for if he ever found out that he hadn't there would be the devil to pay! Twin brother or not, Vincent would seek his revenge.

His eagerness to see Karita and know for certain that she was all right was enough to make Vincent wake up early the next morning. But his impatience to be on his way to Whispering Willows did not stop him from going to see his Grandmother Lucia as he'd promised.

There in her room a very sentimental interlude took place, and one that endeared her very much to Vincent. He knew that Karita would feel the same way, for it told him just how much his elderly grandmother cared for the woman he planned to ask to be his bride.

Her wrinkled hand took a stunning ring out of its

velvet case. Vincent had never seen a more beautiful ring. A brilliant emerald was encircled with diamonds. He could not recall seeing his grandmother wear this ring, but then she had a vast collection of jewelry.

He gave a deep sigh of admiration as he took the ring from her hand. "Your grandfather, Victor, brought this to me at the Palace the night he asked me to be his wife. I've enjoyed it all these years, so now I wish your Karita to have it, Vincent. It is my wedding gift to her. You see, she and I have so much in common."

While he was stunned by her generous gift, he understood what she was trying to tell him, so he put the ring back in the case and placed it in his pocket. A twinkle came to his eyes as he took her small hand in his and held it tenderly. "Now, I know why I lost my heart to Karita Montera. She must be that special kind of lady—like my Grandmother Lucia."

She gave a little chuckle, "Now I know why I loved you so dearly, nieto. You have that irresistible charm of your grandfather. He could charm a rattlesnake."

"Well, that's the nicest compliment you could pay me."

"Well, now you quit wasting your good time here with me and get to that pretty young lady, Vincent Navarro," she gently ordered him.

Vincent did not delay complying with her request and left to be on his way to Whispering Willows.

Two hours later, Vincent was riding back to Silvercreek with the ring in his pocket, for Karita was not at Whispering Willows. Karita's younger sister's comments had pleased him when she'd said that she

427

knew Karita was eager to get back to Austin and to him. "She could find no contentment here after she arrived to find out that mama was not as ill as Victor had led her to believe."

"Did Karita tell you this, Cara?" Vincent asked her.

"Karita was very concerned that mama was seriously ill but all that ailed mama was worry over Karita. Her first night back here made a big change in mama."

Vincent was secretly wondering if Victor had appointed himself to come to Austin and whisk Karita away. Now he thought that he might know the reason for his brother's sudden departure; he had been caught up in a web of lies. But then Victor had always been a liar. Many things had happened over the years that Vincent had never told his parents and had kept to himself, for he never wanted to hurt them.

But there had been a time, when his father was a senator back east, that Vincent became convinced that Victor had inherited the weakness of his uncle, Damien. There was a destructive quality about him. As tempted as he'd been to go to his father to have a serious talk about Victor, he'd been reluctant to do it. But he'd regretted many times that he had not followed through on the impulse to do it. He could have enlightened his father that Victor had boasted that he had no plan to do anything with his life, for he intended to just wait out the time when he would share the inheritance of the Silvercreek Ranch.

At least Vincent rode back to Silvercreek with the wholehearted approval of Yolanda and Abeja after he told them that he wished to ask Karita to be his bride.

There was one thing for certain, and that was that

Karita Montera had given him a merry chase. The next time he caught up with her, he vowed that she wasn't going to get out of his sight until he made her his bride.

His family were all very understanding when he departed the next morning to head back toward Austin after his disappointment at not finding Karita at Whispering Willows.

Vincent would have found it amusing if he'd known that the afternoon he'd paid his call at her home to find her not there, she had dashed away from the White Palace to go to *his* home, only to have Aspasia tell her that *he* was not there. "He goes to seek you, señorita. I think you two young people should not wander off so much. Then maybe you would not always be missing one another along the way," the little Mexican housekeeper told her with a grin on her face.

"I think you might be right, Aspasia. I promise you that I won't be going anywhere, so when Vincent returns, will you tell him I came here?"

"I shall tell him, señora," Aspasia promised.

Karita returned to the White Palace but her spirits were high and her mood was a happy one, for Vincent must surely care very much for her. This was all she needed to know to make all the other unpleasant things of the past fade away.

The happiness she was feeling was reflected on her face as she galloped toward the gambling hall. The same radiance and glow were there when she went to sit at the poker table that evening, but it quickly faded when she saw Adolfo at the table with his friend, Lucas. Karita sensed immediately he was there for good. The scowl on his face deepened when he looked at her. Lucas was his usual friendly self.

429

Karita came to the table and gave her usual welcoming greeting to all the gentlemen sitting there.

All of them except Adolfo gave her a warm smile as she took her seat. She decided to ignore him as much as she could. But she could tell, as the game went on, that her indifference was firing his anger. He was certainly not concentrating on his cards and he kept making foolish mistakes. This was costing him a huge sum of money.

It was an endless evening for Karita and she thought it would never be over. She had no knowledge of the vicious scene that had taken place between Vincent and Adolfo and that Vincent had quit the law firm.

She welcomed the moment when the last card had been played and the evening was over. All the gentlemen rose up from their chairs to stretch their legs. Some had enjoyed the evening, for they had won more money than they'd lost. But Adolfo and another player had lost a tremendous amount of money, so the look on both their faces was not too happy.

His fierce black eyes glared at her as he ambled out of the room with Lucas, and his voice hissed like a viper when he told her, "Tell your lover I want the keys back to my front office door, Karita, or I'll turn him over to the authorities."

She stood there, feeling stunned and embarrassed that he would have been so rude because she knew the others heard his comments.

Now, she was in a quandary as to what Adolfo was talking about. Had he fired Vincent or had Vincent quit, she wondered? Many questions were whirling around in her head as she gathered up the mountain of bills on the table to take to Margie's office.

Margie McClure was flabbergasted by the take the poker table had yielded tonight. She flung several bills down on the desk before she put the rest into her safe. "That's yours, honey. You deserve it."

"This much, Margie?" Karita questioned as she picked them up, counting them.

"I didn't bring in this much in the three nights I worked your table. Yes, that is yours," Margie declared, as she closed the safe. "We must have had some losers out there tonight."

"We did. One was Adolfo Martinez and he was in a very foul mood."

"Lucas is fine but Martinez makes me nervous. He was here one night when you were gone and I didn't like the feeling I had about him. Beware of him, Karita," Margie warned her.

"Oh, I plan to." Karita took her earnings for the evening and told her goodnight, for it had been a very exhausting day. She was ready for the quiet of her bedroom and some sleep.

As she slept through the morning hours until mid-day, Vincent was already riding back toward Austin, but this time he was riding Dorado. There had been two reasons for taking Dorado back to Austin: He could travel faster if he rode his fiery stallion instead of the horse he borrowed from his father. The other reason was that Vincent spotted the thinned strips on Dorado's golden rump which had not had enough time to thicken up since Victor's harsh lashes with the quirt, even though the young Mexican boy had given him daily care.

Danton told his son the truth when he angrily marched into his study to demand an explanation. He also told Vincent what he'd told Victor: that he'd be tossed off the ranch if he ever took the palomino again.

It was enough to make Vincent realize that the truth was long overdue; he must tell his father what he was dealing with where Victor was concerned. He'd covered up for him far too long. So he told him about Victor's latest lie that he'd learned when at Whispering Willows.

"He lied to Karita. He made her think that her mother was desperately ill to get her to leave Austin with him immediately. That is why she rushed away with him, I've found out. Victor is sick, father—sick in the head! I can't wait to get back to Austin to see just what else he may have done. I will tell you this, though. If he tried anything with Karita, I'll kill him—brother or not!"

"I understand, Vincent," Danton told him, even though it was hard for him to say. He was a fair man, and he knew what Vincent must be feeling.

Oh, God, maybe there was a curse on Navarro twins! It surely seemed so to Señor Danton Navarro as he watched one of his sons take his leave to return to Austin.

Danton bowed his head and covered his face with his hands to pray that Vincent would not find that his brother had violated the lady he loved.

Chapter 47

Riding back to Austin astride Dorado was enough to mellow the mood he was in when he'd left his father's ranch. The palomino was certainly ready for the wild, furious pace they made all the way back to Austin.

When they arrived at the gaming hall, it was ghostly quiet and the saloon was deserted. Vincent marched on through the saloon to mount the stairs that would take him to Karita. But since he did not know which of the rooms on the second landing was hers, he opened the doors to the rooms belonging to Maria, Gerta and Estelle before he came to the bedroom where he found his beautiful Karita lying in bed, sleeping soundly, her black glossy hair fanned out over the pillows. He slipped quietly into the room and locked the door behind him. For a moment, he stood there to savor her glorious loveliness. He finally sank down on the bed beside her and felt the sweet warmth of her still body. His fingers could not resist removing the curling wisps of hair falling over her face, and she stirred slightly. He saw the sensuous swells of her breasts in the sheer nightgown she wore. Slowly, her thick lashes began to flutter and her black onyx eyes were looking up at him. A lazy smile came to her face as she drawled, "I—I was dreaming about you, Vincent."

"Well, you don't have to dream any more, querida. I am right here." His dark head bent down to capture her lips in a long, lingering kiss. When he finally released her, he grinned, "You're too hard to keep up with, Karita Montera. Now that I've finally caught up with you again, I'm not going to let you leave me again. Besides, I don't want my wife working at the White Palace. I'm a very possessive, jealous man!"

Karita stared up at him wondering if she had heard him right or if she was still half asleep. So she said nothing for a brief moment.

"You will marry me, won't you, Karita mia?" His green eyes were dancing over her face.

Did he possibly know that this was the romantic dream she had for so long? How many times she'd sat on the banks of the river and daydreamed that this would happen! "Oh, Vincent are you sure?"

"I've never been so sure of anything in my life, mia vida. I think I've known it since the first week I arrived back here from the east. Remember the night of the fiesta?"

She smiled, "How could I forget it! It was the first time you held me in your arms."

His arms went around her, pulling her closer to him as he huskily muttered, "And forever these arms are going to hold you and love you as no other man could possibly do."

He felt her petite body arch against him and she had no need to answer him, for her body spoke for her. He

434

wasted no more time as he removed his own clothing and her nightgown. It was so sweet to surrender to the exciting touch of his caress. Unhurriedly, he made love to her as he never had before and Karita found she had never experienced such ecstasy as she did in this interlude of rapture they were sharing. She felt a liquid fire flooding her as he finally sank down between her thighs to sate her wildest desires.

It never ceased to amaze Vincent how this beautiful angel-faced girl could so quickly turn into the most sensuously exciting woman he'd ever made love to. His own passion soared to lofty heights as their bodies moved to a perfect tempo.

Both of them knew that their hearts and souls were forever bound together as they ascended to that peak of passion where no one existed but just the two of them.

It was only as they lay cozily in one another's arms, coming back into the world of reality, that Vincent once again told her, "I'll be taking you with me when I leave here, Karita mia."

Vincent could not see the pleased smile on her face. She wanted nothing more, for she never wanted to be separated from him again. "I've a few things to attend to, Vincent. I've got to talk to Margie and pack my things," she told him.

"I'll help you and I'll wait for you to go talk to Margie," he quickly offered.

"Well, then I guess I better get out of bed and get dressed so Margie can prepare to sit in my place tonight, Vincent," she declared, leaping out of the bed. Vincent lay there for a few extra moments allowing himself to savor the bewitching sight of her nude body scampering around the room to gather up her clothing and prepare to dress.

"That's a fine figure you have, chiquita," he smiled.

"Vincent Navarro, you're a very wicked man," Karita giggled.

"Only with you, Karita Montera! Only with you!"

"I shall constantly remind you of that, I promise."

"Come here," he beckoned to her for he had now got out of the bed and slipped on his pants and shirt.

"Now, Vincent, I—I can't—I don't have ti—"

"No, no—that was not why I wanted you to come over here. There is something I have to give you." He urged her to hold out her hand to him. She did as he asked and he slipped Lucia's ring on her finger. "For my bride, querida. It was my Grandmother Lucia's. My grandfather gave it to her one night at the Palace in San Antonio. Now, some fifty years later, I'm presenting it to you here at the White Palace. She wanted this to belong to you, Karita."

Karita looked at the exquisite ring on her finger and her first thoughts were that the brilliant emerald stone was the same sparkling green as Vincent's eyes. She was speechless for a minute. "So she knew that you were going to ask me to marry you, Vincent?"

"I announced my intentions to both of our families, Karita, before I left there to come back here, so you see you must marry me or I'm going to look very foolish." He laughed as he swung her around in his arms.

She stretched so she might kiss him. "I love you, Vincent, as I could never love anyone else."

"And I shall remind you of that constantly, Karita mia! Now, let's get out of here as soon as possible."

It did not take Karita long to pack all her belongings. She left the fancy gowns hanging in the armoire, for those had only been hers to wear for the job she'd performed downstairs.

Impatiently, Vincent waited for her to seek out Margie McClure. As he waited, he puffed on one of his long cigarrillos and paced back and forth in the small room.

Margie did not welcome the news Karita had come to tell her, but she was wise enough to know that the beautiful girl's stay at the White Palace was going to be a brief one. She was not a Greta, Estelle or Maria. No, Karita Montera was destined for a different life and Margie had always known it. Besides, she would have done nothing to mar the glorious radiance on Karita's face.

"Come back and see me sometimes, will you honey?" Margie told her as they said goodbye. But she doubted that this would happen, for she and the wife of Vincent Navarro would be traveling different paths.

While Karita promised that she would, and Margie knew that she sincerely meant it, she also knew that it would not work out that way. But she also knew that she'd never forget the little black-eyed girl she'd invited into her saloon one stormy afternoon.

She watched the two of them ride away from the White Palace and it was a striking couple they made. Somehow, she knew that the beautiful face of Karita Montera would be known here in the capital city of Texas in the years to come. But Margie's fondest memories would always be when she shared a time in her life here at the White Palace.

She sincerely wished her a happy life with the handsome Vincent Navarro. Rarely did she shed tears, but she did this late summer afternoon.

*   *   *

A very excited old Jules and Aspasia greeted their new mistress, as Vincent introduced her when they arrived at his house. Karita had not realized how serious Vincent had been about never letting her out of his sight again now that he had found her.

Once he had taken Karita up to his suite of rooms, he sent Jules to the parish to see if Father Valdez would perform a quiet ceremony that night at eight. Vincent felt sure he would, for he had all the necessary papers. This he had done a few weeks ago when he'd decided that Karita was going to be his wife. Besides, Father Valdez was an old friend of the Navarro family, going back to his father's time back in Austin.

When Jules was on his way, he ordered the special dinner he wished Aspasia to prepare and he also requested that she go into the gardens to cut the lovely white gardenia blossoms with their green waxy leaves for Karita to carry or wear in her black hair.

They would later go through another ceremony for the benefit of their families, but Vincent had no intention of taking her back to Blanco County and being separated from her by the miles that divided Whispering Willows from Silvercreek.

When he finally dashed through the door with a look of boyish enthusiasm on his handsome face, he told Karita, "We'll be married before the night is over if all goes as I plan, Karita."

She looked at him with confusion, for she could not imagine how that could be. But he quickly explained how it was possible. "Aspasia is starting to prepare us a wedding feast, and Jules has gone to seek the priest, so now I am going to leave you to make yourself beautiful. I shall be in one of the guest rooms, so you can have my room."

She stood there with a smile on her face and there was certainly no doubt in her mind about how anxious Vincent was to make her his wife. Nothing could have made her happier! She had to make a quick decision as to what she would wear. She'd brought none of the fancy gowns Margie had bought for her at Francine's, but she had bought a couple of gowns herself from the wages she'd earned.

It was the daffodil yellow one she decided to wear tonight with its delicate white lace ruffling on the short puffed sleeves and around the low scooped neckline. The clock told her that she had two hours to have a bath and get dressed before the priest would be arriving.

She enjoyed the refreshing warm bath and sat at the dressing table wondering what to do with her hair when Aspasia arrived at the door with six lovely gardenias in her hand. Karita thanked her, for now she knew how she would fashion her hair.

She made a spellbinding vision when she joined Vincent in her gown of yellow trimmed in white lace. Her glossy black hair was pulled back with gardenias pinned at each side of her ears. Small wisps of black curls teased her temples.

Vincent swore that no bride was ever more beautiful than Karita. Father Valdez performed the ceremony and Jules and Aspasia witnessed it. Vincent's finest wines were served and the elderly priest shared their wedding dinner before Jules escorted him back to his parish.

Señora Lucia's ring had served as the wedding band that bound them one to the other as they took their vows, and both Karita and Vincent knew that this would have pleased her.

When they traveled to Silvercreek, they were man and wife just as Vincent had planned. When they arrived at Silvercreek to announce that they were already married there was a gasp of disappointment that they had not waited to be married here on the ranch, but Vincent quickly quieted them when he told them that they planned to go through another ceremony now that they were home.

Danton could not suppress an amused smile and he glanced over at his wife. They both recalled that time in their lives, so they knew exactly why Vincent had planned things the way he had. They could hardly fault him for that.

A week after Vincent and Karita arrived back at Silvercreek they went through another wedding ceremony. A more gala fiesta had never been held in Blanco County.

For this occasion, Karita wore the wedding gown that Vincent's mother Kristina had worn when she married Danton Navarro. It was a most exquisite gown of white satin and delicate French lace. Once again, Vincent swore that she was the most beautiful woman in the whole world as she came to him on her father's arm. On her ears and around her throat were the magnificent pearls that Florine Whelan's husband had given to her on the day they married.

As for Karita, she had to believe that a young romantic girl's dreams could come true, for hers had. She was married to the handsome young man she'd always daydreamed of marrying as she'd sat on the banks of the Pedernales River.

Vincent felt that he owned the whole world, for he had the woman he adored and wanted to share all the rest of his days with. Until he'd met Karita, he had wondered if he would ever find such a woman, for his idea of the perfect lady had been Kristina Whelan Navarro. He could never have settled for less.

Kristina prayed only one prayer for the two young lovers, and that was that they would not be the parents of twins. The curse had now been cast on the last two generations so she prayed that Vincent and Karita would be spared.

Fate was kind to them, or perhaps it was Kristina's prayers that were answered, for a year later their firstborn was a beautiful baby girl with a crown of black ringlets.

Karita had only to look at her beautiful daughter and know that no woman could possibly yearn for more. She had a handsome husband who adored and worshipped her and now they'd been blessed with this beautiful daughter.

The flame and fever of their love seemed to glow brighter and brighter. She knew that it was an eternal flame that would burn and glow forever!

Chapter 48

During the year after Karita had left the White Palace to marry the man she loved, Margie McClure heard the gossip through the various patrons who came to her poker games in the back room. It was obvious to Margie that Karita was enjoying a happy life as the wife of Austin's most promising young lawyer. Everyone seemed to be raving about the stunningly beautiful wife of Señor Vincent Navarro! Always, Margie smiled smugly when she listened to the gossip among the gentlemen players in the back room.

Adolfo Martinez was to quickly realize that he had a very formidable adversary, for Vincent delighted in taking a case that would pit his skills and expertise against the dapper Martinez. He worked tediously to win, and he usually did!

But it was more than his work that inspired Vincent to be the best, for he was a happy man and his wife was expecting his child once again. He still found that he was guilty about the miscarriage of his first child because he had been so thoughtless. So to Karita he was a most devoted hsuband and saw that she was pampered during the months of her pregnancy.

To him, she was never more glowing and radiant as

she blossomed with his child within her. He wanted to give her the whole world and an even larger house, but Karita would not hear of it, for she loved the house they lived in especially the little courtyard and the fountain where she enjoyed sitting during the afternoon, waiting for Vincent to come home.

He never voiced any of the fear he harbored all those nine months that she carried the baby—the fear that she might have twins. Like his mother, he also prayed she wouldn't!

In the middle of September in the early morning hours Karita had her baby, and much to the delight of her husband it was a beautiful little daughter. So his and his mother's prayers were answered. Just to watch him sitting there by her bed, holding his daughter so lovingly in his arms, was enough to tell Karita that he was going to be a most devoted father.

She had smiled warmly at him as she told him, "Next time maybe we will have a son, Vincent."

He had looked up at her with a grin on his face, "Oh, I don't know. Think I'm kind of sold on beautiful daughters."

When she told him what she would like to name their daughter, Vincent agreed that it was a beautiful name. He was so overwhelmingly happy that he would have agreed to any name she wished to call her wee daughter whose head was covered with black ringlets.

It was a special tribute that she wished to pay to her sister Cara and to Margie McClure by naming her daughter Cara Margarita. She owed both of them so very much. She could never forget what both of them had done for her when she'd needed help so desperately.

After all the months they'd been married she had

never discussed the horrible incident that night by the riverbank when Victor had attacked her, and she didn't know if she ever could.

After all these many months the Navarro family had had no word from Victor. Danton and his wife accepted the possibility that he might never return to Silvercreek.

Some weeks after Cara Margarita's birth, the Navarro and Montera families came to Austin for a very special occasion—their first grandchild's christening. Cara could not have been more thrilled to hear that Karita's baby was being named for her.

All the bedrooms in Vincent's house were occupied for the weekend and he hired an extra woman to help Aspasia.

The day after the christening Karita asked Señora Lucia if she felt up to taking a jaunt with her in the buggy. "I've someone I'd like you and little Margarita to meet this afternoon."

Señora Lucia eagerly accepted her invitation and the two of them left in the buggy with the baby nestled in a little wicker basket placed between them in the buggy seat.

When they stopped in front of the two-story white frame establishment, and Señora Lucia saw the large sign with White Palace scrolled across it, she knew where Karita had brought her.

Margie McClure sat at one of the tables in the saloon looking over the books and the receipts from the night before. She was taken by surprise to see the two elegantly dressed ladies coming through the doors of her establishment until she realized it was Karita with an elderly white-haired lady.

"Dear God, Karita—it's you!" she shrieked and

445

jumped up from the table. She rushed to give her a warm embrace and glanced in the basket to see the adorable baby wrapped in a pink blanket. "Oh, my God—your babe!"

"Yes, Margie—my little daughter," she smiled proudly. "I've brought Señora Lucia Navarro here to meet you as well as my little daughter. Señora Lucia, this is Margie McClure, the dear lady I worked for here at the White Palace."

Margie was rarely at a loss for words, but she was for one fleeting second or two. "Oh, señora—it is an honor to meet you," she stammered, holding out her hand to shake Señora Lucia's wrinkled hand. When she thought about that hand being the one that had so expertly dealt and played cards in the famous Palace in San Antonio, she was awestruck.

She urged them to have a seat and offered them something to drink. Karita placed the basket atop the table as Margie assisted Lucia into one of the chairs. Only then did she take another look at the baby to declare to Karita how very beautiful she was. "What's her name, honey?" she asked Karita.

"Cara Margarita. Margarita for you, Margie," Karita grinned.

"Oh, Karita—you named her for me?" A mist formed in Margie's eyes and it was a rare time in her life, for she didn't cry easily.

Lucia felt as if the years had been rolled back, sitting in a saloon again and talking with Margie. Margie told her that Karita had told her about her being the renowned Lolita. "But I never expected to meet you in person like this. Oh, Karita, I didn't even know that I'd be seeing *you* again."

"I promised you, remember?" Karita gently reminded her.

After they'd chatted for another half hour, the baby began to fuss and Karita figured that Señora Lucia might be getting weary, so she told Margie that they should be going.

"Oh, honey—seems you just got here," Margie declared.

"Oh, we'll come again. I'll have to bring little Margarita back for you to see from time to time."

As Karita prepared to get up from the chair and attend to the baby, Señora Lucia remained in the chair and announced to Karita, "I think I shall stay here a while, Karita dear. In fact, I'm going to try to get Margie to play some cards with me if she will."

"It will be my great pleasure, señora," Margie excitedly declared.

"All right. You take your babe home, dear, and send my grandson here in a couple of hours," Lucia told Karita.

Karita left the White Palace to return home, and when she announced to Vincent that he was to pick his grandmother up in a couple of hours at the White Palace, where she was playing cards with Margie McClure, he exploded with laughter.

He also found it amusing when he thought about the sight of his beautiful Karita, his grandmother and baby daughter entering the White Palace. He suddenly realized why Karita had chosen the name Margarita for their baby. It was for Margie McClure.

"It was for Margie you named the baby, wasn't it, Karita? Damn! I'm surprised that I'd not thought about that until now!"

"Yes, Vincent. It was for Margie," she told him as she placed the sleepy baby in her crib and removed her bonnet. "She took me in off the street when I had nowhere to go and I shall never forget her for that."

Her words pained him deeply and he strolled over to where she was standing in front of her dressing table to smooth back her hair. His strong arms went around her as he murmured softly in her ear, "Oh, Karita mia—never as long as I have a breath of life in me will you ever find yourself like that again. I vow that to you, querida."

"As long as I have you, Vincent, I won't worry about anything or ever be frightened again."

His lips caressed hers but he dared not linger kissing her honey-sweet lips too long, for he knew the beguiling spell she could so easily cast on him and time would be forgotten. So he gave her an affectionate pat on her hips to make a quick exit from the room, confessing to her why he was leaving with a devious glint in his green eyes. She laughed as she watched him go through the door.

At the appointed time he picked his grandmother up at the White Palace and she was in the grandest spirits. Vincent was having his own private musings as they traveled back to his house. His grandmother and his mother had certainly been rebels. Karita had certainly been a little hellion. With a heritage like that, little Cara Margarita was bound to be the same.

Karita had told him that she'd never worry about anything as long as she had him, but he feared she would. He figured that both of them would have a few nights of worry and concern, for Cara Margarita was going to be a little beauty like her mother. He'd wager that she would also be a rebel like her grandmother and great grandmothers.

Life was never going to be dull, he figured!